Blue Falcon

Terry Lloyd Vinson

Published by Rogue Phoenix Press, LLP
Copyright © 2021

ISBN: 978-1-62420-610-8

Credits
Cover Artist: Designs by Ms G
Editor: Christie L Kraemer

Prologue

No Rest for the Weary

14 February 2004

2339 hours

The Droopy Eye Inn, six-point-three miles west of Pine Bluff, Arkansas on Interstate 530

She leans in until he smells a sickening, nauseating mix of recently leaked blood and evacuated vomit. Lips atremble, she peeks through the narrow slit of her left eye, swollen roughly half as grotesquely as her right, which resembles a ripe melon split partially in half.

"Wh-what's he waiting on? Why don't he j-just finish i-it...us a-already?" she stutters in a hoarse whisper and he feels a faint mist of warm spittle coat his exposed neck. Looking at her, he thinks it's a miracle she can speak at all, considering her lips have burst like stomped grapes and several teeth have been violently extracted.

"How the hell would *I* know? Afraid the ol' telepathy radar is currently on the fritz," he barks harshly, his anger and frustration fueled not by the foolhardiness of the query but the constricting binds of fear currently squeezing his midsection like a fleshy vice. In a pathetic attempt to make amends, he reaches back with a free hand, groping momentarily before eventually discovering her own sweat, blood and puke-coated mitt.

"Listen, just concentrate on shielding the kid. Once that door's breached, cover her with your body, look for an open space to dart through and take off. I'll do my best to play human barricade."

In lieu of a verbal response, she gives his hand as tight a squeeze as she can muster.

"Wish I at least knew her name," she finally manages in the almost deafening silence, the last word more a choked garble than actual word.

"Plenty of time for proper intros later," he replies with a matching squeeze, two sets of intertwined fingers fusing as one.

The trio squat together in a bathtub that strains to hold their combined bulk, the man on one knee, the woman on all fours, the child sitting with her back to a badly discolored tile wall: the six-by-eight bathroom and its flimsy, faux-mahogany door the lone source of blockade between themselves and the room within.

"He's probably just reloading," she decrees with a resounding sigh, the limited confines of the tiny space reeking equally with spilt fluids and desperation. "Piece of shit coward."

"Right," the man nods, the constant throbbing at his bloody scalp fighting for pain domination with the open, slowly seeping wound at his left shoulder. At the moment, it is a dead heat he chooses not to rate as victor, lest his weakening sanity pass them both in a wild sprint to the finish line. The mini-Louisville Slugger curled into his free hand sits propped atop the opposite shoulder, the handle slick with sweat.

"M-maybe he's out of ammunition," she continues with nary a trace of sincerity, wincing painfully as if to affirm the idiocy of such awkwardly out of place hopefulness.

Turning towards and shooting the crouching child—her face as pale, slack and emotionless as when the attack had commenced—a quick, steely-eyed glance, the man's expression and tone are dismissive without undue arrogance.

"Not likely. Dude appears supremely confident, like he's been plotting this or some other similar raid for a lengthy spell. Skidded into that parking lot doing at least forty but the heavy chains on the tires prevented even the slightest damn skid. Armed lunatics of a similarly warped mindset are notoriously meticulous planners."

"H-how about your friend? You think he's...he made it? Maybe he's hiding out like us in one of the last few rooms down the line."

"Yeah, well, maybe," the man replies unenthusiastically, recalling the mercifully brief but graphic image of Terrance reeling back with a grunt, eyes-wide with shock as a softball-sized hole appeared at his ample midsection. "Seemed like a tough old bird, for sure. We can hope, anyway."

After a half-minute's silence, during which time the only discernable sounds are that of their own ragged breathing and that of falling sleet pecking the motel's tiled rooftop, the woman responds in a dull, robotic monotone as if speaking to herself while applying increased pressure until he feels jagged nails dig a groove into the back of his hand.

"H-he's was just shooting blind into the windows and doors of every room. Just pointing and s-shooting. But then, no witness left b-behind, right?" She grins, a sad, horrible parody of a smile that the man doesn't have to actually visualize to know exists.

"Why n-no sirens? It's been what, ten minutes since that nine-one-one call?"

"County badges are probably a half-hour drive away in *good* weather," he counters calmly as to lower the rapidly rising frustration of her tone. "Interstate's like a hockey rink out there. Side-roads are twice as slick. They're probably slidin', slippin' and stumblin' all over and around each other trying to get here."

"Never th-there when you need 'em, r-right?" she huffs, thumping the side of her head lightly against the shower tile. "Small-town cops more...used to busting stills or chasing down...chicken thieves. Jesus wept."

Figuring diversion to be the best course to deflect a building tsunami of hysteria, the man largely ignores the comment and instead dons a mask of bravery, albeit one forged from the thinnest of iron wills. Chest pumped, clinched jaw set tight and chin jutted with a wholly false bravado that nonetheless appears genuine, he finds falling back into a character he'd long since abandoned remarkably easy considering the real-world circumstances at hand. He twists around and peers into tear-filled eyes, their foreheads mere inches apart.

"Hey, we *got* this. Trust me. I'm no stranger to what appears to be unsurmountable odds. Just follow my lead, all right?"

She nods in silent anguish, her damaged lower lip trembling uncontrollably even as her death grip eases. The man couldn't help but think there was a rather attractive young lass beneath all the swollen, bloated bruises and open wounds presently on display.

"Okay, I'm thinking he'll blast the windows and outer door open for drama's sake, just like all the others, like something from the eighties B-movie the crazy bastard *thinks* he's starring in.

"After a quick scan, he'll more than likely plant a boot against the john door as to conserve ammo. First appendage that floats into range..." he pauses with a wink towards the upraised bat, "...and I'm swinging for the fences. I'll either pull his ass in here to commence the pounding or shove 'im back out. Either way, you snatch the kid and dash the hell past wherever we're not. My Jeep is better on mud than ice, but it'll take you to safer climes as long as you don't gun 'er too severe or lead-foot the brake. Road's flat enough going west to get you into Pine Bluff without grille-planting a ditch. You got the keys, right?"

The woman nodded, her breathing visibly calmer than when his spiel has initiated.

"Shouldn't we wait, I mean, on you?"

"Negative, sister. If I score the knockout, I'll wait around for the county boys. If not," he shrugs casually, forcing a shaky grin, "well, you sure as hell don't need to be in range in case he exits this room looking to thumb a ride."

Yet again resembling a pain-induced grimace than actual smile, the woman strains mightily to match his level of optimism, however faux. The child, eyes wide and unblinking, thin lips pursed to a purple tint, shifts just slightly in the woman's grip before releasing a weak gasp as if to acknowledge an understanding of the conversation. The man gauges her age at between perhaps five and seven, a rail-thin waif with marble-round, gleaming brown eyes and a shoulder-length, tar-black coif whose fleeting existence was now hopelessly distorted for whatever timespan remained.

"The name's Fowler, by the way," the woman whispers, gently tonguing a deep, raw chasm at her ravaged lower lip in the aftermath. "Dana Fowler. Not exactly the Valentine's Day celebration I h-had in mind."

"Barrow," he replies with the wink of a badly bloodshot right eye, his thick mustache moistened from melting snow. "Deron Barrow. Same here. Not a damn thing sweet to see here, right? Still, pleased to make your acquaintance, ma'am, though I sure as hell wish it was under better circumsta—"

The initial blast echoes like a detonated bomb, the man instantly leaping from the tub and planting his back flat against the wall in the limited space between the shower and bathroom door, the woman's shrieking wails lost in a follow-up explosion that opens a fist-sized hole at the center of their flimsy barricade.

"Showtime, soldier," the man groans between gritted lips, inhaling deeply and holding it with the mini-slugger poised at shoulder-level, his free hand reaching back, palm out, like a fleshy red light for his charges to obey.

Terse, tension-packed seconds pass as if sporadically freeze-framed to move forward in fragmented puzzle-pieces, the man's squinty gaze frozen on the smoking ruin of their shattered blockade.

So, this is it: reality warfare revisited, all these years later, he ponders as the pulse at his temples pounds a frenzied solo. *The life-and-death real deal, up close and personalized, only this time with a different twist. Not just my ass on the line this time around.*

The broken door sails inward with a vicious jerk at the insistence of a square-toed cowboy boot with a snake design running its smooth, suede length from tip to heel.

Wouldn't you just know it? Shit-kicker heaven, the man muses, lunging forth with a booming roar as the bat uncoils in a blackened blur.

One

Into the Think Tank
(From the Private Journal of Deron Joseph Barrow)

August 2019 Entry

Boone's Crossing (four miles east of Holly Springs), Mississippi

That mid-morning in late April—might as well have been mid-July as far as my sweat glands were concerned—as I sat slumped over my trusty old Selectric II, pecking away at a snail's pace, started out like most. The day's second cup of coffee sat cooling to my right, parked just inches from the piled pages of the initial draft of what was fast becoming a manuscript of doorstop-size proportions; a half-eaten bagel with cream cheese took up the opposite end of the scar-infested oak typing stand, the latter purchased for a cool three bucks at a Corinth flea market a few years previous. Last but not least: a half-emptied tube of Ben Gay propped on a nearby window seal, its pungent scent radiating from an exposed left knee that still, despite three early-morning coatings, throbbed and pulsed like a rotted molar.

It wasn't until I detected the faint sound of tires rolling over the gravel drive to the north side of the property that normalcy and routine were fated to take a permanent powder, though I was as yet ignorant of that fact. Looking back, it wasn't as if a sudden surge of telepathy would've changed what was to come. Some things are just meant to be, no matter the timespan between that first domino falling and the last following suit. What one sows, he or she shall eventually reap. Cliché city, I know, but truer than a dozen of the most prophetic fortune cookies. As one learns when youth becomes middle-age and beyond, twenty-one years is but a flash on that ever-spinning wheel of time.

I spotted the mystery vehicle, not nearly as covert once its humming engine grew closer, as it glided slowly between the aged elms at the east end. The roaring engine cut off even as it continued its final roll, leaving the unmistakable guitar chords of AC/DC's "Back in Black" thumping from the stereo to pick up the slack.

Rising from the rickety high-back that had served as my writing throne since the manuscript's inception, the sharp cracking of my knees—one in particular—managed to temporarily drown out both a stiff mid-morning breeze and the glorious bellowing of Brian Johnson.

Radio silenced, a vehicle door soon slammed. Heavy boots or similar foot apparel crunched atop loose gravel.

"Greetings and salutations from civilized society!" shouted a familiar, gravelly voice, "Where ya at, partner?"

My own voice, having gone several days in mute mode from a welcome lack of human contact, croaked and cracked like a pubescent teen.

"Coming at you, Tank. Long time, brother."

He stepped around the Ram thirty-five hundred's sleek, massive hood just as I hopped down from the shack's lower step.

"I'd say. Three, four months, right?"

"At least."

Matching grins: the sincere, comfortable kind shared only by those whose bond is forged not just merely by time but circumstance. It'd been two, maybe three months since our last jawing session. I found I welcomed this particular intrusion. Lance "Tank" Garrett was without a doubt one of very few I could say that about.

We shook hands firmly and strolled silently towards the main house, where a matching set of recently refurbished rocking chairs awaited atop the front porch.

"How's the knee?" he asked, head tilted to study my gait as we ambled along.

"Nuts and bolts still holding firm but I won't be entering a marathon anytime soon. Hey, I've got a semi-fresh pot of java brewed up," I offered as our destination was reached and we soon began rocking away in almost perfect unison.

"Had plenty. More than a cup these days and I might as well tote a porta-potty on my back for easy access."

The shared nod executed was also with almost supernatural sameness.

"So what ya been up to out here in the middle of blessed nowhere, Deron Joseph?"

Two sentences and I was already dead-letter certain this wasn't just a social visit.

"Stopped by the station on the way. Locked up tight. What gives?"

Without breaking stride, Tank pulled a pack of smokes from a front shirt pocket and proceeded to light up. Five years my senior—meaning he'd tipped just over six decades of earthy existence—the man's weathered face appeared carved from granite. His slim features served as a clever disguise for the rock-hard muscle worn as an outer shell.

"Lost my slot, at least 'til they figure out how to retool to something more hip. In other words, probably tap city as far as my future employment goes. No sweat, really. More time to tap the keys."

Tank grunted, and we rocked in brief silence as, in the distance, a semi's horn echoed like the foghorn of a lost schooner. Being that the main highway was a four-plus mile ride from the homestead, the wind on rare occasions would serve proof of the four-lane's existence.

"You still that certain someone's favorite charity, I take it."

"By the tenth of every month, like clockwork."

"So no pressure to bring home the weekly bacon then. At least there's that."

I'd often pondered how a man's perspective is altered if his reasoning to maintain gainful employment is tied only to the time it fills and not the necessity of the salary earned. In the almost fifteen years since my last bona fide "to eat or not eat" job, I wondered how many life decisions, especially the bad ones, might've gone the other way if that certain financial buffer hadn't existed. Luckily, I also realized that obsessing did little nothing to solve anything so utterly hypothetical.

"So," I switched gears quickly, the previous subject birthing a tidal wave of unease and mild shame, "how goes the security biz?"

The earlier breeze having evaporated, Tank's face was temporarily cloaked in a stagnant cloud of fag smoke, the pungent stench of which served as a flagship of memories both haunting and treasured.

"Honestly dude, didn't Lucky Stripes stop production in the late eighties?" I jabbed, frantically waving both hands to clear to air between us.

"Hilarious as ever," he retorted, just the hint of a smile denting that granite visage. "Though I recall last time you told that joke it was Chesterfields.

"As for the aforementioned query, there is definitely no shortage of crime on the mean streets of the Rock, partner. Gangs are basically runnin' three-fourths of our fair city."

"I foresee no issue with job security for, say, the next century or thereabouts."

"Correct me if I'm wrong, but weren't you thinking of hanging it up around this time last year?"

"Yeah, well, it's kinda embarrassin' to confess, but I'm not exactly humpin' it from dawn to dust these days. More like a series of weekly cameo appearances to make sure things are copasetic at the home office. Not an easy thing givin' up a slice of cake that rich. 'Sides, I get the feelin' that a permanent reassignment to the homestead might just cause some serious dents in my own marital status."

I reached over and tapped a heavily tattooed forearm with a tip of an elbow.

"You hinting that Wendy might prefer you keep busy and out from under foot?"

"Hinting, *hell*. Nail on the head, brother. Anybody ever ask me about the secret to a thirty-plus year marriage and I'll tell 'em it's keepin' your distance for the majority of said span. Give each other ample space.

Wendy and I have found a Grand Canyon-type area agreeable."

"Nice. Wish you'd have shared such invaluable wisdom around two wives back," I ribbed, tossing up both arms in faux exasperation.

With that, Tank scanned the surrounding grounds as if expecting the sudden teleportation of a familiar face.

"Speaking of which, where's Jenny? I was hopin' for some of those special eggrolls of hers."

"Lumpia?" I inquired indifferently, understanding the tap-dance he'd initiated.

"Yeah boy. Mouth-waterin'."

"Afraid you'll have to hop a bird to Cebu, dude."

"Oh, she visitin' the homeland, is she?"

"You might say that."

Tank's rocker hit the brakes, obviously breaking our paranormal rhythm. I didn't have to glance over to imagine the dramatically tilted head; the squinted eyes; the characteristic sneer of befuddlement.

"Aw, crap. Don't tell me. Trouble in paradise, partner?"

"A fool's paradise if it ever qualified to begin with," I replied, noticing with no small amount of embarrassment the disorder of the front yard. Knee-high grass infested with crabgrass and dandelions that hadn't seen a mower blade in what appeared like a solid month. On either side of the mailbox—a good thirty-yard walk down the dirt/gravel (mostly dirt) drive—leaned a pair of rust-ravaged garbage cans overflowing with tattered bags that somehow, miraculously, had been spared the local raccoon population's curiosity. Lucky thing the nearest neighbor was old man Pruitt a half-mile up the road or I might've found myself victim of a surprise midnight garbage bonfire.

"Is it any wonder? Jeez Louise, the place is a sty *unfit* for pigs. Can't remember the last time I hauled the trash away. For that matter, the last time I dragged a bag from the kitchen."

"So she left your lazy ass for not takin' out the garbage?" Tank snorted while rejoining the rocking party and, within seconds, falling right back into a steady cadence.

"Tip of the separation iceberg."

"'Zat so?"

"Let's just say Jen didn't consider Holly Springs the American dream she'd envisioned, much less Boone's Crossing. Can't say I blame her. Not exactly a thrill a minute."

"Well, it ain't like you didn't do some travelin' in, the what? Five or six years since she flew over?"

"Almost seven. Yeah, if you consider Jackson, Biloxi and Orleans a proper representation of the country as a whole. Kind of pathetic, in retrospect."

"Didn't you trek over to Gulf Shores a few winters back?"

I nodded casually, though in truth the very fact I'd completely forgotten that specific trip underlined my indifference to the subject as a whole. Bottom line, I hadn't cared enough to resolve the problem of my latest, soon-to-be ex-wife's boredom and overall dissatisfaction with small-town life.

"Biloxi, Mobile, Orleans; same thing really. A natural beach lover that one, for obvious reasons. Me? I couldn't give a rat's hairy hind end if I ever saw another spec of sand."

Never a big fan of secondhand cancer-stick smoke, even in my heaviest bar-hopping days, I nevertheless found myself appreciative of its company when compared with the drifting stench of neglected trash.

"So, pray tell old buddy, what *does* Deron Joseph Barrow give a rodent's ass about?"

"Same as the last time we chewed the fat, I reckon."

"That book thing, ya mean? Holy cats, man, you've been hammerin' away at that for what, three years now?"

"Four, but who's counting?"

"Well, right off the bat I'd say your better half."

We traded sly grins, tendril-thin smoke billowing from each of his dramatically flaring nostrils.

"Touché, partner."

"So, she purchase a one-way ticket?"

"For now, yeah. We'll see. We've been face-timing on Skype every other day or so. Maybe she just needs some time. Maybe we both do."

The casual jawing session having apparently run its course, we rocked quietly for a full minute. Knowing Tank like I did, and thus figuring waiting on him to get the actual purpose of his visit might mean rocking on that front porch until the passing of summer into fall, I quickly caved.

"So what's up? I can't imagine you made that multi-hour drive just to swap tales of marital woe."

"Tell ya what, I might just have a cup of joe after all," he replied with surprising sternness while staring straight ahead into nothing. "You might want to pour yourself something a tad stouter."

With that, we relocated indoors to the living room, which was, sad to say, not much of an upgrade in terms of neatness from the disaster of the front yard.

"Maid's year off?" he cracked while clearing a space from the couch as I searched the kitchen cabinets for two clean cups.

"Hey, feel free to commit a neatness if the urge arises," I managed to volley despite a building trepidation.

"Brother, I'd have to rent a backhoe."

The old hacienda, built in the mid-seventies, far past its prime and bought on the cheap by yours truly nearly a decade past, was most definitely missing its mama. Jenny was, if not quite your basic OCD neat freak, not one to tolerate the overt slob tendencies I'd acquired in her absence. During our Skype sessions, I'd at least possessed the common sense—and survival skills—to strategically clean up whatever area might pan into camera range.

Moments later, with steaming mug of Death Wish in hand, Tank sighed heavily, looking as blatantly ill-at-ease as I'd witnessed in our almost three-decade friendship.

He sipped noisily, eyeing me with a pained scowl as I took a seat in the recliner directly across from the couch.

"Dang good joe. What ya got there, a White Russian?"

I raised my cup—a large black mug with a faded Mississippi State Bulldog gracing its bulk—and executed a semi-toast.

"You know I cut out the booze years ago. Well, all but the occasional brew. Now, what's this dreadful news that you seem to think will shove me, arms flailing, right back *off* the souse wagon?"

As Tank paused for an additional sip and accompanying grimace, I felt my heart skip a beat. I hadn't felt such a rush of dread since a certain military court proceeding that concluded quite negatively for yours truly.

"Well, maybe I am bein' a bit of a drama king in that respect. You be the judge."

Maybe it was living relatively stress free for such a lengthy spell, but as my old friend sat his cup aside, folded his arms, leaned back and commenced with his tale, I was only able to quell the shaking of my own hands by squeezing that MSU mug to the point of implosion.

"A few weeks back, I had a potential client request a meetin', a client that had requested me by name as their first contact. Not exactly a regular occurrence these days—I'm more of the on-site consultant type after the sale—but not altogether bizarre either.

"So meet 'em I did, for brew and nachos down at Carlito's downtown. Straight-laced and very professional, as clean-cut, stone-cold serious and to-the-point as any I've met. No beatin' around the bush with those two. A man and woman, the former tall, slim and bespectacled, a walkin', talkin' CPA if I ever saw one, the latter sweet-talkin', strikingly attractive and upper-class elegance personified. Turns out their interest in me had beans to do with security, and everything to do with the fact that I might steer 'em to *you*."

And there it was. In the aftermath, every ounce of pre-explanation stress and concern were vanquished, snuffed out like a candle flame in a monsoon. Two quick sips of brew—unlike Tank I preferred a little coffee with my sugar and cream—and a quiet belch later, I regarded my old friend with a deep frown birthed from utter disbelief.

"And this was supposed to trigger a mental meltdown? Damn, Tank. You really consider me that unstable? Don't tell me, media types digging for that exclusive front-page story? Better yet, internet bloggers with far too many slow news days of late that caught wind of a potentially hot take? You *do* understand that this is far from a new phenomenon in the last decade-and-a-half or so? Hell, If I had a ten-spot for every jackass junior-grade TV producer or B-grade novelist that proposed to give my story the 'fair, unbiased' angle it deserved, you and I wouldn't be parked in this shithole but some Pacific island mansion with a staff of buxom, scantily-clad servants providing refills along with unlimited eye-candy."

My rant had little or no effect, as Tank's expression remained as hard and stoic post-rant as it had pre.

"You ought to at least listen to 'em, Deron."

"And why the hell should I? What separates them from all the others just looking for a quick cash-grab at my...at the expense of those who lived it?"

Tank leaned forward, eyes squinting as if he were staring directly into the midday sun.

"You consider me a pretty decent judge of character?"

I nodded, albeit stubbornly hesitant. Lance Garrett was, in truth, probably the best judge of people I'd ever known, but I wasn't about to lose the argument, even in the face of such cold, hard fact.

"Well, I can't really explain it but they were just...different. As you recall, I was present at more than a few of those previous, um, offers, through the years. These two were, well, sincerely passionate, for want of a better term. Besides, I think you need to consider at least a courtesy listen for other reasons."

Here it came, right on cue. Even if I wasn't in the mood to hear it. The truth is known, very often, to hurt. This was no exception. Still, logic and good sense be damned, I didn't have to like it.

"Look around ya, buddy," he continued, in the tough-love, tried and true 'schooled-by-Tank' mode that I'd witnessed countless times as a casual observer but rarely been the target of. "It ain't squalor, sure, but it does bring to the forefront that you could, and should, be doing better for yourself, and to Jen for that matter. Not-so-mystery monthly allotment aside, you don't *have* to just scrape by. Plus which, twenty-plus years is a long spell to be fightin' a battle when you're both the one throwin' the haymakers and catchin' 'em on the chin.

"Besides, if the story is told the factual and correct way, why shouldn't you cash in? From my corner, I don't see a damn thing to be ashamed of. Truth to told, I never have."

Sure, I wanted to get mad, go berserk and start throwing shit while screaming at my oldest—and perhaps only *true*—friend to take his advice and opinions and shove 'em. Instead, I calmly sat back and sipped quietly as he did the same. We traded slurping noises—dueling smacks, if you will—for several surprisingly mellow moments, the ticking sound of a nearby wall clock the lone distraction other than our own swigging.

"So tell me what impressed you so much about this pair," I finally said, potential berserker mode having quickly passed.

Perhaps relieved at my relatively easygoing response and openness to the prospects, Tank retrieved yet another smoke and parked it between bared teeth. To this day, it amazes me no end those possessing the almost supernatural skill to belt out lengthy speeches with a cigarette bouncing wildly atop a lower lip as if stapled into place. I swear Tank could negotiate hurricane winds without misplacing a single spec of tobacco.

"Well, if I was to put my finger on it, it was the fact that they weren't pushy in the least. Cool, calm and professional with nary a single hard sell tactic. Then again, it could be they're savin' all those peculiar techniques for you. Bottom line, the lady in charge simply stated they had an idea for a project that wasn't about demonizing the bad guys or sanctifying the good. Fair and balanced story-tellin', I think she put it, written to cover all the dramatic bases with one-hundred-percent honesty and without the usual Hollywood sweetener or punch-ups. They weren't promising the moon, just asking for a fair shot to tell a story that deserved tellin'. I tell ya, Deron, my inner BS monitor was as quiet as a church mouse for the duration of the interview. No easy feat, advancin' years and fadin' superpowers not withstandin'."

"Agreed," I replied, pausing for a trio of sips of rapidly-cooling java. "But like you said, they might be saving up the PR push for yours truly, complete with the requisite promises of fame, fortune and infamy. Remember those assclowns from Full Moon? Their suits spouted the same crap and the final script draft read like some soft-corn porn serial killer space opera."

Tank nodded knowingly while finally torching his smoke. Pretty subtle, hardly noticeable at all, but that was the first time I took note of a slight tremor of his left hand.

"Or that independent crew out of Santa Carla that offered to fly me to Amsterdam for a month of unlimited booze, dope and carnal sins, all for the right to change my character into some kinda Bizarro-World hybrid of Dick Clark DJ by day and transvestite vigilante by night. Of course, the fine print of their contract also stated this would constitute full payment for my permission to thoroughly butcher reality."

"Yep, seems I do recall you tellin' me about *that* particular offer," he cackled softly, tendrils of smoke spewing from both nostrils. "From what I gather about these two, they're strictly documentary flick-makers dedicated to their craft. That was one thing that struck me as original about 'em. They confessed right off that any budget would be of the shoe-string variety and whatever money was paid out in the aftermath of the project would come from profits made on home video and streamin' services. Apparently, they do have some seriously tanked-up PR folks in the company bullpen that have the capability to take such a project and slowly turn it into a hit on the home market."

Lying to myself was pointless. There was a twinge of excitement at the possibility. A faint tingling at the scalp, a spattering of butterfly wings tickling the inner gut. Conversely, a palpable sense of distrust remained firmly intact. Not nearly a virgin to such conflicting emotions since the late nineties, there was but one way to declare a clear winner: tally up the pros and cons of either taking a dive or retreating back to square one.

"I dunno. Trust is a hard thing to come by, especially considering that most days I'd rather not be reminded about the subject matter at hand. Time hasn't altered that mindset. I may not be the hothead of yesteryear, but the level of stubbornness has increased ten-fold. I get what you're saying about the money and closure and the need to stop beating myself up over the whole deal but allowing a group of strangers to have the final say is, to me anyhow, comparable to tip-toeing barefoot and blindfolded through a field littered with claymores."

"I got'cha, boss. I'd be similarly cautious, if not more so," he said between huffs before pausing to paw through his wallet, though not before donning a pair of reading glasses to aid in the search. I couldn't help but smile at the sight, tempted to bombard my old friend with assorted geezer jokes. That is, 'til I recalled my own rapidly deteriorating state.

Pocketing the bifocals, he leaned up and over with hand (complete with barely detectable shake) extended, a black and gold business card pinched between thumb and forefinger.

"Still, here ya go. They said take your time, but not too long, whatever the hell that means."

Solid in stock—no Vistaprint dot com special here—with bright, vibrant blue lettering inside a dark crimson border, it read simply "Dragon Lady Productions, LLC" and provided phone and fax numbers along with an email address and website URL.

Tank pushed himself from the couch, having tossed what remained of his smoke into the coffee mug, which briefly shook so vigorously I thought he might accidentally toss it across the room.

"How long?" I asked, gesturing towards the clutched cup, now clasped in a double-fisted death-grip.

He briefly regarded his own grasping mitts as if they belonged to someone else, obviously having grown accustomed to playing dumb, before remembering to whom he spoke and coming clean with a resounding sigh.

"Funny. The right started shakin' first but now the left has passed it by in both consistency and frequency of tremors. Didn't cave to see a sawbones 'til 'bout six months ago, and not even then until Wendy threatened to slip a mickey into my mornin' java and haul me there herself. Parkinson's runs in the genes from way back from my ma's side. Guess I was hopin' it would skip more than a single generation. No such luck, Chuck."

"Prognosis?"

"Not good, señor. I'll fight the bastard all the way though. This you know. I worry more for Eric and hope like hell it does at least skip the next one."

Eric, currently a junior at Memphis State and the couple's only child.

I nodded, smiling as broadly as possible despite feeling as if I'd been gut-punched.

"For now, worry about yourself. Goes without saying you can count on me for anything you or Wendy need."

"Good for now, but the offer is duly noted and appreciated."

No doubt desperate to switch channels, he tip-toed over and around the assorted piles of organized mess littering our path towards the front door.

"Say, since I drove all this way, how's about an early lunch?"

"Sounds like a winner. Take your pick: the Sonic drive-through or Maggie's Munchables."

"Maggie's still servin' chicken 'n dumplin's with cabbage and pinto beans?" he grinned mischievously. Same old Tank. Never one to forget a plate of top-notch grub, despite, if I recall correctly, only visiting the source of said spread a single time in his lifespan.

"Best in the state, maybe this part of the country."

With that, Lance "Tank" Garret, former security police specialist, non-commissioned officer and participant in many an armed conflict and all-around tough guy, smacked his lips like a drooling toddler at the mere prospect.

"Well by all means, soldier, lock up this here hooch and let us make tracks. Promise to get ya back to your precious typewriter before dark."

As had been the case for the duration of our friendship, said promise was kept, as was the continued oath we'd unofficially reestablished while shaking hands upon his departure.

From there, I had some serious decision-making to undertake. No better place than behind the keys of my trusty Selectric with a fresh cup of steaming joe parked nearby.

Two

The Proposal
(From the private journal of Deron Joseph Barrow)

This latest and certainly greatest debate about whether I should or shouldn't—take the plunge or remain dry as dust—didn't take nearly as long as I'd initially thought it might. As Tank had mentioned, twenty-plus years of gestation is a heck of a wait, though the fact that I'd spent the last four tapping out my personal version of the tale, or tales, if one prefers, probably did as much to motivate as the simple passing of time. Simply put, it had gnawed at my gut 'til I was risking a basketball-sized ulcer. There was also, deny it as I might, the question of my age. Fifty-four *going on dead*, I had silently quipped of late. To quote an oft-overused cliché, this boy wasn't getting any younger. It was a matter of now or never, and while someone remained interested enough in the subject matter to dedicate it to film.

Of course, I did what I'd promised myself, listing the pros and cons of dedicating myself to the process. Unlike all the other times I'd covered the same ground, the landslide of pro over con was as new a development as my sudden excitement over said results. Yep, it was definitely a matter of striking while the mental iron smoldered. As I saw it, and this had been a staple from many days past, the biggest con would be, most likely, the end of the run of relative anonymity I'd treasured so much through the years. Sad to admit, but a part of me would probably root for a commercial and critical flop in hopes of an easy transition back to life as I knew it best. Also, there was the potentially volcanic reaction from a certain involved party or parties who might not be so agreeable with the finished product and the fallout sure to ensue, be it positive or negative. Regardless, the pros won not by unanimous decision, but via a brutal TKO.

As a formality only, I did take the time to discuss the issue with my better half over three nights' worth of intense Skyping. Never a proponent of my officially going public with the story, Jenny eventually relented to go along, mostly since she'd be out of the country for the majority, if not all, of the process. She'd always feared public scrutiny and never seemed to give a damn about a potential windfall, financially. That, and though it remained unsaid and the subject never breached, I'd always figured there was a jealousy factor involved in that the story to be told was long before she'd become a part of my life.

Jen had never thrilled at tales of my former lives or the female companionship that played significant roles therein. A film treatment, be it a straight documentary or semi-autobiographical drama, might possibly shine a light on details she'd rather have ignored for the duration of our marriage. Still, Jen finally caved with a sigh and stiff nod while wearing a stoic, stony, stern expression I'd long associated with disgust and/or disappointment. Talk about your shallow victories: it felt like a textbook case of winning a single battle when the war itself had long ago been a lost cause. I told myself that, in the aftermath, when all was said and done, properly documenting the past could only improve prospects for the future, including my failing marriage. Hard sell that, but hey, sometimes it's the thought that counts, however self-delusional.

Decision made, the next move was to reach out to my potential new partners and get the wheels rolling. Strange, not to mention a tad troubling, how both the hand holding the business card and the one cradling the cellphone shook in almost synchronized harmony when that fateful moment arose.

~ * ~

20 May 2019

Little Rock, Arkansas

Excerpt from *The Mask beneath the Mask: A Memoir,* by Deron Joseph Barrow

Little Rock was a stranger to me. Weird, being that I'd spent a great deal of my life trudging around within its storied city limits. Maybe it was the five-plus years since my last visit, but it was hardly recognizable to me. More likely, like the negative memories of a bad marriage, I'd blacked out a large portion of the years I'd invested. Along the same lines, perhaps it was akin to meeting up with an ex in an awkward attempt to reconciliate.

The restaurant, as chosen by my potential suitors, was a Cracker Barrel—couldn't help but think I was, right off the cuff, being age-range stereotyped—off River Mountain road, just a hop, skip and jump from my old employment stomping grounds. Not at all an accident, I'd presumed, but a preemptive strike to what they hoped was the sentimentalist that remained locked deep within yours truly. Clever, if not the least bit subtle, I had to respect the effort.

Hand extended, the young man introduced himself as Ronald Dixon, a late twenties-early thirtyish-looking, sharply dressed individual whose button-down appearance screamed public accountant or law student. As he was bespectacled, clean-shaven and slightly moist of hand, my first impression of Ron was that of a well-bred, ultra-professional whose presence was little more than that of representation only, as if to officially play the role of witness to the proceedings. Though his handshake and accompanying smile were warm enough, there was a hint of cold indifference and insincerity that, to the seasoned such as I, was easily enough detected upon first contact.

As for the young woman, that initial vibe was the complete opposite. Diandra Chang, or *Dee-dee* as she preferred, could only be described as a five-foot (or less), bean-pole thin (though not entirely curve-free) strand of live-wire femininity. Obviously Asian in descent (I would later find out she was Amerasian, with an American father and

Korean mother), her dark-brown eyes shone with a fevered excitement upon clasping my right hand and—without hesitation or a tint of shyness—literally hugging the stuffing out of me, the top of her head lightly bumping my chin. Dressed in casual slacks and a flowery cotton button-up, her tar-black hair tied into a tight bun, she appeared less professional negotiator *slash* film producer than carefree mall shopper. Upon separation, I noted a buildup of moistness at the edge of both meticulously slanted eyes. I was going to like this one, I recalled thinking. I knew this although not five words had yet passed between us. Dee-dee, a film school grad who, within minutes of intros, volunteered her age only to the specification of "mid-to-late-twenties," sat directly across me from in the back booth they'd chosen before my arrival. D.D. and D.J. conquer the world, I thought crazily as coffee—easily my favorite item off the CB menu—was ordered all around and menus glanced over.

"It's just amazing," she beamed, arms folded and thus her chosen meal utterly ignored as she tilted her head slightly from side-to-side, studying my features as if already placing me within the camera's roving eye. Weird, but I could register no unease whatsoever at the intrusion.

"It's been how long? Twenty-six years and other than the extra growth of lettuce and cookie duster, the difference is remarkably minimal."

"Lettuce? Cookie duster? Ma'am, how old did you say you were again?" I said, lifting my cup for a fresh sip but unable for the wide smile I was finding impossible to wipe free. Usually a master at pinpointing a person's home field by whatever accent they sported, I was finding hers a hard shell to crack.

"Oh, *that*. Afraid my, our last film is still affecting my vocabulary," she said, beaming back at full force, a radiant, toothy thing of beauty that held the seductive power to instantaneously de-age a man of my advancing years, at least temporarily.

"And what was that?" I inquired, forking up a bite of country fried steak.

"Three months of filming inside a nursing home in Norman,

Oklahoma. Hard to shake the verbiage, considering we chopped roughly sixteen hours of interviews to just under ninety minutes."

"Would I know it? I mean, is it on DVD?"

"Amazon picked it up last November for a short streaming run," Ron Dixon chimed in matter-of-factly, apparently for no other reason than to remind me he was still seated at the table, *Gray Matters*, with the 's' bracketed. More a study of how families deal with aging parents and the decision to have them housed, but also an inside look at the facility itself. Not exactly ground-breaking, but the majority of critics received it positively enough."

Illinois, I decided once this mini speech concluded, dry and robotic in a Public Service Announcement sort of way, perhaps Michigan. Definitely Northeastern-Yankee slanted.

"Got'cha. So you're strictly documentary makers then?"

"You'd be our third, Deron. Do you prefer Deron or D.J.?" Dee-dee asked, digging into a salad with little interest.

"Deron is fine. Only my mom and grade-school teachers called me D.J., usually when a butt-scorching was in order."

"Matters followed a shorter film concerning a star high school football player from Alabama who killed his own brother over an ounce of pot," she continued, obviously missing my jab at her geezer-themed dictionary talents with the 'butt-scorching' remark, "It…I found it such a grim, depressing experience I ended up taking nearly a year off and worked in retail just to distance myself from it and filmmaking in general. To be honest I didn't really know if I wanted to attempt another project. The nursing home story came to me through a relative. Not exactly uplifting, but a still a step up the ladder. Mister, um, Deron, are…so those are real?" She gestured towards the exposed tatts on my right forearm.

"They're not stamped on, ma'am."

"Wow. I mean, I just thought they were, you know, for show, at the time, I mean. Forgive my babbling."

"Not a problem," I shrugged, secretly digging her girlish awkwardness, "So yeah, the skin ink is as real as the, well, the lettuce and the cookie duster."

She giggled like a schoolgirl, briefly covering her mouth, those almond eyes glittering. Lord, to have been twenty years younger! Well, maybe thirty, but who's counting. Then again, there was also present an undercurrent of guilt at these occasional bursts of lust. Call it "dirty old man" syndrome.

"I've so looked forward to starting this project, you cannot image. Of course, we knew of your past hesitations on the matter. Ron and I have been searching diligently for months to come up with something different to follow up what we think of as our 'duo of downers.' Don't get me wrong, we're proud of both films, but one more trip down misery lane and I'd probably turn in my laptop and camera equipment for a nametag at Home Depot."

"So, you're both producers?"

Dee-dee delivered a light forehead slap to herself before glancing over at Dixon, who shrugged while wearing a tight-lipped smile.

"My sincerest apologies, Deron. While Ron and I do both co-produce, he also serves as cameraman extraordinaire and editor. I'll be your script-writer and director."

"Got'cha, just so I know where I stand," I said with an amiable nod. Nagging reservations aside, there was no denying I was enjoying her company, as well as the raw excitement at the prospect of many similar meetings to come, rubbing elbows to complete a film that up until a half hour earlier I still held serious reservations about.

"Yes, well, I will of course be depending heavily on your personal recollections, the timeline of events, etcetera. To that end, you will of course receive a co-writing credit."

"Co—oh, well, that's great. I do have a few notes put aside. Scribbled 'em down over the years just so things didn't get so foggy as years roll on. Never thought they'd ever come in handy," I lied, thinking of the roughly three hundred pages stacked in my shack and secretly thrilled to the marrow they might actually be used for something other than gathering dust and/or rat droppings.

"As you no doubt have heard, there have been previous offers."

"Oh, you mean the Bad Moon people who preferred a B-movie

horror flick?"

"*Full* Moon, and yeah, they were one of many. One fly-by-night outfit did mention a docu-drama style but wanted to include vampire hookers and a mystery serial killer to the mix to 'spice things up.' Needless to say, I backed up and punted in each case. Nice to hear you folks prefer truth to fiction."

"Complete honesty without speculation, that's our motto," she replied, flashing me the three-finger Boy Scout salute. "We're not about sensationalism and we make that crystal clear to any and all potential backers. Gotta say, it hasn't been easy with the subject matters we've chosen thus far."

I saw Dixon check his watch between shifting the food on his plate from one side to another and decided to start whittling away on a few of the questions posted in a mental checklist I'd memorized since deciding to listen to the offer.

"Yeah, well it ain't exactly like you're about to stroll onto the highway to laughter, love and eternal happiness with this latest venture. Why me, and maybe more mysterious, why *now*? Many, many years have passed after all and you'd think I'd be second-hand news."

"I truly don't see it that way," Dee-dee said, pushing her plate aside and propping her chin atop clenched fists. "I see it...your story as not only fascinating but timely. Think about it: both chapters occurred before the internet boom. Well, not so much the second but it wasn't nearly as prevalent as today.

"You see in these days of social media how even the most nonsensical, unimportant drivel imaginable spreads like wildfire, only to be relegated to old news in a matter of minutes as the next post takes poll position. Stories like yours are untold gems for *several* generations of web surfers. Sure, *they* garnered a few headlines at the time, um, *times* of occurrence, but then TV spots and newspapers were the lone sources for the first incident. Just to be able to share your experiences as if they happened yesterday and not decades ago is what gives it sizzle."

Dixon chimed in between sips of iced tea, his voice finally sounding less robotic, his movements at least a shade more animated.

"She's right, Mister Barrow. I know I was just a kid at the time the events took place, but in asking around, I couldn't find a single person around my hometown or beyond that had heard of either, much less the names of those involved."

"I see. Where might this hometown be, Mister Dixon?" I couldn't help but pry, if for no other reason than to rate my earlier assumption concerning this accent.

"Lansing originally. Make my home in Champaign these days, though sometimes I wonder if I might as well have my mail forwarded to Holiday Inn Express headquarters."

"And you, Dee-dee?" I pressed on, chest already semi-swelling with self-pride at nailing at least one of their origins, "That is, if I'm not being too for—"

"Born in New Mexico but moved around a lot as a kid. Spent my formidable teen and early adult years in Sperryville, Virginia just a few hours outside of D.C. Can't really claim a hometown, though I've grown partial to Savannah these past five years."

While on somewhat of a roll, grilling the grillers so to speak, I figured one more couldn't hurt. Fair is fair, I figured, as soon enough the spotlights would be blistering my hide but good.

"Soooo, you two a couple or just business partners?"

The two shared a brief, perfunctory glance that explained exactly nothing. Much to my chagrin, it was a suddenly talkative Ron Dixon who offered first response.

"We dated for bit but decided friendship made for a better relationship if we were to make films together."

As for Dee-dee, her suddenly sullen expression spoke volumes, as if I'd not only struck a nerve, but sliced right into the spleen of that exposed sucker.

"Afraid I'm married to my career."

Dixon nodded between alternating hands to applying a vigorous neck message, as if attempting to rub away a building tension.

"Ditto. For now anyway."

So much for my next question, which was to inquire of marital status.

"Got'cha." I nodded Dixon's way, who returned the gesture, his cheeks flushed crimson, "Probably for the best, considering all the time you both spend away from home."

With that, both cleared their throats and resumed stabbing at the mostly untouched portions still taking up space on their respective plates.

"Speaking of better halves, how did our offer go over with one Miss Jennifer Bajao Barrow?"

The query itself—delivered with renewed spunk, the gleam returning to Dee-dee's eyes upon delivery—didn't as much catch me off-guard as the use of my wife's full name. No way Tank had referred to her as anything more formal than Jenny or perhaps Jen. Attempted clandestineness be damned, sometimes it all seemed for naught.

"She was less than thrilled initially but warmed up over time."

"Filipino, isn't she?" Dee-dee probed through a floss-thin glare.

"Correct."

"Well, I certainly look forward to meeting the woman behind the man."

"Well, about that," I paused, feeling suddenly cornered for some inexplicable reason. It wasn't as if Jen's absence factored in with the overall story, being that we hadn't even met until years following the incidents. "Jen's visiting family and probably won't be back for the duration of the filming."

"Pity. We were hoping for an interview for the concluding cut, or at least a special features chat."

Desperate for an about-face, I quickly shifted gears to what I'd rated second in importance from the inner checklist.

"So I take it the format is gonna consist mostly of personal interviews?"

Dixon answered, android-ish monotone firmly back in place.

"That, and video footage."

"Video footage?"

That toothy smile reemerged, effortlessly offsetting the Vulcan-esque traits of her bland cohort.

"We have at least one hundred hours of the show to peruse. I've been going through footage for a sample taste. My god, Deron, what ya'll did. Absolute *gold*. Nothing like it, before or since, at least in that genre."

This time, it was my cheeks heating up.

"Thanks. Haven't heard such accolades since, well, *never*. But..." I paused with a raised forefinger, "...please tell me none of that hokey dramatization crap. Damn, but I detest reenactments."

"Fear not," Dee-dee reassured, reaching over to pat the top of the hand not raised in potential protest. "We've got ample real footage from the station. That coupled with actual news footage and interviews both past and present will provide all we need to fill the running time, and then some. Honestly, the hardest part with a project like this is all the prime tape that ends up on the cutting room floor. *Gray Matters* was, like, two hundred sixty minutes before editing. Final run time was just over ninety-four, I believe."

Which birthed the question that was, at the time, burning like a runaway wildfire at whatever part of the mind-controlled curiosity.

"These interviews, um, other than myself, who've you lined up?"

For the first time, I felt the positivity vibe of our chat derail to something closer to, if not creeping negativity, a definite cloud of doubt.

Folding slim arms, Dee-dee leaned back, briefly bit into her lower lip, inhaled deeply and drove ahead, full-spiel ahead.

"I should've said, *prospective* interviews. To be honest, we've struggled a bit lining up a few of what we've deemed our prime targets. Make no mistake, it's gonna be an arduous process. To get what we want, the finished product just the way we envisioned it, the three of us will need to dedicate approximately eight months to a year of our lives."

My curiosity not yet sated, I attempted to blast through the brick-solid barrier of mystery from another angle and fired away.

"Understood. I figured it might be a chore to not only locate many of the principals, but that there was a pretty decent chance a few had even passed away. Also, I can think of a few that would probably rather undergo multiple hemorrhoid surgeries without benefit of anesthesia than speak of yours truly, be it favorably or spitting bile."

The pair exchanged yet another knowing glance and I realized I'd hit pay-dirt.

"Well, there was one individual in particular that, well, sort of spoke of you in both lights simultaneously," Dee-dee continued, her hands dancing an energetic jig, her naturally tan cheeks practically aglow with a fresh rush of enthusiasm.

"To confess, I've been holding back for the right time. We weren't really sure how you'd react but like we've discussed, we are going for one-hundred-percent authenticity here, right?"

I nodded without verbal response just as Dixon cleared his throat noisily. Oh Lord, I thought crazily. They dug up one of the many interns I'd hooked up with back in the day.

"The truth is, I did want to give you a heads up on one specific individual we secured for part one, or segment one, if you prefer. Former Master Sergeant, now retired, Conrad Boland."

At first, relief; a moment to reflect, not so much. Regardless, I did my dead-letter best to remain as emotionless as humanly possible despite being forced to take a sizeable bite from a crap-sandwich of such a mighty magnitude. Conrad blessed Boland. Well, if this was going to be about honest storytelling, you take the bad with the good.

"Oh yes. Ol' Smiley Boland. Quite the coup with that one. Surprised the grumpy bastard is still above ground." I smiled, shooting Dee-dee as playful a wink as I could manufacture without my eyelid sticking with blatant insincerity. "I guess it's true what they say about that rare breed that refuse to pass on like most, but instead just kinda nasty away. Boland and his army of goose-stepping cockroaches are probably fated to rule the earth post-apocalypse."

Even as Dixon cleared his throat and rechecked his watch, Dee-dee displayed enough zeal for the both of 'em.

"He was something all right. Kind of all over the map and hard to keep on subject. Of course, he is in his late seventies and from what I understand was quite a man with the bottle during his prime. With a little, well, a *lot* of editing, I think his contribution can be a major segment of part one."

"So, you've already interviewed 'im?"

"In all honesty, it didn't start out as anything official, but once his rant began, I just instinctively knew it was potential gold and there might not be a repeat performance. It seems we caught Mister Boland in a rare, well, sober *and* coherent state. It might've been jumping the gun a bit, but it leads us to this, Deron, for now, *this* minute, what we need from you is the official go-ahead sign to commence pursuing leads and distributing sources."

"Well, much as I hate to broach the subject," I replied, pausing in hopes one or both might catch the drift of where I was headed. It was Dee-dee, of course, who did just that, with a playful palm-slap to her forehead.

"OMG, I'm so sorry. Your upfront compensation is nothing to write home about, I'm afraid. A meager one-thousand-dollar check, mainly just for permissions, though once the production is wrapped there will be an additional ten-thousand-dollar payment and of course a contract will be drawn up naming your estate for the customary fifteen percent for DVD, Blu-ray and streaming."

Maybe I should've given it more thought. Maybe trek back to the house, brew a pot or three of Joe and just mull over the pros and cons one last time. Maybe even give Tank a ring and chew the fat with the one other person on God's green earth I trusted for an opinion on the whole shebang. Or, off-kilter as it might sound, even jaw with Jenny one last time. After all, her future was also apt to be altered by how the end product was judged, despite having no direct involvement. In the end— and it took all of three seconds of hard thought, I reached over the table with an extended hand, nary a twinge of regret at the time at such an impulsive act.

"I'm all in. You say the contract is being drawn up?"

While Dee-dee beamed, eyes ablaze and toothy grin intact, Ron Dixon—who at least did manage a firm enough handshake and perfunctory, if less than convincing smile—appeared, for the most part, weirdly indifferent and aloof in the aftermath, as if he'd just been handed the same excrement-filled club sandwich I'd previously chomped.

"Outstanding! Welcome aboard, Deron Joseph Barrow. As for all those wheres and wherefores, if you'll kindly provide me with an email addy I'll zap you a copy upon completion by the production company's team of legal eagles. Feel free to take it to the attorney of your choice for proper translation of all the legalese and we can add the official John Hancocks at our next meeting."

Pulling a cheap Bic from my front shirt pocket, I scribbled my Hotmail address onto a folded napkin and laid it into her waiting palm.

"Sounds good. You guys staying in The Rock for the duration?"

"We'll be booking a room for the duration of filming once contracts are signed," Dixon answered dryly, having already slid out of the booth for imminent departure.

Dee-dee added, "I'll be working on an itinerary ASAP and shoot it to you at the same address."

"Cool beans, people," I said, standing with a sharp retort from both knees, "Look forward to getting started, at long, long last. Um, one last thing."

I lightly patted my gut with bare palms.

"How long before we get to my interview, I mean a filmed version?"

"Depends," Dixon replied, stretching out both arms as if waking from an extended nap, "Pre-production can take three, four weeks. Video footage will need to be gone through and edited. Could be as long as two months."

Her grin cat-like, Dee-dee flexed a thin arm to show off a surprisingly muscular bicep. "Thinking of going into training, are we?"

"Bingo. The years—not to mention about ten million carbs—haven't been kind. Hoping to have time to tighten up ship and post some fresh muscle underneath these archaic tatts."

"No prob, Deron. If need be, we'll film your segment last."

"Much appreciated, my lady and gentleman."

With that, Diandra Chang practically sprung forth, arms flailing and outstretched, to administer yet another lung-constrictor of an embrace before backing away with the slight tilt of the head and an ear-to-ear grin filled with mischief.

"Before we part, Deron. I *need* to hear it, just once."

"Hear it?"

Her head tilted the opposite direction, her lips pouty and full.

"You know."

Of course I did. It wasn't the first such request, just the first in at least a decade. Cornball and cheesy as it was, I have to admit it was a rush just to be asked. Snapping to attention, arms tucked tightly at my sides, I complied with honors.

"And remember, boys and girls, whatever the conflict, never, *ever* surrender, as the white flag has only one use to a true warrior, a true soldier, and that's to drape over the lifeless corpse of your enemy. Until the next revalue, this is Buck Sergeant Ace Claymore saying lights out, you knuckleheads!"

No doubt more than one observer figured the middle-aged white dude had flipped his lid, but in extracting even the tiniest smile from the lips of Ron Dixon, professional tight ass, the mission had obviously been a smashing success. As for Dee-dee, she shuddered as if from a sudden chill and we exchanged a joyfully spastic high-five before saying our goodbyes.

On the drive back to Boone's Crossing—radio silence observed, a true rarity from the classic rock station that normally accompanied my travels—emotions ran the gamut from cautious optimism to trepidation to outright dread. In excavating the bones of past triumphs and tragedies, an expedition I'd purposely avoided for over two decades, there was always the possibility of the bad aspects overwhelming the positive. Depression was a state I'd battled on and off for years due to memories of the former, and though many a head-shrinker preached the benefits of facing one's fears, I'd taken many a psychological ass-kicking from same. Also, the chances of drudging up a memory long since repressed—perhaps from some random interview or news spot—hung out there like a waiting noose.

In the end, I'd accepted my decision to participate as sound, figuring it was about damn time for a soul-cleansing of the whole mess in one gigantic, lump-sum serving. Only time could dictate how wise or unwise my choice.

That night, I slept soundly enough, though dreams came fast and furious and filled with faces and places from a life that seemed so far-removed as to be pure fantasy.

Three

Rehab, Rewind and Rehash
(From the private journal of Deron Joseph Barrow)

25 June 2019

Boone's Crossing

"Whoa, partner, look at you, all buffed and puffed. You ain't injectin' any of that illegal muscle-juice, now are ya?"

Tank leaned against my home-gym squat rack, casually toking on a freshly lit smoke. Having announced a recent diagnosis of summer cold virus, I'd directed him to a far corner for quarantine purposes.

"Nah. You know my distaste for needles. Mostly just raw egg whites, baked chicken and pounds and pounds of brown rice," I huffed, leaning up from the weight bench, where I'd just concluded a set of three presses at two-hundred-five pounds—a new high since starting the daily regiment just over four weeks past—and reached nearby for a chilled bottle of H2O.

"One thing for sure: hoisting these things in one's fifties births potential dangers I'd never even considered decades previous. Last week I cost myself two days training just from jerking a twenty-five-pound barbell from the rack."

Pausing to sneeze between tokes, Tank giggled, resulting in the evacuation of twin contrails from each flaring nostril. There was a definite jolt of both mental and physical rejuvenation just from spending time with someone other than myself—Skype chats with Jen not withstanding—for the first time in several weeks.

"Know the feelin'. These days I can pull a muscle just poppin' a squat on the toilet. Still, looks like it's payin' off in fine style there, Schwarzenegger. So this is how you've been spendin' your days since agreein' to the deal?"

I answered in between dumbbell curl reps, doing my best to correctly regulate my breathing. False modesty aside, I had to agree with Tank. Since transforming the spare bedroom into a home gym almost immediately following the pow-wow in Little Rock—in addition to the squat rack, water-based hard-bag, manual treadmill, weight bench and over three hundred pounds in free weights, I'd also mirrored an entire wall—a decade-plus of flab buildup and bodily neglect had slowly but surely witnessed a fairly dramatic renovation. I'd chiseled away three inches from my gut while donning a tightly muscled shell the likes of which hadn't been sported since my mid-to-late thirties.

"Two to three hours a day on average, the rest out at the shack. Hardest part has been cutting out the junk food. Sodas, chips and cookies are on the permanent ban list, and I've even cut back on the carbs. Not at easy task for a man used to putting away about a pound of white rice a day. Dropped twelve pounds of flab so far, what with fruits, nuts and bottled H2O dominating the menu. I do manage to sneak in a cheeseburger every now and then."

"I hear ya. Man's a natural carnivore, after all. Hey, speakin' of nuts and bolts, how's she holdin' up?" he asked, gesturing with the smoldering cancer-stick at my brace-covered left knee. I'd taken note of the slight tremor, not nearly as pronounced as his last visit, of the accompanying appendage, and would bide my time on inquiring a status update.

"Stronger by the day, as long as I keep it braced. Doesn't hurt that I squat about as much as your average sixth grader. These days, it ain't about the tonnage but the reps."

Curls complete, I reseated on the bench while using a towel to wipe a stinging buildup of perspiration from each eye.

"How's about the great American novel? Still got blisters on your blisters?"

Instinctively, I glanced at the fingers of both hands, as if half-expecting to see each digit mummified in bandages.

"Second edit still in process but the gist is done and done. The powers-that-be even said they'd give it a once-over and pick over any specific segments for possible reference into the script."

"Only fair," he replied following a lengthy exhale that temporarily blanketed his face in a floating black cloud. "I mean, she is your story after all."

"Yeah, there is that. Hey, did I tell you they secured funding for a pretty decent budget?"

"Cool. Who and how much?"

"Some independent outfit called Foul Play Films offered just over one point five mil. From what I've gathered, that's a pretty healthy price tag as far as documentaries go."

Tank had strolled over to the free-weight rack and scooped up a ten-pound dumbbell and proceeded to execute a set of curls with one hand while tending to his smoke with the other. He would occasionally lean over and exhale out the cramped room's lone source of air circulation, a window I'd propped open with a triceps bar. Maybe it was just his all-black ensemble—jeans, muscle tee, Orleans Saint's ball cap and work boots—but he appeared to have lost a ten-spot or more since our last face-to-face. Still, I didn't think the timing yet right to hit him with a series of random health questions.

"Million and a half, huh? Jeez, I would figure half that would easily cover a flick consisting of folks sitting around answering questions. It ain't like you're gonna be crashing Lamborghinis, blowin' up castles or shootin' CGI lasers at pretend flyin' saucers. Where in blazes does all that cash go?"

"I figure the majority for marketing," I replied with a shrug before rising with a groan, pulling on a pair of padded gloves and sizing up the punching bag. "I was told they're building a mock-up set of my old KATV studio. Should be interesting."

"No shit, you thinkin' of tryin' on the old uniform again,

partner?" he said, grinning and trading the ten for a fifteen before switching arms. Weight loss or not, the well-defined bicep on display was anything but puny.

"Yeah, well, Dee-dee kinda talked me into it. Said it would add a real jolt of nostalgia for former fans of the show. I balked at first but then figured what the hell? Might be a hoot at that."

"She's a fire-plug, that one. Pretty sure she could talk me into sky divin' off Mount Everest if so inclined." He winked, taking a seat on the bench with what little remained of the cigarette bouncing off his lower lip like a fleshy feeler.

I nodded knowingly and delivered a series of jabs to the bag, concluding with first a left and then right hook that sent it spinning sideways on its bulky base. As I backed away for a breather, planning on a set or two of squats to finish off the workout, Tank resumed with a notable darker tone.

"Her partner phoned me last week at the office. You know, Don or Ron somebody: the snobby suit who sounds like he's bein' forced to jaw at ya at gunpoint. Anyhow, he asked for an interview sometime around the first week of August. Said I'd be receiving a contract sometime beforehand that would promise a small percentage of sales. Some such malarkey. I, well, just wanted to clear it with ya. You know, get the official thumbs up or down. It's your call, partner."

Stepping over, I placed a gloved hand on a gaunt but well-defined shoulder.

"Tank, you don't need my permission. I'd deem it a true honor to have you in my corner. Hey, as things pan out, you might be the lone representative for that particular category."

Standing with an unsteady gait, he delivered a gentle jab to my right shoulder while casually flipping the butt of his thoroughly spent smoke through the nearby window.

"The honor will be all mine, partner. Far as I'm concerned, it's long past overdue that folks know the truth, especially all those who took shit at face value all those years ago. I guess the whole fake news phenomenon didn't originate in the 21st century, right?"

"Not by a long shot. Speaking of interviews, Dixon mentioned they'd already completed the first, that being my first ex. Supposed to drive up to the station next week to give it a preliminary look-see. Should be interesting, so say the least."

I concluded the workout in relative silence, biding my time until we'd retreated to the front porch with frosty bottles of Gatorade in our respective mitts. I finally broached the subject.

Between wet sneezes and with all the outward concern of a man discussing a bothersome bone-spur, Tank said the doctors were treating him with something called Carbidopa-levodopa, a natural med that works with the brain as a suppressant. With a sad grin, he shared Wendy's persistent worries and penchant for turning stone-cold taskmaster where his treatments were concerned. A wonderful woman, he confided with a wink, but also a mega-worrywart who held the power to drive him up one wall and down the other on a daily basis. Eric, home until the fall semester, was the exact opposite, choosing to ignore his father's failing health as if doing so would somehow provide a cure. Having grown up and been raised in the presence of such a strong, ultra-manly influence, watching the gradual deterioration of said influence had to be the hardest thing he'd faced in his young life.

"No shit, partner, she is forever clamping my hands and checkin' 'em for even the slightest shake, forcin' me to repeat every other sentence to make sure I ain' slurrin', and makin' sure my arms swing normally when I walk. I swear I can't hoof it out to the damn mailbox without her videotapin' my every friggin' step. Jesus wept, but she's the absolute limit."

Translation: He'd be utterly lost without her. To think I'd known the man when the term 'settling down' was considered outright profanity. Somewhere along the line, the former Wendy Peterson from Corinth, Mississippi had come along hauling custom-made shackles fated for the wrists of this self-proclaimed lifelong bachelor. Three marriages and I'd never found a jailer close to her ilk. My loss, for certain.

"Uh-huh, and you're damn lucky to have her and you know it."

He raised his Gatorade in toast and we gently tapped bottles.

"No denials there, partner. Speakin' of better halves, how's Jenny takin' all this?"

Thoughts of our last Skype chat, two nights previous, shot to the forefront. The chats, as they were, had grown less frequent and shorter in duration in the past month. Weeks before, they'd been talks of her flying back for the fourth of July. It seems her family had talked it over and decided her involvement in the film held much potential, at least financially. Knowing Jen, I'm sure they'd been fireworks but, in the end, at least in my wife's country of origin, family held the face cards. Just a few days later, there'd been a shift in plans and the trip canceled. Unless she changed her mind, the film would more than likely be completed sans an interview with the current spouse of its main character. Deep down, I was somewhat relieved, as it could've been both painful and embarrassing to watch Jen put on the happy face and strain to keep it from slipping off like a cheap Halloween mask. Plus, I could do without all the 'mail-order bride' crap likely to follow.

"Keeping as low-profile as possible. Really not that hard to accomplish being nine-thousand miles away."

Tank cocked a brow quizzically and sneezed yet again as a light rain began to descend, the first such shower of any kind in several weeks, filling the air with the scent of scorched dust.

"Figured the family might've intervened, what with her...hesitation. Nice people, I'm sure, and no offense, but they ain't exactly the Royal Family."

"None taken. I'm sure they made their feelings known, but Jen has enough stubborn in reserve to fight 'em off, at least temporarily. Personally, I think she's just stalling them until the shoot's over."

"Dude, she really, *really* doesn't want anything to do with the whole business. Gotta give her credit for sticking to her guns against that crew."

Between tokes on a fresh smoke, Tank grunted but remained silent.

"Spill, dude," I chided before finishing off the Gatorade in three quick swallows.

"You think much about those times?"

"Which, in particular?"

"Those years, playin' the character? Did...does it seem real to ya? I can't imagine what it must've been like, especially how it, well, ended."

Before I could begin to reply, he turned to me with palms upturned apologetically.

"Hey, if I'm oversteppin', don't hesitate to tell me to leap into the nearest body of water, ya hear? More than ever these days, I seem to have misplaced whatever filter my mouth once he—"

I immediately waved him off, sincerely amazed he thought there were bounds between us, considering our history.

"Hasn't been a single day since they did end that I haven't thought of 'em. You know, we hear certain things our entire life, what my granddad used to call 'sayings' or 'wisdoms.' Well, there is one golden nugget of yesteryear that sticks out to me like gospel about now."

Pausing for effect, I didn't expound until I saw Tank's gray-tinted brows cock in curious anticipation.

"You never know what you had until it's gone. I missed it...severely. Not the notoriety or whatever small sample of fame I'd acquired, but the show itself and especially all the quality individuals it allowed me to meet, hang with, and build a friendship with. No better example of the latter than your leathery hide, you old warhorse."

Grinning as one, we traded shoulder-jabs, albeit much gentler than those of our youth, and fell into a comfortable silence known only to those who share friendship of the most tried and true variety.

It would be almost six weeks before I'd see my best friend again. Neither knew at the time how unrecognizable each would appear to the other when that day arrived.

~ * ~

Excerpt from *The Mask beneath the Mask: A Memoir*, by Deron Joseph Barrow

My father, newly acquired communications degree from Ole Miss in hand, had hired on as a morning DJ at KHLT in the late sixties, about the time anti-war, pro-sex and drug-use rock anthems became all the rage. My memories of his early days at the station are blurry at best, but I recall he and my mom—the stereotypical suburban wife of the sixties, quiet, dainty, classy to the max—embroiled in many a late-night kitchen debate concerning the pros and cons of moving on to greener pastures, career-wise. As years flittered away and his paycheck increased with the popularity of his primetime slot—he'd of course started at the bottom with graveyard shift duties—all talk of transfer faded away.

I'd rarely visited the station before my pre-teen days, but this changed around the same time I earned my driver's license and Dad helped me purchase a very used Ford Granada with roughly a zillion miles beneath its rust-coated hood. It was, as I became a regular hanger-on behind the scenes in the DJ's booth, and not merely exclusive to dad's six PM-ten PM slot, that the bug bit, chomping to the bone of my being. By the time graduation day at Hawthorne High arrived, my plans were set in cement. Radio was gonna be my game, be it spinning records, reporting the news, weather or sports of the day, or as coffee and donut courier.

Though there had been several factors in my decision during those easily influenced teen years, the most severe symptom the aforementioned bug had inferred was on that rare occasion when my dad had allowed me to fill in spinning the hits. One particular night stood out as my personal trial-by-fire, as he'd been struck by a stomach virus so severe the night janitor had discovered him passed out on the toilet, leaving his barely seventeen-year-old offspring to fill a full two hours of airtime. Though restricted from actually speaking to the audience—such a disaster would've meant my old man's instantaneous firing despite the circumstances—I pulled the half-shift without a hitch, timing the ads and tunes perfectly with nary a moment of dead air. Strangest thing, but I recall zilch in the way of pressure. As was spouted so freely those days, I'd thoroughly 'dug it.' From there, I was hooked, even if I didn't yet know it.

Following graduation, and my grades being of the average sort, I decided on a local community college to kick-start my calling as America's—or at least Arkansas'—most recognizable rock'n'roll DJ. Bradberry Community College was not only close by, allowing me to live at home and thus dodge full-blown poverty, but had a pre-journalism course my dad had heard was top-notch. Mom was, of course, just happy to have me home. It was when I was entering my second semester that I made the chance acquaintance of Miss Lori Jean Givens, the chance being that she'd only been on campus for a three-day candy-striper course for beginning nurses. As fate would have it, we bumped lunch trays in the campus cafeteria line, and, upon sharing similar opinions concerning the credibility of the main dish, took a seat at the same table and struck up what would soon become a serious coupling that would dramatically alter both our young lives.

LoJo, as I would so affectionately refer to her in the early years, and I would marry within eight weeks of that first meeting, a dual decision made in youthful lust, haste and blissful ignorance. Needless to say, Mom and Pop were devastated as I dropped out of Bradberry and instead, upon talking with an old high school mate and being thoroughly impressed by his finely pressed uniform and tales of worldly conquests, cruised on down to the local recruiter's office. Newly married and working nights at the local Winn-Dixie stocking shelves, the military promised better money plus valuable educational benefits, not to mention providing a one-way ticket out of Little Rock. It wasn't until I spoke to the Air Force rep—that dude could've sold space-heaters to the Iraqis—that I'd known my young bones to even possess a traveling Jones. The mere prospect of sharing such exotic lands as Japan, South Korea, the UK or Germany with an equally wide-eyed bride had sent this boy's head to spinning like a top.

Basic, followed by technical job training, had flown by in what now seems like the blink of an eye, and soon enough LoJo and I found our initial assignment in Idaho. Not exactly the exotic locale I'd envisioned, but at least it wasn't Arkansas.

It would be just over three drama-filled years before I'd refocus on broadcast journalism. By that time, I was possibly the oldest twenty-three-year-old in history, at least psyche-wise. Sinners can learn too, even those prone to the most extreme of transgressions. A leopard can change his spots. You can indeed teach, well, a *young* dog new tricks anyhow. The time comes when you do wise up. Unfortunately, in my case it was usually after the hammer had dropped but good. You live and you learn, somebody much wiser than I once uttered. My problem was, and always *has* been, the learning portion of said cliché. As the curtain closed on the Year of Our Lord nineteen-eighty-four, I'd find myself detoured, by pure accident, yet again, landing directly onto a meteoric star fated to burn out in the most tragic fashion. Sometimes, the ride alone is worth it, I'd often heard. Even now, over three decades later, I have serious reservations about that statement's validity.

~ * ~

Video Interview with Lori Jean Caldwell (formerly Mrs. Lori Jean Barrow)

(Introduced—via subtitle *Lori Jean Caldwell–ex-wife*—while sitting cross-legged in a padded recliner, dressed conservatively in floral-print blouse, blue jeans and flat, brown pumps. Background showcases retro Air Force recruiting poster with tagline *Aim High.*)

Well, it's an old story, I guess. An all-too-familiar one for so many at that age, I suspect. The simple truth was that Deron and I were far too immature for marriage. Neither of us even had a clue *how* to be a couple. At the time we met, I'd had the grand total of one steady boyfriend, and even that relationship lasted less than six months my senior year in high school *(Insert shot of assorted high school photos; Lori solo; Deron solo; a trio of couple photos).*

Other than that one steady, I believe I'd been on maybe a dozen dates. I'm fairly certain Deron's experience level was equal if not less than my own. He was a funny guy, and charming in a clumsy way that, at nineteen, I found irresistible. In hindsight, we obviously should have dated through college and, if the relationship persevered through four years or more of constant temptation, perhaps proceeded to that next level. I take equal responsibility. Cannot lay it all at his feet, as I was as much a woman-child as he was man-child *(Insert photos from wedding, several including assorted members of each family)*.

Once he made the decision to drop out and join the service, I naturally followed his lead. I figured I could continue nursing school anywhere. Again, we should've spent more than a few fleeting evenings convincing ourselves it was the right thing to do. I think we were both caught up in the moment and in many ways were just craving adventure somewhere, anywhere, other than our Arkansas roots. While I closed out things back home and packed our meager belongings, he attended basic training and tech school in San Antonio, where he spent the next fourteen or fifteen weeks *(Insert photos of Deron in both a green fatigue Air Force uniform with numerous other airmen; shot of Deron in dress blues, rank of Airman Basic)*.

Looking back, we thought it ridiculous when his recruiter announced his test scores best suited him for a career in base security, SPs I think they were called, but it wasn't like he had a choice. Deron had requested Broadcast Journalism but when informed that specific career field was overcrowded and he could either carry a revolver or a pencil behind the ear as an administrative specialist, he chose the former for its, now how did he put it? Oh yeah, its potential for shenanigans *(Insert photo of Deron wearing green fatigue uniform—displayed rank of Airman 1st Class—wearing SP beret with M-16 propped on left shoulder)*.

The recruiter had apparently talked it up as the wiser of the two, and Deron was in no position to argue.

Funny, the memories are so vivid that even thirty-plus years cannot blur. I recall a collect call from Deron—I'd temporarily moved in with his folks while he was in Texas—and discussing which bases on his 'dream sheet' we'd prefer. If I remember correctly, there were five or six slots, including two or three for overseas assignments. In the end, the orders not only ignored the bases we'd listed, but the regions of the country as well. At that time, I'd have been hard-pressed to name a city in Idaho, much less an Air Force Base. In the end, it didn't matter, not really. We were young and eager to travel and meet the mystery of Mountain Hill Air Force Base head on. The major disappointment was not the base itself, but the surrounding area. Mountain Hill was a relatively small town and, in all honesty, there just wasn't a lot to do. Little Rock was the Big Apple comparatively. On occasion we drove to Boise for that 'big city' feel *(Insert various photos: Deron in fatigue uniform—displayed rank of Airman 1st Class—standing guard at a base entrance gate; Deron and Lori together, each holding fishing poles— with mountain peak in background; Deron and Lori mugging for the camera with a lake and mountain range landscape in background).*

From what I remember, Deron's job duties consisted mostly of walking a flight-line or checking IDs at the main gate. Not exactly the action or excitement he'd anticipated. But we had each other. After a time (*sighs*), I found out he'd had *others* as well. It was just as well, as I was slowly finding out that playing the role of housewife just wasn't my bag. The closest nurses' training was in Boise, and being that we could only afford one car, continuing my schooling was temporarily out of the question. Two and a half years passed in a blink, as they are apt to do at that age.

Ignoring his occasional transgressions out of, I guess, nothing more than blatant apathy, I didn't give a second thought to *not* accompanying him to his next assignment.

If forced to attach a book title to my experiences with Kunsan Air Base, South Korea, I'd lean towards something like 'The Season of Abandonment' or 'Welcome to Purgatory, Pacific-region.' As Korea was what they termed a remote tour, meaning a year with dependents not invited to the party, I discovered the one thing worse than mistrust in a marriage, that being a black cloud of loneliness.

While Deron was off, please pardon the crude, whore-hopping and getting boozed up for his country (*clears throat*), among other things, I moved back near my folks and secured an apartment. After a few months, I managed to find work at a local market and scraped by on my meager salary and what little he sent home *(Insert photo of a smiling Lori and her parents standing on the porch of the latter's home).* Deron would call only sporadically and wrote even less, citing long hours on the flight-line, the fourteen-hour time difference, constant war games, blah blah blah. My mom, rest her blessed soul, always had a keen intuitive power when it came to her baby girl, and even though I hadn't mentioned any of Deron's previous hijinks, she knew there were problems. Once the news broke—a call from the Wing Commander, no less—neither she nor Dad showed anything resembling shock and were clearly relieved when I called it a day on a marriage both had secretly deemed, well, a doomed fiasco from the very start.

I guess just about everyone has a time period in their lives they wish they could magically erase from memory. For me, this was it. It was that bad. The single worst year of my life, no contest, and in recent times I've battled breast cancer while my husband and I both lost our parents. Between the cheating, drinking, and of course, the...that *incident*, it's hard to define a single calamity as the worst. Once it finally did end, I felt absolute numbness but, in time, absolute relief. The marriage had been a sham past its first few months, and ended as it should have, with a resounding whimper. Finally, I was able to enter real life with at least a semi-clear head.

As far as Deron, we haven't spoken since the divorce was finalized. Soon after I moved to Baton Rouge and resumed my nursing education. Of course, I did read about his...that other incident. Can't really say I felt much one way or another. Just disassociated, I guess. By then he was just a stranger. I got my first job in nursing a few years later in Shreveport and have spent over twenty-five years in the field, mostly around Shreveport but also New Orleans and Gonzalez. Met Jerry in the summer of ninety-one and, well, three kids and now two grandkids later, my time with Deron has, fortunately, faded to near nonexistence *(Insert photo of Lori, husband Jerry, their grown children and grandkids).* No hard feelings really. Who has time for such? If one lives long enough, they come to realize there are several distinct stages, the early to midstage normally being the rockiest. Graduation from the school of hard knocks allows one to live and learn. Luckily my diploma was earned fairly early in life.

~ * ~

Excerpt from *The Mask beneath the Mask: A Memoir*, by Deron Joseph Barrow

17 July 2019

Little Rock

"So, what we're thinking is injecting your response to each subject's interview."

Sharing couch-space with Dee-dee and Ron Dixon in the sparsely furnished, two-room apartment *slash* office space they'd rented as shoot HQ, I felt a cold chill trail the whole of my spine despite the clammy interior temps of the cramped space. We sat facing a flat-screen Samsung plasma with assorted gizmos of unknown origin flanking it on all sides. In a far corner leaned a tripod setup and what appeared to be video equipment of assorted sizes, the latter appearing to give birth to enough multi-colored wiring to quality for jungle-vine status. We'd just previewed my first ex's interview, taped just three days prior in the smaller of the two rooms, which had been set up specifically for shooting those either living in the local area or willing to travel—I found out later Lojo and one other interviewee had their travel expenses paid, as well as receiving a separate check for participating. It's almost as if I could sense her presence, even days removed, as if she might spring from a nearby closet at any moment. Dee-dee continued while I fought to escape the self-imposed daze triggered by my ex-wife's shockingly haggard appearance—lord, the years had not been kind: the overly-plump features, the gray hair and puffy, drooping eyes, though in fairness over three decades had passed since I'd last laid eyes on her. Of course, she'd also mentioned a bout with breast cancer and recent passings in the family, and lord knows such jolts can age a person.

"The other option is to save the entirety of your interview for the film's conclusion, but this would probably mean a much tighter edit to save time. I'm thinking the instant reaction format is more effective, as viewers are apt to forget earlier details of what you're responding to if we just lump it all together in a single narrative."

"Um, yeah, whatever you think. You folks are the experts," I managed to babble, still foggy in reflective thought. Dixon, as usual, displayed all the emotion of a houseplant while Dee-dee was all waving arms and sparkling, darting eyes, as if riddled with a myriad of thoughts and ideas, all competing for immediate attention.

No doubt sensing my unease, she extended an elbow to deliver a playful tap to my shoulder.

"Hey big guy, I know this isn't easy for you, but we did discuss both the good and potential bad of rehashing the baggage."

"Yep, indeed we did." I shrugged, reaching for the fast-cooling cup of Mickey-D's coffee I'd brought to the party, "Sad part is, Loj…um, Lori's recollections just barely scratch the surface of the tidal wave to come. Have no fear, my skin just needs time to thicken between bouts. It isn't as if she were even remotely stretching the truth. If anything, I think she came off as, well, politely restrained.

"So, you guys want my immediate reaction to Lori's words? Wish I'd thought to dress for the occasion."

"No real hurry," Dixon chimed in indifferently, having already rewound Lori's segment, "We don't want it to sound like a debate. Better it doesn't come off like some stale question and answer segment. We can film your segments back-to-back when the time comes, after you've viewed the others, and that way it'll sound less like a rehearsed rebuttal than a live, ad-libbed reply in your own words."

"Well geez Ron, whose words would they be *other* than my own?" I shot back, a bit perturbed at the snotty millennial vibe of his naturally condescending attitude. In typical fashion, he seemed wholly unfazed.

"Bottom line is, we need a natural response and not one fueled by the emotion of the moment. Dee understands the semantics."

"He's right, Deron. You're apt to be responding solely to her recollections. On a different day with a fresh perspective, you'll be providing your own. We didn't bring you here today for taping. We'll schedule that weeks ahead of filming. Oh, by the way," she paused, slapping me lightly on the knee with the back of a hand, "The set we talked about is well under construction and should be a done deal in a matter of two weeks, maybe less. I was going to show you some pics I took on my cell but decided to save your reaction for a live shot. We also have the replication of your old uni. From what I'm seeing," she paused to flex her biceps and then gesture towards my own, "you're gonna pour into 'em just like old school week. Buffed and thoroughly puffed."

On the verge of blushing, a bona fide rarity that, I felt obligated by modesty to respond in kind, despite the stone-cold truth of her description.

"Still a work in progress but coming along."

I stroked the salt-and-pepper stubble at my chin with one hand while running a hand through my grayish mop with the other.

"Gonna have to perform some serious man-scaping before the filming, at least to get fully back into character. Speaking of which, you guys know of any local makeup gurus for hire?"

"Makeup gu..." Dixon mumbled, obviously perplexed.

"Oh, got'cha," Dee-dee practically shouted after a short pause, snapping her fingers as the answer clicked. "The famous battle-scars. Oh yeah, no worries. We'll make some calls and line someone up the morning of the shoot to fix you up."

Though I shrugged casually, this seemingly small detail had given me some cause for concern. If I was going to recreate ol' granite jaw, I wanted it to be as realistic as possible for a re-intro that was almost three decades between appearances.

"Great. I guess if we're gonna do this, we might as well do it right, yeah?"

"Darn tootin'," she said with a girlish squeal, raising an arm airborne and displaying the flat of one palm.

"Damn straight," I countered, finishing up the high five with a light tap and feeling less awkward than I had any right to. The young woman's enthusiasm was as catching and she was fetching, as Tank might quip.

"Oh, how goes the self-edit on that door-stop autobiography?"

"Slowly but surely. Been splitting time between polishing it up while doing the same for this withered old physique."

"Sure would like a sneak preview," she chided with a slight head-tilt. "Nothing like personal insight from the source to avoid missteps along the way."

"Well, to be honest I'm kind of anal about anyone's eyes scanning those pages 'til I know they're completely error-free, and not just grammatically and typo-proof but memory-wise."

"We get it, Deron. Don't apologize for being a member in good standing of the perfectionist club. You can take a seat right next to yours truly."

She continued only after lifting a forefinger thoughtfully.

"Don't delay too long, though. It would be one heck of a boon to release a companion, tell-all book in conjunction *with* the film version."

I nodded in tentative agreement, figuring my writings were probably eons removed from being professionally written enough for actual publication, at least without a year's worth of rewriting and countless edits by those infinitely more qualified than myself. Still, the thought of a dual release was a tantalizing one.

As was the norm, Dixon managed to shatter whatever momentum had been built with his robotic monotone and lackadaisical body language, pulling himself up from the couch with all the gusto of a sloth on a Nyquil drunk.

"We've scheduled Mister Boland for early next week. Offered to fly him in but he punted, stating, and I quote, 'it wasn't worth the effort to leave his couch' and that if we were aiming to romanticize the man being spoken of in any form or fashion, that he'd 'sue us until our future in filmmaking would be limited solely to the field of infomercials'."

Jaw muscles working like well-oiled pistons, I nonetheless

managed to maintain my cool despite the urge to put my fist through the nearest wall.

"Yep, sounds like the cranky old bastard. The one constant in an ever-changing world, ol' shit-heel Boland. Am I gonna be graced with a similar sneak preview in the aftermath?"

"Indeed you will, Mister Producer," Dee-dee answered, as upbeat as ever despite surely feeling the sudden shift in vibes blowing in like a fevered breeze from my general direction. "As well as editing rights, if you feel the need, potential lawsuits be darned."

"We'll be flying out to his ranch in Arizona. Just an overnight stay. I take it you'd rather remain at home base?"

If it had originated from anyone else, I'd have surely taken Dixon's question as snide, sarcastic and downright insulting. As it was, par course pretty much summed it up and I took no offense whatsoever.

"You assume correctly, young man. Put me and ol' grumpy-gums in the same room and I'm liable to forget he's old enough to have signed the constitution. Not claiming angel wings here, the story is what it is and I'm...*was* guilty as charged for the most part, but Boland will no doubt embellish at every opportunity just to stick it to me as often as possible. If he and I are ever fated to share space, false teeth and adult-diaper be damned, I'd still beat his fossilized ass to ashes and thoroughly enjoy it."

To that, even Dee-dee remained conspicuously silent. We parted with a hug (Dee) and limp, generally uninspired handshake (Dixon) and I cruised back to the homestead with a fresh cup of Joe parked in the center console while rewinding and critiquing Lojo's interview. By the time I reached the hacienda, I'd accepted, as stated earlier, that the majority of what she'd said had been as right as rain. I had been, for the most part, a complete asshat upon our assignment to Mountain High, the jack-wagon behavior only escalating to new levels of debauchery in Korea. I had, admittedly, treated her like access baggage, a hindrance to my newfound lifestyle, and she'd done nothing to deserve it. All that confessed, it was to her credit she came off so forgiving, at least in deportment. Deep down, I'd never meant to hurt her, my first love. Well, maybe *lust* is more apt, but at that age it's kind of a po-tay-to/po-tah-to situation. Doesn't forgive my horse's ass behavior, but it's true. It almost made me wish she'd dished out the entire buffet of vile instead of just a single serving.

Settling back in with my feet kicked up, a freshly heated frozen dinner smoldering atop the TV tray and the glow of the boob tube lighting up the living room, I briefly thought of phoning Tank but reconsidered. For some inexplicable reason, I thought of this as a weird form of tampering. It wasn't as if my oldest comrade held some agenda, but I didn't want him thinking I called to somehow coerce with his interview next in line. Instead, I choked down a bland slab of roast beef and equally tasteless mashed potatoes—washing down what I'd foolishly purchased as a 'cheat meal' from my recent health kick with a chilled glass of OJ— and Skyped my estranged spouse. Half an hour later, whatever positive vibes I'd received from that day's meeting with the production team vanished in a cloud of cool indifference. It appeared the grim reaper of divorce was yet again aiming his scythe my way, and no self-serving documentary was apt to stave off that bad boy's razer-sharp edge.

Four

Land of the Morning Calamity
Excerpt from *The Mask beneath the Mask: A Memoir*, by Deron Joseph Barrow

That initial infidelity occurred fairly quickly, maybe three months into the Mountain Hill assignment. Lori and I had rented an apartment less than a mile's ride from the main gate, a cheap-as-dirt, dilapidated crap-hole that we used to joke was being held up by an army of roaches living rent-free. Being that we could only afford one form of transportation, a '77 Le Sabre in the twilight of its existence, she stayed home and played house while I, as a newly assigned Airman Basic (no striper), routinely put in sixty-plus hour workweeks. The troop's name was Pamela Fries, a busty, ultra-cute red-headed Airman First Class assigned to the same security outfit and, personality-wise, the polar opposite of my quiet, reserved and sometimes emotionally stilted newlywed spouse. Pam Fries could hold her own with any of her male peers in terms of work output, alcohol consumption, overall physicality and, both shockingly and hilariously, was a true Zen master in the art of profanity. I'd never met anyone like her and honestly, she blew my socks off. My biggest crush, possibly of all time, but surely for a highly impressible, barely twenty-one-year-old. It started out innocently enough with a few beers at the base airman's club after a long shift of walking the flight-line like a pair of fleshy automations. By our third or fourth such outing, we ended up in her barrack's room and well, such was the beginning of the end for that first ill-fated marriage. Approximately six or seven weeks later, the new had worn off and it ended as quickly as it had begun. Oh, we still worked many of the same shifts and occasionally tipped beer mugs at the club or some of the local bars, but that mostly involved a group dynamic. Pam went on to other affairs—rumor had it she even briefly shacked up with our unit NCOIC—before receiving orders to Guam. Toot sweet, we never even said goodbye.

Wish I could claim she was the lone discrepancy, the single mistake that could be chalked up to youthful curiosity, hormones, untamed horniness. Not...even...close. There were countless others, including yet another co-worker at the end of my tour whose name, I'm ashamed to say, completely escapes me. Then there were the numerous one-night-stands, normally kick-started at one of two local watering holes near the base's main gate that catered to base personnel and thus whose female clientele consisted mostly of what the young airman referred to as 'camp tramps.' Over time—about the time I'd earned my second stripe—I found my personal favorite to be a country-western dive with the laughably cornball moniker of *Thirsty's*, only because the majority of my conquests originated from said tavern. This boy wasn't picky, not in the least, especially after six or seven rounds of libations.

Many was the night I'd stagger home—if I found my way home at all—wearing a drunken grin that poor Lori was forced to endure along with the lies that accompanied it. I apparently had no shame in cheating on her so openly, and though I never gave it much serious thought at the time—I was literally on a never-ending carny ride of work vs. play with no time in between—there was little doubt I was purposely sabotaging the marriage. All these years later, there is shame but, sadly, little regret. Surely Lori would echo this, wherever she may be. Selfish lug that I was, I can't help but reflect on that expression of off-kilter bewilderment that often clouded those baby-blues, even in the supposed 'good times,' what few there were.

The orders to Korea were the nail in the coffin from the day they were slapped in my sweaty little palm. Lori had hoped for England or Germany for my initial overseas base, and I'd even lied in telling her I'd filled my assignment dream-sheet with nothing but the best the European theatre had to offer, and only those deemed 'accompanied,' meaning three to four year tours with dependent travel paid in full. Instead, I'd listed such popular remote locales—meaning the twelve-month type where family members did not qualify—as the Philippines, Korea and even Greenland. Obviously, I was craving a little 'me' time, that whole 'til death do us part crap wearing mighty thin as year three since those initial vows approached.

Kunsan Air Base, South Korea: *The Kun*, The *Land of the Morning Calm*. More like the *Land of the Daily Debauchery*. Make no mistake, you worked your ass off—we were, after all, supposedly a mere nine minutes from the grisliest of deaths via chemical warfare if the enemy from the north deemed it so—and partied like it was your last night on the planet when the opportunities arose. Needless to say I accomplished both, in spades.

Though base regs required all those below the rank of E-5 (Staff Sergeant) be assigned a barracks room, it took me less than a month to *unofficially* rent a room off base near the narrow, winding streets of the 'Ville, more infamously known as American Town, or *A-Town,* a party-haven located a few scant miles from the main gate and allegedly built with DOD funds to give off-duty GIs a place to blow off steam. Modestly put, this boy could've shoved a loaded freight up Mount Everest with the steam I blew off, despite my stay being so cruelly, but justifiably, cut short. From the moment I deplaned to the overwhelming scent of garlic-laced kimchi, that place was equal parts magical mystery and sinner's paradise. From the readily available prostitution to all-night clubs to street vendors selling all manner of exotic foods, this southern-born, southern-bred boy was a space-traveler trekking atop a planet of unknown origin and discovering all manner of carnal delights.

I often came to the conclusion during one of the many drunken escapades inside A-Town's gated walls that I never wanted to leave. I figured I could continue to extend my tour until they literally dragged me onto that Freedom Bird back to the states, a flight the majority of Kun inmates began to anticipate from day one of assignment, especially the married of the species. In my nine-plus months on-site, I saw many a marriage crumble as those so happily wed and loyal to their displaced better-half upon arrival fell lustful victim to the ample charms of some local seductress. In fairness, I didn't qualify for said category, being that my marital status was teetering on the edge of collapse *upon* arrival.

The Korean word was 'yobo' for lover or live-in partner. In my sadly truncated tour, I managed to move in and play house with two different yobos, although unlike so many of my doe-eyed peers out shopping for engagement rings and filling out stacks of acquired-dependent paperwork, my own agenda was purely physical, baby. Sewed on my senior-airman stripe about mid-tour and with the accompanying raise—laughably miniscule in retrospect—I felt like I'd secured rock-star status, at least among the bar girls that had become my personal entourage. Well, that and a natural talent for black-marketing everything from American smokes, booze and even select grocery items from the base commissary. I was, at least until the big implosion, one of the made men of the 'Ville, a smooth-talkin', fancy-walkin' dude with the cheesy grin, fat wallet and perpetual erection.

Looking back with less innocent eyes and a modern take, it was like comic-book geek's wet dream: hard-ass 'Ville cop when duty called—as base security, we were also tasked to police up the A-Town bars, which usually meant breaking up drunken brawls or yanking a horny GI off some unwilling, extremely pissed-off bar girl—and town Romeo without-a-conscience whenever out of uniform. More importantly, I had plans of becoming the unofficial mayor of GI town, that is, the guy who could get you anything for a price. Those plans did not include the shitstorm that soon followed: a level-five tree-bender that left me stripped of not only whatever imaginary status I'd achieved, but as the dominos slowly toppled, a potential career as well.

~ * ~

November, 1987

Gunsan City, South Korea

American (A) Town

"Yo, Hairy-back! Let's shag! Sounds like some trouble over at the Phoenix," the senior of the two airmen barked, his grimacing mug temporarily shielded by a virtual cloudburst of breathe vapor. The Indian Summer of just days before had given way to a brutal winter stretch that had seen temps plummet into the low twenties and the severely cracked pavement coated in fresh snowfall. Just minutes earlier, a trio of drunken airmen had half-jogged, half-stumbled down the narrow path between the Paradise and Young 11, catching Barrow's immediate attention as he'd exited the Wolf's Den, the loudest and perhaps more sober of the three pointing north and stating they'd just witnessed a skirmish of some sort inside the Phoenix. Barrow, having recently sewn on senior-airman stripes, might have normally ignored such inebriation-laced chatter as a potential prank, but on this night—a Wednesday, usually a fairly tame night in the 'Ville—found himself pegged as highest-ranking SP on duty and thus had no choice but check out any and all such claims. His partner, a recent arrival at the Kun at just over three weeks in country was a wide-eyed, baby-cheeked, rail-thin Airman First Class with the unfortunate name of Harry Bachman, thus the charming nick.

Decked out in the required camo fatigues, baseball-cap styled cover, black gloves and regulation jacket of choice—Barrow in a camo field jacket and his subordinate in a supply-issued parka—the two fast-walked it up the slick incline, negotiating mostly deserted streets as familiar tunes echoed from the surrounding bars; John Mellencamp's "Cherry Bomb" mingled rather clumsily with Heart's "Alone" as they passed between the Golden Butterfly and The Stereo Club and Whitesnake's "Here I Go Again" meshing meticulously in sync with Guns 'N Roses "Welcome to the Jungle" as they split the Long Beach and Savoy, respectively.

"What a night to pull this garbage detail," Bachman groaned between labored huffs. "Cold as a freakin' coven of witches' tits. Maybe we can claim a dark corner inside the Phoenix, huh? I need to thaw out my privates."

Having taken point by several steps, Barrow briefly turned to regard his charge—his junior by surely no more than a calendar year—with a pained scowl, nostrils flaring as if offended by a scent even stronger than the overwhelming stench of raw garlic, rotted cabbage and cooked pork which seemed to permanently permeate the entire region and country as a whole.

"Best learn to love it, bud, being as you just barely crawled from the shell. You ain't seen shit until you've spent a summer walking this beat. Best invest in a pair of pliers once June hits, as you'll need 'em to peel off your undies at the end of shift."

As they veered left past a small shop advertising women's shoes, though widely known by all as one of many 'cash to won' exchanges, on the right and VIP club on the left—Survivor's "Burning Heart" rattling the outer walls—a middle-aged local Barrow instantly recognized as the Phoenix club's manager sprinted past, literally skidding to an awkward stop with arms waving wildly.

"Whoa, Mister Cho, where's the fire?" Barrow inquired with arms raised in mock surrender. Meanwhile, Airman Bachman busied himself by digging into his parka for a fresh smoke.

"He michyeosseo! Break tables and chairs and throw bottles against the stage! Glass go everywhere, some into Miss Young's eye! Michyeosseo! Then he drag Miss Leah outside but punch her first many times!" the man, slightly cockeyed and crooked of nose, screeched and spat, emphasizing the Korean word for crazy with the trademark dragging out of the final word of each sentence.

"And you say he was mechiso, do ya?" Barrow jabbed, hardly able to maintain a straight face as his sidekick leaned against a far wall and casually toked, utterly indifferent.

"He owe me money!" Cho continued to rant, a fine misting of sweat coating his cheeks and forehead despite the bitter cold, veins as thick as cable cord protruding from each side of his slim neck, "He owe me maybe fifteen, twenty thousand won! I no pay Miss Young bill if she have to get glass taken out of eye! I *no* pay! She might have to miss many days and I lose more money. Weekend coming and GI stay away without

Miss Young!"

Miss Young, Barrow knew, was Cho's main attraction as far as his stable of dancers went: nice, round butt, perky boobs, a toothy smile and exquisitely slanted brown eyes that lit up every crotch in the house. Not your everyday bar girl in a thong; the Phoenix wasn't liable to rise any time soon without her to feature.

"Yeah, yeah, I get it, I get it. Tell you what, we'll take care of the crazy GI and you head on back to your club and total up the damages for our report. We'll be back..." Barrow paused to push back up the glove on his left hand in order to reveal the watch-face underneath, which read twenty-one forty-six hours, "...either right before or right after you close, get it?"

The slight little man—decked out only in a thin Member's Only jacket—the cheap knockoff version sold so commonly in nearby Kunsan City—wore a perpetual scowl, which only increased in pinched fury at the senior airman's blandly delivered instruction.

"But how you know *where* to find?"

"Yeah, DJ, what *he* said," Bachman chimed in between puffs, strolling up to stand beside Cho while failing miserably to drudge up anything close to sincere interest.

Reaching up and over with the speed and dexterity of a veteran gunfighter, Barrow snatched the cigarette from between the younger man's clenched teeth and flicked it down a nearby alley, all in one fluid movement.

"Smoke 'em if you got 'em only when off-duty, bud. As for the suspected perpetrator, let's just say I've got a hell of a hunch."

"You bring that shabolnoma to me! I make him pay what he owe! I bring my brothers and they fix that Michinom!" Cho continued to rave, waving spindly arms counter-clockwise as if to attempt flight. Such liberal use of such Korean profanity staples—at least those most GIs learned quickest, usually from being referred to as such—had little to no effect due to their overuse, except perhaps to elicit humor. If not for the brutal conditions, Barrow might've played along and even egged Cho on ever further into a lip-foaming, bug-eyed lather. As it was, he just wanted the screeching little weasel—whose breath reeked of kimchi and soju—out of his face.

A stout gust finding every available crease in order to properly chill his bones to the very marrow, Barrow pointed directly over the smaller man's shoulder in the general direction of the Phoenix, replying with a purposeful curtness he hoped would nip a continued performance directly in the bud.

"Otishe, we will take *care* of it. Now get your scrawny ass back to the club, arasseo?"

"Okay, but you come later?"

"I said we would. Now go. Take care of your people."

With that, Mister Cho grunted in obvious disdain before trekking back up the hill with his hands tucked in the imitation brand-name jacket's pockets. Barrow briefly peered past the quickly ascending man to the double-door entrance to the Phoenix, where a trio of individuals stood, their frames propping each side half-ajar. While two were obviously blue jean wearing patrons, a naked, shapely brown gam IDed the third as none other than the delectable Miss Young herself, a bandage as snow-white as that falling from the blackened skies held snugly over her injured orb.

"You owe me a smoke, man," Bachman grumbled before following Barrow's slightly bandy-legged lead into a nearby alley.

"Sure, bean. How much for a pack of Pine Tree these days? Two hundred won I can spare without contacting my banker," Barrow replied with a thick layer of smart-ass, secretly reveling in the use of the 'bean' reference at every opportunity, the term short for 'green bean', defined as a new arrival to the peninsula.

The younger troop kept a three-step distance, dragging his boots lazily along the narrow, half-cobblestone, half-concrete walkway, the surface of which was growing slicker by the minute due to a sudden infusion of larger flakes.

"Pine Tr—are you serious? I don't buy that local roll, man. Takes a flamethrower to light 'em. No sir, that was a Marlboro. Made with care and true cancer-concern in the good old U.S. of A."

"Yeah, yeah, remind me to scribble out an IOU once we're off shift. For now, keep focused on the task at hand. The dude we're about to face down isn't apt to greet us with anything other than extreme malice."

Ducking a drooping clothesline hanging shoulder-level between neighboring hooches, Barrow could just make out Bachman's whispered mumblings.

"Issues, airman?"

"Just saying it's horseshit," the younger man growled, amping up the volume enough to at least be audible while executing a semi-limbo to avoid being clotheslined by the similarly named strand of rope.

"Specifics, bean. Speak freely but with a sense of urgency, as we're nearing the hooch in question."

"Fine. Remember you asked for it. Specifics be, well, the whole shebang basically. Don't know about you, but I didn't sign up to play marriage counselor for a base full of drunken GIs and their chosen whore lesser-halves. Honestly, D.J., I'm finding it hard to give a good shit what they do to each other on their own time.

"If a man wants to screw up his life by getting tied down to some slant-eyed Jezebel and sire a busload of half-breeds, who are you or I to stand in his way? Hey, as long as I don't have to fund their hijinks, I'm cool, but being forced to wade between 'em whenever they 'miscommunicate,' I call horseshit with a steaming capital H."

Barrow paused beneath the plank awning of an abandoned food stand, openly smirking as he turned to face his younger partner.

"Damn boy, sounds to me like you're in desperate need of some down and dirty time with one of the very warm-bodied cuties you claim to despise."

Arms crossed defiantly, frosty streams of vapor pumping from each flaring nostril, Bachman's creased facial features were altered dramatically by the dim lighting, temporarily giving him the appearance of a man twenty years his senior.

"Never said I despise anybody. I just don't agree with...mixing bloodlines with the locals. We're us and they're them, simple as that."

"Geez Louise, Harry. You're from where again, Pennsylvania?"

"Ohio. Fairborn. Why?"

Flashing a wide, toothy grin, Barrow reached over and planted a firm slap to the smaller man's upper back.

"And here I'd always been taught we southern boys had cornered the market on such racist thinking."

"Raci—hey, I didn't say, I mean, what I meant was...that...got nothing to with being, or t-thinking..."

"No need to birth a cow, bean. A man's entitled to his opinion," Barrow mercifully interrupted, stepping back into the alley and eyeing the trail ahead, now completely snow-covered and adding a slightly improved measure of illumination, "Even if it is better suited for a Nazi concentration camp or pre-Civil War plantation. Now c'mon, Airman," he continued, waving a gloved hand forward in animated fashion, as if leading a war charge, "We've got some serious couple counseling to do."

In the aftermath, Barrow wore a mask of sly satisfaction despite his obviously offended subordinate's barrage of barely audible cursing, the word 'asshole' easily comprehensible. He'd decided he didn't particularly like the mouthy little prick, and would, in turn, do his dead-letter best to use those confessed prejudices against him at every opportunity.

As they crested a final hill in what appeared a never-ending maze of tiny, thatch-roofed dwellings, Barrow paused to survey the pathway ahead. Bachman moved up to his left with a pronounced grunt, braking hard and nearly falling to one knee from the effort as his left boot slid forward awkwardly.

"Hang on," Barrow announced wearily, yanking the bulky radio from his belt. "Gonna call this in before we step any further into some potentially disorderly family shenanigan."

Moving conveniently out of his partner's line-of-sight, he verbally, and perhaps a bit too loud for sincerity, announced to HQ their approximate whereabouts and the mission at hand, all while never actually engaging the send button. He did this with steely-eyed resolve, as if such blatant noncompliance to regulation was as routine as natural obedience.

Upon exiting the alley, and while casually reattaching his radio onto its preset slot, he nodded towards the path ahead and forged purposely forward.

Three additional twists and matching turns through the seemingly infinite rat-maze of miniature abodes, boarding houses and abandoned street vender tents later, Bachman's groans, grunts and assorted moans of disgruntlement finally evolved into a genuine audible pronouncement.

"Holy crap already! Are we *there* yet? Feels like we've covered about ten clicks over the same winding alley. We get any further from the 'Ville and we're gonna need a passport," he moaned, alternating lifting each knee chest high as if running in place.

Ignoring this latest bitch-rant, Barrow stepped directly in front of the smaller airman and, an expression of grim, stone-seriousness set firmly in place, spoke in a low, deliberate tone he normally utilized solely for shock value amongst his peers.

"Listen up, Harry-Oh. This dude's name is Brookens. Len Brookens. E-seven, Master Sergeant type; an NCO within our own unit. Works mostly perimeter road security and bomb dump. A real hard-ass when he's sober and a just plain ass when he's tanked."

"He's an SP supervisor? How do you know this is the same guy Cho was yapping about?"

"Let's just say our paths have crossed a time or three. The Miss Leah that Cho mentioned is his bride-to-be and a former dancer at the Phoenix. I'd heard Brookens had a helluva of a temper, especially when lit. Guess it was only a matter of time before he went off the deep end on my watch."

The younger troop licked his lips nervously, both gloved hands clenching and unclenching in time.

"Listen up, Barrow, since they've retreated to their hooch, why bother with the report at all? The sarge can sleep it off and we can act like we gave 'im a good scolding, end of story."

"You forget the damage, personal and property, back at the Phoenix? Dude, a scolding ain't about to pay Cho for the busted furniture or his main attraction's medical bill," Barrow countered, digging beneath the lower edge of his field jacket into his utility belt for a quick non-visual inventory. "Don't shit a brick. If things get heated, I'm a walkin', talkin' popsicle, dig?"

Harry Bachman's hesitant nod didn't exactly exhume confidence.

"Worst comes to worst, pull the mace and ready the cuffs, but do not, I repeat, do not even *think* of reaching for either until I say, got it?"

"Yeah, sure," Bachman retorted curtly, swallowing hard. "And if the whore extracts her claws? What then? Don't know about you, but I don't want to spend the rest of my tour in a local eight-by-ten being corn-holed by every Tom, Dick and Mister Lee craving a little American gluteus maximus."

Forced to break eye-contact, Barrow's upper torso briefly tremored from suppressed laughter, a low gurgling sound emitted from beneath the glove cloaking his mouth. He managed to retain the majority of his composure—devilish grin not withstanding—fairly quickly, twisting back around to relock orbs with his subordinate, whose bony frame had stiffened with a building rage.

"Just follow my lead and I guarantee to keep that precious virginity intact."

"I'm serious, asshole!" Bachman brayed, fists shaking at his sides.

Slapping an open palm firmly against the smaller man's upper chest—the thick parka taking the brunt of the force—Barrow's gaze alternated between Bachman's sneering mug and the hooch to their immediate left, approximately twenty feet away, where a dim light shown from beneath the lone entrance.

"So am *I*, airman. Now clam up, grow a pair and do your damn job. Geez, Harry, just chill the hell out and remember your training. Let's go do this."

As if prepping for some imaginary bell to ring for round one of a prizefight, the younger man shrugged his shoulders, inhaling and exhaling several times, filling the surrounding snowflake-filled air with a trio of perfectly rounded vapor clouds.

"Right behind you, Ace."

Taking point as promised, Barrow managed to maintain a purposeful, dutiful gait and unemotional, unreadable expression despite feeling his gut constrict like banded steel and an icy chill race down his spine, the latter having little to do with the frigidity of the night air.

~ * ~

Excerpt from *The Mask beneath the Mask: A Memoir*, by Deron Joseph Barrow

Blame it on the weather. Blame it on being partnered with a still-moist-behind the ears partner. Blame it on lack of experience from a non-NCO on his first night as A-Town security patrol officer in-charge. Deep down, all the above answers would be greeted with a resounding buzzer and, in bold red font, a bright, blinking neon light proclaiming '*INCORRECT—Try Again*'. The sad truth was, and whatever argument or excuse I might drudge up would be as stale as year-old brew, the royal screw-up of base policy and procedure on that specific amateur night was due solely to yours truly. The reason for such bone-headed non-decision making? Well, it wasn't nearly as accidental as many might speculate. Truth was I wanted to maintain as much secrecy as possible and thus involve as few up the chain-of-command as possible. The reasoning for such a blatant, boneheaded attempt at confidentiality would become obvious in the aftermath of the fiasco to come but at the time, at least within the mostly hollow brain-shell of this boy, it truly seemed like the lone option.

As far as the mistakes/missteps go, there were many, but two stood out like sequoia-sized turds floating in the proverbial punchbowl:

Hulking miscue #1: Upon contacting complainant (Mister Cho), should have immediately had Bachman take a statement while radioing for backup. Upon backup's arrival—usually only minutes in duration—return to the Phoenix and survey damage, both property and person, tasking backup SPs to take any additional statements.

Hulking miscue #2: Assuming the tasks of miscue one were complete, radioing base HQ would've been strictly policy, considering the circumstances of multiple assaults and substantial property damage, mostly to ensure an NCO of at least Tech Sergeant rank report to the scene toot-sweet and take over the investigation. Said NCO would then decide who and how many town SPs would track the potential suspect to his hooch, or perhaps call in troops assigned to base detail for a knock-and-talk at the Brookens' abode. Being that the suspected perpetrator was himself an E-seven assigned to base security in a supervisor role, the latter would've probably been the logical call, with at least another Master Sergeant leading the posse.

In retrospect, such pathetic non-calls, though subliminally sound to the warped mind, were but the first hairline crack in a dam nearing total collapse.

From the time Bachman and I began what seemed at the time like a slow-motion walk to that hooch entrance, I'd instantly forgotten just how frigid—the coldest I'd felt since my arrival at the Kun—that night had been. It was like a toxic mix of stress and apprehension hit me like a tidal wave, coating me in an almost-suffocating shell of searing heat. This would be the only explanation to the thick layer of sweat that, despite a wind-chill factor near the single digits, didn't instantly freeze my eyelids, nostrils and lips shut. With my severely disgruntled, green as freshly prepared Bok Choy partner acting like a frightened pup—he alternated this with an annoying lack of devotion to the job at hand—I remember thinking I'd have been better off handling it alone. That was, until the cheap particle-board hooch door swung open and I was allowed that initial peek inside.

FYI: The majority of Korean homes back in the day—at least those I'd frequented—were heated via Ondol system, that being the baking of stones beneath the floor via lit charcoals that, depending on the dwelling, served to heat either single rooms or the entire abode. Odorless for the most part, the invisible fumes can be deadly if leaks are left unattended. Maybe it was the arctic temps of that mid-November night— I seem to recall being told later it was a record low for that specific month—but the breeze that slapped my face as I stepped inside the living space of Sergeant Len Brookens and his bride-to-be Leah Mai, it was like sticking one's face into a live furnace. I'd fibbed, of course, about only knowing the good sergeant in passing, unless one spoke of on-duty meetings only, which had been limited to a handful. No, it was off-duty where Brookens and I had become acquainted, though in an indirect, non-personal way, and to my eternal regret. I was, admittedly, a cocky, brash SOB in those days, the kind of smart-ass slickster who truly thought they were beyond the reach of those who enforce the rules. Needless to say, the Air Force had many regulations covering anything and everything considered conduct unbecoming, and not just for those labeled 'commissioned.' Didn't know it at the time, but I was about to be introduced to several, some of which I didn't even know I'd broken. It all began with the leering, grinning face of Len Brookens, bloodshot eyes spinning like pinwheels, greeting me at the door, the sounds of a whimpering, sobbing female voice echoing in the background.

~ * ~

"Well, it's about time, boys. Colder than Minot in February, I got it, but I also figured you might've stopped off for a smoke and maybe a bowl or two of jungle-juice just to prep for this little conference call."

His eyes darted and rolled like a BB in one of those hand-held carny games where the purpose is to land 'em all inside strategically placed holes. Standing barefoot on the cold stone of the hooch's foyer—occupied by an ondol firebox, two-burner stove, a trio of restaurant-style, high-back chairs with accompanying wooden dining table and a faded gray top-freezer refrigerator—the Master Sergeant's ensemble consisted of faded blue jeans and light brown tee, a slight rip at the collar of the latter, which also appeared to hold several dark spatters at the breastbone and upper abdomen, spatters Barrow instantly deduced as freshly applied, thus recently extracted.

"Evening, Sarge. You, um, mind if we come in and jaw? Not exactly sit on the porch and sip lemonade conditions out here," he asked, surprisingly without even a tint of apprehension despite the bass-drum pounding at his temples. One glance at Brookens' bug-eyed, spastic expression and Barrow recognized the symptoms, as well as the probable suspect responsible for said condition as a depressingly familiar one.

Backing away with a slight bow and wave of a pale, freckle-infested arm, Len Brookens' slug-like lips curled into a parody of a smile: a single, circular droplet of clear mucus hanging from the tip of his bulbous nose like insect larva. Though Barrow had seen the man out of uniform several times before, this was a new level of dishevelment. Brookens was tall, big-boned and doughy, and his preferred eyewear—thick black frames, coke-bottle-thick lens—brought to mind the spectacles issued to the seeing-impaired during basic training, sometimes referred to as 'birth-control glasses' for their undeniable butt-ugliness. With his prominent snout, close-set eyes (complete with caterpillar-like unibrow) and square, dimpled chin, he gave the impression of being at least a decade older than he really was, which Barrow would later learn to be a recently turned thirty-eight.

"Why certainly, Airman Barrow. I have to say, you, sir, are indeed a sight for sore eyes. No offense, but I kind of figured someone of higher rank to be out front on this thing. And who is your baby-faced partner here? Seems we might've crossed paths briefly, but I can't quite put a finger on any particulars."

Harry Bachman stepped timidly forward, politely thumping the heels of each boot on the welcome mat just outside the foyer entrance. In the background, the soft whimpering of who they presumed to be Leah Kim was slowly mutating into a series of wrenching sobs.

"Airman Bachman, Sergeant," he nodded, turning to gently reseal the entrance door at his back and twisting back around to resume. "Not sure we've met unless it was at a commander's call."

"Perhaps we did, Airman. I rarely forget a face. Green bean, are we?"

"I'm reminded daily, yes." Bachman shrugged wearily.

"Ah well, this too shall pass. Well, where are my manners? You fellas kindly remove those clodhoppers and step right on in. My home, that is, *our* home, however humble, is your home."

Exchanging an awkward glance, the younger of the two airmen shrugged towards the only slightly older one as if awaiting proper direction.

"Afraid it's not a social visit, sarge," Barrow stated amiably enough while careful to maintain eye contact with the senior NCO. "The boots are gonna have to stay put for now. Maybe you've got a rug we can park 'em on inside?"

Surprisingly, Brookens' demeanor did not harden, nor change in any visible way, though Barrow knew this might strictly be med-related.

"Oh, I'm sure me or the old ball-and-chain can dig up something. Hold that pose, boys. Back in a jiffy."

With that, the sergeant darted inside only to reappear just seconds later, having spread a dark blue shag carpet across the threshold.

"Entre vous, boys."

Swell, Barrow thought randomly, *Barrow, Bachman, and Brookens: the three Bs of the apocalypse.*

As they stepped cautiously inside, senses instantly assaulted by myriad of scents, to include the familiar—garlic, kimchi, curry—and the not so common, one of which might've been recently evacuated vomit inundated with a slight odor of OB beer and perhaps an overabundance of Soju.

The hooch itself was of the two-room variety, the type usually associated with those of higher rank, of conservative decoration and not overly crass or downright gaudy, as many troops were apt to prefer. A leather sectional centered the living room, fronting a thirty or perhaps thirty-two-inch Samsung TV, VCR and matching stereo system with moderately-sized wall-speakers, while a nearby three-tiered entertainment center housed assorted hardback novels, and VHS and cassette tapes.

Barrow shot a quick glance at the television, presently muted, to see the popular Korean program *National Singing Contest*—a staple of regular viewing with the locals—being broadcast. Meanwhile, the Bryan Adams tune *Heat of the Night* could be heard echoing faintly from the stereo, obviously tuned to the peninsula's lone American station, Armed Forces Korean Network (AFKN).

Though the paneled walls were void of any sort of painting or portraits, assorted houseplants took up the slack from separate corners. Only a single item seemed obviously out of place: the couch's matching ottoman sat askew between its parent and the entertainment center, flipped onto its side with a pair of plastic coasters with USA flag designs and a single empty drinking glass scattered nearby. To the right as you entered was a sliding glass double-door leading, presumably, to the bedroom and the hooch's lone bathroom. Beyond those stained-glass doors, the cries and whimpers had diminished to the occasional hitching sob.

"I know it's not exactly regulation, but how about a beer? Got some recently purchased OB chilling in the old ice box," Brookens offered after collapsing onto the couch and leaning a bare foot onto one corner of the overturned ottoman.

"Now you know better than that, Sarge," Barrow lightly chided, standing at the far end of the couch even as his partner struck a casual pose with his back facing the double glass door, "Now, you catch me off-duty and I'd gladly accept. As far as the reason for tonight's visit, well, um..." he paused to gesture with a gloved hand towards the ottoman, "...doing a little late-night redecorating?"

Upon hearing Bachman's nasally grunt at his back, Barrow reached back and exposed the flat palm of a gloved hand. As for Brookens, he merely shrugged and spread both arms wide and high as if prepping for an impending yawn.

"Hey, sometimes a reminder is necessary, fellas." He concluded with a playful wink, "You'll understand in a few more years."

"Reminder of what exactly, sergeant?" Bachman inquired in an openly snarky tone, his senior partner's jaws visibly tightening in the aftermath.

"Of who's in charge, boys. The little woman has a tendency to forget. They also seem to make a habit of forgetting who's buttering their bread. Some might even seek out...butter of a different *brand,* if you catch my drift. Now, granted the necessary corrections are not something I enjoy dishing out..."

Adjusting his gradually descending glasses from the rounded edge of his purple-vein-infested nose to the upper bridge, the sergeant's demeanor appeared to shift ever so slightly as the rambling rant continued, his fists clenching sporadically, his voice gaining a measure of gravelly edge with each spoken word. Instinctively, Barrow's gun-hand groped for the mace spray hooked onto his belt.

"...just a necessary evil in these turbulent times we live in. Like I said, one day you'll get it. Well, you either will or you will not, and in that latter case, you might as well head on over to the BX and purchase the least chafing dog collar they sell, since you'll be wearing one for the duration."

Barrow turned and regarded Bachman with a stern nod, a clear non-verbal for the younger troop to ready himself for the worst. In turn, Bachman side-stepped over as to block the exit while reaching beneath the bulky parka with both hands, seemingly to seek out his own can of pepper spray.

"If you say so, Sarge. We'll also need to discuss an alleged scuffle of some magnitude originating at the Phoenix Club. There was a report of some random damage and a separate assault. You mind confirming your presence there at around, say, twenty-three hundred hours?"

"Affirmative, Airman Barrow. Indeed I was. As was, before you even inquire, Miss Mai."

"Fine. We'll get to the details in due time, then. Point of order, I'm kind of walking Airman Bachman through the interview process. You know the drill."

As if only half-listening, the sergeant merely nodded sheepishly. From the stereo reverberated the familiar rhythm and riffs of Eddie Money's 'Take Me Home Tonight.'

Reaching over and back, Barrow placed the flat of one hand against one of the glass doors.

"With that in mind, could we possibly have a word with the little woman? I mean, proper reporting technique dictates we get both sides of any story."

"Proper *reporting* tech—" Brookens howled, tossing his head back wolf-like and seemingly unaware his glasses had flown free to smack against a far wall.

"Fellas, be my guest. If you can manage to pry a coherent word from her Royal Highness of Happy Medicine, the floor is *all* hers," he bellowed through a gruesomely wide, slowly mutating grin with the potential to eventually split his suddenly beet-red face into two separate but equally maniacal sides.

"Let me know how that goes for you. Meanwhile, think I'll treat myself to that aforementioned brew."

"Might not be the best idea," Bachman injected with surprising firmness while holding up a gloved hand, palms out. "The clearer the heads, the better, am I right?"

Struggling to push himself erect, once Brookens was able to stand, albeit shakily, he stumbled forward towards the entertainment center and bent forward with groping hands as to pick out a particular tape, be it movie or music related.

"Airman, I'm thinking that particular boat sailed hours ago."

Bachman, fisting the pepper spray in one hand while the other dug at his utility belt for a pair of plastic cuffs, struck a defensive pose while, to his immediate right, Barrow tugged at the glass double-doors leading into the bedroom.

"Sarge, ugh, Sergeant Brookens, we're...I'm gonna need you to sit back down while Airman Bachman takes your official statement," Barrow babbled, briefly struggling to separate the sliding doors.

"Yeah well, about *that*," Brookens replied, trailing off once overcome by an impromptu fit of cackling giggles, before twisting on a bare heel and displaying a grace and fluidity one would've thought impossible just seconds earlier.

Two things happened in almost perfect synchronization: both equally unexpected and, in at least one case, shockingly tragic.

~ * ~

Excerpt from *The Mask beneath the Mask: A Memoir*, by Deron Joseph Barrow

Ask any troop stationed in the Pacific Theater during the same period as my own tour and, unless they were one of a small minority who spent their time voluntarily shackled to the limitations of strictly on-base living—there were those unfortunate fools who actually feared the 'mass sinning potential' of traversing off-base—they'll either be honest or lie like dogs and refuse any knowledge of the black market. As for myself, it's way past the time or need for fibbing. I not only had extensive knowledge, but personal dealings, at both Kunsan and Osan air bases. As a married E-4, securing an extra income wasn't about pocketing some extra cash for partying—well, not entirely anyhow—but downright survival from month-to-month. Selling assorted groceries or the odd household item to the locals, all acquired at the base BX or commissary and otherwise unavailable to them, was fairly routine for most troops, mass denials be damned. I was there. I saw. I participated. One of the biggest sellers—and easily the most abused of all black-market items— was whiskey tagged with labels from the good ol' US of A, most notably fifths of JB Scotch, Johnny Walker (*red* being the most popular) or Crown Royal. Being that we were only allowed four such 'units' per month, it wasn't always easy to refrain from drinking up some or all of your prospective profits. Alas, no such quandary for yours truly, as I did most of my serious drinking in the A-Town bars.

Still, even with all the above to sell off in the back rooms or alleys of Gunsan City, A-Town or, on that rare excursion to Osan to, well, expand one's market, Pyeongtaek City, I found myself struggling to maintain a workable monthly budget, especially considering I was sending roughly half my base pay home to the little woman.

It was around the one-hundred-day mark of my tour that a co-worker, well, actually his Korean yobo and former club dancer, introduced me to a potentially lucrative alternative to the everyday, mundane black-market pusher: the world of pill pushing, specifically the

Korean version of amphetamines, and more specifically the south peninsula version of American *Black Beauties*. I had, for better (initially) or worse (soon after) found my cash cow.

The whys of how I became a 'Ville pusher were, obviously, financial. The hows were reasonably simple and required only a woeful lack of respect for both local and military law. Sad to say, at least at that time in my life, I possessed both in spades. But then, maybe lack of respect is not quite the right term. More like, woefully apathetic. Regardless, I gave very little thought about getting caught or the possible ramifications. Dove headfirst into a boiling cesspool of potential disaster without so much as an hour's lost sleep, such was the level of my greed. It was yet another bar girl that introduced me to what she so lovingly referred to as 'happy medicine,' without which, according to her at least, the majority of the dancers could not perform on a nightly basis, either on or off stage. Opinions on that latter tidbit of info vary, as several of my other female contacts vehemently disagreed, at least with the overall number of those wholly dependent.

The meds themselves were, for the most part, the Asian twin of our little black beauties back home, only manufactured in an assortment of colors: blue, maroon, green and of course the most popular seller amongst the ladies, hot pink. Now, it should be known that Korean pharmacies were strictly off-limits to all GIs, and this is one regulation that was rarely, if *ever*, broken, as being caught even traipsing about inside such an establishment was, according to the MCJ (Military Code of Justice) akin to first-degree murder. Yes, this is a bit of an exaggeration, but from what we were told, not by much. Of course, being off-limits for the GIs did not mean off-limits to their better halves, be it spouse or just live-in yobo.

As for how I went from casual user to minor and then major distributor was not nearly the laborious transformation one might imagine. Yobo introduces me to her dealer, who in turn offers me a deal I could not refuse but definitely should've. He would first buy in bulk from some crooked local pharmacy, pass said bulk onto me at a set price, which I would place on the local market, at an increased cost, of course, to an ever-growing list of willful buyers. This contact—a middle-aged citizen of Gunsan City who dressed and acted as if he'd just left the set of an American mob flick: slicked-back hair, cool shades, big, open-collar shirts, plaid jeans and black wing-tips and enough gold bling hanging around his bony neck to sink a destroyer—spoke just enough English to make the deal, though usually my girl would play negotiator on my behalf, for a cut of the profits, of course.

As for said buyers, I'd first enhance with the oldest sales technique known to man, that is to provide a free sample or two before the regular charge for said item commenced. Needless to say, not many walked away fully satisfied with that meager sampling. Speed meant increased energy on those weekend nights in the 'Ville when sleep was viewed as a hindrance. Never mind the dangers of mixing the happy meds with copious amounts of booze; I never claimed to be a pharmacist. Pop at your own risk, I'd tell 'em. Just grease my palm and be on your happy, reckless, partying way. Stupidly, I had no qualms about who I sold to. That is, rank meant nothing. I did sell to the occasional officer, usually a butter-bar Lieutenant visiting the Kun on temporary duty and looking to make his off-time payoff with the blurriest memories possible, but for the most part it was the lower-grade airman or NCOs who partook on a regular or semi-regular basis. Did I fear being narked out? Was there always the possibility of a sting? Sure, but I didn't allow myself to dwell on it. Days and nights at the Kun (and subsequently the 'Ville) passed at warp speed. Ask anyone ever stationed there. It was like being on a treadmill that never powered down. Kunsan Air Base, on and off-base, was not for the faint of heart or high of morals. You literally worked one ass-cheek off and partied the other into the same state of non-existence.

A smarter man, or man-child, would've surely seen the signs of trouble lit up like a bright red neon-sign at the end of that cash-green rainbow. Not this boy. With less than one-hundred-days to go on my tour, I recall even considering an extension. After all, it wasn't like I was really missing my wife or the ultra-dull life we'd led, and while the Kun wasn't exactly gravy as far as military assignments go—war games were lengthy and exhausting, especially those involving donning chem gear that stunk of decades-long sweat—the off-duty rewards were plentiful and more important, damned profitable. Like I said, not exactly med-school material, this kid.

They say that, if possible, it pays to learn life's hardest lessons at a relatively early age in order to learn from the experience.

That said, I was about to be taken to a fictional woodshed previously found only in the most graphic of horror novels.

Five

The Three Bs of the Apocalypse
Excerpt from *The Mask beneath the Mask: A Memoir*, by Deron Joseph Barrow

As the glass door finally slid free from what Barrow had naturally assumed was a warped or blocked track, a figure leapt from the shadows and past him, the object that had led their charge swooshing mere inches from his jutted jaw.

At the same time, a loud gasp of unknown origin was soon followed by sound not unlike a sudden burst of air forced through a narrow hose.

Barrow alternated wide-eyed glances, first to the scantily clad female executing a clumsy combat roll onto the living room floor, the claw hammer she'd been wielding sailing from a blood-slickened hand to land with a muffled thud against a far wall, then to the stumbling back-pedaling of his assigned partner, who had managed to back into the foyer while clutching his chest with both gloved hands as if suffering a massive coronary. Bachman's head twitched and jerked atop his scrawny neck, his eyes bugging and lower lip trembling uncontrollably even as a low whining sound—Barrow thought crazily about a Klaxon's incessant ring—escaped the back of his throat.

"Bachman, what? What the hell's w-wrong with y—"

He halted in mid-sentence upon seeing his subordinate's tightly clenched, gloved hands turn a dark shade of red, a wide circle gradually forming around the younger man's breastbone. It would, Barrow knew instantly, take a major leakage of bodily fluid to saturate through three layers of clothing, most notably the thickness of the outer parka.

Reaching into the thin air between them as to miraculously plug the hole from afar, Barrow discovered his lower body had taken the high road and automatically down shifted into neutral, as complete a paralysis as he'd ever experienced.

"Je-jesus, H-Harry, just hang on, m-man. I'll...I'll call it in and get s-some...he—"

For a split second, a single blink in time before logic dictated the horrific truth, Barrow thought a large, round black bug had used Bachman's forehead as a landing strip. It wasn't until the young airman titled forward to land headfirst onto the cool rock floor, his limp form hanging half-in, half-out of the living room, that the condition of the hooch's front door painted an altogether more gruesome narrative; a splash of gray/reddish gore dripped freely down its cheap wooden frame as, in the forefront, the young man who'd involuntarily provided its wet, technicolor glory appeared to slip his mortal bonds with a final series of foot spasms and a single twitch of his right hand. As surreal as it was fitting, AFKN's on-duty DJ had picked that very moment to kick-off Kenny Loggins' 'Danger Zone.'

"Believe this or not, I was hoping there'd be no such collateral damage," Brookens mumbled, bloodshot eyes darting spastically back and forth between the fallen airman and the one still upright. Standing in the center of the room, he held the unidentified handgun—from such a close distance, Barrow could tell it definitely wasn't the base armory issued thirty-eight—in the classic shooter's position, with the left hand cradling the underneath of the right, the latter aimed directly at the remaining airman's upper chest. The woman, wearing only a torn, blood-spattered white tee and purple panties, had managed to retain the hammer and was creeping up from behind Brookens on all fours. As she'd sailed into the room in a blur and landed face-first in similar fashion, Barrow hadn't been allowed any particulars of her physical or mental state until now. Leah Mai's face was a maroon mask, her left eye swollen the size of a golf ball, her open, gasping maw revealing several missing front teeth. From her chin, which appeared weirdly off-hinge, hung a glutinous string of mucus, spittle and blood. Just as she crawled to within reaching distance to her once-future husband and obvious abuser, rearing back the hammer as if to, at the very least, reach his exposed upper thighs or lower back, Brookens flung back his bare left heel, effectively mule-kicking her in in the area of her already shattered jaw. In the aftermath of the muffled crunch of possible facial bones, Leah's arm collapsed like a felled limb from the parent tree, the hammer spinning away to vanish beneath the nearby entertainment center. She lay face-up, a fresh stream of drainage, as black as motor oil in the relative dimness, flowed from her shattered chin and down her slim neck—Barrow silently wondered if a pulse still beat somewhere thereabouts—to fill the narrow space above her collar bone.

"The innocent type, that is. I guess it *was* silly of me to ever think they'd send a lone officer, but hey, you have to give me credit for thinking positive in such a severely negative situation. Now," Brookens continued unabated, gesturing with the barrel of the firearm—a thin tendril of smoke barely visible through whatever archaic silencer cloaked the barrel tip—towards the couch, "Kindly take a seat, Airman Barrow. We have much to discuss and not a second to waste."

Swallowing hard, Barrow peered down at his right hand and was openly shocked to see the two-way radio held there, while, just as unexpectedly, his left was conspicuously empty, the small dispenser of mace previously gripped there having magically teleported to parts unknown.

"S-she needs help, man. Might bleed out if y—if you don't let me radio for help."

"Oh, she's fine, airman. Believe you me, my Le-Le is so much tougher than she appears," Brookens replied wryly, allowing his fallen fiancée a quick once-over. "Takes a licking and keeps on ticking, you might say. Airman Barrow, I'll only ask you once more, at least *politely*," he chided, gesturing yet again at the couch, the previous attempt at a smile now a strained grimace.

"While you're at it, I'll have that radio."

His thoughts as scattered and frenzied as his movements were stilted and robotic, Barrow considered the possible scenarios that might allow for his survival, number one with a bullet being to toss the two-way with fastball strike efficiency with one hand while pulling his thirty-eight free with the other. It was, while he was working out the proper angles and probable time allowed for this particular action that the potential target for said attack made up his mind for him, with extreme prejudice.

When later asked, Barrow would testify that the pointing, aiming, and discharge of the ancient peashooter, later to be identified by a local Gunsan historian as a WWII-era Webley revolver, appeared to transpire not in real-time but extreme slow-motion, although he would also confess to his own movements being helplessly locked into the same bleary realm of severely segmented animation. Screaming "NO!" at the precise moment the silent round shattered his left kneecap, Barrow 's radio was inadvertently flipped over his right shoulder as both arms wind-milled wildly.

As he fell back through the glass double-doors into the bedroom, a wave of darkness soon descended upon him like a black curtain. The numbness that enveloped not only his left leg but left side as a whole was rapidly graduating into the stinging of a thousand highly pissed-off wasps, their syringe-like stingers embedded to the very bone.

Upon awakening—Peter Cetera's sappy but undeniably catchy 'Glory of Love' providing the backdrop—he discovered a relocation had transpired, as he sat directly across from Sergeant Leonard Brookens, his wrists snugly cuffed by his own hardware with his hands resting at his crotch. Upon conducting a quick, blurry-eyed inventory, he found his knee had been bandaged by what appeared to be thick cotton gauze secured by several layers of gray duct tape, the camo pants beneath his knee drenched to the calf. As for the pain, it had mercifully returned to its initial state of numbness, though with an accompanying throbbing sensation, the almost complete lack of expected misery likely due to an extreme banding of the tape around the wound. Such a cutting off of normal circulation, Barrow knew, was a double-edged sword of good and bad, the good being the bleeding was under control, the bad meaning practically no circulation to the lower leg. In time, he also knew, this could mean dead tissue and possible amputation. Leaning up and back with great effort, his head lolling as if balanced on greased ball-bearings, he studied his assaulter through droopy eyelids and an equally sagging lower lip which dripped saliva in a stringy, yo-yo-string-like spear.

Decked out in his dress-blue jacket—four full rows of assorted medals with gold and oak-leaf clusters on full display—with the same blood-blotched tee underneath, Brookens leaned back with the Korean-model revolver in one hand and a more familiar government-issued thirty-eight in the other. Barrow could only assume it was Brookens', though there was little question that his own holster, if checked, would be conspicuously empty. Gradually shifting the barrels of each weapon towards either side of his captive's chest, the sergeant's floss-thin squint had seemingly lost the power to blink beneath his glasses' comically thick lenses, nor did his horribly chapped lips part as he spoke, as if he'd been transformed into some mad ventriloquist's dummy come to maniacal life.

"Well, glad to have you back, Airman Barrow. I do regret that last little measure of security, but I had the distinct vibe that you weren't going to participate willingly. I get it, Airman. I *get* it. I was your age once. Not that terribly long ago, in fact. Underwent the same training and taught the same philosophies. I'd have probably chosen fight over flight back in the day, as well, especially considering the sudden lack of backup. Now, what say we get down to brass tacks? There is a riddle I've been trying to solve all day that I hope you can help me solve."

Unlike his captor, Barrow blinked rapidly and continually in an attempt to clear away the swirling cobwebs coating his vision like a windblown spider's web. Perhaps as a foreboding precursor for things to come, AFKN's tune of choice for that moment was Peter Gabriel's bombastic 'Sledgehammer.'

"Sarge, a backup patrol will be h-here any...any time. Make it easy on yourself and..." Barrow paused for a deep breath, his eyes briefly shifting to his partner's legs splayed on the floor to his immediate right, the tips of Bachman's spit-shined boots pointing in opposite directions, "...you c-can't...won't win in a firefight. You *must*...know th-that."

"Barrow, allow me to nip any further attempts to talk me down firmly in the bud, yes?" Brookens replied gruffly, teeth no doubt gnashing to the point of shattering despite remaining utterly hidden behind seemingly super-glued lips. "I've got two questions, you see. I want you to answer them without undue dialogue. In other words, Airman," he hesitated, raising the Korean revolver and extending its dull-gray barrel to shove it flush against Barrow's sweat-coated forehead with enough force to leave a circular mark in its wake.

"Nod if you copy what I've spelled out, but not too forcefully, boy. I've found this particular gat of Gook manufacturing possesses a hair trigger of epic proportions."

Barrow did so, as gently as if to jiggle or quake any harder might yank the pin from an attached grenade.

"Outstanding," Brookens replied, wearing a tight-lipped smile while pulling the revolver away and resting it, still barrel forward, on the tabletop. "Now, to question number one: Have you, Airman Barrow, regularly provided my sweet, adorable but undeniably rascally yobo with a steady supply of amphetamines?"

Somehow, miraculously able to remain expressionless despite said query hitting home with the blunt force of a Louisville Slugger to the breadbasket, or in this case a red-hot steel slug to the center of the kneecap, Barrow momentarily—and completely out of character—thought of coming clean. As it was, this too passed, much like the aforementioned slug through flesh, cartilage, and bone.

"I did...have *not*, sir."

For the first time since coming to, Barrow saw the other man blink, though this was executed at warp speed and only once.

"So, you deny supplying said medications in and around the 'Ville, Airman Barrow?"

Poker-face still magically in place, Barrow tilted his head slightly to the left as it to punctuate the sincerity of the statement.

"I didn't say...not saying that at all, Sergeant. I'm saying I never supplied them to *her*."

"Fair enough, and your honesty is much appreciated."

The sergeant leaned in, lips spreading to almost Joker-like proportions, while pointing the barrel of the thirty-eight downward and to the left, indicating Barrow's right leg.

"In all honesty, I was fully prepared to let the air out of that other knee at even the slightest hint at denial of your dope-dealing ways. The scuttlebutt has been all over the unit for months. Fact is, I'd heard either Chief Bolan or Major Ford were one additional rumor away from busting your chops. More than once I've personally overheard Bolan hinting at hauling you up on charges, only to be overruled by the major due to our present personnel shortage."

Barrow nodded agreeably, releasing a well-hidden sigh of relief as the revolver was hoisted up and back onto the tabletop.

"Interesting. I never suspected they were onto me. Maybe...intervention is just what I needed. Maybe not this...extreme, but hey, whatever works, right?"

"Precisely, Airman, and let me say I am beyond impressed with your attitude. Now, and even more vital to this rather unpleasant scenario, question number two: Have you, now or ever before, and to avoid the common, crude vernacular, bumped uglies with my fiancée?"

Left eyebrow dramatically cocked, Barrow's expression conveyed utter befuddlement, as if his captor's quiz had been delivered in some ancient or even alien dialect.

"Sir? Excuse me, but...bumping...uglies?"

"*Sex*, Airman Barrow. Have you ever had participated in the act of carnal knowledge with that unconscious concubine sprawled out in the next room?"

The throbbing sensation at his ruined knee kicked in suddenly, as if a numbness-inducing tourniquet had been cut free from the source.

"Sergeant Brookens, not sure you're aware, but I'm a married man."

A short pause, wherein Brookens' bloodshot orbs—the pupils shrunken to pinpricks—bore into Barrow's own as if waiting for even the smallest sign of deception, while the Korean-made peashooter was lifted from the table and inched gradually forward until its front sight lightly tapped the cuffed man's chin.

"Son, you know as well as I do that a ring around a man's finger means absolutely jack squat on this peninsula of degradation. I make it a point to learn the reputations of those of lower rank within my own unit. Yours, like so many others, is that of heartless Lothario: a moral-less pack of hormone-infested Don Juans spreading their seed as recklessly as your basic dandelion struck by monsoon winds. So, spare me all the loyalty and true-blue faithful garbage and just answer the question, please."

The revolver barrel moved away just enough to allow free jaw movement, Barrow managing to visibly ignore its ominous presence and not break eye contact with its possessor. The momentary silence—the very air thick with a toxic mix of malice, misdirection and misgivings—allowed Duran-Duran's 'A View to Kill' to provide, sadly, the evening's perfect theme song.

"Sergeant Brookens, I have not had such...relations with your fiancée. This I swear."

Searching the younger airman's increasingly pale visage for a random twitch or a sudden buildup of nervous perspiration, the sergeant remained frozen in place for a full thirty seconds before reeling in the revolver and leaning back with a resounding grunt, tipping the high-back chair until it lightly smacked the wall to the left of the hooch entrance.

"So far, so good then. If you are indeed fibbing, I'd surely categorize the level of skill, if you will, as pathological.

"Wish I could take your word as gold, Airman, but I'm afraid there is still a test of sorts that remains to be passed before I can fairly pass final judgement."

Barrow's mind raced. Whatever survival skills training he'd received were instantly forgotten in the face of a scenario he'd never imagined possible. This was no riot, hostage or sniper situation, and workable options appeared nil. Despite facing such dire, seemingly insurmountable odds, at least one decision had been made and, no matter how things progressed, set in impenetrable stone: he would perish with dignity. There would be no begging, no pleading, no whimpering prayers. In that regard, strange as it might sound, he almost envied Harry Bachman, who'd perished fairly quickly and with minimal pain. Watching Brookens lay the thirty-eight on the tabletop with its barrel still positioned towards his upper abdomen/lower chest while using the freed-up hand to dig into his dress jacket's inner pocket, he felt the faint beginnings of a plan begin to force its way to the pole position of the jumbled traffic jam making up his current thought pattern.

"The little item here is the root of the problem," Brookens resumed, pulling free and then slapping the object onto the center of the table, the thirty-eight briefly shaken airborne with the force. "Oh, I'd had my suspicions over the last few weeks, you understand. A man instinctively knows when another has been plowing on his land, so to speak."

The SP beret was standard issue, its size impossible to gauge from the partial fold and severely dented top portion, the familiar '*Defensor Fortis*' patch mostly hidden.

"Found it in the bottom drawer of her dresser just this morning while she was stir-frying some octopus out in the foyer. Imagine my surprise. After all, at the time I was only seeking out a misplaced sock."

"Not yours, I take it?" Barrow asked with a tad more sarcasm than intended, eyes shifting smoothly from the headgear to the thirty-eight and finally Brookens, who, perhaps picking up on the vibe, reacquired the firearm.

"Affirmative. Roughly a size and a half too large, and it isn't as if I'm dragging around a witchdoctor's shrunken head. The fella this belongs to is what we used to refer to in base supply as a real melon-noggin."

The plan not quite at the completed stage, Barrow groped desperately for ways to extend the dialogue.

"Supply, huh? So, you weren't a-always an SP?"

As hoped, the sergeant's eyes shone with a fresh glimmer, growing instantly distant and staring past Barrow through some unseen time-tunnel

"Cross-trained about six years back while at Wright-Patt and for my troubles got back from training with orders for Clark Air Base waiting. Met and married my first ex there. Lesson not learned, obviously." He paused, glaring into the living room to where his fiancée's prone body lay. "But hey, it's been a wild ride that I've never regretted. Supply was, well, I just never figured bullet-counting as my true calling."

"The PI huh? I've heard the stories. Fact is, been giving some serious thought to following up this tour with a little excursion to Clark myself. What do you thi..."

"Duck your head down and forward, Airman," Brookens interrupted, the dull, lifeless glare having returned. This expression, so far removed from the tic-infested, goo-goo-googly eyes from their initial greeting just minutes before, Barrow rated as easily the more frightening of the two. Relegating the thirty-eight to the tabletop yet again, Brookens used the free hand to hoist the beret airborne and, with a single, vicious snap, smoothed out its dents while simultaneously raising the Webley and pointing it directly at the center of Barrow's face.

"And be quick about it."

"Not gonna fit, Sergeant. I can tell just by look—"

The barrel tip struck his front teeth with a muffled thump, the blow buffered by a top lip now split and spewing its content onto the table in thick, dark maroon droplets.

"Disobey just once more, Airman, and it surely will *not* fit a head missing a large majority of its previous bulk, do we understand one another?"

"Y-yeb, y-yes, s-sirb," Barrow managed, the ruined lip rapidly swelling.

"You know what?" Brookens announced curtly, eyes squinted floss-thin while yanking the beret back as if first tempting a small child with the promise of candy only to refuse awarding said treat for punishment's sake. "You can just hold your water, mister. Let the sting of that love tap sink in for future reference. In the meantime, though I have my doubts, I have one other noggin to check for possible malfeasance."

As Barrow leaned weakly forward, a veritable torrent of fresh leakage spattering the tabletop between his propped elbows, his mind continued to race with all manner of potential actions: actions he now understood might be his lone change of survival. Brookens hadn't just sprung a minor leak from his inner reservoir of sanity but spewed forth the entire kit-and-caboodle in a tsunami-like projective barf of epic proportions.

Perhaps the wife's extra-curricular activity mixed with regular amphetamine abuse teamed to snap that final twig of reason, or it might've been the aforementioned combined with a long-simmering nervous breakdown. Regardless, Barrow knew his minutes sitting upright with a working pulse were now severely limited. He would get one chance, tops, to nip the six-stripped reaper of his untimely demise squarely in the bud, with several obvious roadblocks to mission success, the cuffs being the most glaring, along with being outgunned two to none and finally and maybe the most egregious of all, combating someone whose blatant insanity was fueled by jealous rage. Then again, he pondered, perhaps the latter could be used to his advantage if manipulated properly.

Tucking the thirty-eight beneath a tucked armpit, Brookens kept the archaic revolver trained in the general vicinity of Barrow's head and upper torso while pushing away from the table and, with none of the uneven gait of earlier, side-stepped gracefully over Harry Bachman's splayed legs.

"You just stay comfortably seated there, Airman Barrow. Make a run for the door and I won't hesitate in stopping you, read me?"

Barrow nodded acknowledgement without speaking, thus hoping to temper the steady flow from the badly split lip. He could taste the coppery twang of his own life source on his tongue, sliding down the parched path of his throat with alarming regularity.

"Good boy. This won't take but a second, then we'll see about clearing you on the main felony charge on tonight's docket."

Upon watching the sergeant vanish from the foyer into the living room, Barrow briefly tensed his thighs and calves before doing the same with his biceps and shoulders as to gauge the reserve of strength and energy in each for what was to come.

"Yep, just as I thought. Kid has...*had* a half-kegger when the cover here calls for the full variety," he heard Brookens mumble from just around the edge of the living room entrance, having obviously attempted to fit the beret on the dead airman's blood-soaked head.

"Well, hey there, babe," he continued, voice fading while relocating further into the hooch to address his battered better-half. "Looking a tad worse for wear, I must say. Might need to schedule that nose job after all, yeah? Just don't expect me to foot the bill, Snookums."

As the sergeant continued the decidedly one-way conversation, interrupted only by the occasional grunt, groan or sob—so weak as to barely qualify as audible—from its intended target, Barrow dug in the heels of both combat boots while flexing his buttocks in an attempt to slide back the chair just enough to allow for the space to arise. One perceptible squeak, he understood, would more than likely send the sergeant in a sprint, the vital element of surprise lost forever and most likely, fatally. Fortunately, the radio's constant blaring, faint as it might be, provided a thin cloak of sound to prevent total silence. Currently, the Moody Blues' 'Gemini Dream' provided just enough of a blanket to successfully overlap any and all squeaks and squeals his movements birthed.

Half-inch by begrudging half-inch, he slid silently back until both knees—his left screaming with newfound misery with even the slightest shift—cleared the edge of the circular table, his butt and thighs on the verge of cramping from the strain. As all dialogue had abruptly ceased, along with all accompanying movement, he froze in mid-squat, fearing that upon resuming, one or both knees might pop and crack like detonating fireworks, or just as damning, the excruciating pain linked to his ruined knee would produce a window-shattering banshee-cry of unbridled anguish. Teeth gnashing to the point of cracking several molars, he resumed his steady uprising upon hearing Brookens' scolding—remarkably calm and steady of tone—continue.

"Wish I could find it in my heart to regret my part in tonight's debacle, but sweet plum, you must agree that all the anger and subsequent fallout was, pardon the law enforcement pun, fully justified. If you recall, that first blow was yours. Right there in the club for all to see. Pretty solid left hook, I must say, even loosened a tooth or two, I do believe. Wasn't for your pal's timely intervention, I would've surely returned the favor. Well, timely for you, not so much for her. Anyhow, have to admit a bit of a turn-on just witnessing my little *Tigress of Punsan* make such a fiery return to form. Just wish it had been under better circumstances."

Barrow stood upright, balanced solely by both hands balanced with the palms flat on the tabletop, allowing their gradual release only when the sergeant tossed a final verbal haymaker his downed fiancée's way.

"We're not nearly done here, peach-cheeks. I'll be back in just a few so we might discuss the rather unpleasant details of our mutual breakup. Here now, allow me to take that nail-blaster away before you get any further ideas. In fact, while I'm at it, I'll need to discourage any random thoughts of additional aggression."

The grisly sound that ensued, two rapidly executed blows, like piston-strikes slightly muffled, reminded Barrow of meat being tenderized atop a butcher's cutting board. In the aftermath, a series of low, throaty moans of the purest angst, the cries of one who has suffered the final indignity as all hope fades to blackest despair. The *Tigress of Pusan*, Barrow feared, might have just relinquished ownership of her fast-fading soul to whatever deity might claim its battered husk. Hooking curled digits underneath the top half of the high-back chair and lifting it gently airborne, his teeth remained tightly clenched while taking that first shuffling, half-step towards the entrance, this time fueled as much by rage as the incessant throbbing of his wounded appendage.

Less than a foot away from the open entrance, his right boot planted firmly against Harry Bachman's right thigh, Barrow fell back against the cool stone with the chair—shaking slightly as a mild spasm wracked his left shoulder—cocked back and coiled to strike. He would get but one chance at liberation, he realized grimly, left eye ticking wildly in anticipation, before being either filled with nickel-sized holes or hammered into fleshy pudding, perhaps both. Inhaling deeply as a sense of his prey's impending arrival neared, Barrow held the air as if prepping for a deep-sea dive and felt the trigger mechanism in his shoulders begin to involuntary unhinge. If not for the cuffs, he could have alternated arms or better yet, used the chair as a battering ram held at both ends. As it was, he'd be allowed one clumsily executed swing and pray it landed with enough force to do the necessary damage.

Just as it had aided in his escape from the kitchen chair, the stereo was now his enemy, as any approaching steps were being successfully drowned out by Boston's sloppily sentimental but irrefutably haunting 'Amanda,' a tune Barrow instantly associated with a recently separated yobo of his own as one of her current favorites.

"Upsy-daisy, young man," he heard the sergeant whisper just as the dead airman's legs were yanked through the threshold and out of sight. *Clearing the runway,* Barrow thought, *probably doesn't want the bodies to pile up like cordwood in case he needs to make a sudden dash for it,* his thighs, shoulders and biceps burning with equal fury and begging for sweet release.

"Well, at least here's one I don't have to worry about your seducing, my Tigress," he heard the man resume, a faint dragging sound accompanying his voice, each cutting off at roughly the same time. Just as Brad Delp smoothly crooned, "*It's now or never, and tomorrow may be too late,*" Barrow detected a rapid succession of bare feet slapping stone, as if the originator had broken into a wild sprint.

As he broke the perimeter between living room and foyer at a brisk trot, the sergeant had led with the Webley's barrel, holding it out like a divining rod in search of a wet-well spring. Fortunately, for a second earlier or later most likely would've cost him his life, Barrow had pushed from the wall and swung the chair across just as the extended arm had appeared over the threshold, the cheap veneer and particleboard chair meeting metal, flesh and bone with a sharp crack as parts of the former practically detonated upon contact with fragmented portions sailing off in all directions.

Forward momentum forcing his stumbling frame into the foyer in a clumsy lurch, Brookens cradled his damaged right hand even as, on the fly, his left swung the claw hammer back and forth as if attempting to swat a pesky fly. All the while, the sergeant—eyeglasses hanging slightly askew from a badly-warped temple—alternated pained cries of anguish and the enraged growls of a predatory animal caught off-guard by a prey it had mistakenly considered hapless.

He bounced off the blood-spattered front entrance like a human pinball, landing on his right side and onto a knee-high pile of used ondol charcoals, one of which he quickly snatched up with his lone remaining uninjured hand.

Barrow, still holding a jagged portion of chair leg in both clenched hands, took a single step forward to continue the attack and immediately regretted the attempt, his left knee practically unhinging as a flash of searing agony threatened his very consciousness. Temporarily staggered, he leaned against the wall for support, lowering his chin onto his chest and inhaling deeply. A split-second later, his bowed head arose as the room was engulfed in a virtual cloudburst of blackish dust that filled his nostrils with the overwhelming scent of spent charcoal. Barrow could only deduce that, in his downed state, Brookens had utilized the charcoals as a makeshift cloaking device, perhaps tossing them against the wall or straight up to the ceiling.

"O-oh, you sneaky Pete y-you," he heard Brookens whine through the drifting haze, only the fallen man's bare feet clearly visible. "Guess I really should've...c-cuffed you at the...back, yeah?"

Kneeling onto his one good knee, Barrow watched the bare feet rewind into the drifting dustbowl and a large shadowy image rise to full height less than two feet away.

"Oh well, they say hindsight is *always* twenty-blessed-twenty, right?"

The single blast echoed like cannon-fire, its deafening effect no doubt amplified when compared to the barely audible rounds fired from the Webley, Barrow instantly ducking down and to the right as a sharp stinging at his left shoulder joined a growing list of recently-inflected pains.

Figuring a second shot was soon forthcoming—and at such close range the odds of another minor graze being slim and/or none—but still partially blinded by the dust coating his badly tearing eyes, Barrow bulled forward with his head lowered and elbows extended in textbook human battering-ram position. Just before impact, a resounding thump and ensuing crunch that could only be the result of fractured bone, Barrow thought he heard the veteran non-commissioned officer yelp as if taken completely off-guard by the assault.

Barrow awakened with a start, his throat tightly constricted and his breathing limited to heavy panting from flared nostrils semi-clogged from the thick mucus packing each. Len Brookens seemed to levitate over his prone frame, the Master Sergeant's face a mask of reddish seepage, his eyes bugging as to pop from their respective sockets, his crushed nose bent sharply to the left, his teeth, save one of the front two, conspicuously absent and, along with the misshapen proboscis, evidence to the apparent success of the blindly executed head-butt. Those obvious facial injuries aside, Barrow would have surely testified that, despite the sergeant's badly broken right hand, the fore and middle finger of which were horribly discolored and bloated like overlooked sausages, the pressure being applied to his voice box was being doled out in equal measures.

"F-fit li-like a g-glove, y-you bastard," Brookens mumbled, bloody spittle ejected from equally smeared lips, his badly swollen, rapidly blackening eyes appearing saucer-wide. "L-like the d-darn thing was m-measured for t-that blocked me-melon of y-yours."

Able to tug and yank his cuffed hands from between their matted midsections, Barrow felt his remaining energy reserve—the tank already dangerously close to bone-dry—ebb to near blackout stage. The head-butt, for all the damage it had incurred, had apparently opened a rather substantial gash at his upper forehead that had, along with Brookens' continual drip and spat overhead, painted his visage as effectively as a liberally applied gallon of dark maroon paint.

"Should've...b-been a bit m-more cautious of...l-leaving such da-damning evidence b-behind, Airman!"

Fading fast, his vision spotting to the point of visualizing Brookens through a fishnet of static, Barrow reached up, wedging folded hands between his assailant's wrists, the cuffs sliding smoothly over the squared chin with aid from the slickened flesh until the cuff's twin rings dug in just underneath the man's disjointed yet still widely-flared nostrils. Coincidentally, the pressure applied to his windpipe subsided just enough to add an extra jolt to the internal battery.

"J-just l-let it happen, boy," the sergeant continued, his voice noticeably nasal as the cuff's bit deeper, "N-no need for...all th-this pointless s-struggle. You're ju-just g-getting what y-you d-deser..."

Realizing it was most likely his final shot at survival, Barrow applied a final, vicious shove upward, instantly transforming the other's man sputtering spiel into an anguish-filled shriek at the distinct sound of fractured cartilage and shredded flesh, the cuffs having literally removed the majority of the man's left nostril while forcing selective bone fragments through the bridge of his nose like bony antennae. As squeezing hands departed his ravaged throat, Barrow found the strength to roll to the right and directly into the ondol stove, where a pair of steel tongs sat propped with its twin blunt ends buried into a fresh, unused charcoal.

With Bob Seger's stirring 'American Storm' as a concluding backdrop and heard only between Brookens' guttural growls and sobbing wails, Barrow gripped the tongs—surprisingly weighty and solid, like a quality nine-iron, he surmised—and, taking advantage of their stoutness, used them for leverage in rising onto his good knee.

Spinning around with as much haste as his battered frame would allow, he heard the sergeant's wet, lunatic's giggle, the uncontrollable cackling of the utterly unhinged.

Brookens sat yogi-style, the thirty-eight held in his shaky but mostly unscathed hand and pointed, if not directly, within the general vicinity of Barrow's fully exposed torso.

"Yo-you g-got m-moxie, boy," he spat through a veritable

crimson river pouring onto his lips and bared teeth, the revolver's shaky aim moving wildly from side to side, its barrel nearly within Barrow's reach, "Ca-can't take...that away from you. Re-real potential to...cl-climb the ranks, yes s-sir. Well, if n-not for th-that pesky drug habit that...tragically transformed you into...a r-rapist and murderer, obsessed with a s-superior's wife to the degree of k-killing your own...partner and the g-girl herself before...finishing off the...competition."

The pair kneeled and posed respectively, less than three feet apart, locked eyes and, like living statues, froze in place as best they could, considering the plethora of injuries present. From a distance, one might've naturally assumed each had fallen victim to some comedic workplace accident involving copious amounts of red and grayish dyes, the latter smeared like war-paint onto their blood-saturated flesh in the aftermath of the earlier ondol explosion.

His voice a grating croak, Barrow executed a slight head tilt without breaking eye contact.

"Won't fly, Brookens. You're...obviously off your rocker, but even so, you can't really...think anyone's gonna buy into that...shoulder-high pile of h-horseshit."

Grinning broadly, the mere act initiating a fresh, bountiful leak from the raw ruin of space that previously held his right nostril, Brookens' aim appeared to waver more upon speaking, a note quickly filed away by his potential target.

"Chances a-are better t-than decent, I'd w-wager. Wh-who they gonna believe...d-drug dealing airman or dec-decorated NCO? Besides, only one...of us is going to...be around to tell the tale, and it won't...be you, boy."

The tongs were growing heavier by the second. Barrow realized, with no small measure of sheer terror, that all viable options had been exhausted. It was, in every literal sense, time to do it or die. He'd always known, as do all servicemen, that such a dire, potentially fatal dilemma might arise, though he could have never dreamed that when his personal moment of truth came, the enemy he would face would be of the same uniform and would have taken the same exact oath at enlistment. Head throbbing, throat raw and bruised, his left knee a screaming banshee of primal anguish, he sucked in what might be his last lungful of life-sustaining air and, having recited several possible lines in his head with frenzied, rapid-fire speed, blurted out the one chosen as number one with, hopefully, *not* a bullet.

"Leah *hated* you," he barked through a tight smile he hoped didn't appear too forced. "I mean despised your crazy ass. Especially, well, the sack-time she referred to as more work than it was w-worth, if you get her drift. You see, sarge," he paused to shoot a playful wink that was much harder to execute than normal due to the eyelid being practically glued down by the build-up of semi-dried blood layering his brow, "guess she needed a real man to occasionally, well, lay the...proper amount of pipe, so to speak. I was...as you've probably guessed by now...just one of so...*very*...many."

The reaction he'd prayed for was instantaneous: a wide-eyed, lip-twisting rage, as was the predicted side-effect, as the revolver's barrel strayed wide left from the suddenly spasm-racked hand gripping it.

"*FUCK y-you and that f-fucking WHORE!*" Brookens bellowed, tilting forward as the weight of the revolver had thrown his entire frame off-balance. The thirty-eight's thundering retort coincided with Barrow's two-handed tomahawk-like chuck of the tongs, which ricocheted off the top edge of Brookens' scalp just as it had started its bowing descent. His own equilibrium thrown off by both the force of the toss and, most vital, ducking away from the short-range blast, Barrow felt his right shoulder ignite as if a lit match had been lain across bare flesh. Managing to ram the opposite shoulder into the hooch's entrance door frame, he somehow remained semi-upright with the majority of his body weight forced upon his good knee for balance.

Hands instinctively raised in front of his face in case of a follow-up shot, Barrow squinted cautiously between splayed fingers, only to gradually drop this admittedly sad wall of defense once it appeared obvious no such counterattack was forthcoming.

Though propped on all fours and steadfastly holding position for the moment, Len Brookens appeared well beyond attempting any type of retribution. With almost surgical precision, the tong heads had sliced away a wide, pizza-slice section of scalp, the skin and attached hair—more stubble due to the buzz-cut style—flapping freely over onto the opposite side of his head to showcase an expansive patch of crimson rawness underneath, his cartoonish-wide, unblinking eyes filling to the brim from the accompanying spillage. The sergeant's breathing was harsh and raspy; his pale arms flexed and released in two-second intervals as if on the very edge of impending surrender.

Once Barrow's own blurred—and growing hazier by the moment—vision noticed the thirty-eight laying just inches from Brookens' left hand, a lower gear of survival skills was discovered he hadn't previously known he possessed: a purely-impulsive, adrenaline-fueled gear that kicked in before logical thought could toss in a wrench of hesitation.

The heel of the combat boot landed with a resounding crunch, Brookens releasing nary a whimper or sob despite his remaining good hand being so graphically mangled.

Falling back from the effort—his own mutilated left knee having been forced for temporarily leverage—Barrow's upper back smacked the opposite wall near the hooch entrance and, sighing heavily, he slunk slowly down as if being lowered by some unseen puppeteer.

Eyelids suddenly leaden, his entire body a bloody tower of throbbing misery, he watched with sober fascination as Master Sergeant Len Brookens remained miraculously posed like some abstract canine statue: brutalized, beaten and bludgeoned, but magically held in place by nothing more than dogged stubbornness or, more likely in this case, unfathomable madness.

Though the sergeant's frame did eventually collapse to a belly-flopping, face-first collapse, Barrow was hapless to decipher the time elapsed due to his own fight with remaining at least partially conscious.

By the time he was aware of the sound of multiple combat boots pounding the stone path outside, followed soon after by the hooch's outer door flying inward with an echoing crash and finally a plethora of jumbled, panic-leaden voices filling the space, Barrow found the simple act of lifting a single eyelid akin to hoisting the whole of the Korean peninsula.

~ * ~

Excerpt from *The Mask beneath the Mask: A Memoir*, by Deron Joseph Barrow

The first question that comes to mind, or at the least the most provocative in some eyes, is the easiest to answer: true enough, the beret did indeed fit. A bit snug however and not nearly the perfect match that was insinuated at the time. In other words, Brookens' accusation wasn't nearly as incriminating as it sounded, being that roughly a third of the Kun's security force were issued similarly-sized headgear in that Year of Our Lord nineteen eighty-seven. Not sure if such records still exist in this era of 'going paperless,' but if so, I can pretty much guarantee this was the case. Yes, I had known Leah Mai, but strictly as a buyer of the wares I offered. Was she physically attractive? Yes, in spades. Would I have obliged if a different type offer had arisen? I can't honestly say, at least not at this advanced age. I truly believe we are different people at certain stages in our lives. The older me can only speculate that the younger, infinitely more naïve and undeniably reckless me probably wouldn't have hesitated to jump her delectable bones if she'd so desired. I can't honesty recall there being a single watt of electricity generated between us. Along those same lines, I can't remember ever hearing she was the unfaithful type. Sure, she'd traveled to Kunsan and eventually A-Town from some faraway peninsula town, and like so many of her ilk, usually running away from some similarly traumatic family situation. She'd danced in several clubs before catching the eye of Security Police Technician Master Sergeant Len Brookens, who quickly paid off her bar bill and began the paperwork to whisk her away to the land of milk, honey and the big BX.

As for how Leah and I became acquainted, she'd heard through the grapevine I could get her a cheaper price than her local pharmacy and we did business on a monthly or so basis. Always blew my mind that so many of the town girls, as we referred to them, couldn't work out their own sweet deals with the hometown drugstore, especially considering their natural aptitude for negotiating. After all, Korea was widely known as the land of spirited bartering.

I'm not feigning wide-eyed innocence here; I knew good and well that the majority of the 'Ville ladies that partook of my services were passing on the meds to their government-issued partners. Hell, I sold to the troops as well, so I was obviously about spreading the pharmaceutical happiness, so to speak. Actually, what it was all about was cold, hard cash slapping my palm on a regular basis. How I thought there would not be a hefty bill to pay I can only chalk up to blatant greed and stupidity. I would throw in the naïve aspect again as well, but I knew damn well that distributing illegally obtained meds was as illegal as illegal can get on the peninsula, and we're not talking a light wrist-slap-type misdemeanor. This wasn't nearly in the same minor-league as selling a fifth of Canadian Mist or handful of bananas in some downtown alleyway. Nope, this was black-marketing on steroids, baby. We were talking, at the very least, loss of stripe and some serious correctional custody, basically the Air Force version of house arrest. At the most, loss of *several* or all accumulated stripes followed quickly by a plane-ride back to the states for immediate court-martial, perhaps bookended by a lengthy stopover at Leavenworth Military Institute to specialize in making little rocks out of big ones with a ballpeen hammer.

At the time, I thought the punishment doled out in the aftermath of that frigid winter night in the 'Ville to be a prime example of UCMJ (*United Code of Military Justice*) overkill: the chance to hang me out to dry while simultaneously holding me up as an example to others who dared bend their precious rules. I was just the scapegoat the brass needed to nip drug use directly in the bud. In retrospect, I got exactly what I deserved and, considering the tragic circumstances directly associated with my actions, I can only now see how they might've actually pulled their punches, perhaps figuring that drug use is a two-way street. Dealers need users, after all. Len Brookens, he of the multiple commendations, achievement awards and even a Purple Heart earned as a young Airman serving in Vietnam, had developed quite the jones for amphetamines. Scary stuff, considering the man was a noted weapons collector, always in search of retro firearms or combat cutlery, thus his ownership and eventual use of the vintage Korean revolver and homemade silencer. Seems he'd even rented a storage space in nearby Kunsan City that held numerous popguns, knives and even a machete or two.

In the sergeant's specific case, this over-indulgence on beanies had gradually led to some seriously troubling personality quirks and severe bouts of both depression and paranoia. The latter played out in the form of suspecting his fiancée was secretly humping every horny GI running the 'Ville. The mysterious beret you ask? Issued ten months earlier and officially signed out at base supply by one Len Brookens. A beret a size larger than his own, which he'd reported misplacing during a base exercise. No jive. No joke. The mad bastard had signed out an extra beret simply for accusation purposes. One his subconscious knew would not fit him and, naturally, birth the necessary suspicions required for proper allegations.

All this was speculated upon and ultimately penciled in as the probable cause for Brookens' mental meltdown by one of PACAF's (*Pacific Air Forces*) most respected psychiatrists, a thin-faced, balding colonel with jug ears and constantly wringing hands whose name escapes me. All told, and I remember being informed of these particular stats during my own court martial, fourteen troops had been indicted for the use of the banned pharmaceuticals I'd supplied. It seems a base-sweep, or at least a company-wide one, had ensued once the dominoes began to tumble on my little part-time cash-grab, mainly targeting those labeled as my regular customers. Being that I probably sold to at least seventy-five or more pill-popping airmen during that ten-month period, the total busted was fairly minor. I'd heard that many lost stripes and most received sentences in correctional custody, but that I'd been the only one discharged. Fitting and totally justified, no argument.

Decades later, I cannot honestly say what triggered such horse's ass behavior. It wasn't as if I'd been a winged angel of all things righteous while serving in Idaho, but something about the total, unbridled freedom of overseas duty had released the beast, a personality I'd never revealed or even been aware of housing. Maybe it was the unshackling of a failing marriage, just being out of both eye and earshot of the old ball and chain. Well, that would certainly explain the extreme boozing and blatant infidelity, but not nearly the dealing of dope as such a casual pastime. I want it noted here, for whatever it's worth, I never dealt while on duty, nor did I ever shirk my duties while either patrolling A-Town, performing flight-line or gate duty. Also, I refrained from ever even *discussing* said extra-curricular activity whenever my boots trekked atop base grounds. Moot points all, at least on the surface, but it proves I did possess a semblance of pride, however miniscule.

My court martial, conducted at Travis Air Force Base approximately three weeks following the incident—I'd spent the first ten days in recovery at the Kun base hospital, this following major reconstructive knee surgery, as well as numerous stitch and sew procedures to both my right shoulder (Brookens' final shot had dug a fairly deep groove) and right calf (no blessed clue, perhaps from one of many falls onto the hooch's concrete flooring)—lasted a scant two and a half hours and led to a loss of all stripes and immediate discharge under the Honorable *Under General Conditions* umbrella, which, while it wasn't exactly confetti and champagne worthy, sure beat the alternative of swapping the '*honorable*' portion for its evil cousin beginning with the letters '*dis.*'

My court-appointed barrister—a peach-fuzz-cheeked butter-bar with a horrendous overbite but a headful of smarts—had apparently done a bang-up job in citing my exemplary record sans the Kun assignment, explaining that it was pretty much a proven fact that a short tour in South Korea had brought down many a young troop while also denting the perfect record of many veteran NCOs and officers alike. In the end, the hand-picked jury of mostly Tech, Master and Senior-Master Sergeants had agreed, and I was spared the embarrassment of having both my psyche and permanent record stained with the dreaded badge of dishonor.

As for the other players of said tragedy, Len Brookens had first undergone a trio of surgeries of the reconstructive type, including resewing his peeled scalp, rebuilding his shattered nose and finally restoring his badly fractured right hand. Following a brief rehab at the Kun—we had obviously been housed at opposite ends of the facility—he had been shipped to Osan Air Base for not only the physical rehab from said procedures but also to shake his addiction to amphetamines. From there, he'd been flown to Vandenberg Air Force Base for trial, where it was, approximately three months removed from two attempted murders and one successful execution of same, he was sentenced to an indeterminate span at a mental health facility in Van Nuys; one that specialized in treating combat-trauma veterans. I'd heard he'd been released less than five years later, but this wasn't confirmed as cold, hard fact until a few years later, with obvious ramifications.

Leah Mai was treated for numerous broken bones, to include both collarbones and the hand that Brookens had hammered as I sat cuffed, bleeding and desperately plotting at that dining table. Needless to say, the brass saw fit to pay her medical bills in full. I heard she remarried a year or so later, to some fresh-faced airman no less, and relocated to the States soon after for a life happily-ever-after. If so, good for her, but I have my doubts the events of that night are easily forgotten no matter the passage of time or carefree existence resided within. As for Brookens' many accusations of her unfaithfulness, it was determined by many a character witness that she had been nothing less than the poster-child of loyalty to the maniac that had nearly killed her.

Harry Bachman's body was flown back to his hometown, where he was buried with full honors and a twenty-one-gun salute, while being survived by a young wife and an infant son. Sad to say, I hadn't a clue of the man's personal life at the time of our teaming.

Selfishness is its own muted box, I've heard it said. If so, the *see no evil, hear no evil* model I was be-bopping around in during that time was the soundproof prototype of the future. No excuses here, just a lifetime of self-bewilderment on how or exactly *why* I'd ever transformed into that stranger.

Inexplicably, the gods were kind, and I was spared any form of military jail time other than what was deemed as 'time served' before the court-martial. From Travis, I was allowed the cost of a plane ticket to the U.S. destination of my choice. Believe it or not, I seriously debated expunging not only the city of Little Rock, but also the entire damn state of Arkansas from the list of probables. In the end—and this took many hours of contemplating—I decided that to not at least face Lori Jean face-to-face with an explanation would've been the ultimate copout: the chicken-shit equivalent of sacrificing an innocent to purgatory in order to preserve one's own worthless hide. Low-rent piece of excrement I was at that time, even I wasn't capable of leaving her hanging in such a hideous form of purgatory. Not surprising, our reunion was less than heartwarming. LoJo was, justifiably, cold and distant. I'd attempted a half-hearted apology, which she'd instantly read as so much insincere bunk, and correctly so. In truth, it was more about my own regret and guilt at being caught. Listed as my emergency contact, she'd been contacted via wire concerning the incident and, soon afterward, the charges I was facing. Apparently, it wasn't long after she'd already filed divorce papers—her parents, never thrilled with the marriage from day one, footed the bill—and we parted as complete strangers, which, sad to say, we pretty much were.

From there, I went the only place left anyone would have me. A barely twenty-four-year- old unemployed disgrace returning to his childhood home for some much-needed tough love. Sounds like some cliché-riddled TV movie, I know, but it's weird how often such familiar, overly dramatic scenarios often mirror real-life. Turns out the issue was going to be experiencing the 'love' part of that equation. The toughest part was right there in my face from minute one of my arrival, courtesy of my rage-filled, red-faced father, who cursed me first for not informing either Mom or himself of my issues at the Kun, much less the fallout of said issues. I was scolded, scorned and scoffed at repeatedly over a full evening's counseling session, mostly over the fact that they'd had to hear all the dirty details from Lori Jean's folks. Making it worse were their fervent denials of what they'd deemed nothing more than nasty rumors, obviously created by some mysterious source from the base that I'd made an enemy of. They remained in stanch denial for a matter of weeks, attempting many times to contact me through military channels, only to be left shell-shocked and hopelessly embarrassed when said rumors were substantiated as fact via an official, notarized and duly stamped U.S. Air Force letter.

My mother, always the quiet avenger of the clan, the emotional anchor with her quiet strength, was less vocal but just as disappointed. I could read it in her eyes, the sagging of her shoulders. Even as she attempted to encourage, there was a sense of going through the motions, as if she'd resigned herself to the fact that her only son's once-unlimited potential had bellyflopped directly into an impenetrable barricade.

Sure, as a family we shared the same space, but for that first month or so, it was like my folks viewed me as nothing more than a shadow figure that emitted a rather unsavory odor. Hey, as with my ex-spouse, who was I to blame them? Talk about not having a leg to stand on. For those first few months as a reintroduced civilian, I was practically limbless.

I moved out after finding not one but two gigs: stocking groceries at a local Winn-Dixie full-time while also part-timing as a delivery driver for an auto-parts dealer. The apartment was a tiny one-bedroom job with little in the way of amenities and not in one of the better parts of town, but it might as well have been the Taj Mahal for the peace of mind it provided.

Life pretty much stagnated for a spell: no doubt just what I'd needed at the time considering all the drama and negativity that had proceeded it. I was, at least for those few months before everything tilted back to the theatrical, satisfied with the routine of being just another average working Joe, paying the bills, keeping his nose clean and steering clear of any of the sinful trappings of that land so far, far away in the Pacific.

It was my father, bless *and* damn his well-meaning soul, who was responsible for discovering his boy's future path via the simplest of requests. Given additional time and, more importantly, ample space apart to study on it, he'd apparently decided I wasn't yet the lost cause my recent mistakes had implied. I guess twenty-four *was* fairly young to be written off as dead weight. Of course, I've always thought it highly probable that Mom had a say in his sudden resurgence of confidence in yours truly.

As for the alteration to come, it wasn't of the gradual sort, but meteoric, your classic overnight transformation. Talk about your hybrid entity destined to be equal parts gift and curse. What would start out as a simple lark was destined to be the ultimate example. It was the winter of nineteen eighty-eight, and I was about to become, for want of a better, less egotistical term, a celebrity.

Six

ACE of Spades
(From the private journal of Deron Joseph Barrow)

3 Aug 2019

Holly Springs, Mississippi

I could only hope my face didn't give away the shock I felt at seeing my old friend for the first time in almost six weeks. Tank was no longer an appropriate nickname, unless it was of the fractured Tonka variety. In the relatively short span since late June, he'd not only lost considerable weight but the perpetually toned, muscled appearance of old had disintegrated to literally a shell of its old self. Slightly slumped and shambling forward with the considerable help of a walking cane, Lance Garrett appeared a full decade older than just a few short weeks past.

"Dang, brother, you *must* have a legitimate fear of safety pins with that new physique of yours. One errant poke and you'll be flyin' around the room like a burst balloon!"

"Hey, if I was gonna resurrect the good sergeant, it wasn't gonna be as some flabby couch-tater," I countered, the smile I forced easily the most difficult I'd ever manufactured. "How you doing, dude?"

He nodded with a slight shrug, as if to say, 'Isn't it obvious?"

I'd spoken to Wendy via text before she'd dropped him off and she'd warned me to prep for his appearance, which was far beyond anything I'd envisioned. As if the Parkinson's diagnosis wasn't enough, recently submitted bloodwork had added anemia to a growing list of ills that already included sleep apnea. The latter two explained the sudden weight-loss well enough, though not such a rapid decline or the shocking frailty of his overall deportment.

"What say we grab a booth and order up a couple of cold ones?"

"Sounds like a plan. Lead the way, McDuff," he replied, shuffling past with surprising vigor, as if to show me he hadn't yet reached invalid status. He picked a booth at the rear of the place, four spots down from the nearest patrons. Years ago, or perhaps it was nearing a decade past, the joint had been called the *Hit the Spot*, but a recent management change brought with it the moniker *Suds 'N Spuds*, touting the coldest brews and best-tasting French fries in the free world. It had been many a moon since Tank and I had tipped a few within its dimly lit walls. A retro jukebox in the corner once dominated by country western was currently showcasing a classic rock tune from the either the late '80s or early '90s. The smell of stale cigarettes and spilled brew permeated the walls, though use of the former had been banned for at least a decade.

We both ordered Bud Lights, the brief, stilted silence that followed allowing for brief clarity of Huey Lewis and the News belting out 'Jacob's Ladder' from the 'box.

"Guess you heard. Goes without sayin' with my newly forged Crypt Keeper looks and all."

The forced smile, this time easier to flash but just as difficult to maintain. Staring into my old friend's eyes, drooping with obvious fatigue but glistening with quiet desperation, the hardest thing was not breaking contact.

"Wendy told me. Said you'd been on hiatus from the salt mines for several weeks. So, what's the plan, sawbones-wise? They thinking about putting you on a clear diet of strictly hops 'n barley? If so, I'm thinking a full recovery is in order."

"Appetite's for shit these days. A pack of saltines can fill me up. Worst part is the sleep deprivation. Tell what I've found out, what with spendin' all this quality at home."

"What's that?"

"You remember they used to call television the vast wasteland?"

"Yeah, very well, more so once I became a small part of it."

"Truer words have never been spoken, partner. Two hundred channels and absolutely nothin' on. You'd think with twenty-eight movie channels, Net-tricks, Amazon Pro, Ho-low and the rest, a person could eventually rest their eyes on a flick worth watchin', right?"

I couldn't help but laugh aloud at Tank's network butchery, par for the course for a man who'd probably watched less programmed entertainment than a stadium full of Apostolic Pentecostals.

"Color me clueless, dude," I shrugged once back under control. "We view via antennae only. Get about six channels clearly and three of those are of the shopping variety. Eric still staying with you guys?"

My old friend's eyes dipped at the mention of his lone shire, not a positive sign.

"You know Eric. Like most his age, the boredom of bein' around his folks all summer got to 'im. He and a couple of his college buddies took off for the left coast a few weeks back to see some sights. Sowin' some oats, as is natural for that age, remember?"

"Yeah, the memories fade but I do seem to recall the cabin fever those homegrown cave walls triggered," I said with a wink. Tank grinned in the aftermath, though the hurt reflected in his eyes remained uncloaked to one who knew him as well as I.

"He spoke to Wendy just yesterday from 'Frisco. They're flyin' back in a few days. As for the litany of ills, I'll lick 'em. I'll lick 'em all. 'Least, that's what Windy Wendy keeps tellin' me. That sweet lady has always been the glass-half-full type to my glass-fully-drained."

"Well, I'm not dense enough to doubt her," I replied with a wink, "Looks like you've dropped a few pounds since we last jawed. Daily milkshakes and a half-dozen peanut butter and banana sandwiches might do the trick. Remember that? The too-skinny for duty G.I. diet?"

Tank's croaking laugh, concluding with a harsh series of hacking coughs into an open palm, were painful to both the ears and eyes, the lines around his eyes and mouth as pronounced as that of a man twenty years his senior. My old friend was wasting away before my very eyes. My gut coiled. Still, I had to suck it up and avoid giving him any hint of inner turmoil at this plight. I knew the man well enough to understand any level of pity at his expense was not acceptable behavior.

Our beers arrived, each suitably frosty and foamy, and we sipped in lieu of gulping, as men of our advanced bracket do to avoid that initial of inevitably numerous treks to the little boy's room.

"Affirmative. That same menu saved many a budding career back in basic. Buddy of mine arrived at Lackland about as thick as your basic mop-handle. They force-fed his bony ass a similar thrice-daily in-between 'snack' until the buttons on his fatigues were tremblin' on the edge of poppin' free. Afraid I'd end up spendin' the majority of my days atop the latrine throne if I hopped aboard that particular diet-train."

As we nodded in time and shared knowing smiles, I gazed over Tank's rounded left shoulder towards the jukebox, where a gray-haired gent with a scruffy, similarly tinted beard was gesturing wildly while conversing with another man, obviously a few decades younger. Apparently the pair were discussing the state of modern rock/pop music, said subject-matter most likely tied to what must've been the younger man's choice of tunes, a bass-heavy rap offering of some type, the older participant no doubt pointing out the dreadful state of same. Three things were a sure thing in this life: death, taxes, and each passing generation claiming the music of their era was the best the industry would *ever* have to offer.

"Had my interview for the flick last week. Guess Wendy told ya," Tank finally offered, if for no better reason than to divert the subject of his present health, gaunt hands folded atop one another atop the table with no sign of trembling present.

"Spoilers? Not sure I wanna know, dude."

"Not givin' anything away, partner, unlike most movie trailers these days. I'll just say it wasn't the chore I'd built it up to be. Once the questions were asked, I found myself flowin' pretty naturally. Seems the old noodle," he paused, jabbing his own forehead with a probing and only slightly shaking forefinger, "is still fairly flexible even as the body beneath her shrivels and puckers like a slowly rotting orange peel."

"Cool. Hope my own goes half as smooth," I countered dryly,

suddenly very anxious to view Tank's interview, pre-edit if possible, if nothing else to hear how he perceived me back in the salad days. Sometimes, those close to you can offer surprises both good and bad.

"Headed over to the studio early next week to see the mock set and then over to view Boland's interview. Can't say I'm that stoked about hearing the latter. That old bastard wanted me hung from the short hairs back in the day. I can't imagine the passing decades have done much to mellow that level of animosity."

"Safe bet, partner. Still, you never know."

"Oh yeah I do, and so do you."

He smiled wryly, a smudge of beer foam hanging from his lower lip like pre-popped soap bubbles.

"Yep. That was one feeble attempt, I must confess. Hey, wanna try some of those world-famous fries? For the first time in weeks, I think my midsection's constant grumble is due to actual hunger pains. Man cannot or maybe it's *should not* live on fresh veggies and fruit juices alone, ya know?"

We did just that, two large orders and a house bacon cheeseburger on the side for Tank, whose eyes had suddenly grown larger than his rapidly shrinking gut. Who was I to argue? The man obviously deserved to sneak in as many guilty pleasures as possible, since the multitude of ills that had taken hold weren't apt to release their grip any time soon, if at all.

"So, since asking you any direct questions about the interview is considered strictly off-limits, allow me a simple query of my own," I inquired a bit later between chews of steaming hot potatoes. If not the world's best, possibly a few surrounding counties could justifiably be claimed.

"Shoot, partner," Tank mumbled through an overstuffed maw of his own. "I'm all ears, well, and at the moment, teeth."

A sip of brew later and holding a partially bent fry between two fingers like an unlit smoke, I inhaled deeply and let 'er fly.

"Okay then, I want you to hop into the magical wayback machine and travel all the way back to the first time we met. What were those initial thoughts? Don't hold back, dude. I can take it."

Reaching to scratch through a comically disheveled coif with one hand while gripping his own mug of suds with the other, Tank appeared simultaneously amused and bemused.

"Wow, that is quite the backward trek alright, and you're askin' a hell of a lot for a man of my limited memory banks, the majority of that inner vault havin' gradually emptied out over the years. Hoooo-kay, lemme think. That would've been, winter of '88, correct? Or was it '89?"

I interjected only when he seemed hopelessly stuck on trivial trivialities.

"Early November eighty-eight, exact dates long forgotten but I do know it was a few weeks before the base Turkey Day celebration."

"Yep, sounds 'bout right. You were screenin'...now don't tell me," he paused, holding up a hand palm out, "Rambo Two, yeah?"

"Three, but close enough for government work, and you haven't answered my question."

"I'm gettin' to it, I'm gettin' to it. Sad thing was, most of the troops had already seen Sly's latest months before. Manila was always a popular overseas spot for previewin' flicks weeks before they landed in the homeland. Seoul, Toyko, Laos the same. Guess the suits needed early reviews to gauge U.S. box office. Probably still do."

"Clark Air Base, check. So we have a correct location and timeframe. How about a straight answer, Sergeant Garrett?"

A long sip, echoing belch and foamy grin later, he finally conceded.

"Honestly, I wanted to dislike or at least dismiss your smooth-walkin', slick-talkin' ass as a Hollywood wannabe out to make sport of the troops, what with the regulation cut, Sears-best muscles and undeniably impressive but fake-as-shit military deportment. I was hopin' for a reason to bust your chops but good. Happy to say, ya *never* obliged. In a Reader's Digest nutshell, there ya go, partner."

A moment of brutal honesty here: my lifetime has seen very few true friends, the kind you know you can truly depend on when the chips are down, your hand held out for aid and praying for a little human compassion. The man sitting across from me was at the top of a very short list, but even so I'd always dreaded the answer he'd just divulged. It felt, cliché be damned, like an anvil roughly the weight of an Arkansas razorback had just slipped from my shoulders.

"Sears-best muscles?" I managed, the accompanying smile and laugh strictly to mask the emotion bubbling beneath. "Smooth-walking *and* slick-talking? Dude, you saw through me like a lace curtain."

"Well, you proved from the git-go to be the real McCoy. I ain't much at math or chemistry, but I could always read sincerity. Those tours of yours were for the right reason, and we all appreciated the effort. Yeah, the troops dug the show well enough, but it was mostly that you folks cared enough to travel halfway around the globe to put it on. Partner, you and that crew of yours were our version of Bob Hope's Vietnam-era USO clan."

I had to look away, back towards the jukebox, from which an old Johnny Cash chestnut echoed, to avoid the rapid buildup of moisture in both peepers escalating into an unstoppable torrent. As archaic as it might seem to younger generations of males, men of our era still held to the belief that openly weeping was a sign of weakness. We do and act as we are taught. Still, it took all I had *not* to reach over and deliver a bear-hug squeeze to my cherished old friend while sobbing like a Girl Scout with a skinned knee.

"Goes without saying it was the very *least* I could do, Tank, and thanks."

"Besides, it gave us *something* to look forward to other than the booze, hookers, and war games," he concluded with a sardonic wink, as if sensing my inner struggle to control the waterworks.

Yep, machismo aside, I loved this dude like a brother and I often wished we'd served together when I'd worn the uniform for real and not just for show.

A comfortable silence ensued, wherein we sipped our respective brews between chews.

"So, I know we probably covered this same terrain back in the day, but for my own peace of mind, I need an updated answer," I finally said, having successfully drained my mug.

"Whoa, ESP moment," Tank replied, playfully wide-eyed.

Remaining respectfully silent, I tilted my head questionably.

"What was the initial gut feelin' concernin' your sordid past?"

"Precisely, Einstein."

"Same now as then, buddy-boy. All that rig Amaroo was dead and buried before we ever met. The way I figured...figure it, a big part of the man you've become wouldn't have surfaced without survivin' that Kunsan shitstorm. I respected, and still respect the man I *know*, not that foolish young airman I did not. Sound familiar?"

Indeed it did, and for the second time in a matter of ten minutes, I could have hugged the stuffing out of that tough old bastard.

"Almost word-for-word, I do believe. Gracias yet again."

We ordered a second round of brews and fell silent yet again, that is until the fresh set of overflowing mugs arrived and we each silently nodded our appreciation to the waitress.

"So how's Jenny?" Tank inquired cautiously.

The very subject the ultimate downer, I was either unable or unwilling to mince words.

"Indifferent. Uncaring. Uninterested. In other words, the same as the last time you and I jawed. I think she's just waiting for me to tell her the documentary is wrapped to fly on back and file the D papers."

"Seriously?"

"Yep. Truthfully, at this point I could sign away without hesitation. Things haven't been right between us for so long I can't remember the last time they were."

"Sorry, partner. Truly. I was hopin' this one was the one for ya."

"My fault as much as hers, if not more. There's nothing worse than when a cliché as old as 'we just grew apart' is probably the most apt. Saddest part is, I'm not at all certain we were ever truly together."

I shrugged and we sipped, the subject happily locked away that quickly.

The beers were soon gone, the conversation following suit. I drove Tank back over to Boone's Crossing while nursing a not-unpleasant buzz, cautious to obey speed limits along the way just in case being slightly over the limit became, heaven forbid, an issue. Two blessed beers. Amazing how one can go from a heavyweight to lightweight in the span of a few short decades.

It was just past twenty-one hundred hours when I handed Tank off to Wendy, who'd kindly allowed us our time while visiting an old schoolmate in town. I gave them both a hug as we parted, the fragile feel of Tank's frame as shocking, if not more so, than his appearance.

I feared greatly for my old friend and promised myself I would phone him more often in the coming weeks while simultaneously staying in closer touch with Wendy concerning his condition.

On the short trek back home, I contemplated many things, my thoughts frenzied and jumbled and mostly tied to both the film and my latest failing marriage. I was meeting with Diandra and Ron Dixon in three short days at the studio apartment to view several interviews and discuss my manuscript and its chances for publication in concert with the finished film. Funny how issues that seem so major at the time can be so abruptly minimized by a single twist, a fractured moment in time that transforms the universe you think you knew into a bizarre plain of unfamiliarity. Such was the dramatic change ahead that, if I'd known was just over the next bend, a mad jump from the tracks would've surely been in order. Sad to say, we almost never see them coming in time to make that faithful leap.

In my case, the word *almost* can safely be omitted.

~ * ~

Excerpt from *The Mask beneath the Mask: A Memoir*, by Deron Joseph Barrow

Appointed to station director at KHLT in late eight-six, Dad still enjoyed spinning discs as a part-time Dee-Jay, usually on weeknights but occasionally on weekends to spell the regulars if needed. Being that I'd subbed for him—effortlessly and without formal training, I might add—

he asked if I wouldn't mind taking over the part-time slot. Again, I have my suspicions that Mom had planted that particular nugget for his perusal. My dad was not a stupid man, and logically thinking men know where their bread is buttered. Thus, I was immediately able to give up the delivery job and settle in as the fill-in DJ at KHLT-FM, the *Rock of the Rock*. Soon enough, the two-night, four-hour gig (Tuesdays-Wednesdays, 6PM-10PM) expanded to Tuesdays-Fridays and finally the primetime weekday gig was mine and mine alone. It seems my natural style and penchant for choosing just the right playlist—the station wasn't about current top-forty but more of an early pioneer for what would soon be commonly referred to as a 'classic rock' format—meant an instant upswing in local overnight ratings. Adopting the DJ moniker *Dan-Jammer*—Dee Jay D.J. would have admittedly been comically redundant—I was soon receiving more fan mail than the weekend spinners, a rare feat at that time in the business.

Less than six months into this personal resurgence, an even better opportunity knocked, though at the time I can't help but recall how, well, damn silly the whole idea sounded. Through the decades, Dad had secured many contacts in both local radio and TV, the most prominent of these a former college chum who had, by that time, graduated to program director at KATV, KHLT's sister station, and the Rock's ABC affiliate. Don Olivia was, by all accounts, a stern but fair taskmaster with a flair for the outlandish: a creative dude who often clashed with sponsors for what they considered 'content unbecoming,' the mostly hardcore Baptist, Bible-thumping, God-fearing market. This latest brainstorm wasn't going to win him any fans amongst such tight-ass conservatives. For this alone, I admired the man without reservation.

The idea (in general): Dating all the way back to the '50s, local TV stations had found inventive ways to fill the early-morning and late-night timeslots, one of the most popular being the creation of horror and suspense film 'hosts.' These were usually heavily disguised local Dee Jays and unemployed stage actors with the gift of gab, utilizing dime-store-budget sets to introduce cult flicks while cultivating a core audience who would tune in more for their act than the movie itself. By the late

'60s and well into the '80s, such camp luminaries as *Vampira*, Bill *Chilly Billy* Cardille, *Dr. Creep* and *Svengoolie* had become household names, at least in their specific area of viewership. Don, a paunchy, balding man in his mid-to-late fifties infamous for his walrus mustache—it always seemed to be housing remnants of his latest meal—duck-like shamble and boisterous persona, decided that KATV needed such a gimmick to kill time and draw in new sponsors for the ten-thirty to midnight timeslot on Saturday nights, but with a decided twist.

Instead of horror, horror-comedy or horror-suspense movies—many within these catalogues popular only for their campy badness, the stereotypical 'so bad they're good' subgenre—Don decided a new kind of movie host was needed as a potential substitute for the same-old, same-old. Being a big fan of historical conflicts, Don suggested that KATV be home to the very first War Movie Host. From what I heard from several present when the idea was presented to the station manager, this went over like the proverbial turd in the punchbowl. Don, ever persistent and, rumor had it, not above threatening to relocate his programming talents to a rival station, eventually emerged victorious, but only for an initial run of three episodes and a shoestring budget of the floss-thin variety.

Obviously, such an undertaking involves a daunting checklist just to get off the ground. An office, abandoned for years, had been chosen from several similarly deserted spaces on the third floor of the KATV building and a set drawn up with the most economical of local carpentry specialists enlisted for the job.

Interviews were soon scheduled for script-writing duties as well as a director and perhaps most vital, the choosing of the show's on-screen host. Don, along with his assistant, a highly enthusiastic and energetic young lady named Maggie Jensen, would conduct said interrogations.

The station manager had given them less than a month to complete all pre-production before the initial program was to air Saturdays in the less-than-coveted ten-twelve PM slot, lately dominated by either reruns of *Hawaii-Five-O*, back-to-back *Sanford and Sons* or the occasional infomercial.

The original set, blue-printed at cost by a local stage-play designer, depicted what was supposed to pass as the interior of a World War Two-era bunker, complete with sandbag and concrete block (faux) walls, an antique—rented from a local surplus dealer—RCA-brand 1935 RAK and RAL receiver radio and transmitter with accompanying headgear; a Woodstock-brand manual typewriter; an enamelware coffee pot and of course, a cache of assorted weapons to include a Thompson sub-machine gun, M1A1 flamethrower, the M1911 single-action Colt pistol and a handful of Mk2 grenades. Toss in the accompanying furniture, assorted tables and chairs, all nicely scarred and fittingly aged in look and purchased from similar dealers of ancient goods, and it successfully captured the necessary look, especially when filmed in grainy black and white. Color, Don declared, and all would later agree upon experimentation, was apt to showcase the cheapness in a way that black and white effectively disguised. Toss in a pin-up or three (to include the infamous *Texas Rose, Keep 'em Flying* and *Cowgirl Blues* posters from that era) and the initial set was, well, set. Not sure how accurate, but I'd heard the total cost had been under five thousand bucks. Not a bad sticker price for a twelve-by-twenty mockup, even for the decade in question.

Next came the scriptwriters, rumor had it chosen after a single interview. Chad Bottoms and Chris Markum, both Vietnam-veterans from the Army and Navy ranks, respectively, and long-time comedy scribes for a slew of radio and TV stations in the South and Midwest.

A director was hired with less than two weeks remaining until that initial shoot, though this caused little panic since the job only really entailed they be on set to direct the episode as if it were a live program, with at most one to two days of actual filming. Sixtyish but sporting shoulder-length gray locks usually snaked into a ponytail, Gregory Tate had helmed countless commercials in sixteen states, to include political ads, fast food and, before such bits were banned, hard liquor and cigarettes. A short, chubby Alabamian with a deep drawl, Greg ruled on set with an iron fist and quick temper, though over time it was obvious his deep-south bark was far worse than the slight overbite of his dentures.

Then came the casting. The first round was held approximately a week before Tate's hiring and drew three dozen or so hopefuls—I've since been told the number was closer to well over fifty—and consisted mostly of local stage actors and wannabe auteurs from at least six states, with Don and Maggie being the lone interviewees. From what I heard—second-hand info at best at the time—none really captured their fancy enough to snag the role outright, though there were a select few that stood out for follow-up auditions.

Don was all about personality, natural charisma, while Maggie was more concerned about the character—still unnamed at the time—possessing the right look.

As for how I got involved, it was straight out of some of the cheap, B-movie scripts we would soon be mimicking with regularity. The day before round two of interviews for the role, Don had stopped by KHLT to speak with my dad over some unrelated programming issues.

Now, no one better than I understand that the following sounds like something out of one of those ancient Hollywood pulp mags, but I've often volunteered to place my hand on a head-high stack of the good book variety that it's fact. Don would often second this—several YouTube videos from the late eighties and early nineties can be perused and viewed for proof—when asked, with very little variation in plot.

As memory serves, my moment of 'discovery' occurred as Don, pacing the station in search of my father, strode casually by the DJ's booth—a routine Saturday night around nine PM or thereabouts—briefly spotting me and offered a brief nod in passing. Though some of the smaller details escape me, there are two that stand out to this day; the tune presently spun had been Cheap Trick's 'Surrender' and, for some inexplicable reason I cannot explain to this date, the return gesture I'd chosen to match Don's casual tilt of the head had been, inexplicably, a military salute, no doubt my first such use of said gesture since being so ceremoniously fired from their official ranks over a year earlier. Next thing I know, he's backpaddled down the hall and into the booth. There, surrounded by the rock album covers of the day adorning every available inch of wall and inner-door space, I was asked to stand, come to attention and repeat the movement. Now, it must be injected here that I was, at that time, fairly buffed as far as physique went.

Point of order: Probably out of boredom and more-so sexual frustration, I'd started hitting the weights at a local Y a few months earlier, adding a twenty-spot of mostly muscle onto my previously toned but overly trim frame. A buddy was a personal trainer and had helped me work out a regimen to bulk up in the shortest time possible. Apparently, I had decided that the chicks dug muscles and was eager to test the rumor.

Toss in the fact that, on the very day Don afforded me a personal audition at my place of work, I'd decided to sport a two-sizes too small muscle-tee and, to top it off, had previously shoulder-length locks trimmed to damn near a military regulation cut, and voila! The role of war movie host was mine to lose. This despite as far as acting chops went, I'd never so much as taken on a role in an elementary school play. As far as Don was concerned, my DJ experience—he pointed out my natural gift for gab and talent for ad-lib—would serve to carry the day until some on-air experience helped work out the kinks of whatever awkwardness arose on set. Needless to say that once the shock of even being considered wore off, I had my doubts. Don had asked that I come to his office the next day and meet with Maggie and himself to seal the deal, if I was so inclined to accept. To this day, I find it hard to believe I was hand-picked over a simple salute and a set of buffed biceps. It certainly wasn't about unproven talent, and even though it wasn't exactly landing the lead in a Hollywood blockbuster, I couldn't help but initially suspect that dear ol' dad had played a part.

About an hour or so after Don had offered me the gig, my shift ended and I recall sprinting down the hall to and finding my father in the station breakroom, calmly sipping a cup of Joe while casually reading over some paperwork. He not only denied any involvement, but I thought *I* was going to have to swear on a Bible that I wasn't pulling *his* leg. In fact, he'd spoken to Don just a half hour earlier and the man had mentioned nothing to him about the job offer. For some reason, that non-act by the veteran program manager had garnered instant respect from his soon-to-be lead actor. As for my dad, he was, at the very least, astonished. That night, I spoke to both him and Mom about the offer, and, considering that it wasn't apt to interfere with my regular schedule in the booth, we all agreed in principle that it was one of those 'nothing to lose' scenarios. If I bombed from the outset, nothing lost. If, on the other hand, I succeeded, it might mean additional avenues of future employment. Easy enough. Decision made. At the time, not exactly filed away as one of your monumental types. Time would dictate otherwise, and rather quickly.

The meeting was at noon the following day in Don's office at the TV station. As to step directly into character—whatever character that might be—I dressed in camo jeans and matching tee (again, at least a size too snug), and high-glossed black boots. That morning, I'd not only hacked off a mustache I'd been cultivating since my discharge, but for the coup de grâce, stopped by the Y for a half-hour free-weight workout binge just to ensure the bod was fully pumped.

Maggie's first impression as I marched into the big man's office could've been taken as either awestruck wonder or comical horror: all wide-eyed and lower jaw unhinged shock that soon enough transformed into a droll smile, approving nod and congratulatory glance Don's way. Without uttering a single word, the job was mine. As much as I'd like to claim a smug, knew-it-all-the-time coolness in the face of such instantaneous acceptance, every expression and bodily movement that followed was accompanied by a fluttering swarm of butterflies assaulting my gut with razor-sharp wings. A production meeting was called for that very afternoon, just an hour before my next scheduled shift in the dee-jay booth, with Chad Bottoms, Chris Markum and Gregory Tate in attendance.

Top of the agenda: Two of the most important details as far as the program went, both involving me specifically.

The first would be my character's name, the second, and maybe most vital of all, his personality traits. As for the first, I hadn't nary a suggestion.

As for the second, I most certainly did.

~ * ~

Video Interview with Maggie Carpenter (formerly Maggie Jensen)

I have to confess to having quite the crush on Deron right from that first encounter in Mr. Oliva's office. Lust at first sight, you might say. As time and experience progressed, that crush did naturally wane, as such instinctively physical attractions are apt to do. Deron and I became friends, although I cannot honestly claim to share the same feelings for that...for the *character* he portrayed. If anything, we agreed to disagree on most topics. I was, and still am, a liberally minded individual. That...character was, well, let's just say I used to half-jokingly refer to him as Archie Bunker with stripes. Wow, *that* reference surely dates me, doesn't it (*laughs)*?

Anyway, since Deron was responsible for most of the later scripts, I often found myself arguing with his character's words and opinions, and it was strange that I seemed to knowingly separate the two as if they were indeed two different men. Not that I held any expertise in what made a good TV script. My job as assistant program manager was more about personnel issues and dealing with feedback and criticisms of ad spots. I'm of the belief that Don included me in the mix just in case a female opinion was needed amongst all that testosterone. Hey, it might've been the late eighties, but I still considered myself a bit of a trailblazer, baby *(laughs)*.

Don and I had juggled several names between us for that character, most of which sounded pretty comical in retrospect. Fortunately, I can only remember a select few of the funnier ones. Don loved *Axel Stone*. I think the rank was Captain, and even admitted that his older son had been a big Sergeant Rock fan from sixties and seventies comics. In the end, we both agreed it was a little too close to Sergeant Rock, though today it sounds more like a man's deodorant or maybe a body scrub *(laughs)*. I laid a few eggs myself, but the lemon of them all had to be *Ryker Steele*. Sounds like a Pittsburgh-based metal manufacturer, but hey, I wasn't exactly knowledgeable in the ways of manliness (*laughs*). A few days into tossing around similar tripe, we were a cat's whisker away from a radio contest to pick the moniker when who else but Deron himself stepped up with a winner. It was what the younger generation refers to these days as a no-brainer, and both Don and I instantly knew it was the one.

A few weeks later, the world, well, at least the small patch labeled middle Arkansas, would be formally introduced to *Sergeant Ace Claymore*. Sad to confess that Don had to explain the claymore reference to yours truly. As for just how Deron came up with his own alter-ego namesake, it was pure military logic. '*Ace*' represented both Navy and Air Force flyers, while *Claymore* mines were well known by all of what he called 'the ground pounders' or 'ground grunts,' that being Army or Marine troops. Personally, the whole process was a heckuva learning process. No war buff was little old me, obviously.

Now that we had the proper label, the character itself needed to be fleshed out. For that, we brought in the writers and director and sat through many a brainstorming session. Wow. It wasn't always pleasant, especially the vast difference of opinion between the writers and Deron. We're talking Grand Canyon wide. I remember being surprised that Deron was so, well, passionate, considering his rather low position on the decision-making totem pole, at least at the beginning. Got to say, he scaled that sucker in no time flat. I was just as surprised by Mr. Tate's low-key, non-participation. I mean, he was about as involved as the furniture. I found out later that Gregory was just that type. He saw his job strictly as director of a completed script. Now, he could be a grade-A horse's butt on the set, but as far as scripts went, he wasn't about tweaking or re-writing. He expected the writers to do their jobs and the actors to do theirs.

If I recall correctly, Don and I made very little suggestions other than what films might be plucked for viewing those first few episodes. Honestly that was almost all Don. I had ideas about slight alternations to the set depending on the chosen movie, but mostly I just sat with extinguisher in hand just in case all the flying sparks ignited a larger blaze (*laughs nervously*).

The main gist of disgruntlement: Deron did not want the Ace character played strictly for laughs or parody, as he saw the writers were hinting at with the first draft of that initial episode. Chad and Chris had written Deron's role—a five-to-six-minute intro sequence, followed by four separate two-to-three-minute pre-commercial interludes and finally a four-to-six-minute closing—with Coppola's *Apocalypse Now* as the sample flick, complete with Ace cracking wise on Brando's weight, Duvall's infamous 'smell of napalm' quip and even Martin Sheen's off-screen heart attack, all the while hinting at the blatant stupidity of U.S. involvement.

Gotta say, Deron took serious offense to the majority of not only the wisecracks, but the buffoonish Foghorn-Leghorn accent he was to bring to the proceedings. Though a born southerner, he was told to 'up the ante' on his natural drawl to the point of sounding like a hillbilly hybrid of Jethro Bodine and early Andy of Mayberry. He fought that tooth and nail, I tell you, and I respected him for not backing off. As things progressed, it was obvious he was right to do so. Just an opinion, but I don't think the show would've ever reached such heights if he'd played it so stereotypically broad.

We sat through two or three additional roundtables, each more heated than the last, until a compromise had been reached in terms of Sergeant Ace Claymore's overall deportment. Several test screenings were shot with that first script, though the only clear memory I have of them is the set itself. At first glance, I remember thinking, 'rock and roll! How awesome is this?' Seriously, I'd seen less impressive set-ups on network television. It was like a freaking war museum!

A week or so later, Chad and Chris delivered that initial pilot script and my involvement in the show all but ceased. Maybe ten or twelve days after, we all gathered in the screening room to check out the finished product. The preview movie chosen, fittingly I must say for the times, was the last sixties hit *The Dirty Dozen* with Lee Marvin, Charles Bronson and Ernest Borgnine. My father had loved that movie, for reasons that always escaped this girl.

Now, I'm no movie critic, especially of the genre in question, and while the *Dozen* is considered a classic, I secretly caught myself wishing there had been less of it and more of our chosen host. I didn't find out until the end credits ran that all present had felt a similar urge to fast-forward to Deron's spots. Sure, the script takes a share of the credit—no performance can shine without the right words—but Deron Joseph Barrow was a true natural in front of that intrusive lens from minute one. The voice, gravelly and gruff without being forced—think Clint Eastwood aping Tom Selleck—the performance itself utterly flawless: tough, stern but with a playful wink that spoke to the audience in a *don't take me too seriously here, folks. Then again, too lightly and I'll happily have your ass tossed in the brig.* Greg Tate, a man rumored to have graduated from the Stanley Kubrick school of a never-ending takes, admitted in the aftermath that every scene was completed with a maximum of two. For at least that opening prologue, I think it ran the longest in duration...maybe six or seven minutes, they dressed Deron in this vintage flight-suit and Ray-Ban shades. Kind of a *Top Gun* for the World War Two crowd (*laughs*).

They even had the station beautician add a pretty darn realistic fake scar starting just under his left temple, running the length of his cheek and ending just beneath his chin. War scar or no, it was Tom Cruise country all the way, standing at attention next to a wall adorned in the stars and stripes like Patton making that famous opening speech. And boy howdy, that delivery! Stone-cold perfection. I had chills, I tell you! For the remaining spots, he'd peeled away the flight-suit to reveal an extremely snug camo green tee. I recall jabbing Don about going after that female dynamic and of course he denied such sophomoric tactics (*laughs*). Clever as a fox, old Mister Oh!

The wrap party was at this local steakhouse and I only recall two things clearly: Deron sucking down Seven-Ups one after another and as chatty and apprehensive as his alter-ego was cool and collected. Seems he'd given up booze for Lent, well, for sugar and caffeine at least, and was convinced everyone's praise was unwarranted. Funny how things can change so rapidly. A month or so later you'd have thought he'd fisted multiple Oscars or was at least deserving of such. Then of course, the inevitable crash to Earth. Of course, in Deron's case, it was like the ultimate flame out: crash *and* burn. To a crisp, baby.

Anyhow, back to that first taping. The premiere ratings didn't exactly break any records, but compared to the previous programming, it was absolute gangbusters. Reviews from the local news-rags were positive, though not as glowing as our own. Predictably, all had pointed to Deron's performance as the main draw, calling it 'quirky' and 'hilariously droll,' if I recall.

Don was thrilled to the marrow and decided to bombard (*laughs*), pardon the combat pun, the channel with promos for the second episode, even sneaking several in during primetime. Not exactly cheap PR, but he really believed we had a potential hit on our hands. Who was I to disagree? The sponsors were happy enough with the numbers, so my bread was sufficiently buttered.

Episode two started the trend of filming live and was centered around John Wayne's ultra-patriotic *Green Berets* and ushered in the first hint at controversy behind-the-scenes, which, we all understand in the business, can be a very good thing as far as the creative process goes. Critics had long since panned Wayne's version as leaning so hard left politically to qualify as parody, especially considering the liberal landscape cloaking the late sixties. Chad and Chris had written the skits with a similar vibe, but Deron didn't, well, quite cooperate, going off-script so severely that the two writers threatened to resign afterwards. I remember watching it and, even not having read the original script, I could tell Deron had injected some serious ad-lib, painting Wayne's vision not as patriotic tripe but just the opposite, standing tall at attention with that flag flying high. Sergeant Ace Claymore, eyes moist and voice cracking with emotion, bowed with pride to the image of John Wayne as the ultimate true-blue American his movies portrayed. Cornball perhaps but hey, that was Deron. He wasn't acting and took a stand against the guys' gentle poke at the Duke's ideals. The guy wore his heart firmly on sleeve in matters of patriotism and apparently decided from the get-go that the sarge would follow suit. But hey, ratings darn-near doubled as the audience seemed to agree whole-heartedly.

Letters began pouring into the station with two distinct patterns forming: the male audience, mostly the thirty-five to fifty demographic I believe, loved Ace for his pro-American stance and hardline conservative politics. As for the females (*laughs*), well, I seem to remember this only made up about twenty percent of the audience or thereabouts, well, they were crushing big-time, little hearts all a-flutter over the sarge's bulging biceps and gruff, manly deportment. By, I think, episode four or five of that first season, the female demo had increased substantially to around thirty or thirty-five percent of the overall audience, no doubt proving that political differences can be overlooked in the face of, well, the charms and magnetism of the opposite party (*laughs*).

By the time we got to episode five or six, there was talk of moving the show to primetime. Can you believe it? They were talking about the coveted eight to ten PM slot, thus preempting network programming. In the end, it was deemed both too costly and risky, but that should give you some indication as to how popular *Ace's Flick Picks: Cinematic War Stories* had become. Oh, by the way, the show title is the one contribution I can partly claim (*laughs*). Well, at least the Cinematic War Stories part. Even that stubborn old tight-lipped Gregory Tate warmed to it immediately.

Well, by the time *Platoon* was featured as the season finale, Chad and Chris had already given their notice and Tate was also talking of jumping ship. The former pair fumed over Deron's continued on-air alternations of their scripts, while the latter was, reportedly, fed up with being caught in the middle of the weekly bitch sessions that had become the norm. Scuttlebutt had it that the straw that snapped the camel's back was Deron's criticisms of Oliver Stone's controversial take on the Vietnam experience, even referring to the noted director as a 'shameless doper whose participation in the conflict seems to have been limited to getting high or raping the locals' while blaming politics for his own criminal behavior. I'm pretty sure I have that down verbatim, even after all these years. Scout's honor *(laughs; raises right hand in three-fingered salute)*, that is from memory only and not from a sneak peek at those recently re-released DVDs of the show. Well, I heard the writers had an on-set kitten over their 'star's' choice of words and actually feared being sued for something they hadn't scripted. There had been, allegedly, some pushing and shoving off-screen, though I can't verify since after the second episode I watched from home and not the screening room. Anyway, Chad had requested to Don and me that all future episodes be taped to prevent Deron's antics and was flat-out denied without much discussion by Mr. Oliva. I had to agree, though I never got the chance to verbalize these feelings, that something vital would be lost if the show went to tape. There was a rawness, a dangerous, rough-at-the-edges style to the live shows that we both felt would be lost if the format had been tweaked even slightly, much less such a major alteration. Bottom line was that Deron's going off-script had been a strength, not a weakness. When that red light flashed, Deron Barrow became Ace Claymore. I don't know any other way to describe it. It was a live soul-possession that taping and re-recordings would only serve to homogenize, to tame. The change would be obvious to the audience, and ratings would begin to tank. That was our biggest fear. KATV had caught lightning in a khaki-green canteen (*laughs*). History dictates that you simply don't fix what isn't broken in this business. Ace Claymore was cracked in many ways perhaps (*laughs*), but we weren't about to break him by tempering the momentum he'd built that first season.

Ten episodes in and the letters continued to pour in, the majority extremely positive. Not surprisingly, Chad and Chris did not agree with future plans and resigned almost immediately. For better or worse, you decide (*laughs*), the bulk of the script writing was soon handed to the man who knew the Claymore character best, that of course being Deron Joseph Barrow. Seeing that there was a pretty massive built-in audience by that time, screwing up would've been quite the achievement. Well (*sighs*) as we all know, there was a dramatic drop coming. Historic in its rapid descent, I'd venture to say, and of course it had nothing to do with the writing.

With a few months off to take a breath and revel in the show's shocking popularity, I was able to pick and choose the second season's potential sponsors, a heck of a switch from season one when I was mostly trapped in *beggars-can't-be-choosers* mode. Of course, that follow-up campaign is when the show took off like a rocket, what with nationwide syndication and the live base shows. My clearest memory is sitting in Don's office after the syndication deal was finalized with WGN and TBS, the big guy wearing this mask of joyous disbelief which I'm sure I mirrored from the across his desk. It was like, how did this happen and so darn fast to boot (*laughs*). I can't claim much in the way of actual involvement from that point to the beginning of the third season other than lining up new sponsors. Not exactly a Herculean task, to say the least. By then it was basically just a matter of choosing the highest bidder. Well, all that changed before the curtain was raised on a fourth campaign, except for that one episode that in retrospect turned out to be an ironically fitting swansong. Oh well (*sighs*), they say all great runs come to an end, and boy-howdy, did it ever. But then, it was a heck of a run.

~ * ~

Video Interview with Chad Bottoms

Barrow seemed a nice enough kid at the beginning: cocky but never disrespectful to either Chris or myself. I mean, we weren't exactly Neil Simon and Billy Wilder, but we'd been continuously working in the business for a full decade, and he treated us, at least initially, like mentors. Took instruction well enough from Greg—that man wasn't apt to take much in the way of shit, and the kid obviously knew it—and seemed to just be taking it all in. (*Laughs*) Well, all that went to hell in a big hurry once that camera light shone. Suddenly, the young dude knew it all and we were all just a grouping of human barriers to his stardom. I mean, he took a big old dump on our very first script, ad-libbing roughly half that initial skit. Wish I could say this sudden rush of ego-maniacal behavior was just a temporary glitch, but if anything, it went downhill from there. Chris and I were helpless to keep him from butchering our words and/or themes, what with the live format, and could only sit there and stew as he played war-hero for real. Being the more level-headed of our partnership, there were several occasions I thought Chris was going to scoop up one of the prop weapons and attempt to relocate the leading man to a nearby infirmary, if you get my meaning (*laughs*). We tried to hang on to the gig, especially once it caught fire in the ratings, but having one's words twisted so severely trumps paycheck after a time, so we walked. Can't speak for Chris, rest his ornery soul, but it was a decision I didn't regret then and certainly not now. I was never a believer in karma until the hammer fell on Deron Barrow's little scam, but you know (*winks into camera*), I guess there is something to that whole 'what comes around goes around' thing.

~ * ~

Video Interview with Gregory Tate (recorded in 1995, courtesy ABC-TV)

I had very little issue with Deron and have always felt very bad for the young man. At the time of filming those episodes, I thought him a raw but viable talent with a bright future. The program itself was very little work, to be honest. It was, to my experience, much like filming a series of elongated commercials. I rather enjoyed the compensation, especially that final year. I would've definitely signed on for more (*laughs*).

~ * ~

Video Interview with Donald Oliva (recorded in 1995, courtesy KATL)

Of course, when it came to light, it was like a supernova. But ya know, the show itself was kinda like that in a way. Meteoric in rising and like a fallen star, the descent equally sudden. Biggest success of my career, no contest, and the money wasn't bad either.

As for Deron, sure, his britches got a bit roomy for his butt there for a while, but I never got the feelin' he took any of the success for granted, and he always made it a point to give credit to the crew. As for some of the off-set antics, hey, he was still in his twenties, for cripes sakes! I will say, despite how things ended, we did some great things with that little show, especially those live gigs on the bases. We made the day for those troops, without a doubt. Just watch the tapes. They loved every minute of it! No denying that we made a cultural dent there for a while. A minor one, maybe, but a dent!

~ * ~

Video Interview with Conrad Boland, Senior-Master Sergeant USAF, Retired

Purely accidental, it was. I hardly ever watch war movies and the like. Just too damn unrealistic, except for maybe some of the combat scenes in that *Finding Private Ryan*. Hollywood is the last damn place that understands the art of war (*Scoffs*). They can hang their PhDs on the wall if you're talking protesting those fighting and dying for their freedoms, but lifting a finger to defend those same rights? Fat chance. Anyway, the channel just happened to be turned to that particular program that evening and despite the cheap disguise, sacrilegious dress and blatant steroid use, I recognized 'im easily enough after a squint or two. (*Grins, raising a hand airborne*) No doubt about it, outing that fraudulent jackass was my pleasure, thank you very much. I only wish I'd sniffed 'im out sooner. Hell, these days the way they glorify antihero types, he'd probably be the toast of Hollywood. The media would've crowned him a fun-loving rebel or some such horseshit, though I still have doubts the masses would completely approve. Tells ya what a difference a couple of decades make, right? Lying bastard was toast practically overnight, as well he should've been. There had to be some base commanders wiping eggs from their faces once the truth got out, including the one I served under at the time at Yokota. Fate can be one cold-hearted bitch, but especially to those deserving of her wrath.

I'd attended the show at the base that night by sheer happenstance, that being that my wife at the time worked behind the scenes on the set as a volunteer. Folks still find it hard to believe I recognized 'im from how he'd looked before versus the show-business version. What I tell 'im is, and I know it sounds like so much clichéd garbage, Conrad Boland never forgets a face. In Barrow's case, I'd trailed 'im at the Kun by maybe a year and, working in security at that time, we'd all been well-versed in his escapades. Hell, part of our in-processing was ogling a dozen or more training films of the base history and such, which by that time of course covered the infamous case of Len Brookens and murder of the Bachman kid. Their pictures, along with that of Deron Barrow, were burned into my subconscious from that moment on. Sure, his show-biz persona was bulked up and adorned with a fake scar and jarhead buzz-cut, but it's the eyes, ya see. The eyes are not only the windows, but to me they're also the true IDs to the soul. Maybe if he'd thought to wear some color contacts I'd have never made the connection, but that's just a maybe. Ya see, it was more than just that. The pics I'd seen of his younger version mirrored the same exact smile: a tad crooked with a severe curl of the top lip. Unmistakable. Knew it the first time he flashed it at the crowd.

Now, I have to admit the prick was a showman and a damn good one. He had the act down by that time, I reckon. The boys loved 'im unconditionally for the tough-guy act and the girls swooned at what they must've perceived as charm. He had the knack for jibber-jabber, no argument. The movie they screened was a Chuck Norris vehicle, one of the ones where he rescues the war prisoners in Vietnam. Title escapes me. Not a bad choice, considerin' how popular Norris was with the troops, him being a former Air Force vet himself. I recall Barrow's act included him breaking separate stacks of boards with his fists, feet and finally his noggin, all the while decked out in martial arts duds and crackin' wise. 'Bout every half hour they would stop the flick and he would invite a few troops onto the stage to interact, mostly asking them their hometown, favorite foods, booze of choice, and how much they were missing home before thanking them for their service. SOS as far as visiting entertainers go, but very effective in building comradery. Jackass was a natural. Too bad he turned out to be such a royal scam artist. My blood commenced to boil as the truth was revealed, this only after I gave myself an invite backstage after the final curtain fell and most of the troops had exited the theater.

As we shook hands, he flashed that smile and tilted his head just so, confirming what I'd earlier suspected from sitting thirty yards away. I was slapping palms with Deron Joseph Barrow, former disgraced airman and present charlatan of screen and military stage. A true Blue Falcon if I'd ever laid eyes on one. Um, Blue Falcon meaning the kind of worthless, soulless troop that cares absolutely nada, *zilch*, about his fellow soldiers and will sell them down the river in a heartbeat if it somehow benefits his own selfish cause.

Well, my blood immediately commenced to boil, especially in the knowledge that in the previous three days before gracin' us with this fakery, he'd had the cast-iron testicles to complete a similarly fraudulent display not only at Osan Air Base in the ROK (Republic of Korea) but returning to the scene of his greatest crime. Hard to believe, but Kunsan Air Base had seen the return of one of their most infamous prodigal sons, though obviously unaware of said fact. How he had the...gall to show his ass back on that peninsula is beyond me and mine. The next day, after receiving permission from my own CO to do so, I stomped on over to the Wing CC's office, still blowin' smoke from both nostrils, and laid my suspicions on the line. Happy to say there was little resistance from the colonel, who initiated an immediate investigation to include having Barrow's party held at Gimpo airport as they prepped to fly down to Guam for another show. The rest is history. I will give Barrow credit for not dancin' around the truth and confessing right away, though I kinda suspect that look of sadness he wore at the press conference was more about getting caught than any sincere guilt.

I say all that to say *this*: what happened to 'im in the aftermath is neither sad nor surprising to me. Bad shit follows bad people, period. I'm just proud to say I helped to permanently alter his deceitful existence. He was hoodwinkin' an entire nation and it just wasn't right. I did and still do feel some sympathy for those who lost their jobs once his ride ended. They didn't deserve to take the fall with 'im, but in such a situation there is always gonna be collateral damage. I'll go to my grave knowing I did the right thing in unmasking a person so undeserving of his success when so many good men and woman that served with honor go unnoticed and unheralded. Enough said.

Seven

And nothing but the truth
Excerpt from *The Mask beneath the Mask: A Memoir*, by Deron Joseph Barrow

6 Aug 2019

Little Rock

"I'm surprised at the man's conciseness, actually. Thought he'd ramble on for hours. You sure ya'll didn't take the editing clippers to his interview and hack off a few hours?"

Dee-dee smiled before sipping from a tall paper cup of iced coffee adorned with the Starbucks logo. Little lady definitely had a rehab-worthy java jones, as this was her second such mug-full in less than an hour. She'd spent the first few minutes of our latest reunion poking and jabbing my biceps and chest with an extended forefinger, though with little force in fear of what she prodded might initiate a sudden 'deflation' of my newly resurgent muscles. The last six weeks of daily workouts—twice a day except on weekends—and drastic change in diet had produced surprising results, especially for one so long-in-the-tooth as yours truly. With that in mind, the overly snug, sleeveless black tee I'd chosen for this latest visit was certainly no accident. Apparently, a man's ego might diminish with the passing years but never completely evaporate. Caveman crude as it might sound, I had admittedly gotten quite the charge from Dee-dee's wide-eyed attention.

"Well, he did tend to ramble and rant off-camera, but as soon as the mic was put in place and the camera powered up, that was the gist. Any initial thoughts? Of course, we're still planning on recording your reactions before initial edits."

The studio apartment had filled up substantially since my last visit, various cardboard boxes and assorted filming and recording equipment of every size and shape. I'd arrived around nine AM, an hour earlier than scheduled, mostly due to waking up too early with a swarm of butterflies swatting my gut with enough mini-jabs and right and left hooks to prevent further snoozing. Thus I'd left the house much earlier than expected and had even stopped off for a six-pack of steaming java from Dee-dee's favorite brewer before arriving. Dixon, dour as usual, greeted me with a quick nod before diving back in with both hands on whatever complicated surgery he'd been performing on one of the standing cameras. Dee-dee, cute as a button in a light green tee, blue jeans and white sneakers, tar-black hair tied into a ponytail that hung freely between her shoulder blades, nearly joggled the coffee-pack from my hands with an exuberant hug and light kiss on the left cheek, her perfume happily overtaking the stout scent of breakfast blend. A half-hour of light chit-chat later—topics included the steamy-as-always Arkansas summer, a horrific pile-up on the nearby interstate the previous night, and the latest update on a possible completion date for the film—and curtains were pulled and lights dimmed for the latest screening.

"I'd say surprised, not only that you managed to dig up Maggie but that she ever had a crush on yours truly. Sweet gir—woman and very talented. I hope Don knew how lucky he was to have her on the team. As for Chad and Gregory, nothing either said comes as much of a surprise. Chad and I never clicked. Fine writer but he just didn't understand the concept of what we were going after. They both hated my either altering their lines or ignoring them altogether. I got it. Writers are supposed to write and actors act, but their vision of Claymore was that of a big-mouthed clown so full of hot air an F-16 jet wasn't even necessary for 'im to take flight. Basically, Will Stockdale in a flight suit. I maintained and still do that if we'd gone with that concept, the show wouldn't have lasted more than a handful of episodes. My version of the fictional sergeant struck a chord, as the ratings bore out."

"What chord specifically?" Dee-dee pried as, distractingly, Dixon cursed under his breath every few seconds while struggling with a handful of tangled wires.

"Patriotism, to a degree. Sure, my take on Claymore wasn't without campiness, but deep down I saw the dude as the type whose Fruit of the Looms featured the stars and stripes. You know, a man who hadn't just fought for his country as orders and paycheck dictated, but who bled the ink of the Constitution. He didn't get that scar tripping off a bar stool, but from an enemy's attempt to take away his, *our* freedoms. I think the audience sensed that he wasn't just flapping his gums, and actually came to appreciate his criticism of some of the anti-American themes, subtle or not, in the film being showcased."

"*Apocalypse Now* in particular, correct?"

"One example, yeah. *Platoon* got the most reactionary mail, as I recall. Hey, I personally served with many Vietnam vets, many of whom agreed that although Coppola and Stone got a lot right, they also severely crapped the bed on other issues."

Leaning back with a heavy sigh, Dee-dee's smile was a wide, toothy delight to behold, and though I had nary an inkling of its source, entirely contagious.

"What?" I asked with a goofy grin of my own.

"I was just thinking this exchange would be perfect for the film. Let's just hope it's this relaxed and engaging when we tape your portion for real."

Sipping from my own ice brew, I briefly broke eye contact with Dee-dee and glanced over at Dixon, who appeared to sporadically wince at a random remark before diving back into the camera's guts. Shrugging it off, I refocused on Dee's sparkling brown eyes—she seemed to hang on every word—and found myself easily lost within their magnetic gleam. The girl was a walking, talking fireplug, her energy and upbeat attitude wholly contagious.

"Have no fear. If anything, I've been pulling punches so far, candor-wise."

"Really? Wow, can hardly wait for the unedited Deron Barrow. Back to the interviews, please continue. I think we were up to the programs main director, Gregory Tate."

"Greg was a professional hired gun, nothing else. He didn't involve himself with politics. Just get the shi...um, stuff on film and pack it up for home. I heard him state on many occasions that he compared our program to a series of infomercials he'd cranked out at the same time. As far as Tate was concerned, we might as well have been selling cleaning products. He was invested as long as his paycheck cleared, no more."

"And Donald Oliva?"

My involuntary wince was just that. Perhaps the most painful outcome of the entire aftermath, at least as far as the old crew and relationships went. It was hard, nearly impossible, to hide the disappointment.

"Don, bless his heart, was *all* about the bottom line. M-o-n-e-y, baby. Loud, boisterous and about as sincere as a wall-plug. When the whole thing collapsed, I couldn't find the guy. Wouldn't take my calls and basically treated me like a leper. Sad really, since I'd considered him a father-figure of sorts that first season. I got it. Distancing himself from me was the best for business, his career and reputation, but it didn't make it any easier to accept. Awkward for my dad as well, as the two had been friends for decades.

"I don't make a habit of speaking ill of the dead, but Don turned out to be kind of a fraud."

"And finally, Senior Master Sergeant Conrad Boland?"

"A blustery hot-air balloon with an axe to grind, for sure. Probably lived a sour life and had the demeanor to match. I have no doubt mine was not the lone target of his disgruntlement through the decades. From what I've heard, he'd been through three marriages and to this day has grown children who pretend he doesn't exist. A real peach of a guy, as long as misery, negativity and defeat dominate the conversation. All that said, he called me out and was probably right to do so. It's taken me a lot of years to stop fighting and arguing myself into a corner and just admit it. A jackass like Conrad Boland would be far from my chosen accuser, but he did deserve the bust."

"Locked and loaded, D. Finally," Dixon announced, rising with a groan and standing with hands propped atop both knees as if he'd just scaled Mt. Everest.

"Great! We've got one more to show you, Deron," Dee-dee added, practically levitating off the couch and fast-stepping it down the hallway towards the john, no doubt persuaded by the half gallon of iced coffee she'd ingested since my arrival, "That is, as soon as I return from the little ladies' room."

Left alone with Dixon, an awkward silence prevailed. The perfect time, I deduced, to poke the silent bear.

"So what's your take so far, Ron?"

Having finally straightened to a standing position, his button-down dress shirt untucked at the back, I had the distinct feeling the young man's perpetual scowl wasn't merely sore muscle or stiff bones related.

"Come again?"

"Do we have a winner here or what?"

"No way to know at this stage, but if quality matters, it certainly has the prospects to make a ripple."

I couldn't refrain from a final jab as the faint sound of a flushing toilet echoed down the hall.

"Gut feeling. After all, not your first rodeo."

His expression, normally as bland and stoic as your basic Vulcan, lit up with an animation previously unrevealed but unfortunately, equally unreadable.

"I think it'll serve its purpose *very* effectively."

"Well, that's, um, good to hear, I…guess."

Dee-dee collapsed onto the couch beside me, soon to be joined on the other side by her clearly schizophrenic partner.

"We saved perhaps the best for last. That is, following all that one-sided narrative, here is one for the good guys," she beamed, gesturing with an enthusiastic nod to Dixon to punch play.

Once the mystery person's face filled the small screen, I couldn't help but smile, albeit a tad nervously.

~ * ~

Video Interview with Master Sergeant (retired) Lance Garrett

"Clark Air Base was, as it turned out, to be not only my last overseas tour, but next-to-last tour period. Turned in my badge, gun and non-commissioned status less than twenty-four months later at Eglin in Florida and almost immediately went into the private security sector. As for that initial face-to-face with Sergeant Ace Claymore, the base CO called me into his office on a characteristically humid November day to inform me I'd be in charge of babysittin' some jackass *act-tor* and his entourage for some live show that was part of their Pacific tour. Now, we're comin' off a five-day base exercise, meaning sixteen-to-eighteen-hour shifts wearin' full chem gear as a second skin with temps already high enough to fry bacon in our shorts as command played its latest round of war games. Once the white flag waved, all this boy wanted to do was crawl into a few dozen bottles of chilled brew while actively, though maybe not consciously, participatin' in a weekend's worth of debauchery. Instead, I'm assigned to playin' nursemaid to some spoiled thespian and his gang of paid butt-smoochers. To say the very least, I was not a happy camper. A decade and a half-plus of security trainin' of the highest caliber and this was my reward. *Sheesh.*

Upon their arrival, I met 'em on the flight-line with a hand-picked crew of SPs—all of which were as thrilled as I, as I recall their sour expressions and profanity-laced comments—and there I got my first look at Mister Make-Believe War Hero: a beefy-lookin', regulation buzz-cut wearin' dude decked out in a jean-jacket with the Kunsan Air Base 'Wolfpack' symbol sewn across the back, faded blue jeans and cowboy boots. He shook my hand firmly and thanked me and the boys for our service, and damned if appeared as if he wasn't just plying his chosen trade but actually *meant* the words that were comin' out his mouth, pronounced and very authentic southern drawl and all. Bein' an old southern boy myself, I felt an instant kinship with the big lug. It wasn't awe, as one might naturally assume, that googly-eyed star-struck garbage that blinded those beneath its spell. Hell, I didn't know the goofy bastard from Adam, nor the show from which he'd gained fame, but there was an instant connection; a substantial vibe that hinted strongly that we weren't makin' the glorified acquaintance of Ace Claymore, but a normal, everyday Joe named Deron Barrow, which is exactly how he introduced himself.

Now, those that knew me back in the day will attest to the fact that I wasn't exactly an easy guy to get to know. As assistant NCOIC, that's Non-Commissioned Officer in Charge of base security, I took no assignment lightly, much less one pinned on me by the head honcho of Clark Air Base, Philippines, Pacific Theater. Hard-assed and tight of jaw, I instructed my guys—mostly a collection of newly assigned A1Cs, that's Airman First Class, and Senior Airmen, of the temptation to let regulations slide for visiting dignitaries, and that anyone caught doing so would find my size eleven steel-toe inserted into their backsides via extreme force (*laughs*). Well, forty-eight hours later I was contemplating the same-said punishment be doled out to yours truly. Kickin' one's own ass is never an easy chore, but I kinda figured the massive hangover I'd sported for the better part of three days was punishment enough.

To backtrack a bit, the show had been on a Friday night at the base theater and damned if that place hadn't been packed to the rafters. Now this bein' despite two-hundred or so troops comin' off a week's worth of wargames, most of 'em surely itchin' to start their weekend by slammin' the downtown bars but deciding instead to take in a flick most 'em had probably seen at least a half-dozen times. Personally, I was never much of a TV or movie guy, so *Red Dawn* was new to me, as was the Ace Claymore show that I'd been told was some kinda cable sensation back in the States. Nearly two decades in the service and I'd never seen a group as fired-up as that one. I'm talkin' clappin', screamin' and yellin' to beat the band and it didn't have squat to do with the flick. Mister Barrow marched onto that stage and the small-town goober with the hillbilly grin was gone. Sergeant Ace Claymore had entered the building and taken full command, brother. Prancin' around in a fatigue-green tee, camo pants, spit-shined combats and wavin' a flag the size of a tractor-trailer around like a toothpick while beltin' out a speech that would've put Patton to shame. (*Laughs*) I felt sorry for the bar owners once that crowd was unleashed. It was like nothin' I'd ever experienced. The guy had somethin'...I hestitate to use the word *power* but it was like he'd cast a spell of, pardon the corniness, of well, newborn patriotism on the masses, who, after a week of playin' war, were likely damn fed up with the subject. Personally, I rarely felt a stronger jealousy for any and all civilians than right after a base exercise. Still, he riled 'em up like gangbusters. As many had told me who were familiar with the TV show, he was funny and profane in equal measure, havin' gauged their mood right from the get-go, and from there the crowd was putty in his hands.

Once the curtain fell and the yelpin' and cheerin' crowd dispersed, I thought of pawnin' off further chaperonin' duties to my second-in-command, then reconsidered in lieu of hangin' out with this walkin', talkin' phenomenon just to see what really made 'im tick. Well, two days of balls-to-the wall, hearty-partyin' later, I found myself passed out in not one but two separate downtown brothels, I still didn't have a blessed clue but I *did* know this: I'd just spent the better part of two days livin' on the very edge with the Pacific Theater's version of Elvis the Pelvis. More importantly, I'd found a lifelong friend, even if we'd never cross paths again for the rest of our days.

Ya see, sometime between twelve midnight and four AM on that second night of alcohol-drenched shenanigans, three of us found ourselves backed into a dark alley with a half-dozen switchblades openly displayed and pointed our way. Seems myself, a young troop and fellow Clark SP named Logan and Deron Joseph Barrow himself had accidentally wondered far off the beaten path from the downtown bars and into an area infamously known as *Blow Row*, an area where inebriated airmen were open season for both everyday muggers and local malcontents less-than-thrilled by the foreign presence. The reason such places were placed off-limits were well documented, but dumbasses such as yours truly and his party of idiots had stumbled drunkenly into the fray without a friggin' clue we'd done so until it was too late. There I was, a respected supervisor who'd written up countless GIs for the same offense I was now guilty of, several of which had lost stripes and many others done time in correctional custody, the Air Force version of the poky. Sheesh, talk about talkin' the talk but not walkin' the walk. I was sooooo busted.

Anyhow, there we stood—well, maybe leaned is more apt—three loaded goats about to get properly fleeced when a bona fide miracle occurred. I kid you not, this was as close to a supernatural occurrence as this man has ever experienced or hope to. Just ask Deron. He'll confirm. As for Logan, I haven't a clue of that boy's last name, if I ever knew it to begin with.

There were at least eight of 'em, maybe more (*laughs*), then again maybe less bein' that I was probably seein' double, and they were a mule's whisker away from ropin', robbin, and probably rapin' us and leavin' us naked and bleedin' in a Manila back alley when one of 'em practically took flight and provided us a human barrier. Bony little dude probably no older than eighteen or nineteen, screamin' and wavin' his stick-thin arms like he was helpin' land a jet.

Now, other than a select list of profanities, I wasn't exactly fluent in Tagalog, but the English he mixed in was easily comprehended. What I saw and heard, plain as day despite the blurriness of both eyes and ears, was 'Ace,' 'Sergeant Claymore,' and 'American bad-ass,' and though a few of our erstwhile muggers appeared oblivious to their pal's rant, two or three got it immediately and joined him while voluntarily pocketing the cutlery.

The miracle of which I spoke came next, with our fate still hangin' in the balance, as Deron did his best Jekyll/Hyde routine, transformin' into that fictional Air Force Sergeant in a blink, this despite bein' boiled like an owl from bar-hoppin'. Now, how these back-alley thugs from the area's lowest-rent district even knew of the show and/or character is beyond me, though Deron did speculate later that maybe they'd run across a bootleg tape at one of the countless video rental stores in the city.

However they knew, Ace Claymore sauntered up and began to speak in that well-deep baritone, shakin' hands and slappin' backs like he was gonna make a run for Marcos' seat until a few of 'em actually had 'im signin' the backs of their shirts with a magic-marker. I shit you not, we went from potential shish kabob to celebrity status in the time he takes to rattle the air with a Red Horse belch, um, Red Horse bein' a popular local brew. Hell, they even had me and Logan chicken-scratchin' our John Hancocks, figurin' since we were hangin' with the King, we must've been somebody important (*laughs*). Once they startin' speakin' mostly English, we were bein' offered all kinds of amenities to hang with 'em for a bit. One of 'em (*laughs*) even offered up his own sister as some kinda kinky sacrifice to Deron, who politely declined, though not without brief consideration. He might deny that part, but (*laughs*) I saw a slight hesitation. Instead, we shared a brew and some grilled pork at a local stand before sayin' our goodbyes to the damndest fan club imaginable.

So, as it was, though we had escaped an almost certain death solely on the well-worn sleeve of Ace Claymore, there still lay a challenge ahead that, in many ways, was just as treacherous for yours truly. Ya see, we'd been spotted down at The Row by the roving security patrol, headed by a Tech Sergeant named Will Quiggly, a sniveling weasel in sheep's clothing who I'd been butting heads with ever since his arrival on station a few months before. Born narc that he was, the jackass wasted little time in turning me into the squadron commander, a Bible-thumping do-gooder named Watson, a captain of the strictly-by-the-book mode. Well, I figured my goose was cooked, bein' as Wilson detested the whole bar scene as one big well-spring of sin, though in my past dealings with the man he'd been nothin' but fair. Being named Barrow's official chaperone from minute one of his arrival on station, I'd been tasked with daily reports to command anyhow, and since I'd already gotten wind of Quiggly's report, I had little hope to be departin' the captain's office with a full set of butt-cheeks, as the man was said to have one helluva temper when it came to those foolish enough to wonder off-limits.

I remember walkin' into the CO's office the not-so-proud

possessor of quite possibly the worst hangover I'd ever owned and, take my word for it when I say that is no small feat, and almost gaspin' aloud at the sight.

It seems Deron had somehow anticipated that I might be in for trouble and had beaten me to Wilson's office to offer a report of his own. This mostly fictional account included how myself and Airman Logan had saved his carcass by trackin' 'im to The Row, even going as far as describin' how we'd managed to shoo away a gatherin' of possibly nefarious locals lookin' to score some easy American greenbacks via force. This, of course, completely flipped Quiggly's damning narrative and, (*laughs*) if you can believe it, Logan and yours truly even received commendations at the next commander's call. If I hadn't mentioned it before now, Deron Joseph Barrow was, *is*, one heckuva underrated actor. Saved this man's bacon and possibly a stripe or two in the process, all the while sportin' a potentially fatal hangover. It was, as we jawed over some ultra-stout java just hours before he and his crew were scheduled to fly to Guam, that I swore that I'd pay him back for savin' my hide, twice mind you, if it took me a lifetime. We shook hands and promised to stay in touch, not figurin' to ever really do so, though by chance we'd been raised only a few hundred miles apart so the odds of a future reunion weren't as improbable as most. But then, you know how it is. In the service, people fly in and out of your life like a conveyor spinnin' at warp speed. Most you know you'll never lay eyes on again but the promise is made nonetheless.

It was nearly a year and a half later, a few months after Deron's trouble and the show's axin', that I took it upon myself to look 'im up, figurin' he just might need to lay eyes on a friendly face, even if it was as butt-ugly as my own.

A few months earlier I'd hung up my service badge permanently and was in the beginnin' stages of settin' up a private firm, its headquarters based, coincidentally, very near Mister Barrow's stompin' grounds.

Once the news come down, I hit up a few sources to just where he might be hidin' out and wasn't at all surprised that he'd left Little

Rock behind for the rural Mississippi countryside. Took a bit of doin', I ain't gonna lie, but I convinced 'im to head on back to the hometown and work for me at the firm. By that time, he'd remarried and was scufflin' a bit on what exactly he wanted to do with his life, not surprisin' considerin' the previous circumstances, and he struggled mightily before cavin' in and joinin' the firm. He'd also been cultivatin' a beard and bushy mop of hair as if recently placed in witness protection, which I'm sure he kinda felt he had at the time. From very humble beginnings, Deron helped me build the business into the success it would become. We worked together for almost a dozen years, all told, before he packed it in for more peaceful climes. Durin' that time, he'd divorced for the second time and it had obviously taken a heavy toll. He said he needed time to regroup, but I think we both knew he was packin' it in for good. I hated losin' 'im, not only as a friend but as a one hell of a reliable right hand. We'd seen each other through some bad times in those years, as all true friends do. Through the years I've tried numerous times to coerce 'im back to the business, but once he settled into the country life, it wasn't gonna happen. Can't blame 'im, and I thought of doin' the same many a time myself before my present situation kinda, well, forced the issue. We both make an effort to break bread and sip a few cold ones a few times a year, relivin' the past as old-timers are apt to do.

Earlier you folks asked me if the reveal of his military record all those years back changed my opinion of the man. The honest answer is no, which might come as a surprise to some but ponder this: why would he make the supreme effort of flyin' halfway across the world to entertain troops as his alter-ego when he confessed to me many times that he funded the trips himself on his own dime? The answer is simple and damn logical if ya dwell on it. Deron saw the opportunity to make amends, to both himself and his country, both of which he knew he'd shortchanged as a young airman, by utilizin' the shot of fame Claymore afforded 'im.

I respected 'im a heck of a lot more for spendin' untold thousands of dollars to entertain our men and women of uniform while also standin' up for what they stand for by openly criticizing Hollywood's sometimes warped take on exactly what that *is*. Might sound strange, but Deron and myself never even openly discussed the subject of his forced discharge or what it stemmed from. Hell, it wasn't until the news media jumped on 'im like starvin' piranha that I found out. Couldn't care less then and care even less now. The man doesn't owe me a thing, nor anyone else as far as that goes, but apparently, he owed himself and went to great lengths to make amends.

As far as that other thing, I cannot express my level of... (*pauses; sighs deeply, clenched fists visibly shaking*) ...disgust on how the same media slime that helped shred the man's actin' career seemed to overtly revel in makin' him the villain in that tragedy, as if he were actually at fault, or could possibly be at fault in any way. Absolute scum of the earth. Dirt-bags and lowlifes, the whole rotten lot of 'em. Anything to sell papers or, I guess these days, corral readers. Personally, I trust media types about as far as I can heave 'em, present company excluded...I *hope*. Truly (*leans in, smiles, crossing fingers on both hands*), I hope and pray you guys are givin' Deron's story a fair shake. The man was far from perfect, but who among the human race is, right?

~ * ~

"So, first impressions?" Dee-dee inquired a split-second after the picture faded to black.

Luckily, the relative darkness of the room's interior effectively hid the building wetness at the corners of my eyes. Tank's blunt honesty and strong outburst of emotion hadn't as much surprised as touched me, as openly sissy as that may sound. As he'd said, we'd never broached the subject of my discharge and until hearing him speak on camera in front of total strangers, not usually considered the ideal situation for spilling one's guts, I'd never before known his true feelings.

"Hey, he's my friend and as a friend, he's naturally gonna have my back. I, well, it was kind of strange watching him put into words things we never personally spoke about in over twenty-five years."

"It's hard to catch there, the edit is clean and without a noticeable break, but had to cut it short once he went into his...that media rant. He stepped out onto the balcony for a smoke," Dixon said blandly before standing and walking stiffly to eventually disappear down the darkened hall.

"Ron's right, he was shaking and his voice trembled with obvious anger," Dee-dee added, hopping up and strolling over to reopen the curtains. I'd strategically used these few seconds to wipe each eye with the back of a hand.

"Tell me, do you agree with Lance's assessment of the media's treatment of you following the incident?"

In truth, I'd only heard what I'd been told by others, the majority of which matched Tank's appraisal almost verbatim. Probably not the answer Dee-dee wanted to hear, but I'd sworn eons ago against embellishing anything concerning my past.

"I did my best to ignore any and *all* news for what must've been several months. Just wasn't in the mood, if you can dig it."

"I can only imagine," she replied, retaking her seat and digging into a nearby briefcase for a large yellow notepad, to which she perused with great intensity.

"From the microfiche clips we dug up from local libraries around Pine Bluff and Little Rock, the local papers played fair for the most part, not dwelling so much on the lurid or wild speculation but sticking to the facts as they knew them. It was mostly some of the northern periodicals, *New York Post, Cleveland Plan-Dealer* and *USA Today* who leaned hard towards sensationalism."

"Guess I lucked out that the Puffington Host hadn't yet seen the light of day, yeah?" I injected, unable to wipe the grin from my face in the afterglow of Tank's interview.

"Huffington Post," she corrected with a girlish giggle, reaching over to land a light tap to my right shoulder, "And no truer words have ever been spoken. By the way, to switch gears before it slips my frazzled mind, what's the story on this other ex-wife he mentioned?"

Damn the girl's powers of observation. I was really hoping that the subject of Missy could be one sidenote worth skipping, a real minor nugget as far as chapters go but still a painful one, kind of like recalling the passing of a particularly painful kidney stone. Still, I understood Dee-dee's curiosity, and did my best to bud-nip it once the expected game of twenty questions began.

"Oh, her."

"That bad, huh?"

"That fleeting."

"How fleeting?"

"Eight months, six days, and we spent roughly half that time separated."

"Found out you weren't really compatible?"

"Found out we couldn't stand the sight of one another."

"Oh, well then, I take it there's no reason to seek out Miss..."

"Missy, full name Melissa Jelks, at least once she took her name back, and no, I'd say that's a fair statement. I kind of doubt she'd ever admit to knowing me, much less that ill-fated hitching."

"Fair enough. Subject dropped, locked away and key subsequently tossed away."

"Appreciate it. In a nutshell, Missy and I met in a metal bar and ended up in the sack the very same night. She later admitted to recognizing me from television. We only had a few things in common and nothing you could ever hope to base a long-term relationship on. I was...obviously a disappointment to her, financially. Ended up as we started. Complete strangers. End of story."

With that, Dee-dee merely nodded and mercifully, we moved on. A full minute or two of silence later, I decided to scratch an itch that had spread like a full-body skin rash since hearing Tank's interview.

"So, what's your take, Dee?"

The words had escaped on autopilot with no hope of retrieval, though there had been, since the beginning of the project, a nagging curiosity of what my young biographers' opinions were on the story they'd committed to tell. Dixon's take, be it positive or negative, was of less importance than Dee's, and not solely due to how fond I'd grown of her, but because I simply cared more about what she thought of me and the experiences and events that had brought us together.

Strange as it sounded, I felt a weird obligation to her as the person liable to take the brunt of criticism for not only telling my story, but my side. What I'd initially, and fortunately misconstrued as a physical attraction to a much younger woman, was now clearly defined as more of a fatherly instinct to shield and protect. I didn't want her life or career stained in any way merely via association with yours truly and his questionable life choices and accompanying brushes with trauma.

"What's that?" she's mumbled in reply, obviously distracted by the notepad's shabbily scribbled contents. Smart, witty and attractive as she was, Dee-dee's handwriting appeared to have been accomplished with her feet.

"If the camera was turned your way and the questions concerned the subject of your latest film project, what would be your honest feelings?"

She seemed to, ever-so-briefly, tense as from a sudden shock, her hands curling into her lap as the pad was gently laid onto the couch. About the time I regretted broaching the subject, she sighed deeply and stared straight ahead without speaking for several moments. Reply impending, I felt the infestation of butterflies that had departed my midsection at the conclusion of Tank's interview return to full-blown swarm status.

"Wow. This is unexpected. I mean, I kind of knew you might query at some point, but I just figured it would be once filming was complete."

Having never raised children, I could only imagine the question being akin to a middle-aged father asking his grown children for their opinions of the 'old man'.

"Honesty, Dee. You owe me *that* much," I said, plunging in head-first despite a deep-seeded fear of the forthcoming response, "That is, I respect your opinion and it's, well, kinda been prying at my mind."

"I'm honored it means that much to you. I take it Ron's next in line?"

"Not necessarily."

I was hoping my expressions—squinting eyes, cocked brow—defined my answer. Once she didn't pursue further, I deduced it had done just that.

"I think...you're like the majority of the human race in that you made mistakes, only from those mistakes was sewn a lengthy thread of tragedy. I think...a good man eventually grew from a reckless boy, but unlike the majority whose similarly bad decisions lead to nothing more than innocent life-lessons, fate decided to make an example of Deron Joseph Barrow."

She turned towards me and, as our eyes locked, the aforementioned swarm departed as if magically teleported from my gut. Regrettably, I had no chance to verbally reply as Dixon picked that very moment to rejoin us, sauntering into the room with all the verve of a sloth on downers. If given the opportunity, I would most likely have asked, nay, *begged*, Dee-dee to insert her dialogue, word for word if possible, into the film.

"You tell him?" Dixon asked flatly, essentially shattering the moment while kneeling in front of the same camera equipment he'd been tinkering with on-and-off since my arrival.

"I was getting to it," she responded with a huff, and just like that, Dee-dee had once again buried her head into the yellow pad reset atop her knees.

"Tell me what?"

"We've scheduled your interview for two weeks from today. Twenty August at, say, eleven AM okay?" she asked without looking up, a yellow sharpie balanced between the fore and middle fingers of her right hand.

"Um, yeah, I guess. I mean, I'll have to check my calendar."

Neither responded other than Dixon's mild grunt, my lame attempt at humor obviously sailing airborne to parts unknown.

"Sure, sounds good."

Just like that, I was all but dismissed. What a vicious comedown from just moments before, when Dee-dee and I had shared, at least from my perspective, such a real, raw, human moment.

"Super. Oh, and don't forget, you'll need the full Ace Claymore threads and regalia. They did still fit, yes?"

"Oh yeah, sure. The suit was a little snug in the back at first. Guess I added a little more bulk than I'd planned," I grinned, executing a semi-hulk 'flex' to no apparent affect as she never even bothered to look up. "By the way, where in the world did ya'll dig up those retro combat boots? Somebody did some serious 'Fossils 'R Us' research to find those bad b..."

"Okay then, Deron, it's a date," she interrupted sharply, as if I'd never spoken. "We'll meet up here and drive over to the set."

I stood, both knees popping like small-arms fire and backed towards the door.

"Yeah, see ya then," I practically mumbled, tossing up a hand palms-out in what was an empty gesture in the face of completely apathy. As the door shut behind me with a low click, I felt, quite inexplicably, as if I'd been gut-punched. Maybe it was nothing but a case of hyper-sensitivity on my part, but I had this gnawing sense that, for the first time since that opening offer, I was slowly being relegated to commodity status. I was merchandise, plain and simple, and Diandra and Dixon were the sales force.

In no real hurry to return to an empty house, I stopped off at a local Cracker Barrel for a heaping serving of black coffee, country-fried steak and mashed potatoes—my first such food reward to myself since training had commenced—and couldn't quite shake the vibe that something had gone slightly tilt back at the studio apartment, though there was no pinning it down. It was almost as if Dee-dee had somehow regretting sharing her personal opinion, like she'd broken some type of secret, unspoken taboo of the filmmaker's credo. The awkward parting bugged me to the point of almost calling her up upon arriving home. In the end, I let it slide, chalking up her sudden, inexplicable coolness to overwork. Two weeks: fourteen short days and counting until it was my turn to stare into the camera eye with a hot mic attached to my collar. The physical prep would continue unabated—ego dictated I *would* look my very best—just as easily the most difficult test lay ahead, that being to successfully channel a character I once swore I would never again conjure.

Eight

The Re-Channeling
(From the private journal of Deron Joseph Barrow)

19 Aug 2019

Little Rock, Arkansas

I'd felt like a damn fool, at least until Tank and the rest of the Garrett clan broke out in a hooting, clapping, foot-stomping, full-blown standing ovation. Tank's text invitation, received exactly a week following my last meeting at the studio apartment, couldn't have come at a better time. Nearly two weeks of constant working out and rehearsing had me ready to climb the walls, or in my case, the nearest tree, as I'd recently added a midnight stroll—fueled by chronic insomnia—into the dense woods behind the house to my daily workout regimen. The text had simply read:

hey partner, pack an overnight bag and swing by the house the day before your interview. Moron support is, as you know, my specialty. Wendy is planning a real feast in your honor, pal. Showing up is not an option. Tank

Shenanigans of the highest order, and, if I'd been thinking clearer and not suffering the effects of severe sleep deprivation, perhaps a slight suspicion could've acquired a handhold. As it was, I was effectively blindsided by the entire setup, and most notably the cast involved. I'd arrived at just before sunset, which means approximately nineteen-thirty hours or thereabouts when speaking of late summer in Arkansas.

Tank and Wendy's split-level, brick Victorian—purchased at the beginning of their marriage for what was now a tenth of its current worth—sat at the backend of a cul-de-sac of similarly styled homes for the upper-middle class and was shaded on all sides by an eccentric mix of Carolina Basswood and Black Gum. Once greeted at the door by the aforementioned ovation—if flesh-temp was any indication, my face must've glowed red—I was instantly blindfolded by Tank's son Eric and led through, I assumed, the sunken living room and to an add-on bonus space still in pre-production at my last visit, which I was ashamed to admit had been over a year. Blindfold lifted, I was treated to what, at first impression in the strategically dimmed lighting, resembled nothing less than a mini-cinema, to include old-school theater seating, wall-sized screen and a half-dozen ceiling speakers. Coolest of all I think were the four walls themselves, cloaked in red drapes from ceiling to thickly carpeted floor.

"Partner, this is as boss as boss gets," I exclaimed as the crowd gathered around, the lights growing gradually brighter and allowing that initial rollcall of attendees.

"Two years and at least that many paychecks' worth," Tank replied with a light jab to my right shoulder, practically beaming with pride and looking as spry and healthy as I'd seen him in many a moon. Did my heart good to know that all the praying—not to mention getting reacquainted with the big man upstairs himself solely for that purpose—wasn't for naught.

"Looks like all that's lacking is the industrial popcorn machine," I countered as Wendy snaked past her lesser half to give me a hug and peck on the cheek. Apparently still drinking from that mythological fountain of youth, she was somehow as striking a figure in her late forties as the drop-dead gorgeous twenty-something I'd first met, her flowing red mane and hourglass figure still miraculously intact.

"About time you paid us a visit, buddy-boy," she said, displaying that flawless, dimpled smile that I'm certain helped ensnare my old buddy all those seasons past and lock his heart into a blissful state of solitary confinement.

"Well, I'm kinda like a windblown virus, Wen. I'll pass for a while but there's no known cure."

"Hey, I know Tank's already asked, but I feel the need to reiterate our offer to stay overnight. We have a perfectly good guestroom with your name on it."

"Don't think I don't appreciate the kind offer, but the producers already pre-paid for the hotel and, well, to be honest I'm gonna need my early morning space to property prep for tomorrow's gauntlet."

"Understood," she replied warmly, though I doubt she truly comprehended. The truth was the last thing I needed were witnesses to my own potential nervous breakdown.

Eric, now taller than his old man by several inches and wearing a similar outer shell of taunt muscle, leaned in to slap palms, a ritualistic gesture we'd shared since he'd just gotten out of diapers. It was good to see him back with the folks and, hopefully, starting to do more than just tolerate his dad's plight but provide support for the even tougher times surely to come.

With the more familiar faces fading into the background, a trio of not-so-recognizable types stepped forward, all but one seemingly hesitant to do so without first shedding a thick layer of shyness or, god forbid, fear.

"Well holy crap on a soggy saltine, D.J., you outta rent yourself out as a human recruiting poster! What you answering to these days, Captain Tricep?"

I hadn't laid eyes on Ronnie Jelks in at least a dozen years, not since we'd pulled security gigs together for Lance back in the early two-thousands. Other than adding an extra chin and a layer or three of additional padding around his midsection, he hadn't changed an iota: loud, gregarious and completely without a verbal filter.

"Ron! How you doing, partner?" I countered, blocking a playful jab aimed at my midsection.

"SSDD, bud. Added a grandchild or two since we last jawed but otherwise happily retired with the expanding gut and sagging testicles to prove it!"

As my co-worker continued to blare on unabated—nope, hadn't changed a bit—my gaze drifted over his left shoulder as the final puzzle piece of mystery guests emerged from the shadows and directly into the spotlight.

No doubt noticing the sudden glazing-over of my eyes, Ronnie sidestepped over like a seasoned bullfighter to allow us a clear path of re-introduction.

It had been nearly thirteen years since we'd last shared the same space, that being a cramped interview room at the Pine Bluff Police Department HQ on a frigid February night as the building in which we were being held was slowly being cocooned in a frozen shell of mixed sleet and snow. Despite the many years and the dramatic changes in looks—hers especially, but then growing into adolescence and then adulthood has a tendency to do that—I knew her instantly from those sparkling brown eyes. The straight, tar-black mane of the child had been replaced by that of a shoulder-length, slightly curled strawberry blonde coif.

"Mister Barrow," she practically whispered, offering a shy smile and slim hand palm-down.

"Miss Winslow. I, wow. I can't...this really...I mean, I never expected to..." I babbled, gently taking her hand and shaking it just as mildly. The rail-thin child had grown into an equally slim young woman. Dressed in a flowery yellow summer dress and sandals, the lone representative as far as baubles went a floss-thin gold necklace, she appeared as I often imagined she would: a natural beauty of the 'girl next door' quality.

"You look, well, great," she mercifully interrupted, placing her other hand atop my own.

"You've aged pretty well yourself, young lady," I countered, my grin widening until I thought the skin of each reddened cheek might tear asunder.

"How's the knee?" she pointed to the bionic cap solely with her eyes.

"Rusting away at the same speed as the rest of me, I'd say. All the weight-training of late has added a little volume to its squeak, but a little forty-weight always does the trick."

It was surreal, like striking up a conversation with a fictional character come to life.

"I was afraid you wouldn't recognize me, I mean, after all this time and of course I was just a kid."

"The eyes never lie, Misty, and yours are real beauties, like rough-cut diamonds carved to perfection."

She blushed, the ensuing giggle reflecting the little girl of all those years past, briefly looking away to regroup.

"Mother says hello," she said, patting the top of my hand a final time before our mutual grip loosened and fell away.

"Hello back. And your father?"

"Dad passed a few years ago."

I instantly wished for the power to rewind and thus retract the question.

"Oh, sorry."

"You couldn't have known."

"Was he...had he been ill?"

"Auto crash. Mother had always said he was a bit of a lead-foot behind the wheel. Wisconsin highways in late December can be treacherous."

"Much like Arkansas in February," I nodded and we shared a perfectly synchronized shrug.

"Precisely."

"You still homesteading in Madison?"

"Lincoln, Nebraska actually. Attending NU on scholarship. Hoping to graduate next May."

"A real live Cornhusker? Cool. And your mom?"

"One of Madison's proudest permanent residents. We actually held a vigil at Tammy's gravesite back in March, a slightly delayed fifteenth anniversary thing. We thought of inviting you but didn't, well, know if you'd appreciate the remainder."

To this, I reached over and gripped each of her narrow shoulders and applied a gentle squeeze.

"I wish you had. I'd have been honored."

"As I'm sure she would've been. No telling how many times she's thanked you from heaven for saving her little sister."

She swallowed hard, those gorgeous peepers gleaming with fresh moisture.

"My pleasure, Misty, and I'd wager big sis is beaming with pride at the fine young woman her younger sibling has become. I'm thinking the other angels need earplugs just to muffle her continuous bragging."

A mixed giggle/sob escaped her and we embraced a second time, the spell broken by the hushed whispers at our back, where the others had huddled together as if to fight off a sudden chill with a group hug. We each took a step back and shared a final, knowing nod, Misty using a bare forearm to wipe away the buildup of potential leakage from each eye.

"And hey, thank *you* for coming to, well, whatever this is," I concluded, motioning towards the home theater setup. "That's a heck of a commute from Husker-U."

"Well, I've been staying with Mom during summer break and when Mister Garrett called with the invite, I just couldn't resist."

"I'm glad. Unfortunately, knowing Tank as I do, it's some half-assed *This is Your Life* sideshow."

"If so, I'd be proud to participate," she grinned broadly and for that instant I recognized the frightened young girl from that horrible night in Pine Bluff and the instant she'd realized the terror had passed.

Leaning in, I whispered close to her left ear as voices prattled away at my back.

"I know we're obligated for a little while to other things, but I do need to talk to you about your mom."

Upon moving back to an arm's length and locking eyes one final time before the night's festivities began, the young girl had been replaced by an overly-mature-for-her-age, deadly-serious woman armed with a steely resolve and matching glare: no doubt a family trait.

"The payments *won't* cease, Deron. Grace Winslow labels you her white knight, now and forever. For me to say I disagree would be a blatant lie, and that's not how I was raised."

"Maybe if you let her know I've been donating the bulk to the Wounded Warrior Program for many a year, she might decide to go ahead and choose her own worthy charity."

She shook her head and shrugged at the mere suggestion, as if attempting to convince a small child that their argument, however logical in their mind, just wasn't plausible.

"She doesn't care what you do with the money. I know you consider the amount extravagant, but the...my family is quite well-off. Dad invested like a champ back in the day, not to mention the quite healthy life insurance payoff when he passed. Regardless, I'm convinced if mother was being forced to take a suite at the nearest poorhouse, she'd earmark her last penny to the man who saved her little girl."

I sighed, resigned to a reluctant defeat that in truth I had had little hopes of derailing.

"Well, just make sure to tell her it's going to the most noble of causes."

"Sir, yes sir, sergeant," she replied with a wink, landing a light jab to my left bicep.

"I hear that in addition to the documentary, you have a potential best-seller in the works."

"Oh, *that*. Well, we'll see how the movie is received, I guess. The producer/director team is actually using the manuscript for a...sort of reference for now. It's in dire need of a professional edit, but at least it's past the rough first-draft stage. Many years and countless reams of paper later, I was relieved enough just to finish it. Can't say I'm in any hurry to revisit those pages."

The smile we shared effectively melted away whatever awkwardness remained.

"Well, I for one would love to peruse the finished product."

"Tell you what, upon publication I'll happily sign a copy for both you and your mom."

As if cued by some unseen director's gesture, my old friend stepped up to take center-stage, waving his cane airborne and bellowing like a carnival barker of old, this after whispering in his son's ear and pointing towards a nearby hall that, if memory served, led to the kitchen.

"Ladies and gentlemen, welcome to Garrett Cinemas LLC, for a one-night showin' of an oldie but goodie from the golden age of syndicated television!"

"Oh lord, don't tell me," I moaned, applying a light face-palm as the wide screen lit up and the lights dimmed yet again.

"Now if you'll all take the seat of your choice, the fruit of my loins will soon be offerin' assorted snacks for the choosin'!"

"Fruit of your loins? *Really*? Wendy, I can't imagine you gave your approval to such an inane monologue."

"I wasn't allowed the opportunity to proofread, sad to say," she replied with a Cheshire cat grin, Eric pushing by her with a layered rolling cart full of goodies. As he sailed by, I caught a glimpse (and heavenly scent) of the top bin's contents, which included freshly popped popcorn tucked into individual bags, as well as such old movie-time standbys as Milk Duds, Juicy Fruits and Whoppers Malted Milk Balls. The lower bin held frosty glass bottles of A&W root beer and R/C Cola.

"Good grief, Tank, what drive-in time machine you raid for those munchies?"

"Hey, you know as well as I do that those expiration dates don't mean squat!" he countered with a sneer before turning to Ron Jelks and flashing an enthusiastic thumbs-up. "Ronald, my good man, do you currently cradle that ancient, priceless relic for which I searched so long and hard, sparin' no expense and ignorin' the potential danger to life and limb?"

"Indeed, Lance. Showtime?"

"Affirmative. Please present said fossil, newly added muscles of stone aside, to our guest for his perusal."

Ronnie strode over with a grace and agility that belied his considerable bulk and parked the DVD case mere inches from my probing eyes.

"Ah hell, I *knew* it," I groaned, though unable to halt the involuntary smile creasing the whole of my face, which I could feel transforming to a light shade of crimson. "Sparing no expense, you say? I say you most likely dug up this specific collectable in some cost-cutter bargain bin for the hefty price of at least a single, crinkled George Washington. Probably got some change back to boot."

Featuring my grinning, leering mug with a flowing Stars and Bars as a backdrop, the DVD's title, *The Very Best of Ace, Vol I* printed in bold red, white and blue, I recognized it as one of a four-part series released in the wake of the events of fifteen years ago.

"Oh boy, now that's classy, and not the least bit cheesy. Check out those pearly whites, man. Damn things are the size of railroad ties. Nothing creepy there, no sir."

"Aw, enough with the harsh self-criticism, Sergeant Claymore," Ronnie exclaimed, backing away with DVD tucked protectively to his doughy chest. "No amount of self-deprecation is gonna derail this train. On with the show!"

In truth, I was still receiving a small residual for those videos, being that at the time of their pre-production I'd retained a local Little Rock barrister of reputation, who'd secured me a ten percent across-the-board deal with the company responsible for their release. How strange and downright ironic to once again see a financial gain from playing a role that had been so ceremoniously blackballed just a decade before. Who was I to fight it? At the time, I'd needed the money and found it surprisingly easy to shrug off a mild case of embarrassment in order to properly endorse those checks.

"Yeah, yeah, blah blah blah," I countered with as much faux sarcasm as I could muster despite the warm feeling of pride heating my inner being like a glowing pot-bellied stove. "As I recall, those video treasures contained two shows per disc, and the powers-that-be sure as hell didn't ask yours truly advice on which episode constituted a 'best of.' In other words, don't blame me if the presentation doesn't live up to expectations."

Obviously ignoring my bogus rant, Tank resumed the role of

ringmaster with a slight bow and tilt of the head in my direction.

"As for the guest of honor, we ask that he take the center seat of row one."

Eyeing said row—the theater seating setup included four rows of three seats apiece, spaced perhaps a foot apart—I shrugged and held my ground, arms crossed in mock defiance.

"Jeez Louise, do I have a choice?"

"That'd be a no, Flyboy. If...you...*please.* The blood's runnin' to my noggin' like Niagra-freakin'-Falls."

Moments later, with everyone properly seated and snacks of choice in place—the black-leather padded seats also came with extra-large cup holders and 'goodie' baskets—the screen flashed to life just as the room faded, fittingly, to black.

~ * ~

(*Fade in. Sergeant Ace Claymore, decked out in full combat gear (WWII era), face fully camo-painted and a rifle of undetermined model and caliber gripped in both hands, stomach crawls beneath a two-feet-high barbed-wire barricade*)

Ace (*labored huffs and pants intermediate between spoken words*): "Well, good freakin' evenin' and afternoon, good citizens of the U.S of A! Ace Claymore here, wormin' and squirmin' my way gradually but with purpose towards a Nazi stronghold that the good guys desperately need to take out A S A and P. I gotta tell ya, I never considered myself any kind of natural-born killer while baggin' groceries back home at the Piggly Wiggly, but those bloodthirsty swastika-wearin' krauts sure as hell make the art of execution more fun than it ever had the right to be!

(*Claymore emerges from beneath the barbed wire to sprint full-bore towards a rock wall, the tip of which appears jagged from recent explosive damage. Pinning his back to its slick surface, he shoulders the rifle and yanks a grenade from his utility belt before taking a quick peek over the jagged edge. Descending gradually to one knee, he starts into the camera and sneers*):

Ace *(Pulling a badly bent cigarette from a field-jacket pocket and, after striking a match on the side of his left combat boot, lights it and takes a deep inhale before exhaling gradually from each nostril):* "Yeah, buddy, got the sleep-walkin' bastards right where I want 'em. Cocky and dumb as rocks, the majority of their kind, thinkin' the Allies fear 'em far too much to slink this far into what they deem their turf. (*Laughs*) Ya see, that's the problem with the krauts and that midget lunatic dictator pullin' their collective strings. All that 'superior race' BS comes with a checklist of personality ticks, one of 'em bein' flat-out complacency.

"Before I come off soundin' like some full-of-himself one-man Army type, it ain't only grunts like me takin' advantage. I hear there's this group of hand-picked GIs leavin' a trail of dead goose-steppers piled up in and around South France. Rumor control is that their CO, a hard-nosed but fair Lieutenant Colonel by the name of Frederick was tasked with teamin' a ragtag group of American born-and-bred convicts and malcontents with some top-notch Canuck soldiers led by a Major Crown, the major similarly by-the-book but fair-minded. Despite an admittedly rough breakin' in period, it's turned out to be a dream team of sorts.

"Tell ya what, while I gather my second wind, you good folks so bravely holdin' the fort back home take a gander at what makes their teaming so damned special. The year is nineteen forty-three and the troops in question answer to the name *The Devil's Brigade*."

(The *United Artists* logo appears; opening credits roll)

(At the 28:05 mark—a commercial break, followed by a fade-in as Claymore is shown standing in what appears to be a stone bunker amid a trio of downed bodies dressed in German uniforms, their uniforms torn and bloodied but their faces turned from the camera. Claymore grips a handgun in one hand and a serrated blade in the other, the latter smeared in dark crimson, which drips freely from its pointed tip. His own uniform shirt is ripped on the left side of his abdomen, also drenched in red, the right sleeve torn completely away past the elbow. Claymore is whispering into a radio mic connected to a Torn Fu G

transmitter/receiver unit as the faint echo of distant explosions and gunfire team to drown out his dialogue. Tossing the mic aside, he turns to the camera wearing a pained grimace)

"It sure as hell wasn't easy, but this particular bunker and the adjoining valley beyond is now officially claimed for the good guys. Got a patrol headed this way from just over the next hill who'd been hunkerin' down in a hollowed-out church. Seems they'd been pinned down by krauts like these (*steps over and plants a solid kick to the ribcage of the nearest cadaver*) for the past three days. Glad I could be of assistance in freein' those boys up. Lost a comrade or three along the way, but such are the wages of war. Suit-and-tie-wearin' politicians can jaw and blow smoke up their collective asses all day and night but it's the soldier who ends up solvin' the world's conflicts for the most part, either in open combat or more...shall we say, *secretive* operations. Bein' as I've seen active duty on both fronts, I know of what I speak.

(*Bends down to scoop up an overturned wooden chair and takes a seat with a resounding grunt while propping blood-spattered boots onto the upper back of still another fresh corpse.*)

"The Führer would've been proud of these here goose-steppers, yes sir. Gave the ol' sarge one helluva scrap before headin' off to meet their maker, that more than likely a horn-headed hothead totin' a pitchfork, 'cause much like the brigade you've been watchin', the Devil plays a supportin' role in all things Nazi. Speakin' of those boys and seein' as I've got the situation in hand here, let's get back to the south of France and see if they can stop actin' like a buncha hard-headed whiners and start workin' as a team. Hey, I understand the hesitance of our boys to take aid from a foreigner, even if it is an ally on paper, but if I can learn to fight alongside the French and even the blessed Russians, surely they can suck it up and give those well-meanin' Canucks a break.

"When next we speak, I hope to be bunkin' in more friendly climes and maybe even enjoyin' a short sabbatical from all the head-crackin' with a smoke and a shot of somethin' a little stronger than fire-brewed java. For now, back to *The Devil's Brigade*.

(*At the 73:39 mark, a commercial break, followed by a fade-in as*

Claymore is shown laying on a cot inside an otherwise empty tent with unoccupied cots on either side. Face cleaned of camouflage and dressed in a sleeveless, dark-green muscle tee, camo uniform pants and highly-polished combat boots, he grips a bottle of Vat 69-brand whiskey in his right hand as a cigarette smolders between the fore and middle fingers of his left. A tiny transistor radio sits atop his nearby duffel, Vera Lynn's 'The White Cliffs of Dover' clearly heard between random bursts of static)

"Takin' five, people, and though the original plan was just to sack out for a few hours, this fine bottle of libations was offered up as a personal thanks by the unit left-tenant. Hey, who am I to look such a prize-winnin' gift horse in the mouth? As she stands, I've got *(places cigarette between gritted teeth and checks the watch adorning his left wrist, retrieving the smoke following a deep inhale)* less than four hours before buggin' out with these guys. Seems there's another kraut stronghold five clicks to the south all but beggin' for a good, old-fashioned butt-kickin' *(takes a long swig from the bottle, grimaces; nods and flashes a wide, toothy grin)*. Smooth as mama's milk, ol' Vat-six-nine. It ain't Early Times or Southern Comfort, but it'll surely do in a pinch. Gotta tell ya *(laughs)*, a person can get mighty burnt out on schnapps and vodka. The left-tenant has hinted that once the aforementioned strongholds are terminated and/or captured, we'll be headed to a spot near the German/Belgium border called the *Hurtgen Forest* for what promises to be a long-term skirmish. Rumor control has it somewhere along the lines of forty-thousand dogfaces are movin' that way as we speak *(takes another drink, wipes mouth with forearm, crude skull & crossbones tattoo on his right bicep briefly showcased)*. If so, well, so much for gettin' back to my unit, who last I heard was movin' on to the outskirts of Paris. So be it. All those sweet-smellin', long-legged French putains at the *Le Sphinx* will just have to survive without the Ace for just a little while longer *(laughs)*.

"As for the Brigade of Satan fame, they're preparin' to walk into a Nazi hornet's nest of their own. Despite the crappy odds, I'm puttin' my money on the good guys *(tips the bottle towards the camera)*. While

I take a rare opportunity to sip my way to a much-needed nap, let's get back to *The Devil's Brigade.*

(At the 99:11 mark, a commercial break, followed by a fade-in as Claymore stands just outside the tent entrance, a build-up of morning fog drifting about his ankles. He is decked out in full combat gear: face re-striped in black camouflage, M1 combat helmet w/skull emblem painted in black on each side, khaki ranger vest visibly exposed underneath what appears to be a newly issued, regulation M1943, olive drab-shaded uniform. His Springfield rifle is slung over his left shoulder, while the gleaming black handle of a Colt .45 protrudes from a similarly colored holster hitched to his utility belt, along with a trio of grenades. A freshly lit cigarette hangs from his lower lip, bobbing wildly as he speaks)

"Looks like the Brigade and the unit which has so kindly adopted me have somethin' in common; we all have some sizable mountains to scale. The left-tenant has decided that a little early mornin' climb up a rocky grade to our north is preferable to walkin' the beaten trail leadin' directly to the kraut stronghold, that bein' just in case they have said path heavily guarded, which is a good possibility. Luckily, Lieutenant Thompson, an Okie I'm told, ain't some butter-bar combat virgin right outta Fort Benning. Far from it, as his many scars and battle-savvy can attest. His men fully trust his judgement, and, despite only bein' around 'im for only a few hours, so do I. As his unit's lost several NCOs since landin' in-country, I've been tagged as a temporary squad leader. No sweat, no strain. The men saw my work at that previous bunker, so gainin' their confidence hasn't been a problem. So *(takes a final draw from the cigarette before flicking it away)* it's time both the Brigade and myself start earnin' our stripes. See ya on the other side..."

(End credits roll in the background, as Claymore has relocated to the show's regularly seen bunker, now wearing his trademark flight-suit. Arms folded, his elbows rest atop a stack of black and white newspaper clippings, the first of which he pulls free and holds aloft so that the headline stands directly in line with the camera eye. Published by Stars & Stripes, *the 8 May 1945 headline reads: 'VICTORY: Nazis reveal surrender to Western Allies, Russia')*

"Damn right they surrendered. The Third Reich, which their madman dictator dubbed 'The Master Race' discovered, to the midget Führer's dismay, I'm sure, that the allies could take body-blow after body-blow and refuse to go down for the count. America's armies are infamous, before and since, for more than just stubborn perseverance and a steely resolve but an unknown quality, a 'can do' attitude and 'never say die' spirit unmatched by any peer throughout history.

(Holds up second clipping, this one from the Los Angeles Examiner *and also published on 8 May 1945, sports the large, bolded headline 'NAZIS SURRENDER: Europe war comes to an end' over a snapshot of General Eisenhower)*

"Handed them their asses in the end, sure, but at such a great expense, one that is impossible to measure other than to thank God the freedom and liberties we enjoy were spared extinction at the hands of a lunatic mass-murderer. As for part II of the greatest conflict the planet's ever seen, well, it yielded similar results just a short few months later *(Holds up clipping taken from the* Pasadena Star-News *dated 14 August 1945 which reads 'VICTORY! Japan Quits!')*

Yep, Tojo learned a similar lesson and paid a helluva price themselves in the process. My personal opinion on why the Allies prevailed across the board might sound simplistic but I think fairly logical. I know, I know, not exactly my strong point. Anyhow, ya got to figure the resolve and determination of those tryin' like hell to *preserve* a way of life has gotta be stronger than the ones attemptin' to take it away, right? Just my two cents. Were we better in a scrap? Maybe, maybe not. Did we outgun 'em? Depends on the scrap. Sometimes yeah, sometimes no. Did our leaders have an edge in strategic intel? Again, case to case, though it's damn hard to argue against battlefield generals with names like Macarthur, Patton and Bradley.

"All in all, I think it all came down to what I call the grunt mentality, that bein' what the individual doughboy has in here *(pokes own chest with an extended thumb)* and when it came down to brass tacks, the good were just a might stonier where it counts. We wanted it more than they did and we took it, period.

(Stands, faces the mounted flag to his left and salutes)

"God...bless...America and her allies. History and the good Lord above were on our side...the right side."

(Short commercial break, followed by a gradual fade-in of Claymore, now dressed in civilian clothing: dark brown tee, blue jeans, black high-top sneakers, the trademark scar conspicuously absent; the voice is noticeably softer, the gravelly tone dialed down considerably. He sits behind a dark-stained oak desk that features a dozen or so assorted military caps and hats, all stacked in threes and taking up the whole of the desk's wide perimeter; in the background, covering the whole of the wall, hangs an American flag)

"As a paid actor, I've been proud to play the part of the ultra-patriotic, blood-and-guts leader of men, Sergeant Ace Claymore, and to hopefully bring a sense of realism to what are sometimes campy scenarios in the tradition of the great war comics like Sergeant Rock, Nick Fury and of course Captain America. Toss those guys into a blender and a mold of Ace Claymore is formed.

"What started out, or at least was supposed to be a *parody* of such broad characters quickly transformed into just the opposite: a bombastic flag-barrier whose veins literally ran red, white and blue. To this end, our decidedly alt-right treatment and subsequent criticism of such controversial movies as *Platoon*, *Apocalypse Now* and *Born on the Fourth of July* was met with a firestorm of opposing views and voila! A somewhat reluctant star was hatched and a local show of shoestring-budget fame and throwaway timeslot found itself broadcast on two coasts and even overseas. Humbled I was and still am by the show's success and I'd be lying through these recently reconstructed teeth if I hinted I wasn't enjoying the ride while it lasts.

"All that said, I know my place in the overall scheme. I'm a fake. A complete fraud. I play-act for a living. The role I play is just that: a caricature of the man I wish I truly was if under fire in a combat situation. I have to confess that once nothing more than a lark turned into a full-blown success that a part of me starting thinking I was that man, that the faux tattoos were real and the plastic mold scar earned in battle. I guess that's natural, as least I've heard similar tales of egos gone wild before and just never thought it would ever pertain to yours truly.

"Wanna know how to deflate an overinflated personality in record time? Let 'em keep company with the real deal, up close and personal. Let me tell ya, it worked wonders for this boy, like a surgical needle to a bloated balloon, yes sir. Allow me to briefly preach on it. In the production break between seasons two and three, I got the idea to take the show on the road and even volunteered to foot the majority of the bill to do so. Hey, we'd just signed this extremely lucrative syndication deal and I was rolling in it, so I figured—and was instantly referred to as 'genius' for doing so—that to keep that ratings ball rolling, what better way than offer live showings to the troops on their home turf? The producers and sponsors were enthusiastically on board, and why the hell not considering I was picking up the majority of the tab. So, once Don and Margie worked their PR magic, myself, Gregory Tate and a stage crew of four packed up and hit that tarmac for destinations known (*video and photo imagery of Claymore and crew on stage at assorted US bases, the attending masses largely shown in uniform*). Now, to sit here and spout that I didn't view these strategically placed treks as not merely smart PR but also an excuse to party and raise hell with the troops would be yet another attempt at shameful dishonesty of the lowest order. I'd just been through my second divorce in less than three years and didn't need an excuse for excess, if you can dig it. That said, I wasn't about to shortchange the crowd and, if I do say so myself, stretched my acting chops in a manner only possible with a live show. It was also a hoot and a half being able to ratchet up the profanity and crudity, something obviously not allowed by the TV censors of the time.

"Well, the third show on the docket was Hickam Air Force Base, Hawaii, a choice spot for its obvious charms, not the least of which were all those lovely island honeys (*photo image of a smiling Claymore being greeted as he exits the aircraft by a trio of young ladies in grass shirts, all of which offer colorful leis to hang around his neck*). Talk about getting more than you bargained for. I departed that scenic paradise a different man than the one that arrived, all due to a preshow dinner offered by the local VFW, where I was honored to sit at a table with not one, not two, but half-a-dozen World War Two vets, all six survivors of the Pearl Harbor bombing.

"I gotta say, by the end of that evening, my perspective hadn't just been slightly altered but converted, renovated and mutated. These were real heroes whose aura of dignity was palpable without benefit of ego. They'd lived it, not play-acted it. I was, for perhaps the first time in my miserable life, in awe of another human being. In shaking their hands and staring into eyes that had faced certain death and not only survived but persevered to live quiet lives of nobility, I suddenly didn't feel qualified to shine their boots, much represent their kind on a make-believe set while spewing made-up dialogue.

"On the positive, will-not-ever-forget side, I received what has to be the greatest compliment ever associated with my take on Ace Claymore from one of the Pearl Harbor vets, a bandy-legged, bald-as-a-cue-ball little firecracker with a slight limp who'd made the Navy a career following the great war. Over a couple of frosty brews, he'd leaned over the table we'd shared and whispered beneath the flat of one palm, 'I ran into a few like your Sergeant Claymore durin' my time; one part Jarhead, one part doughboy and half a part flyboy, and I wouldn't never have admitted it then, but they were the backbone without which the war-machine would've needed a wheelchair. Big mouth didn't always equate to big action, but damned if it didn't *most* of the time. You do 'em all proud with that act of yours. Keep up the good work, young man. Lord knows these newer generations need to hear from a few more flag-wavers like your sergeant.'

"The greatest generation. I'd heard that phrase my entire life but until that night, didn't have a clue of its true meaning. May not sound like much, but I have vowed since to try to do them a semblance of justice with my rendition of this fictional character. In the meantime, if you just happen to find yourself in the presence of a war veteran, no matter the conflict, do the very least you *can* do and thank them. Believe me, it'll warm your heart as much or maybe even more than their own. Whether the veteran in question answers to...

(Scene transitions to Claymore dressed in the White Summer Dress uniform, famously nicknamed 'The Good Humor' or 'Milkman' of the U.S. Navy, complete with 'Dixie Cup' cap and neckerchief, the background image that of an unidentified Destroyer)

"...Sailor, Squid or Swabbie. Or if they were once known as..."

(Scene transitions to Claymore dressed in the camouflaged 'scorpion design' fatigues of the US Army, the background image a formation of similarly dressed soldiers standing at attention)

"...Grunt, Dog Face or Ground Pounder. Or if they once answered to..."

(Scene transitions to Claymore decked out in an Air Force dress blue uniform, the background image that of F-16 Fighting Falcon Jets taxiing down an unidentified runway)

"...Zoomie, Flyboy, or Wing-Nuts. Or if they were once referred to as..."

(Scene transitions to Claymore wearing the Blue Dress uniform of the US Marine Corps, the background image that of flag-raising on Iwo-Jima, circa 1945)

"...Jarhead, Leathernecks or Devil Dogs, or even if they once went by..."

(Scene transitions to Claymore decked out in the service dress blue 'bravo' uniform worn by the US Coast Guard, the background image depicting a trio of Coast Guard cutters sailing into foggy waters)

"...Coastie, Puddle Jumper or Puddle Pirate."

(Scene transitions back to Claymore, standing at parade rest with the flag as a backdrop)

"...Whatever uniform they wore, they served under the same flag and fought for the same ideals, and *all* deserve and have *earned* our respect and undying gratitude.

"Good night and God Bless America."

(Fade to black; the home theater lights slowly illuminate)

There was a spattering of clapping, mercifully brief as I'd felt my face rapidly reddening, before Tank broke the silence.

"Impressive, old buddy, truly impressive. I seem to remember the

Devil's Brigade episode but not that monologue at the end, and that's just weird 'cause it *should* be the thing I remember most clearly."

Standing, my reconstructed knee popping like a M-80, as it was want to do following lengthy inactivity, I caught a glimpse of both Misty and, more surprisingly, big Ronnie, swiping the corners of their eyes, the latter as nonchalantly as he could manage without being obvious.

"That's because they canned it. Some of the suits tied to the left coast syndication package considered it a bit, now what did they say again? Oh yeah, heavy-handed."

"Crap on a Ritz," Tank grumbled, shaking his head in disgust as Wendy handed him his cane. "Left coast liberals. Figures."

"I'm surprised at least the Midwest and Southern markets didn't give it the green light," Ronnie said, side-stepping from his aisle to allow Misty a clear path.

"I think it was discussed, but in the end even they caved. Said the length put us over the allotted timeslot."

Tank was at the top of his malcontented game, waving the cane airborne like a dueling sword.

"Load of steamin' cowpies. All they had to do was jettison a car-dealership ad or two, or heaven forbid one of those bogus weight-loss commercials."

Eric, one hand buried in a popcorn bag, used the free one to apply a light tap to my right shoulder.

"That was top-notch, big guy. It ought to be required viewing on all college campuses. I've got friends who don't know beans about military history."

"What surprised me was those acting chops," Ronnie added with a sheepish grin, his eyes still noticeably red. "Correct me if I'm wrong, but didn't I hear you were once offered a couple of acting roles while the show was hitting its stride?"

"Yeah, well, there was talk but only a few actual offers," I replied, hoping for a rapid subject change, as in truth those few 'offers' included a cameo role in a military-themed soft-core disaster and several small parts playing assorted mob-muscle types.

"Hey, never too late for a comeback, partner!" he countered, flashing a double thumbs-up.

"Well, technically to make a comeback, you would've had to be *relevant* at some point."

As if on cue, Wendy stepped up and handed me a frosty bottle of beer of the root variety, the timing of her intervention just what I needed to switch verbal gears to a subject I'd been looking for the right opportunity to broach.

"Why, thank you kindly, ma'am. May I say your lesser half is looking mighty spry this evening," I said, gesturing towards Tank, who stood by the home theater room entrance jawing with Misty and Eric while playfully twirling his cane about like the Penguin.

"He's taking to the treatments much better since they tweaked the meds."

Despite the positivity of her words, the concern behind those baby blues was evident.

"Strongest SOB I've ever known, both mentally and physically," I replied, reaching with my free hand to take her own and apply a gently squeeze. "Plus he's backed by one hell of a support system here at home."

Wendy leaned in, despite no one being within earshot as Ron had strolled over to join the others.

"Eric is still...struggling, though less now. At first he wouldn't even accept the diagnosis. Insisted we get no less than three or four opinions. Now that he has finally come to terms with the medical facts, well, he can't always deal with what's happening to his dad. I'm just so thankful that the sudden regression has subsided somewhat. My god, Deron, those first few weeks were difficult, to say the least."

Placing a slightly shaking hand over my own, Wendy conveyed her personal struggles with her long-time spouse's health in a single pained expression. The dark-haired, slim-figured beauty had a few scattered sprinklings of gray and a few tiny wrinkles here and there but had overall flashed Father Time the middle finger.

"He thinks the world of you, you know. I'm so glad you're able to spend this time with him now. It's like, well, like this movie project came along for that reason. A bona fide gift.”

“Funny that word. Gift,” I said with a grin and dramatic tilt of the head. “I’ve always felt the exact same about the Garrett family as a whole.”

That warm smile belied the slight apprehension in her tone upon broaching the subject of my conspicuously absent spouse.

“I hear Jenny is still back home with the family?”

“For the duration, perhaps.” I shrugged, finding I had grown surprisingly unemotional about the subject. “Our Skype sessions are few and far between these days. Still not exactly sure why, but she seems to be severely embarrassed by the whole thing.”

“She’ll come around. You’ll see.”

“Maybe. Maybe not. I’m living proof that marriage ain’t for everybody. The more I think on it, I can hardly blame her. From the beginning I promised her things I never really intended to provide. I was just lonely and she was an easy fix. Not a *cheap* one, mind you, but an easy one.”

“No evidence you’re the problem. If Jenny’s smart, and I think she is one sharp cookie, she’ll use this time to clear her head and understand what she’s about to lose.”

“Thank you, ma’am. But then, the Wendy Garretts of the world are as rare as a Sasquatch selfie.”

This time, that radiant smile was absolutely sincere.

With knowing nods and a soft tipping of bottlenecks, we joined the others, who’d apparently been engaged in a discussion concerning their favorite war films of all time. Their choices, none too surprising considering their respective ages, were fine as far as the genre goes, though Eric had chided his father concerning his choice of The Duke’s *The Alamo*, asking him if he’d enjoyed his time there serving alongside Davy Crockett, Jim Bowie, etc.

“Bravest men that ever took a stand, son, no matter the hopelessness of that situation,” Tank shot back as serious as a heart attack and without a hint of humor. “Those boys knew they were gonna die. Had the chance to shag ass but deferred. The phrase ‘brothers to the end’ ain't never been more pertinent."

As for the younger Garrett, the more recent *Flags of our Fathers* was received with overall acceptance with Ron having to default in light of never seeing it.

Wendy's selection, Kubrick's flawed masterpiece *Full Metal Jacket* had been covered in season one of the show, where I'd given it a decent flaying for its limp, by-the-numbers second half and *'that's all there is?'* ending. It wasn't the bloated, clichéd message of 'war is hell' so much as the lackluster execution by a man deemed a modern filmmaking god. Still, there was no arguing her stand that the first half, a brutal but sometimes equally hilarious showcase for war-time boot-camp on Parris Island, is unrivaled in cinematic history.

Ron's pick of the original *Red Dawn* was given a decent-enough rating, as shamelessly patriotic as it had been—my personal reason for showcasing it in season two—for the time, it struck a nerve with like-minded folks of our generation who'd been told to expect a Russian invasion at any given minute of the day or night.

Admittedly no fan of the genre, Misty was hard-pressed to come up with a single title, that is until she recalled seeing *Dunkirk* with a blind date the year before. Being kind—I was never really a fan, having been disappointed considering the rave reviews at the time—we all congratulated her for pulling that rabbit out of her hat.

As for myself, the group gathered around as if awaiting a particularly fascinating dissertation, perhaps in the thought that I should be, after all, one of the top experts in the field.

It was with befuddled frowns (Wendy, Eric, Ron), blank stares of incomprehension (Misty) and, mercifully, a knowing nod (Tank, who was long-privy to this particular nugget) that I was greeted upon the casual, no-hesitation-whatsoever announcement of *Missing in Action*, the Chuck Norris actioner which spawned two subsequent sequels. Considered a B-movie at best by most critics, most notably the snobby Hollywood elite types, it was, admittedly, a guilty pleasure, one I'd been forced to all but openly bribe Don Oliva to add to the show roster. The old man had refused until season three, no doubt wary of my constant grumbling and increasingly pathetic sales-pitches in its behalf. As it turned out, I was finally able to host Norris' ultra-badass Colonel Braddock rescuing POWs with a giddy mix of kicks, punches, chokeholds and assorted weaponry while for all the world resembling a seventies-era GI action-figure, complete with Kung-Fu grip and full beard. Ironically, it was also the feature chosen for the live show that saw me officially 'outed' by Conrad Bolan.

When I informed the openly dismayed group, all save a perpetually grinning Tank, that to this day it still frosts me that Don wouldn't allow a showing of the MIA sequels, their respective jaws dropped ever further downward. Well, that is all but poor Misty, who had to be reminded, via Google search, who Chuck Norris even was, and even then was pretty sure she'd only seen him on late-night exercise-equipment infomercials.

This roundtable discussion, accompanied by Cracker Jack in vintage packaging and ice-cold root beers all around, was followed by yet another trip down Ace Claymore Memory Lane, so much of which I'd forgotten or perhaps purposely forced into the catacombs of a rapidly fading mind.

It was Eric who broached the subject, always the curious one when talk of previous eras and the cultural changes that naturally occur, no doubt due to his current student status and the attitudes he encountered on a daily basis on-campus.

"Were there many complaints about the show? The active years were right before Desert Storm, yeah? I just figured, well, it couldn't have been popular with *everybody*. Practically nothing is."

Tank rolled his eyes, which then locked directly on me. He knew very well the story I could tell, as he'd heard it many times over the years. I was debating side-stepping the subject with a quick 'nothing much' or 'not really' but then decided otherwise. True enough, the show hadn't been all peaches, cream and widespread popularity, particularly one warm, breezy afternoon in Southern California.

"Fort Ord," I began, leaning back while cradling the frosty, frothy brew in clasped hands. "One of our last stops on the live tour. Things got kinda dicey. In hindsight we should've realized the possibility, considering the general vicinity."

"Which was?" Wendy asked between crunchy chomps.

"Monterey Bay, California, twenty or so miles south of San Jose," Tank answered for me before partaking in a handful of candy, a portion of which spilled from his overstuffed hand.

"Yeah, and only seventy or so from San Francisco, and even though the early nineties are almost three decades removed, the ideals and ideologies remain fairly consistent."

"Protests?" Eric inquired, sipping from a bottled Sprite.

"More like open harassment. It was pretty damn awkward, especially how random the whole thing was. We'd already visited five or six stateside bases and forts and escaped without a single verbal moan tossed our way, at least as far as we knew."

Naturally quiet and shy for most of the evening, Misty inquired next, one hand buried in a bag of Fritos while the other cupped a can of Diet Dr. Pepper.

"This is so weird. I've got a first cousin that lives in San Jose who's always posting pics of their visits to the Bay. What happened, Deron?"

"Well, on our last night at the fort, the base entertainment director treated us to Chi-Chi's for chow." I paused to address Eric and Misty specifically, who's befuddled looks were hilariously similar. "Yeah, I know it sounds like a south-of-the-border exotic dancer, but it was actually a popular Mexican food establishment back in the day. Fantastic enchiladas, but you didn't want to be around me an hour or so later, if you catch my drift, and believe me that particular draft wasn't one you'd en—"

"Dude, you're driftin'," Tank injected with a light tap of his cane-tip against the table.

"Oh, um, yeah, sorry. Have that tendency of late."

"Probably all that rampant steroid use," Tank jabbed, reaching over with the cane to poke my left bicep. Straight-faced and purposely grim, my lone response was a series of quick flexes of same.

"Anyhow, all told we had about ten or so folks at the table, counting the crew and base escorts. We'd barely ordered, tequila and tacos all around, when I became aware of a commotion at our backs. Being that we'd requested seating at the rear of the place, the source of the ruckus had apparently run a gamut through employees and the restaurant manager to arrive at our location. I remember hearing one of the base reps, a burly captain named Wiggins or Wilkins, rolling his eyes and growling '*Aw shit, here we go*' or something similar before I turned around to see the mass of humanity pouring our way.

"Later I'd heard their number confirmed as twenty-five or so, but in that moment, it looked at least triple that, some of 'em toting signs with anti-war slogans and bloodied, tattered American flags, essentially mimicking banners and poster-board and spouting the same rhetoric you heard during the Vietnam era. In that first minute before things got real, I half expected Alan Funt to crawl out from under a nearby table. Instead, it got real ugly real fast. One of the..." I paused upon spotting Misty timidly raising a hand airborne, as if about to ask permission to use the ladies' room.

"Question?"

"Yes, sorry, but who's Alan Funk?" she asked with a cute grimace.

Tank, Wendy and Ron's respectively guffaws sounded perfectly synchronized, like a TV sitcom soundtrack, leaving Eric to understandably share her confusion.

"Oh geez, my bad. Definitely before your time. Mr. Funk, um, *Funt* hosted a television program way back when called 'Candid Camera' that purposely set up unknowing victims for pranks just to see their reactions before letting them in on the joke."

"Oh, gotcha. So at first you thought..."

"Somebody was pulling our collective chains, yes."

To this, Tank face-palmed his own grinning mug.

"Dude, if you keep usin' references older than my corns, this story is never gonna get told."

This time, it was Eric and Misty that shared a giggle at my

Jurassic-era expense.

"Oh, yeah. I just thought someone had to be playing some elaborate practical joke."

"Better," my best pal concluded with an approving nod.

"Well, you know, I can do modern if necessary."

"Carry on to that thrillin' climax, DJ, before the mornin' sun rises, if possible."

It dawned on me as I resumed that I hadn't been tasked to tell this particular tale in its entirely for a least a decade-plus, that being during one of a dozen or more pressers in Pine Bluff.

"So anyhow, the whole prankster notion vanished as soon as one of the clan poked a forefinger into my spinach dip and proceeded to flick the gooey residue directly onto my buzz-cut and forehead while screaming something to the effect of '*bloodthirsty war whore!*' "

"Blood...whore?" Eric mumbled aloud, apparently unaware he'd done so.

"Yeah, doesn't quite roll off the tongue does it? I still remember the wide-eyes and dropped jaw on that lunatic when I laughed in her face. To put it mildly, she wasn't fond of my taking her lightly all that well, and the guy standing next to her holding a sign that said something to the effect of '*To Glorify War is to ask for War to Repeat Itself*' or some such schlock, was even more butt-hurt. Our camera man, a toothpick-thin but feisty from birth dude named Rich Hansen later told me the guy had reared back his protest sign to cleave my skull. Now, in all honesty that cheap-ass particle board probably would've snapped like a soggy candle against this concrete noggin." I paused for dramatic effect, clearing my throat and gently knuckling my scalp, before resuming. "But, Rich hadn't earned the nickname '*Scrap*' for no reason and took it upon himself to save my bacon by hopping up from his seat, hoisting that sign airborne with one bony arm and sending it flying straight into the guy's upper chest and chin. From there, that tiny corner of Chi-Chi's resembled a full-blown street brawl.

"I recall only a few specifics between all the screams, cursing and bodies being flailed about, one being punched, scratched and spat upon numerous times, throwing a single punch in retaliation and finally, the well-aimed head-butt that ended my participation and shattered some poor jackass's jaw. In the end, myself, Rich and Herb Victor, one of the stage roadies, joined one of the base reps and about a dozen protestors sitting on the sidewalk outside the restaurant's main entrance, cuffed but not-yet-officially-charged. Two, maybe three hours later, I really can't say being that I was toting around one helluva brain-throbber *slash* semi-concussion, we were released without being hauled downtown and ultimately cut loose altogether. This most likely due to some unidentifiable Lieutenant Colonel showing up to speak to Chi-Chi's management completely out of earshot. Can't say for sure money passed hands or the promise of said payment for damages, traumas to employees and non-participating customers, but it would be years before I'd ever heard anything resembling an aftershock of that melee."

"The guy you head-butted asking that you pay for reconstructive dental work?" Ron asked between beer belches.

"Bingo. His grown son hired a lawyer and was requested I pay two-plus years of medical bills, as my well-placed skull-jab had led to his father's chronic facial pain, concussion syndrome, and TMJ. Long story short, we settled out of court. At the time, I wasn't in the mood to fight it."

"Honesty, I'm kind of surprised that was the only such episode," Wendy said, lovingly assisting her husband twist-open a fresh brew.

"Caught me, *us*, completely off-guard. As a rule, we found most bases and posts were surrounding by a supportive community, the majority of which are naturally patriotic by default. Then again, California was always a different kinda beast."

"Pinheaded weanies," Tank growled, evoking a knowing nod from Ron and matching bland, wholly unreadable expression from either Eric or Misty.

"No similar scenes overseas?" the latter asked, much less timidly.

"Nope. The few protests we saw or even heard about were at the Korean bases and those were always about the American presence, period, not a traveling band of TV nitwits."

Ron tossed in a softball, apparently if for no other reason than to actively participate.

"No other controversies since, I mean, other than the well-publicized?"

"Nothing worth mention..." I began only to be cut off by Tank's rich baritone.

"Tell 'em about your secret, sweetheart."

"Stop it," I spouted back, a herculean effort necessary to keep an involuntary smile at bay.

"Hey, fans and non-fans alike are all about the spicy details, dude. It's only fair to your audience that they hear it all: the good, the bad and the brutally ugly."

"You're an ass-wipe of the highest order, Garrett," I replied, unable to halt the low giggle that followed and thus blowing the short-lived straight-faced façade to hell and back.

"No argument," Tank replied with a shrug and tip of his foamy brew, which Wendy had poured into a tall glass. "Now you gonna tell 'em or am I?"

I quickly waved him off, though that joyous, damnable grin would not so easily dissipate.

"I got it, I *got* it, but only because I want to bring forth the absolute truth with no embellishment of the made-up-facts type."

"Oh, I can't wait to hear this one," Wendy announced, leaning in and propping her chin atop clenched fists, those sparkling eyes gleaming with newfound interest.

"So, a few years into working with Tank here at the firm, a certified letter arrived at the home office from a Little Rock law firm, essentially naming me in a paternity suit dating back to the show, so approximately six or seven years after Ace had hung up his flight-suit."

"Ohhhh," Wendy purred, eyes dramatically slanted in my direction. "So there was a little booger-eating, ankle-biting Ace or Ace-et stomping around the first grade *not* knowing he or she was sired by a famous act-tor?"

"Peas in a pod, you two," I groaned, gesturing towards my

favorite couple with an accusing forefinger. "Bottom line, I sacrificed a blood sample and it was, of course, a pathetic attempt at extortion with no basis. The end." Sure, like I was gonna get out of it that easy. Tank could be overheard inhaling for a follow-up even as I'd concluded.

"You forget, partner, I saw your long-lost love, way too up close and way too personal. I still think there's a definite possibility that test was somehow, maybe *purposely*, tainted. Remember, I knew you then. In between wives and lookin' for love in all the wrong places."

"Jackass," I spat between uncontrollable giggles, head bowed and rapidly watering eyes averted. "I'd never met the woman before and you damn well knew it. I...wasn't into her, well, type." I leaned up, vision only partially blurred, to see Tank prepping for yet another snappy return and secretly hoped I had the self-control not to collapse like a cheap tent in its wake.

"What type might that be, partner? I can't seem to recall your bein' that finicky."

"The *unattractive* type. Not to be overly cruel, but extremely unattractive."

"Well, bein' that you were quite the elbow-bender in those days."

"I was never *that* drunk, pal."

"Aw, c'mon now, she wasn't that bad."

"She was a moose in yellow spandex wearing a Dolly Parton wig who reeked of unwiped rump and was desperately in need of a new set of dentures...and *that's* being kind."

All but Tank, an old hand at maintaining his composure during moments of madness, completely lost theirs, including the usually sweet and kind Wendy. Young Eric, who I'm pretty sure didn't even understand the Parton's wig reference, actually extracted fizzy Sprite out of both nostrils. As for the old master, he managed one final jab to my already quivering funny bone.

"Good thing you managed to add some Nestle Quick or Ovaltine to the maternity stew or they'd have been a veritable forest of Moose...*Mooses*?...*Meese*? Headed to their respective barristers to file similar suits."

"Stud Moose was no fool," was all I had as my midsection trembled and ached for release.

"I'd always heard that the life of a celebrity is rarely what it's cracked up to be," Eric said, a bit nasally as he continued to clear the lemon-lime soda from his sinus cavity.

The remaining hour or so—Misty was the first to leave, practically squeezing the stuffing from me in the process—was spent talking about everything but my past, a relief by that point as I was sincerely burnt out on the subject. Such a night would have normally exhausted me more than a three-hour workout, but even as midnight neared and I prepped to leave, I felt as naturally wired as if it were mid-morning, post a full pot of expresso-stout coffee. The source was a no-brainer; after months of sitting in the bullpen, chewing my nails and tapping my toes, my interview was less than ten hours away.

"Knock 'er out of the park," Tank had said as we stood on their front porch, the midnight moon lighting up the distant horizon like an army of flares, "It's easy as peach pie when ya think about it; all you gotta do is tell the truth."

Dude always could cut to the chase in his own homespun way.

"True enough."

"They recordin' you at the apartment or that retro set they built?"

"Both, I guess. Dee-dee wanted me to meet 'em at the apartment and we're driving over to the set together, so it seems Ace Claymore hops behind the mic first."

"Where was this set built, anyhow?"

"Not a clue. She wants to keep it a surprise so I'll provide their cameras a 'live' reaction."

"How very clandestine of them."

"Ain't it though? You're looking better, Tank. Rosy-cheeked and bright-eyed."

Tank shrugged, staring up into a starless sky.

"Took 'em a dozen tries, but those VA sawbones finally hit on the perfect mix of meds. Won't be entering any Ironman contests anytime soon, but the energy level went on a dramatic upswing once I started getting some semi-regular shuteye. Long-term is anybody's guess, but for now I'm just tickled to be up and movin' around with some purpose."

"Wendy looks pleased. Eric, too. That is one sharp kid. Glad he took after his mom."

"Me and you both."

Despite my attempt at witty banter, my old friend sensed the unease not only in my tone, but deportment as a whole.

"What's wrong, partner? I'd think you'd be glad the project was headin' straight for the finish line."

"Tank, my feet aren't just cold, but frostbitten to the point of flakin' away like shaved ice."

"Why suddenly?"

I shuffled my feet and for maybe the thousandth time in the last week, cursed myself for this sudden wave of weak-kneed regret.

"It's been building. I wanna just tell 'im to forget it but, well, with the work and money invested, *that* would be a true horseshit move."

"Bad vibes?"

"More than that. Reliving all this shit hasn't been easy and to think I'll have to endure eternal public and media scrutiny once the movie is released to the masses makes me damn near nauseated." Using his cane for support, Tank leaned over as we lightly bumped shoulders. Somewhere in the distance a semi-truck horn blared a mournful tune.

"A natural response, I figure. If it were me, I'd probably be makin' malted milk in my drawers 'bout now. You'll kill it, no worries. Like I said, all your doin' is statin' facts. Personally, I can't wait to see how ya channel the ol' sarge after all these years."

"I guess you're right. Nothing but damnable self-pride rearing its ugly head."

"Ya may be stubborn and stupid in equal measure, but you're also human."

"Thanks, pal," I said, unable to even fake much in the way of faux displeasure. "Such moron support is always welcome."

As I headed towards my drive, the sound of loose gravel crunching beneath my feet amplified by the near total silence of the midnight hour, my final verbal offering was by far the most honest of the evening.

"I guess the birth, nurturing and even the abrupt passing of Ace Claymore was the one thing in my life I could claim as a success. Bottom line is I just don't wanna make a fool out of myself and, well, soil his memory. Crazy, I know, but there it is."

"Then you go make 'im proud, partner," Tank retorted with a sharp, crisp salute. "Make sure you *both* go out with a respect and dignity that wasn't previously allowed."

That was the problem, you see, that had nagged me like a gradually-rotting tooth since the project's inception: was said respect or dignity *deserved* on either count?

Nine

Rough Cut
(From the private journal of Deron Joseph Barrow)

20 August

As far as harbingers go, waking up to a seventy-eight-degree temperature at just before six AM with an expected high of one-oh-two— a steamy, sticky, sweltering, above-ground Hades annex—I wasn't exactly brimming with cool, pardon the pun, confidence. This sense of foreboding, however unjustified, wasn't exactly boosted by a night of unending rocking and rolling atop my mattress. Eyes bloodshot and sagging from, at most, two hours of uninterrupted shuteye, I make my initial pit-stop at a Starbucks drive-through for a double-shot of expresso and a warm slab of banana bread. Toasty as it was, even with the A/C cranked on high, I'd felt the flight-suit needed a suitable cover while driving, thus a light red windbreaker—the embroidered *Razorbacks* logo badly faded between the shoulder-blades—was given a late-summer reprieve from the hall closet. Sure, it would've made logical sense to change once I got to the apartment and worn a light cotton tee for the drive, but then, the words logic and sense simply did not fit the narrative thus far, so why break formation?

Along those same lines, I'd felt compelled to bring along a copy of my manuscript. A valid reason for doing so escaping me except the distant possibility of comparing notes with the filmmakers as my interview went along. Fat chance, I know, but in case things went way off the rail, fiction-wise, I could at least offer written documentation to avoid full derailment.

As I neared the apartment complex a full thirty minutes before my appointment time, I continually cleared my throat in hopes of wiping away the raspy hoarseness a woeful lack of sleep had birthed. Pulling a semi-chilled bottle of water from the mini-cooler I kept stashed in the back floorboard, I sipped between throat-clearings before testing my voices for signs of normalcy. Voices as in plural: the first representing the man I am, the second belonging to a certain non-commissioned officer of fictional lore. Happy to say, by the time I'd reached my destination, all signs of the previous night's struggles had all but vanished. Probably hadn't helped that I'd spent the early afternoon reading and re-reading, aloud and booming when appropriate, an old script I'd dug out from a hall closet. In retrospect, hour upon hour of becoming reacquainted with the sarge's gravelly tone was, at the very least, extreme overkill. Toss in a mostly sleepless night and a triple-shot of stress, and it was nothing short of a miracle I could conjure his raspy, gruff cadence at even a fifty-percent clip.

Glancing at my watch, it was a quarter 'til eleven. Inhaling deeply through the nostrils and exhaling through pursed lips, I felt several layers of apprehension peel away like a sweat-encased second skin. At that moment, a distant memory pushed to the forefront, that being of a morning so long ago when I'd first donned the costume of and created the personality of the character I was now hoping to reincarnate. Without being conscious of it until I caught my own reflection in the rearview, a wide, toothy grin had materialized, one that, if seen from a distance, probably appeared borderline psychotic. Again, I couldn't help but find said reflection strangely fitting. Back in the show's prime, I remember calling the first day of shooting an episode 'the pod process,' meaning I needed to conjure my inner pod-person of *Invasion of the Body Snatchers* fame to effectively pull off the act. I was about to find out if, staring into the camera's glowing red eye for the first time in eons, my pod twin could still be successfully extracted from its shell.

Role Prep Technique number one was tossing the cloaking

windbreaker aside and daring to expose my long-buried alter-ego to, let's face it, a mostly clueless public. I walked briskly from my ride to the second-story apartment. As a triple-shot of adrenaline is apt to do, body aches were at a minimum despite the woeful lack of shuteye, to include the ol' bionic knee, which hadn't felt as well-oiled and tweak-free in ages.

The note was taped just below the peephole, tucked within a small, brown, unsealed envelope. Scribbled in sharpie was an address and seven words that provided little in the way of an explanation: '*See you there, Sergeant. Bring your 'A' game*'.

It was apparent they'd changed their minds about filming at least a portion of the interview here and instead decided on the set, though I did find it a bit of a head-scratcher that Dee-dee hadn't phoned or at least shot me a quick text and thus saved me a trip. Maybe it had been a matter of technical difficulties or perhaps one of those spur-of-the-moment decisions that such creative types are infamous for. Still, a little common courtesy goes a long way. Heading back to my ride—and setting my phone's GPS for the note's mystery destination—I fell back upon an old auxiliary *Role Prep Technique* that, although rarely used, had always proved damn effective, that being to use apprehension, annoyance or mild anger as a motivational tool of sorts. Absorb said emotion and pack it away for later use when the role called for that rarely seen, pissed-off version of the fictional sergeant. In this case, it was as much about being perplexed as truly perturbed, but it would do.

~ * ~

1756 West Cowen Drive was found to be located, no shock whatever, in the old warehouse district, roughly seven miles to the west of the apartment/studio, bookended by two similarly aged, long-deserted warehouses—each of which held the same signature signs of a decade or more of abandonment: shattered windows, spray-painted gang markings, assorted bullet-holes and wild vine growth on outer walls. The single-story, half-brick, half-siding structure bearing the numbers I sought may have possessed less in the way of overall dilapidation but was still far from pristine in appearance. A faded metal sign reading *'Mobley's Signs, LLC'* hung from a double-glass door entrance which had miraculously avoided the shattered state of its neighbors' entryways.

Spotting no other parked vehicles in the nearby vicinity, I pulled into and slowly covered the length of the building's front lot until seeing a rust-coated chain-link fence and opened connecting gate, presumably leading to the rear of the building. Hoping a criminal trespassing charge was not in my immediate future, I steered through the wide gap and spotted a clearly disengaged baseball-sized padlock hanging from the gate.

There, parked side-by-side and fronting a closed metal dock door, sat both Dee-Dee's red Honda Civic and Dixon's black Jeep SUV. Overly dramatic overreaction aside, my sense of relief was palpable. Backing in next to the Jeep, I found myself utilizing a certain *Role Prep Technique* yet again, one that was fast becoming more routine than rare.

Worn manuscript in hand, I let myself in a side entrance to the right of the dock door, a barely readable notice announcing 'EMPLO EE'S O LY' in badly fading bold lettering and was forced to pause as the outside light provided the lone source of illumination. As I stared into the near complete darkness, the stench of soldered wires and overheated machinery wafted past. As blazing hot as it was outdoors, the interior was fairly comfortable, temp-wise. I could only surmise it had taken a full night's blasting of some Mac-truck-sized A/C unit to make it so, especially considering the overall square-footage involved. With that in mind, I had serious doubts that the same people responsible had somehow forgotten to pay the light bill.

Poised at that creaking door in a faux flight-suit, hair freshly buzz-cut and light brown stache—thank you, *Just for Men*—trimmed to regulation length, I can't say I've ever felt more foolish.

"Hey, who's minding the fort?" I bellowed, the echo which followed reverberating countless times, as if I'd yelled into some bottomless mind-shaft.

"I detect shenanigans meant strictly for yours truly. C'mon now, somebody jump out and yell surprise already!"

I detected a faint clicking sound and accompanying giggle just as the place lit up like a supernova, temporarily cloaking my vision in a barrage of explosive floaters and flashes. Straight ahead, though briefly reduced to a bleary wave of green, opposite sides of a massive tent slowly pulled apart with stage-play theatrics.

"Welcome, Sergeant Ace Claymore, to this *was* your life!" a familiar female voice shrieked, followed by a clattering of handclapping and even a rather pathetically executed wolf-whistle.

The door behind me closed with a resounding thump, but I was beyond noticing once my rapidly recuperating orbs settled in on the scene at hand, or more appropriately, the *set* on hand.

From the scarred oak desk, radio/transmitter set-up and tattered American flag hanging slightly askew on the back wall, all encased in shoulder-high, fittingly tattered sandbags, it was like stepping out of a time portal back to the late eighties. Never one for cheap sentimentality, I have to confess that more than a few chill bumps materialized at the mere sight.

"I take it by that bug-eyed, jaw-hanging-as-loose-as-a-busted-shutter expression that it's up to DOD standards?" Dee-Dee inquired cheerily into an exact replica of the mic my alter-ego had utilized almost three decades earlier. Hopping up from an unpadded high-back armless chair —again, if not the original, a near-exact replica from the original set—she was dressed in season-appropriate attire: a short-sleeved red, white and blue tee, faded blue jeans and white sneakers. It took me a few moments to nail down just why, at least from the twenty foot or so distance between us, she suddenly resembled a grinning teenage girl. It wasn't until she strolled towards me, arms outstretched and hands palms up to receive my own, that I was finally able to nail down the source of such a dramatic alteration. Roughly half of her previously lengthy do had been unceremoniously shorn away, leaving the bottom edges levitating just above her slim shoulders.

"Amazing, Dee-dee. Kudos to those responsible," I replied, taking her warm, slightly moist hands into my own and applying a gentle squeeze. "Appears they didn't miss a single trick."

She backed away and gestured with a slight bow towards the set, that highly contagious smile never wavering, though there was also just a hint of nervousness in her movements, her tone, that was new, at least in my presence. Admittedly, I found a measure of relief in sharing my own apprehension.

"The transmitter was the hardest to procure. Everything else was surprisingly easy, at least according to Ron."

As if on cue, Dixon emerged from between tent folds, his dour expression as bland and hangdog as ever.

"Clay—um, Barrow," he nodded weakly in acknowledgement, decked out in a light blue button-up dress shirt—complete with pocket protector—brown Dockers and Buster Browns. I couldn't help but wonder if the kid ever loosened up enough to pull on a pair of Levis and mud-stained Reeboks. "What you got there?"

He'd pointed at the manuscript, stuffed inside a dog-eared manila folder, tucked snugly against my left side.

"Dixon." I nodded curtly in reply. "Brought along my copy of the 'script, just in case we need a specific reference."

We shook hands, his usual wet-noodle grip relegating the gesture to nothing more than mere obligation.

"Think we've procured the gist."

"Remains to be seen," I shot back bluntly, secretly hoping for some form of verbal retribution which of course never materialized as Mr. Happy strolled casually over to Dee-dee to discuss assorted technical details that held little interest. Instead, I opted to better scan the surroundings. The warehouse in full light proved to be much larger than its outer shell would suggest, with at least a dozen rows of three-tiered metal bins in the rear, a gated-off space roughly half as roomy that had perhaps once served as a bindery *slash* production area, and lastly the space beneath my feet, which I could only speculate might've previously served as the shipping/receiving section.

Here stood a circus-sized green tent and the set underneath, the former stretching out far beyond the latter's limited perimeters.

"Can't help but stare," Dee-dee said, landing a soft jab to my right bicep, Dixon having already trudged back to the rear of the set, where he quickly vanished beyond the tent folds. Soon enough, the sound of rolling carts and whirring machinery ensued.

"At what, m'lady?" I grinned, unabashedly unashamed at flirting with a woman three decades my junior. Such thoughts, inappropriate and un-PC as they might be, were immediately echoed, much to my naughty delight.

"Not my habit to hit on men old enough to be my dad, but you are one chiseled *hunk,* Deron Barrow."

In lieu of a verbal reply, surely to have been littered with stuttering, possibly intelligible mumblings, I shrugged like a red-faced teen.

"The way you fill out that jumpsuit...my-oh-*my*," she concluded with a wink, ultra-cute dimples on full display. Again though, there was a twinge of unease present that I was beginning to think wasn't merely tied to my own. For the first time since we'd been introduced, I felt Diandra *forcing* the cheeriness.

"Could be they shrank in the wash," I managed, unconsciously flexing both arms and my upper body as to further impress. Clicking her tongue, she hooked an arm into the crook of my left elbow and led me toward the set.

"Nope. Not buying it, muscles. I'd say it's more about dedication to one's craft. Hey, I'm even digging the porn stache."

"Regulation porn stache, at that."

"I would expect nothing less, sergeant. By the way, got a surprise for you."

"Oh yeah? Don't tell me...IMAX three-D premiere at Cannes."

"Not quite," she laughed. "But I do like the way you've gone full Hollywood on us in such a short time."

"Beverly Hills hick, that's me."

Giggling, she led me up to and around the desk, releasing my elbow and gesturing towards the chair.

"Your throne, my king."

I sat, the seat's unpadded surface less than soothing on my butt-cheeks, which still ached from the previous day's squat workout.

"Don't tell me you rounded up my last ex," I grumbled, leaning forward to rest my chin atop clenched fists.

"Nothing quite so dramatic or presumably negative. You just hold tight. Back in a jiff."

With that, she bounded away like a magical pixie, practically skipping like a kindergartner at recess. Shared apprehension aside, as had been the case since our initial introduction, the mere presence of Diandra Chang was akin to diving head-first and mouth agape into a bona fide River of Youth.

The 'surprise' emerged a moment later, their mystery form temporarily cloaked by Dee-dee, who side-stepped away to allow a full reveal, Ron Dixon standing in the background with a camera propped atop one shoulder.

"Deron Barrow, this *was* your life!" she bellowed, arms outstretched as Dixon strolled cautiously forward in a slight crouch as to acquire a more evenly filmed shot.

Once the figure steered the wheelchair to a full stop within reaching distance of my position, there was a brief pause before recognition and subsequent identification prompted my jaw to literally unhinge.

"Paul? Paul Holliman?"

Fifteen years since laying eyes on the man, no matter the dramatic changes in appearance, there was no forgetting that face. The strapping young man was long gone, his replacement a severely shriveled middle-aged man with a grayish beard, visage cracked and creased from a decade-plus of health struggles, no doubt as mental as it had been physical. A tidal wave of shame washed over me, gargantuan enough, if a physical presence, to swallow me whole and spit me all the way back to Boone's Crossing.

"Deron Barrow," he nodded amiably enough, though the accompanying smile was as forced as my own, a faux gesture I'd long since mastered.

"It has been a few years," I managed as our hands gently clasped, his grip loose and clammy.

"You look damn healthy, big fella," he replied in that thick Arkansas drawl, the grin wavering dangerously on the edge of pained-grimace status. "For a man of your advancing years, I mean to say."

My mind scrambled madly for an appropriate response; literally anything that didn't reference his appearance. Dixon bouncing and shuffling around in the foreground as if someone had poured fire ants into his drawers wasn't exactly helping soothe my jangled nerves.

"Hey, thanks solely to yours truly, my man. How've you been, Paul?"

There was a split-second of stupefied horror at the potential ramifications of such a moronic question, his eyes briefly gleaming with barely restrained madness and his top lip stuck on an upper plate of freakishly white teeth, before my mind was somewhat eased as his expression quickly softened.

"Oh, you know, living the dream, as it were," he said with the slight tilt of the head.

"Hey, you're a survivor, bottom line."

"If you say so," he shrugged, breaking eye contact and wheeling forward a few feet until I could no longer gauge his expression. I couldn't help but think, in that moment, that Paul Holliman and myself were two novice actors rehearsing lines from some crappy B-movie script. Surreal, sure, but also devastatingly sad.

With a sudden epiphany, I playfully stroked the palm of one hand across my own clean-shaven mug while gesturing towards his ZZ-Top-ish chin whiskers with the other.

"Brother, that is one serious cookie-duster."

"Eight years in the making," he said through a crooked smile, though his eyes held a faint look of bewilderment at the reference, having no doubt long-forgotten my 'Deputy Peach-Fuzz' reference at the press conference all those years ago. "Wife keeps threatening to take a weed-eater to it." It secretly made my heart soar to hear he had someone. My God, what a strong woman she must be.

"Well, I'm glad you could make it, Paul," I concluded clumsily, frozen in my tracks as if temporarily paralyzed.

Once Paul whirled around, the hum of the chair's motor barely audible, he wore yet another mask, this one so unlike the others in that it screamed sincerity. That mask, if labeled for Halloween sale, would have surely read '*The face of regret.*'

"Same here, Deron. I'm just sorry it...took this long for us to reacquaint."

"Same here, man. Sincerely."

In taking a step back, I nearly tripped into Dixon, who'd practically planted the camera eye into my left ear. Fighting off the urge to elbow the arrogant bastard squarely in his exposed ribs, I instead executed a half-curtsy dripping in sarcastic resentment that obviously hit home as he backed away with a free hand held up palms-out in an apologetic manner.

It was, in the aftermath of such a shamelessly orchestrated set-up, that I was finding it increasingly difficult to maintain the façade of positivity. I could only figure that Dixon was behind the whole thing, and sincerely hoped Dee-dee was either a somewhat unwilling participant or simply ignorant of its shameless, reality-TV trashiness.

"I guess an audience of one is better than none," I directed to Dee-dee as Paul wheeled towards the set with Dixon right on his heels.

"Oh, there just might be a surprise or two we've yet to reveal, big fella," she shot back, those adorable dimples on full display. "You ready to reintroduce a certain non-commissioned officer to the world at large?"

With Paul parked silently off to the left of the set and Dixon kneeling on the opposite side while tampering with the camera, I followed her lead with surprisingly little trepidation, as if the ol' sarge was sufficiently locked and loaded for a victorious return to the spotlight's glare.

~ * ~

A little more than ninety minutes later, I paced the warehouse's stained, slightly cracked stone floor while sipping a cool Sprite and rehashing as best I could how the taping came off, Dee-dee's unrelenting praise notwithstanding. I'd always found the art of critiquing my own performance virtually impossible, as from the get-go of Claymore's birth on film, it was like someone else was playing the part, like I'd stepped out of my own skin and into one of those animal-mascot suits. I'd never really felt comfortable 'acting,' probably due to a lack of formal training, and usually viewed my segments with no small amount of embarrassment.

As prompted by Dee's off-screen questions, neither to be heard or shown once editing was complete, the first half-hour or so—later I was told it was a lean seventeen minutes—covered my youth, induction into the service and ill-fated first marriage, to include those initial bouts with infidelity. Taking five—orange juice and banana bread surely hit the spot—Dee wiped away a buildup of perspiration from my mug and patted it down with a light shade of foundation, only stopping short of applying what she called a lip-balm that too closely resembled its cousin, 'stick,' upon my insistence. During this brief sabbatical, I overheard Dee-dee and Dixon discussing what a monumental chore the editing process was going to be, considering that thus far they'd recorded something in the range of two hundred twenty-eight minutes of footage when a maximum of one hundred and four had been the original target. Knowing the industry and their preferred audience, I had a sinking feeling that the lone portions off-limits to the editing-room clippers would be the most garish and ghoulish aspects of the story. Gulping down the last of my Sprite, I made a mental note to discuss said concern with Dee-dee once the day's filming concluded.

Following a short segment, two or three minutes tops, that saw the first *official* reappearance of Ace Claymore in nearly three decades, I shifted back into my own skin and fielded Dee's queries concerning the Kunsan incident. Just a quick comment on the sergeant's rebirth: I'd found it fairly painless, though the first few words uttered in that, *his,* voice did feel strangely forced, regardless of all the previous month's rehearsals.

The three similar segments that followed were performed in a comfortable groove, the last of which had been the longest at nearly five full minutes. I knew I had it fully licked once the initial stiffness loosened and I actually starting *enjoying* letting the character rant and rave like old times, the majority of which was fully ad-libbed, no cue-cards or teleprompter necessary. Just goes to show that although one cannot fully go home again, you can sure as hell pay it an extended visit.

Segment two ran a full forty-eight minutes, little wonder considering the material covered. No surprise that Korea and the fallout took the bulk, and I have to confess to being thrown off balance by Dee's choice to fit in another Claymore segment—this one written specifically to get the old soldier's opinion on today's military as compared to days of old—before breaking to prep for the Pine Bluff episode. I'd hoped to push on through and be done with it, being that it is, without a doubt, the most difficult subject to openly discuss and one I'd only covered in private, first with authorities at the time of occurrence and later with Tank and Jenny as years had passed.

Unlike the Kunsan debacle, talking at length about the happenings at Pine Bluff was not in the least therapeutic. Oppositely, as far as my warped psyche is concerned, it's akin to reliving a particularly painful root canal while simultaneously undergoing hemorrhoid surgery sans the anesthesia. Though I understood Dee's strategy, to allow me a few deep breaths and a moment to reflect, I'd much rather have just barreled ahead and put it in the rearview mirror for all time. Thing is, I'd already sworn to myself that this would be the last time I'd *ever* discuss it, meaning the subject would be placed strictly off-limits for any and all future movie premiere junkets and/or interviews, said proclamation to be shared with Dee and Ron Dixon immediately upon this day's filming.

As Dixon prepped the camera—when I'd offhandedly asked Dixon, he'd identified this particular item as an EOS C300 Mark II—I'd pulled Dee-dee to the side and asked a favor. In my opinion, to discuss the details of the Pine Bluff tragedy while dressed in Claymore's flight-suit would be in extremely bad taste, considering the character in question had long since vanished from the public eye and consciousness by then. Also, and probably more vital, I'd feel like an A-one jackass wearing the costume of such a broad, comic-book persona when speaking of what had been to many, including yours truly, the most traumatic night of their lives. After a short pause to consider said points, she agreed, thankfully not even bothering to discuss it with Mr. Morose, AKA Ron Dixon. I'd brought along a pair of blue jeans and dark blue tee for just such a scenario and was led to a locker room near the plant's former fulfillment area to change. Dee had thought of filming the final Claymore segment before my wardrobe switch but then agreed to proceed with the present plan. She'd no doubt noted the intensity in my eyes and figured the flickering flames might be permanently doused if forced to transform back into character. If so, she'd have been spot-on. After countless years of silence, I had never been so ready to stand atop the soapbox and preach on it.

Back in civvies, amazing how much more relaxed I'd felt almost instantly upon ditching Claymore's duds, Dee-dee, Paul and I shared Styrofoam cups of ice-cold lemonade pulled from a nearby cooler. Dialogue between us was sparse, which was a good thing as my tongue was already growing fatigued with many more verbal miles to cover.

"So, you ready to do this thing, Mister Barrow?" Dee-dee finally asked, rising from where she'd been leaning against the desk just as Dixon strolled back into view with the camera propped on his left shoulder.

"As I'll ever possibly be," I replied, draining the last drop of pulp from my third refill and hoping I'd be able to finish taping without calling timeout for an overfilled bladder.

With that, Paul Holliman rolled away in reverse wearing a pained grimace and, ever-so-briefly, shooting both my biographers a look that could only be described as troubled. Deeply so. At that time, I was far too distracted to dwell on it.

Dee-dee took up position roughly a dozen feet from where Dixon would begin filming, slender arms crossed as her stoic-as-a-marble-slab partner gave a trio of stage-lights a final check.

"No problem at all filming this in increments," she said between nervous gnaws on the pinkie-nail of her right hand. "It's not like we're obligated to one take by any means, so if you feel yourself growing weary, just pause and shoot Ron the high sign."

I took my assigned seat behind Claymore's desk for what I prayed was the last time, though we'd agreed that if needed, I could stand and pace while regaling the tale if doing so eased any building tension.

"Got it. Hoping I can get through it without calling time. I'd sure as hell prefer it that way."

With the lights set and the camera eye and accompanying volume ready at the starting gate, what was scheduled to be the final segment placed on celluloid—DVD and Blu-ray extras not withstanding—launched without a hitch, at least none visible. A small red light flashed on, I took the final of a trio of deep breathes and commenced speaking of an experience I'd once sworn to never audibly repeat ever again, as the almost nightly re-imagings for a decade-and-a-half had surely covered the horrors quite nicely, thank you.

~ * ~

14 February, 2004

23:39 hours

Six miles west of Pine Bluff

The initial blast echoes like a detonated bomb, the man instantly leaping from the tub and planting his back flat against the wall in the limited space between the shower and bathroom door, the woman's shrieking wails lost in a follow-up explosion that opens a fist-sized hole at the center of their barricade.

"S-show time, soldier," the man groans between gritted lips, inhaling deeply and holding it with the mini-slugger poised at shoulder-level, his free hand reaching back, palm-out, like a fleshy red light for his charges to obey.

Terse, tension-packed seconds pass as if sporadically freeze-framed to move forward in fragmented puzzle-pieces, the man's squinty gaze frozen on the smoking ruin of their shattered blockade.

So this is it: reality warfare revisited, fifteen-plus years later, he ponders as the pulse at his temples pounds a frenzied solo. *The life-and-death real deal, up close and personalized, only this time with a twist. Not just my ass on the line this time.*

The broken door sails inward with a vicious jerk at the insistence of a square-toed cowboy boot with a snake design running its smooth, suede length from heel to calf.

Wouldn't you just know it? Shit-kicker heaven, the man muses, lunging forth with a booming roar as the bat uncoils in a blackened blur.

The fat end of the mini-slugger finds knee cap with a resounding pop, though it is more of a glancing blow than Barrow would've preferred, the required torque lost due to his own awkward positioning. With a pained shriek, the attacker backs from the ruin of the door, split neatly in two at the center and attached by a single strip and warped into a V-shape from its ravaged bottom to the equally misshapen top.

"Get behind me...*NOW!*" Barrow bellows, gripping the door's gaping outer edge and pushing inward and in doing so, essentially pulling the tattered remains apart like papier mâché before dashing through the narrow opening with the bat repositioned for a fresh strike.

Bull-rushing forward in a slight crouch, he is immediately transfixed, initially by the condition of the room itself as a heavy mix of snow and ice floats and dances about as if blown airborne by an industrial fan, making the eighteen by twenty-four square foot space resemble a freshly shaken snow globe.

Secondly, and surely the more prevalent of the twin discoveries, is briefly dismissed as some type of stress-induced hallucination, that is until said mirage refuses to mutate or shape-shift to a more logical, acceptable conclusion. The attacker's identity, previously cloaked beneath a full-face, green and gold Green Bay Packers ski-mask, is revealed in all its scar-infested, squinty-eyed glory. The cold truth of the mask's peeling-away exposes a fact every bit as frigid as the wintry mix levitating around its pale, pasty features.

Having dragged himself to a far corner, the attacker holds a lamp table as an impromptu shield while struggling to both re-cock and re-aim the shotgun—a pump-action Winchester, Barrow can only guess without closer inspection—the injured knee pulled in close to his body while the opposite leg splayed outward as if to trip anyone attempting to rush past to the lone exit/entrance, the door itself as fatally vandalized as the bathroom gateway.

Temporarily frozen in mid-lunge from blatant disbelief, Barrow snaps to only upon feeling a rush of air at his back as Dana Fowler and her young charge rush past.

Head tucked, he somersaults forward within the relatively narrow space provided between an overturned mattress and the room's lone furniture representative, that being a worn desk/mirror combo, doing so as more a distraction for their benefit than his own. Rising from the crouch with his forward momentum driving him directly at the attacker, he realizes the six-to-seven-foot space separating them won't allow for reaching the shooter in time to prevent a close-range firing. That in mind, he takes brief aim at the shooter's upper body and head and flings the mini-slugger without breaking stride, dashing for the exit while less than three steps behind Dana and the girl, the former toting the latter piggy-back style. Beyond the shattered door, the landscape is illuminated solely by a single streetlight where the parking lot divides towards the office on one side and the lone existing eatery, a swirling soup of icy winter tears giving it the appearance of a TV screen gone fuzzy and static-filled.

The blast seems to shake the entire room with seismic power, its echo reverberating like a series of explosions, each a bit duller than the last, like a string of lit dynamite tossed down a bottomless mineshaft. Barrow winces at its inception, instinctively shielding his head and face with upraised palms, only to peek through splayed fingers while sprinting even with and then past the open entrance to witness the extensive damage incurred elsewhere.

The hotel door, having previously endured similar mutilation at its center, is missing a sizeable chunk—oblong in shape with blackened, jagged edges—in the space between its knob and top edge. Just beyond that, as the heels of Barrow's boots depart carpet for ice-slickened concrete, his arms briefly pin-wheeling for balance, Dana Fowler lays chest-down in a sparse area of matted, snow-coated grass, a pulpy mass of seeping crimson carnage all that remains of her face from forehead to chin. Dropping to his knees beside the still slightly trembling corpse, Barrow stares first directly into and then past the headlights bearing down on his position, as oblivious to their intrusive presence as the blaring sirens accompanying their arrival. Instead, his eyes dart wildly, squinting through both the sudden illumination and an ever-thickening wall of descending flakes, each threatening to cancel out the other as near total blindness seems a viable threat. It isn't until he spots the girl on the far side of the parking lot, sliding on all fours behind a four-door SUV and appearing no worse for wear, that he becomes acutely aware of two distinct sounds: the first that of a male voice whispering something mostly incomprehensible and repeating the same refrain over and over again; the second the unmistakable racking of the pump-action, although this too is delivered as a dull echo, as if executed behind a closed door. Barrow, still on his knees and wholly unaware of the frigid numbness quickly overtaking his lower extremities, turns to see the attacker posed just inside the room sporting an impossibly wide Joker's grin that is nauseatingly familiar from a previous life. The attacker—teeth impossibly straight and matching the falling snow in level of whiteness—is responding to the mystery male voice, but in a barely audible mumble that Barrow soon realizes isn't due to the pair's restrictive volume level but his own shotgun-discharge-at-close-range deafness.

"Drop it, asshole or I drop you!" the mystery voice, thick with the local drawl, bellows from Barrow's immediate left, a shadowy outline of its source gradually coming into focus.

"If that's my only two choices, you'll understand if I balk on either," the attacker replies, lunatic grin unwavering, a visible tic making it appear that his left eye is executing a continuous half-wink.

"You've got exactly five seconds, mister!" the other counters sternly, stepping free of the headlight's glare, the silver badge on his otherwise dark blue uniform shirt gleaming like a glowing strobe in the otherwise grayish gloom, "Lay the weapon on the ground in front of your feet, kick it forward and drop to your knees!"

The deputy is painfully young, no more than twenty-two or three, tops, Barrow surmises with a building dread, figuring the kid's level of experience in such dire scenarios is more than likely limited to whatever video game he's currently attempting to master. To his credit, Officer Peach-fuzz—as Barrow instantly labels him—displays a steady aim, the tar-black handgun curled into his gloved left hand holding remarkably steady.

Teeth gritting and muscles retracting with a gradual resolution, Barrow knows better than most that no matter the level of expertise the officer has reached at *Grand Theft Auto*, brave voice and posturing currently on display notwithstanding, he was more than likely on the verge of yellowing his drawers.

Crouched between the two armed figures, Barrow inhales a twin lung-full of air so frigid he feels a paralyzing numbness coat his entire torso and tenses, his thighs like coiled springs. Physical readiness aside, there is a major decision yet to be made, as in, which direction to take upon *uncoiling*. The options are basically two: Go for the shooter or for cover. Leave the heavy lifting to the man whose salary he pays to do so or go full death-wish daredevil and mediate the stand-off via a bull-rush directly towards the source of all the carnage.

As he calmly contemplates, arms folded with both hands tucked into the snug warmth of his jean-jacket's armpits, bushy brown coif turned solid white from a steady snowfall that shows no signs of easing up, Barrow's decision is all but made as the two additional actors making up the drama continue to banter back and forth with no sign of actual resolution.

"Time's up, man," Officer Peach-fuzz barks, squinting through the sites of his Glock nine-millimeter, the bill of his baseball cap—dark brown with '*Pine Bluff SO*' stitched in ivory thread not quite as bleached as the rapidly falling precipitation—inexplicably twisted to the back of his head and thus woefully ineffective against the descending elements.

"Backup is on the way. Face it, you've got nowhere to go from here. End of the road. Just...drop the weapon and let's end this peacefully."

Alternating glances from the deputy to Barrow and back again, the attacker replies with all the concern and urgency of a weary traveler placing a food order at a late-night drive-through.

"Deputy, I kindly extend the same offer. My argument is not with you or your...department."

During the short pause between words, the attacker peers slowly back over to Barrow with a slight nod.

"Mister, considering the casualties involved, it appears to me the grudge you're toting around is pretty damn widespread," Peach-fuzz shot back, flashing a faint grin drenched in sarcasm. Barrow, every nerve ending in his body lit, locked and loaded, couldn't help but admire the kid's moxie, if not his blatant recklessness in the verbal baiting of a certified lunatic. From the east of the hotel came the faint sound of multiple sirens, a potential fleet of emergency vehicles whose ETA had been severely delayed by the icy conditions.

"You hear that, Sunshine?" Peach-fuzz resumes while nudging a half-step forward, though executed so gradually and masked by the elements that the actual movement is practically unnoticeable. "They're not headed this way for the continental breakfast. One last time; lay...down...the...wea..."

Despite its shocking suddenness, Barrow used this latest blast like a track runner at the starting gate, this reaction so unlike his cringing, flinching reaction to first. The attacker had fired from his left side without benefit of lining up sites or precise aiming, something normally seen in movies in an attempt to look stylish, but in reality was rarely viewed as an effective choice for shooters desiring to actually strike a perspective target.

Sprinting forward, Barrow was able to determine with a single glance that the attacker's shooting prowess in utilizing such a sideshow exhibition was the exception to said rule. Deputy Peach-fuzz lay on his back, arms sprawled wide and shoulder length as if attempting to create a snow-angel, though a quickly spreading crimson stream gushing from beneath his prone form quickly shatters the illusion. Streaking past, Barrow takes note that the deputy has, for now at least, survived, his mouth agape and lips atremble while alternating unintelligible dialogue and gasping pants.

The attacker, obviously caught off guard by both Barrow's actions and feline-quickness, finds just enough time to swing around and re-aim the barrel but not to effectively re-rack the forestock before being clothes-lined across the chest and driven back-peddling through the open door's threshold.

The two men merge and meld upon contact, their combined weight landing atop and effectively pancaking a narrow wooden ottoman that had centered the room, the back of the attacker's heavily scarred scalp impaled by needle-thin shards that protrude like jagged protuberances.

"Y-y-you....t-t-took...m-my...li-life," the attacker stammers, jerking his bulk violently from side to side in an attempt to topple Barrow, who straddles his midsection as the two wrestle for control of the firearm.

"T-t-there...h-has...t-t-to be...j-jus...j-jus...tice."

Holding the stock and barrel-end with hands slick with sweat despite the glacial temps inside the room, Barrow feels his grip slipping gradually away as the attacker—his own steely grip cloaking the trigger, trigger guard and action bar, respectively—jerks, kicks and bucks with increased fervor.

The faint hope that he can simply hold the madman at bay until additional authorities arrive dissipating at breakneck speed as the plethora of sirens sound no closer than moments before, his eyes dart wildly about the room before landing on the mini-slugger laying within arms-reach to his right.

"Th-th-this...is...your...f-fate, Bah-B-Barrow...w-way past...d-due," the attacker rambles between labored huffs, a bubbling whitish froth coating the corners of his mouth. "...ju-just...accept...it."

Barrow eases his grip just enough to allow the attacker's constant pulling to swing him farther to the left, setting up the predictable, equally forceful jerk to the opposite side.

Waiting until the last possible second, he releases the shotgun and sails free, rolling over onto and then scooping up the bat in one fluid movement.

Poised on one knee, he springs forward while coiling the bat over his right shoulder just as the attacker struggles to rise while repositioning the firearm.

The attacker, having re-racked upon standing, manages to raise the barrel head-level just as the slugger descends, deflecting the brunt of the blow, the lone damage a badly crushed middle and forefinger of his left hand, the latter so severely fractured it hangs from a single tendon and narrow strip of flesh.

Standing no more than two feet apart, the pair square off like dueling swordsman, the attacker swinging the shotgun around like war-club only to see Barrow easily duck beneath its rising arc and, using both hands as if competitively jousting, shoves the bat tip forward into the man's nose and upper lip. A muffled crunch is the result, followed by a free-flowing of blackish-red DNA from each nostril and a severely split lip. Barrow follows this up with a front kick to the man's lower abdomen that lands, if not full-force, solidly enough to exorcise a resounding '*whoof*' as the attacker's lungs are sufficiently drained, a shower of crimson spittle erupting from pursed lips as he flails about in reverse, eventually tumbling back against a far wall and sinking slowly onto his backside.

Barrow, knocked slightly off-balance from the kick, barely avoids tripping over the same ottoman they'd crushed on their way in, and is forced to his knees to recoup even as the blare of multiple sirens grows noticeably louder beyond the open door. The constant influx of freely levitating wintry mix has noticeably weakened since their re-arrival, the gusting winds having died down considerably even as the snowfall grows heavier and increasingly dense, the parking lot and neighboring buildings—the hotel office and Pancake Palace more specifically—having disappeared behind a virtual ivory waterfall.

The attacker remains propped against the wall, head slightly bowed, eyes closed and breath coming in labored gasps while clutching the shotgun to his chest with the barrel-tip jammed against the thinly padded carpeting.

The chorus of sirens and multiple sources of same having finally departed the highway for the hotel parking lot are accompanied by a cluster of churning lights that team to penetrate the dimly lit room like some giant, combination strobe/spotlight. Temporarily mesmerized by the renewed snow-globe effect the sudden burst of illumination has on the rogue snowflakes still drifting about the cramped confines, Barrow inhales deeply and resets his grip on the bat before lumbering forward to land what he hopes will be a final, debilitating blow.

Less than three steps from the intended target, he freezes in mid-step, bat reared back over his right shoulder. The attacker's eyes widen, blood and froth-coated lips parting in a lunatic's grin, the shotgun subsequently flipped up and over with the military precision of a trained rifleman.

At that exact moment, Barrow feels something smack his left heel and hears the mystery object slide away in the same direction. A quick glance provides the answer and, considering the attacker's opossum routine, a surge of renewed hope. Tempting fate but unable to refrain, he risks craning his neck for a peek at the entrance, where Deputy Peach-fuzz's left hand lays just across the threshold, his prone form facedown and without a hint of movement and appearing every bit as lifeless as that of Dana Fowler's just a few feet to his right.

Eyes re-locked on the attacker's own, the latter's narrow squint and fading smile given proof that he'd also obviously caught a clear glimpse of the new arrival, Barrow hurls the bat and dives in and, considering an overall state of battered exhaustion of both body and mind, executes a singularly fluid series of movements.

The attacker, in the process of sliding up the wall and simultaneously swinging the shotgun barrel forward, is forced to drop back to one knee and duck to the right as the bat impacts mere inches above his left ear, a torrent of paint and plaster coating his scalp and forehead.

Remaining crouched, he re-aims just in time to stare down the barrel of a silver-slide nine-millimeter Glock, its possessor standing just inside the entrance and striking a classic shooter's pose—feet apart, knees slightly bent, arms fully extended—that could be showcased in any instruction manual.

"So, just to...be clear: this is...what you *really* want?" Barrow inquires through a tight squint, as if aiming at a faraway target instead of one he could practically reach out and poke with the barrel-tip. Panting slightly, his aim is steady and without a single visible tremor.

The attacker, bloody teeth—a few bent back at angles impossible except for the false type—bared and breath severely labored, winks playfully while centering his aim to Barrow's torso. Similar to the man he was about to duel, there is a rock-like calmness present in both his words and non-movement.

"For...as long as I can...remember, Ace. Seriously, it's all I've...thought a-about for so long that most everything else has been l-lost. I'd wager...you c-can't claim the same."

The Glock's sites squared firmly on the attacker's plaster-coated forehead, Barrow nods slowly up and down in lieu of a verbal reply.

"Yeah...thought so," the attacker concludes just as the blare of a nearby bullhorn fills the room as if from an interior set of wall speakers blasting at full volume.

"*Those in the room, this is the Arkansas State Police! Disarm yourselves and come out with your hands behind your head! Any weapon viewed upon your person will be taken as a viable threat and there will be immediate, possibly fatal consequences!*"

"Well, there you g-go, Ace. *Choices.* There what...life's about when it all comes d-down, right? You can simply toss the p-peashooter aside, turn around and...walk out for assistance. Or..." he pauses, tilting his head dramatically to the right, his left eye blinking solo in the form of a sudden muscle spasm *slash* tick, "...you can, before the authorities rush in and...make the decision for you, stand and face down your demons, or in this case, the plural version."

"Not a chance," Barrow replies, breathing now as steady as the frozen squint and matching aim. "Option one and I take one in the back. By my count, that leaves exactly one option but nil the way of choices."

"The demon it *is* then," the attacker beams, head straightened while the spastic tick kicked into overdrive, the blink so rapid it appeared the eye was trapped in a warp-speed episode of the deepest rim sleep.

"Those in the room, I repeat: This is the Arkansas State Police! You will disarm yourselves and depart the room with hands positioned behind your head! Any variation of these instructions will be viewed as a potential act of aggression!"

Trigger finger strained to the point of cramping, Barrow nonetheless discovers his building rage was only surpassed by a nagging curiosity, a deep-seated itch that would not go unscratched.

"But, why all the innocents, man? How do you justify that....*this* kind of ungodly slaughter?"

"Maddeningly cliché as it...might sound," the attacker responding without hesitation, the left side of his mouth now joining the tick parade, as if full-face paralysis was gradually mapping out its impending dominance, "collateral damage. Well, save your woman and...the child. One should never underestimate that whole mama-protects-her-cub-at-all-costs factor. At least you can gain some assurance in knowing your...legacy lives on, yes? Never did shit for me, I'm afraid, but I've always been somewhat of an exception in such...heart-related matters."

Those in the room, you've got one minute to surrender yourselves or we will be forced to remove you with extreme prejudice. I repeat...extreme prejudice. Sixty seconds, starting...now!

Speaking through gnashed teeth, Barrow's grip shakes, albeit so subtly to be practically invisible to the human eye, from a fresh wave of anger.

"Hate to burst that bile-filled bubble, but that...the woman wasn't my...*mine*...and neither was...*is* the kid. Just more collateral damage, I guess, yeah?"

The attacker shakes his head emphatically—spraying a fine crimson mist in every direction—though remarkably no other part of his body so much as shimmies.

"You lie...*badly*, I might add. No man would risk his own neck the way you did coming out of that bathro..."

"THEY WERE TOTAL STRANGERS, ASSHOLE!"

In the scream's aftermath—and a tidal wave of regret for so willingly taking the bait—Barrow shifts the Glock's aim first back to the center of the attacker's forehead and then approximately eight inches lower and slightly to the left.

"So you say, Deron, but the fury on display is curiously...elevated."

"What am I supposed to do, genius?" Barrow sneers, "Congratulate you on a murder-spree well done? Damn son, you are one hopelessly cracked egg."

"I...suppose not."

The attacker sighs heavily, the tick at his eye momentarily slowing before resuming at full-bore, the shotgun's barrel temporarily dropping several inches before being levitated back upward.

"Regardless, even this late in the game I have to confess a sense of...emptiness. A...hollowness. Wasn't supposed to..." the attacker pauses, a slight hitch in his tone upon resuming. "I just expected, I don't know, something *more*. A sense of...fulfillment, of some dogged, ancient task finally...completed, its banishment miraculously medicating the ills of the past.

"Alas, a lifetime ruined cannot be avenged by inducing similar misery. The man I once was, decades ago, would've known this and avoided all this...unnecessary drama and...inhuman debauchery. Believe it or not, I was a...good man once, though in fairness," he hesitates yet again, a thick, clear discharge spewing from his tick-ravaged eye and trailing down his scar-infested jawline, "the line between fiction and reality concerning this...mystery being has grown increasingly hazy over the years, but what little I recall is a gentle-enough chap, that is unless duty necessitated otherwise."

His trigger finger on the verge of cramping, Barrow grunts angrily.

"Was that supposed to serve as some kinda half-assed apology?"

"Indeed," the attacker replies just as the first of three smoking metal cylinders rolls into the room, smacking a far wall and ricocheting into the center of the room, its journey halted directly between them, "But make no mistake, Barrow, said amends, however moot, were not directed towards you, but *myself.* The bill *you've* neglected to pay is so woefully overdue..." his left shoulder visibly tenses, "...the considerable interest of which, I'm afraid, can be satisfied only with the surrendering of your very soul."

The second and third cylinders bounce and slide into the room, respectively, the air within now a heady mix of flowing flakes and billowing smoke; a whitish haze rising, flowing and drifting like staged vapors from a concert venue.

"And you've...appointed yourself...the collector?" Barrow rasps, his eyes beginning to water at the corners, his throat tightening on the cusp of a coughing jag. He is, of course, procrastinating on purpose, to avoid the fatal conclusion the attacker obviously seeks. With the authorities now out of patience and chomping on their heels, he figures another thirty seconds or so might just turn the trick.

"Who better, Deron? Is there...someone more justified? I think...not," the attacker replies flatly between wet coughs, his lone non-afflicted eye pulled wide even as the other seems to have permanently sealed, "Sooooo tell me honestly...S-Sergeant Claymore, think a...star on the...H-Hollyweird W-Walk of...F-Fame is *still* in y-your future?"

When the attacker's arms visibly tense, Barrow in turn raises the Glock's barrel to its original position with the grave realization that the promise of those extra thirty ticks isn't likely to come to fruition.

"Never g-gave two s-shits...actually," he retorts grimly, his right forefinger finally giving way to the constant pressure.

"*Liar,*" the attacker manages to snarl just as the confined space is rocked by twin blasts ignited, at least if heard from a distance, with synchronized perfection, though in truth there had been a split-second's separation.

Barrow had, upon enduring the Glock's considerable recoil, instinctively ducked to the right. Covering no more than six or seven inches, this reflex born purely of shock and fear had essentially saved his life, as the pump-action's cargo had sailed into the empty space where his head had occupied.

As for the unofficial winner of the impromptu fast draw, the one-hundred-fifteen grain, full-metal-jacket bullet so explosively discharged was now lodged deep within the aged walnut wall previously utilized as the attacker's lean-to. This only after entering the latter's forehead approximately a half-inch over his right eye—a dime-sized hole the result—and exiting the back of his skull, painting the former in a grayish-crimson smear that slides down the original light-green sheen like watery clunks of oatmeal.

The attacker, his right eye frozen agape and staring accusingly, lays on his left side, assorted fingers on each hand periodically twitching as they rest atop the still-smoking shotgun. A wide pool of blood flows out from his ravaged skull even as thinner streams escape each nostril and the sealed left eye.

Having fallen to one knee, head slightly titled and left brow cocked, Barrow stares down the corpse as if expecting a renewed rapport to ensue. The Glock hangs loosely in his right hand, its barrel also smoldering in the aftermath.

Sir! Drop the weapon! A gruff voice instructs from what sounds like some distant locale, though as far as Barrow knows the source could be standing a mere foot away, the confusion tied to a second bout with artillery-fueled hearing loss.

Drop it now!

His movements lethargic, Barrow obeys, the Glock falling free from splayed fingers and bouncing onto the snow-and-ice-coated carpet. Almost immediately after, he is forced to his knees, wrists clasped and connecting arms whipped tightly around to the small of his back, where cuffs are forcefully and snugly applied with that extra level of vigor usually associated with an overabundance of pent-up adrenaline. Shoved forward, the left side of his face is planted onto the snow-coated, thinly padded carpet.

Assorted voices spew forth from all different directions at varying levels of audibility, from harsh whispers to bellowing foghorns as blackened boots—all layered or at least spattered with a clinging wintry mix—stomp nearby, some coming to within mere inches of making contact with his stoutly-pinned noggin.

He is eventually hauled to his feet, his legs wobbly and unsteady, his bound wrists and hands utterly without feeling. Led outside, where blizzard conditions have subsided to light flurries, he is walked past Dana Fowler, the ruin of her face mercifully cloaked in an ivory mask provided so mercifully by Mother Nature. He is then jammed roughly into the back seat of a waiting cruiser, where he leans back, sighs heavily and drops his chin until it nearly touches his upper chest.

Within minutes, aided by the car radio's constant chatter and a well-tuned heating system cranked to its highest setting, Barrow drifts into a heavy slumber interrupted only by a series of disjointed dreams, the most vivid of which involves a winding, strangely familiar alleyway drenched in shadow, muffled voices in various states of duress and the faint scent of well-aged kimchi.

~ * ~

Video Interview with Deron Joseph Barrow

(Opening scene features news video outside the Droopy Eye hotel; a dozen or more vehicles, several with blue lights actively flashing, are parked in a semi-circle facing the hotel room—door agape—as various officers of federal, state and local jurisdictions enter and exit at a frenzied pace).

"Days later, I was told by investigators that Brookens had been trailing me for days and must've been convinced that Dana and the girl were my wife and child and that I'd kept their existence a secret for security's sake. Following the Kunsan incident, he'd been shipped back to the states, given an immediate medical discharge and, from what I'd heard, spent the next decade-plus in custody at various mental health facilities (*Insert still photo of Brookens from a patient ID card from an unnamed facility in Ohio, the institution's title blurred*).

"Then again, I was going through some reconditioning of my own at this same time, so I wasn't really keeping tabs. Now, there hadn't been a single day that I didn't think of Brookens or how his lunatic actions had altered my life, but that many years later, the memories had at least faded from the forefront. Needless to say, that night in Pine Bluff brought it all back in full techno-color. Shit of it was, I had no idea the shooter was Brookens until he cornered us in that bathroom. Up until the minute I rushed 'im with the mini-bat. I'd chalked it up as just another random mass-murderer who'd taken advantage of the crappy weather conditions to corner a dozen or more easy targets in some isolated location with little or no chance of immediate law enforcement intervention.

"Gotta say, he hadn't aged that much considering. Obviously had went under the knife numerous times to sew up and/or repair the many facial and head traumas, and no telling how many dental procedures to replace the missing choppers. As for personality, he was still mad as a hatter, and physically as strong as an ox on 'roids, having definitely trained hard and long for what he perceived as our 'rematch.'

"Goes without saying the years of psychological treatment hadn't taken. I mean, the man had a clear unobstructed shot at me, and chose instead...targeted Dana instead (*Insert still photo of a smiling Dana Fowler, Caucasian female age twenty-six, courtesy of her family, followed by a slightly-bleary video image of a covered body lying on a stretcher being loaded into a coroner's vehicle, obviously taken from hotel the night of the shootings*). Fairly certain he was trying for both her and the kid with that one shot or was even hoping for a quick re-rack. If he'd gone a different route, he had me, point blank. I was a good four feet away when that barrel ignited. The question of why I can't say for sure. I *can* safely speculate this was part of a some long-planned, calculated plan to make me suffer greatly before putting me out of my misery once his appetite for revenge was effectively sated.

"He'd no doubt trailed me to that diner, though how exactly he arrived there is a mystery to this day. No POV, um, personally owned vehicle, was found on the hotel grounds or anywhere near it. No commercial bus-lines, Trailways, Greyhound or similar bus lines were running that night due to icy roads. There was no paper trail found to show he'd booked a room, hotel, motel, boarding house, anywhere near that location. Other than the clothes on his back and accompanying arsenal, no other personal possessions were ever uncovered. His wallet contained a driver's license long-since expired, a few faded pictures of his ex-wife and little else. No credit or debit cards, no receipts, nada. Cobwebs. Nada. Talk about living off the grid. It was like he'd *teleported* outside the entrance of that diner, armed to the teeth and loaded for bear. Well, more like loaded for *Barrow*.

"At some point, Dana had tucked Misty under one arm and sprinted out onto the ice. I recall trailing 'em across the parking lot towards the hotel and falling on my ass more than once. The pavement was layered in fresh snow with probably a half-inch of ice hidden beneath. Not exactly prime traction for someone running for their lives. The hotel being L-shaped with the restaurant centering the compound, the three of us zig-zagged around the few parked cars leading to the last row of rooms on the bottom of the L. Took me but a single solid kick to its middle to access unit thirty-seven. Luckily I didn't bust the lock, as it secured behind us, for whatever good that did.

"I cannot now, or ever could, wrap my head around Brookens' actions that night. He could've easily waited until I exited the diner's front entrance and blown me away. Me, myself and I, no collateral damage necessary. Maybe it was the bitter cold that drove him inside, but once there, why not just saunter on up to his intended target, aim and fire? It wasn't as if I'd been expecting it. On the contrary, I'd been forking up a heaping helping of bacon and eggs when the fireworks started, not dropping my fork until the room shook from that first booming detonation.

"I was later told the headcount inside was twelve, counting the three diner employees. Just how random Brookens had been is up to debate, but damned if there was any logic in it.

"Terry Kinsley (*Insert still photo of Terry Kinsley, African-American male, age thirty-eight, courtesy of his widow*) had his chest blown apart while flipping sausages in the open kitchen, at least ten feet to my west. Misty Winslow's Uncle Jack (*Insert still photo of Jack Winslow, Caucasian male, age twenty-eight, courtesy of his brother*), fatally shot in the back while playing human Kevlar vest for his niece. Her twelve-year old sister Tammy (*insert photo of Misty and Tammy, each displaying a cheesy grin with older sister applying 'bunny ears' to the back of her young sibling's head*) endured a single shot to the chest, killing her instantly.

"A semi-retired trucker from Idaho named Carlton Hansen (*Insert still photo of Carlton Hansen, Caucasian male, age sixty-one, courtesy of his widow*), grandfather of four, his left arm blown completely off at the shoulder, and who subsequently bled out for the unforgivable crime of stopping in for a hot cup of Joe after pulling his rig off icy roads to protect other drivers (*Insert brief video snippets of three separate stretchers, the body's occupying their space covered from head to toe, being loaded into separate ambulances*). Last but not least, Deputy Paul Holliman, spine shattered and forced into a wheelchair at an age when most were just hitting their physical prime.

"Personally, I'd hoped they'd find a journal, a diary, some type of recorded log to explain his actions, other than the obvious revenge factor. In the months following, the Arkansas Bureau of Investigation had assured me that no such manifesto was ever uncovered. Not at his apartment, nor the auto parts warehouse where he'd been employed for the previous year and a half. A check of the trio of facilities he'd called home after the Kunsan incident bore similar negative results. Insane perhaps, but Len Brookens was not a stupid man nor one prone to impulse. I have no doubt his plans for me were as organized and meticulously mapped out as any master field general or cat-burglar. He just kept it all up here (*taps forehead with forefinger of right hand*).

"Other than a few deep bruises and a sprained left shoulder, I escaped that night all but unscathed. They were planning on transporting me to the county SO's office, but since the roads were all but unpassable, decided to conduct interviews in one of the empty hotel rooms. Room forty-eight, to be exact, at the very rear of the hotel on what I came to think of as the grounds' *'dark side,'* as in *'of the moon' (Insert brief video footage of the closed hotel room door, clearly marked 'four eight,' the walkway leading to its threshold recently shoveled as foot-high drifts of snow sit on either side).*

"As I recall, a pair of the bureau's finest conducted the interview while the county sheriff and a trio of his deputies manned the door. Lasted maybe ten minutes tops, as Deputy Holliman *(Insert still photo of a smiling Paul Holliman, dressed in county Sheriff's Department uniform)* had already filled in most of the blanks despite having a large portion of his spine shattered. I couldn't believe the man retained consciousness long enough to do so, but then, he'd already beat the odds all to hell and back by finding the strength to crawl and claw his way towards that room entrance and toss me the Glock. I spent the night in a different room, courtesy of the management, and was allowed to depart the premises the next day once the roads cleared up enough to allow it. I'd barely got home and had just put on a pot of coffee when the phone started ringing off the hook.

"The press conference *(Insert muted video footage featuring four adults and one juvenile seated at a conference table, microphones in place, with a standing crowd of reporters fronting their position; a TV monitor occupies a space on the right side of the table)* was held at State Police HQ eleven days later, with a video monitor hookup for Deputy Holliman so he could participate from his hospital bed in Little Rock. Talk about tough as a twenty-penny nail, that young man had undergone not one, not two but three surgeries in between and still managed to be not just coherent during the interview, but almost chipper, especially considering the diagnosis of total paralysis below the waist he'd been handed. *'Grateful to be alive,'* Paul kept repeating, and there was little doubt he wasn't just spouting dialogue to please the masses. The man was practically glowing.

"Little Misty Winslow was there, seated between her parents, who seemed to be playing protective sentinels despite all the security on hand, at least one of 'em with an arm around her at all times. Considering they'd lost a child, I'd rate their toughness right on par with Mister

Holliman, and though they didn't seem nearly as unaffected as Paul, I think it was more a case of nerves and all the cameras. As the interview wore on, they seemed to relax. They made it a point to mention not only their deceased daughter, but the father's brother Jack at every opportunity. Much like Dana, Jack Winslow hadn't yet seen his thirtieth birthday. Misty seemed mostly distracted by all the fuss, as most kids her age would, this despite losing her big sister, with whom she'd reportedly been very close. I'd always heard that kids adjust much easier than adults, mostly since they hadn't the maturity to process such madness. The good lord certainly knew his onions when it came to how to preset the human condition, from youth to teen to young adult to middle age and finally to elder.

"(*Sighs, briefly glancing away from the camera eye*) Shames me to say my attitude wasn't nearly as upbeat, despite coming out all but untouched and intact, at least physically. I just...wasn't able to separate both outcomes, Kunsan and Pine Bluff, as being twin tragedies tied as much to me as Brookens, maybe *more so* yours truly. I'd never forgotten Harry Bachman and my role in his murder and I sure as hell never forgot his killer, but at least I'd stopped dreaming he was trailing me, sometimes curled under my bed or coiled in my closet. Far from it on both counts, but at least the years had softened the memory of the first and faded the nightmares tied to the second.

"That night in Pine Bluff (*pauses, leans back, briefly bows head*) ...rushing out of that bathroom and seeing that face again, that scarred, aged but instantly *recognizable* damn face, I had a moment, just a blink mind you, but a split-second doubting my own sanity, that somehow a toxic mix of fear and adrenaline had helped replace the real killer's face with Brookens'. It wasn't until he took that first shot that I knew I wasn't scrapping with a hallucination, that his features weren't going to magically reform into someone different, someone...random. His voice was noticeably raspy but all the familiar mannerisms were there, except magnified times ten. The full set of ivory white teeth, ghoulishly oversized and far too straight, and assorted scars aside, this was no doppelganger or stress-related hallucination, alterations be damned.

Identification nailed, it didn't take a rocket scientist to figure out he'd been off his assigned meds for a spell.

"As for the press conference, as awkward as it began, my apprehension had dropped a few notches once the question-and-answer sessions kicked in. That is until that pencil-necked geek from KTHV went all liberal weenie on me, no doubt hoping for his fifteen minutes *(Insert still photo of Ronald J. Miller, former KTHV reporter, currently on staff as investigative reporter at WXYZ in Detroit)*. I won't do him the favor of saying his name, since he'd surely use it as some sort of PR campaign. I understand he's moved on to one of Detroit's stations and specializes in uncovering local government corruption, but also heard he'd been passed on at numerous other Midwestern stations after leaving Little Rock. Now granted, the panel-style Q&A had been chockfull of softball queries up until that time *(Insert video/audio segment showcasing Deron Barrow fielding a question from an unidentified female reporter):*

Reporter: "Deron, how does it feel to be sitting next to the little girl you saved?"

D. Barrow *(Leaning forward with elbows on the table, glances over at Misty):* "Well, for starters, let's give the credit where it's due: Dana Fowler did all the heavy lifting. *Literally,* as in carrying Misty on her back and toting her out. Secondly, without the superhuman efforts of Deputy Holliman, I'd have been just one more victim. As it stands, my role was more as a…distraction. Even then, I fell short or that brave young woman would be up here with us right now."

I'm told the news agencies present had discussed the agenda and agreed to focus on the families and how they were coping and that my presence was more as a crutch for Misty, her parents and the Fowler family. It wasn't about establishing me as either hero, saint or goat. My past connections with Brookens were said to be off-limits until a later date when I alone would stand before the same media reps and give 'em the full scoop from my perspective. In fact, at the time, the case was still active and under investigation, so mum was the word until further notice.

I'd even heard a few of Brookens' next-of-kin had yet to be contacted. So, that in mind, things were surprisingly tranquil—I'd actually felt myself starting to relax—that is until Mister *'watch me stir up some shit in the name of investigative journalism'* decided to go all 'Current Affair.' Make no mistake, it wasn't just about ratings. That asshole was all about making his rep as *Chief Scoop, the Reporter Without Fear.* As it was, he was about this close (*lifts right hand, the forefinger and thumb held approximately a half-inch apart*) to needing some emergency dental work (*Insert video/audio clip of Ronald J. Miller/D. Barrow question/answer segment*):

R. Miller: "So do you feel a sense of responsibility for Brookens' actions?"

D. Barrow (*Leans back, arms crossed*): "Say again?"

R. Miller: "Brookens was targeting you, I understand."

D. Barrow: "Yeah, that's been established, but I really don't think this is the time or place to discuss the man's motives, Mister um..."

R. Miller: "Ronald J. Miller, KTHV. Mister Barrow, it's also been well established that the incident in South Korea involved Len Brookens purchasing illegal pharmaceuticals from yourself and developing a personality-altering addiction to these drugs, leading to the shooting death of your part..."

D. Barrow (*Casually displaying a hand, palms-out):* "Not the place, Miller. Next question."

R. Miller: "Don't you agree that the family of Harry Bachman deserve spots at this table?"

D. Barrow (*Shakes head, briefly lowers it, glances upward):* "This is not about South Korea. Next...question."

R. Miller: "Miles and years aside, there is no denying the two incidents are historically linked."

D. Barrow: "Mister Miller (*clears throat),* such obvious grandstanding is shameful. Does someone *else* have a question?"

R. Miller: "Tell us, Barrow, Does it bother you in the least that you are now the lone adult survivor of two such tragic shootings?" *(Scattered boos, inaudible chatter ensues)*

D. Barrow *(Grins menacingly, points finger directly at Miller)*: "You're a piece of shit, pal. A steaming pile of excrement with a media pass."

R. Miller: "Unlike so many of my esteemed colleagues, I cannot sugarcoat this as simply as hero versus villain: white hat versus black. The history is too bolded; the players not so easily drawn into their respective roles. It appears that playing a hero on television doesn't always equate to real life, does it, Barrow? How about a little recap on your service record?" *(More boos, chattering protest)*

(Misty Winslow's father can be seen rising from his chair and yelling (mostly inaudible) in Miller's direction, even walking in a noticeably aggressive gait from behind the table towards the reporter before being restrained by a uniformed man, presumably security)

It took 'em several clicks to calm the crowd and escort that mouthy blowhard from the premises. Sure, the personal attack surprised me, not so much the content but the timing, but what really pissed me off was seeing Misty Winslow and her mother tearing up and her dad nearly blowing a gasket. Poor guy suffered from hypertension and I was afraid he was gonna seize up right there. Once the dust settled and the slow-pitch questions resumed, a reporter from my old stomping grounds at KHLT caught me completely off-guard with a simple enough inquiry that twisted me in more knots than any Eagle Scout could hope to untangle.

"Deron, do you feel that your actions in Pine Bluff provide adequate redemption for the incident in Korea?"

In response, I wasn't just tongue-tied; I felt temporarily tongue-less. After a much longer pause than anyone could've anticipated, during which time you could've literally heard a feather drop, I mumbled and stuttered before managing to piece together a four-word answer that, in retrospect, made little sense but at least allowed the press to resume.

"Only time will tell," I'd mumbled, which, if dwelled upon, was pretty damn nonsensical. Redemption. Now there's a tricky little word. Break out the old thesaurus and can mean *recovery, refurbishment*, but in this case the definition being chased down was more along the lines of *salvation* or *deliverance*. In the years since, this question has resurfaced numerous times and I could never, nor can I now, provide a definite answer. I can say the very existence of Ace Claymore was a shot at salvation from the tragedy of Harry Bachman's death. Then again, if not for his untimely demise and the events surrounding it, there never would've been a Pine Bluff shooting, thus the succeeding need for salvation no longer necessary. I'd say it's one of those rare enigmas wound tightly inside a mystery. To this day, by its very own definition, true redemption eludes me, and maybe that's the way things ought to be.

"Anyhow, a week to the day later came that other press conference, wherein I was pelted with the same fastballs, curves and change-ups, only with not nearly the level of malice. Hey, I was fair game, no question. Brookens had been gunning for me for nearly two decades and somewhere along the line decided that taking out a slew of innocents would ensure my downfall even if I did manage to survive. Dig it...guilt by association. No denials, I'd been his dealer back in the day, driven by the same greed as all such sellers of illegal or restricted substances. No different than the bootleggers of old or crack and meth distributers of today. In this case, my buyer was a man with barely restrained violent tendencies shoved over the edge by an addictive personality. Hey, my ignorance of his mental state is no excuse (*raises hands as if to surrender*), but no man could ever suspect such...dire consequences could result. I've lost, literally, years of sleep over my role in both incidents. There is no magic pill or words to cure such an affliction. No amount of counseling or man-made chemical, be it in pill, liquid or labeled bottle form.

"Finding the character of Ace Claymore was a gift I didn't necessarily deserve, but I did my best to make a small measure of amends to all servicemen both past and present with my characterization, and yeah, it was a shameless attempt at self-exorcism for the shit I'd done and the damage I'd caused. I didn't have a hell of a lot to be proud of for my own time in uniform, so I tried to ensure Ace was my polar opposite.

"Ace had a deep love for his country and those he served alongside with.

"Ace didn't shirk regulations or shatter military law for his own gain.

"Ace didn't do politics as a rule but had a single rule he lived by: screw with the flag and what it represents and you were his sworn enemy. Plain and simple. He understood there was a price to pay, a fight to be fought and won.

"Ace was a born warrior; a raw-boned, steely-eyed fighter draped proudly in red, white and blue. Ace took no short cuts, no easy outs. The sergeant with the buzz-cut, buffed physique, scarred mug and skull tattoos was everything Senior-Airman Deron Barrow had *not* been. I made sure nothing of myself could be spotted by the camera eye. In the end, I wasn't playing recruiter like many critics claimed. If I'd had a set agenda, it would've been to represent both surviving veterans of foreign wars and the families of those who didn't come back. Those handshakes at Pearl Harbor, man (*pauses, bows head, rubs eyes*), the greatest generation this country will *ever* know, those who earned my everlasting respect, made all the playacting worthwhile. Strange, but as a young airman, being the self-centered little bastard I'd been, I never gave 'em a second thought. Standing there conversing with them, I felt such a wave of...shame. I damn near fell to a knee and broke down. In the end, campy and scene-chewing as I'd come across at times, I think I aspired, however impossible a task, to represent them all; not just the WWII or Vietnam vets I'd come across, but all the men and woman I'd served alongside and embarrassed by my jackass behavior. In a nutshell, the Blue Falcon aspires to become the bald eagle.

"An admission here that I was going to omit but find I just can't. Three or four months after the Pine Bluff shootings, I began receiving monthly payments from an anonymous source, delivered to my door via Fed Ex and without a return address. These payments were always in cash and mailed out in plain brown envelopes. The denominations and amount never differed: fifty-dollar bills totaling three thousand dollars. I had my suspicions as to the donor. Didn't exactly take an astrophysicist.

"It was no secret the Winslow family had bucks to spare, and no doubt figured I was far too proud to ever accept a monetary reward for helping their little girl to escape that hotel room. Very astute, if so. Within a few months, I was able to use a USPS contact of mine to track the mystery packages and confirm what I'd already known. It was no shock to discover they'd been similarly grateful, and generous, towards Dana Fowler's surviving family, even helping secure a college scholarship for Dana's little sister.

"As for my...allowance, I found creative uses, most of which involved assorted charities, both local and international. There was a ballfield at the local middle school the windfall helped secure, not to mention park equipment and a library-annex. Not saying I didn't occasionally cash in a portion for personal use, but that usually involved sporadic medical bills or the occasional truck or house repair. I've since met with Misty, an upstanding young woman with the brightest of futures, and confessed to her my knowledge of her parent's generosity. Whatever little part I played in ensuring that sweet girl's survival, the only reward I'd ever needed was to see, up close, what a fine person she'd grown to be. That was a special day...a special feeling. The *only* thing, the single factor that could've made it even better, was if Dana Fowler could've joined that reunion. Without a doubt, one of the grittiest, toughest, bravest souls I've *ever* met. Gotta toss in Paul Holliman into that very select group. I'd heard the man's fiancée ended up leaving him soon after the shooting. Talk about a double body-block. I honestly cannot claim to have ever been mentally strong enough to survive that level of trauma.

"As for Dana, it makes me wish I'd known her more than a scant half-hour or figured out a way so all three of us could've walked out of that room alive. As for Paul, I know I should've stayed in touch but, well, I just couldn't...face the man *(sighs)*. Couldn't face the man that saved my hide. How *pathetic* is that? I did send him a regular allowance, but in truth that was mostly pulled from the cash Misty's family sent me, so it was more like her gift than mine. If you think about it, it was fitting really. If Brookens had gotten past me and out of that room, more than likely Misty perishes as well. Paul tossing me his hardware saved us both. I think that's what made my skin crawl more than anything when the word 'hero' was tossed my way during interviews, when it was clearly Paul who truly deserved such accolades. Guess it made a better 'story' if a former TV celebrity, even one of very limited popularity, was handed that title. The way of the world, sad to say.

(Long pause; folds arms, sighs heavily)

"Len Brookens did not act alone *(shrugs)*. He had an accomplice, unwilling or not. I know this, better than any media leech, kind-hearted sympathizer or would-be biographer. I *live* with it, have lived with it...every...single...day.

"In the years since Korea, I've sincerely tried to better myself; to consciously wear the white hat, even as the dark angel sitting on the opposite shoulder advised otherwise. Didn't always work—ask the two women I've married in the interim and the hellacious mood-swings they were forced to endure—but it wasn't from lack of effort.

"There are still days I wear the guilt like a permanent shroud; a sewn-on second skin that flat refuses to peel. Fortunately, such days are few and far between, much like the snow and ice that coated Pine Bluff that night *(laughs)*. You know, a buddy of mine that lives there told me they hadn't had a storm like that since. Fifteen years of nothing but light flakes and the occasional sleet, but not enough of either to turn the interstate into a hockey rink.

"Funny, but I was never much for religion until a few weeks after Pine Bluff. Well, I'm sure I did some serious praying after Korea and the rough ride directly afterward, but that was less faith and more about selfishness. These days, it's a lifestyle. If the big guy upstairs decides my dues are paid, so be it. If not, I'll happily stand in line for additional penance to be doled out 'til that particular don is settled up. I would like to think the good sergeant would do the same" *(smiles, flashes a thumb's up)*.

Ten

Alternate Ending
(From the private journal of Deron Joseph Barrow)

"So, what'd you think? Nothing *too* deep now, just your gut feeling."

"First off, why didn't someone hold up a sign that read 'long story *shorter, please'*? Geez, but if you only keep half of all that chatter, it's gonna be more mini-series than movie! Weirdly though, despite fighting off tongue-cramps, it was, well, seemed like I only covered roughly a third of the story."

It was mere minutes since the sneak-peek's conclusion, and I was having some serious mixed feelings. On one hand, I thought my delivery and dialogue had come off naturally enough. On the other, the whole thing felt so...clipped and severely condensed, despite the bloated running time. It was like attempting to explain the finer plot points of a six-hundred-page novel in a two-sentence blurb.

"Natural to feel that way," Dee-dee replied with a sympathetic nod, her chin propped atop a balled fist. We'd viewed the replay on a seventeen-inch monitor sitting atop the set's antique desktop; myself, Dee and Paul, with Dixon conspicuously absent following his setting up the equipment. While Dee had stood to my right as I'd occupied the desk's accompanying set chair—fittingly high-back and creaky—Paul had rolled up to park a few feet to my right.

"I mean, having lived such a traumatic event, I would think everything seemed to move in virtual slow-motion," she concluded, having pulled up a folding chair and inexplicably shot Paul a worrisome glance I could only attribute to a growing concern over the man's present condition. Paul, stroking his beard nervously, was literally sweating bullets despite the relatively cool interior temps.

"I guess that's true. Didn't seem that way at the time. How about you, Paul?"

The man winced as if goosed before regaining a semblance of self-control, the incessant wringing of his chin whiskers slowing just a tad.

"Um, I…can't say for sure. It's always been kinda hazy, except for a few crystal-clear moments that I, well, *wish* were equally blurry," he said in a hoarse, croaking tone, as if my query had shaken him awake from a deep slumber.

"Yeah, I'm with you there, partner. If there were some magic pill to erase shitty memories, I'd be the first to crash the line."

"You'd have to go through me first," he responded behind a weak smile, avoiding my eyes as his hands finally departed the shaggy wave of facial growth to snap down forcefully on each wheelchair handle, the words themselves spat with a noticeable edge of bitterness.

"Personally, I prefer that last segment over all others, including Korea. Something about you shedding the Claymore persona made it seem, well, more personal and sincere. You hit just the right notes. Of course, we'll have to edit it all down to fit the allotted time."

As sweet and accommodating as she was—Diandra Chang seemed utterly incapable of being either insincere or uncooperative—there was something about that last statement that rubbed me the wrong way. How could I have possibly been more *sincere* in either instance? The shit wasn't fictional.

Clapping her hands enthusiastically, Dee-dee the chipper cheerleader all but levitated from her flimsy throne and began pacing behind the desk as if experiencing expresso overload.

"Fine and dandy as caramel candy," she exclaimed cheerily, executing a sweeping gesture with her left hand in the general direction of the same tent opening her partner kept disappearing behind. "Deron, how about a quick tour of the hidden realm?"

"You mean..." I nodded towards the same opening, "...there really is something behind curtain number one? I just figured whoever you rented that tent from accidentally shipped you the Big-Top Circus model."

Her smile, as radiant as usual, lit up that warehouse like a giant, rotating disco strobe.

"Oh, if it were only that simple. Let's just say the truth behind those flapping walls didn't exactly thrill those instrumental in the funding of this project." She paused, twisting around to address Paul, "Deputy Holliman, feel like a second look?"

Waving her off, it suddenly occurred to me how the man had seemingly aged a decade in the half-hour since we'd reviewed my interview. Looking haggard and weary, he wheeled weakly away as Dee-dee clutched my arm and led me away from the set.

Ducking beneath the hanging tarp, we shuffled into total darkness, the air noticeably muggier. Dee-dee shook my grip with a low giggle and I was left to grope alone, that is until a faint clicking noise and the place exploded like a blazing nova.

"Oh, well, *damn,*" I managed once my eyes began to adjust, though faking such enthusiasm is far beyond my limited acting abilities, "This is...unexpected."

"Is it that close to the real thing?" Dee-dee asked, standing to the overturned couch with hands parked sassily atop hips. Her head was tilted slightly, her intrusive, wide-eyed stare making me feel strangely uncomfortable; a first in her pixie-like presence.

"A veritable twin, if memory serves. At the moment, I'd really prefer Alzheimer's."

"Budget-wise, it was fairly economical, believe it or not. Furniture was purchased mostly online and cheap as dirt and the carpenters and painters were hired not from sparkling reviews or word of mouth but solely due to fees of the bargain-basement variety. Still, I do think it came off quite swimmingly considering they only had only grainy, black and white police report pics to go by."

I almost laughed aloud despite a slow churning at my gut. *Did she just say swimmingly?*

From the cheaply painted, sporadically stained walls to the even cheaper Kmart paintings adorning each as well as the aforementioned couch—same color and design—and similarly upturned, sufficiently damaged ottoman, it was a mirror image pulled straight from my deepest, darkest sweat-mares. It was room thirty-seven reborn, even down to that faded, nasty-ass carpet. Probably just an overactive imagination, but I swore it even held the same rank scent of old rat urine and mothballs.

"Can't knock the reenactment skills," I mumbled, shrugging while straining not to sound as mentally off-balance and physically shaken as I felt but still having not taken a single step past the tent's inner flap. "But as far as vibes go, I could've gone the rest of my days without reliving this."

"The plan was a reenactment involving both you and Paul," she prattled on, either oblivious to my very apparent discomfort or, completely out-of-character as it might seem, uncaring. "But, figuring you both might have reservations, in the end we decided video shots of the actual room, both pre- and post-incident, would suffice. Wasn't easy laying our mitts on the latter, I'll tell ya. Pine Bluff PD treated us more like lepers with each subsequent request."

I finally forced my right foot forward and then the left begrudgingly followed. My nostrils flared at the stink I might only have been imagining.

"Well, to be fair, no department likes to be reminded of their darkest days, especially the smaller ones with little to counter with other than the infamy of a mass-murder. Small-town folks are notoriously introverted, and I'd wager that the majority of Pine Bluff's finest feel a similar twinge of disgust as myself at the mere memory of Len Brookens."

"Wow. Until this very moment, I had nary an inkling that Deron Barrow, muscled warrior from another era, could possibly be carrying a single drop of Drama Queen DNA," she countered a bit too sassily, her back to me as she peered out the faux front door into the dimly-lit eastern side of the empty warehouse, "As for Pine Bluff, I would think such a podunk community would be happy to have such a happening...*any* happening, to be remembered by."

With that, I felt my face grow flush with a building ire that, if not soon extinguished, might soon conjure a side of me, significantly darker and prone to profane-filled tirades, that the young woman had yet to visualize. Nor would she want to, or...*would* she?

"Well then, lucky me, I've always had Kunsan to fall back on, right?"

Displaying the grace of a trained ballerina, she spun around on a single heel. Tight-lipped and squinty-eyed, Dee-dee Chang had transformed into full Dragon-Lady mode, seemingly itching for conflict. And here I'd been worried about revealing *my* dark side. Jenny's 'c'mon, let's spar' face had nothing on her, and that's no small feat.

"I take it you'd rather we omit the use of the word 'luck' in further discussions?"

"Little lady," I shot back, arms crossed and suddenly stoked for a little verbal sparring, "Might I define the word sarcasm? As for *this* cheesy shit," I hesitated, arms now wind-milling wildly to all points simultaneously, "what moronic prick figured it would be just peachy to film Paul and I reliving every move of that *very* special night when he permanently lost the ability to walk and I nearly lost my fucking mind?"

"If it's an apology you desire, I'm afraid I'm unable to comply. I'm...we're filmmakers. We make conscious decisions on what might or might not appeal to the core audience of our films."

The level of gall was stretching to picking-at-the-edges-of-the-ozone layer heights, as was my blood pressure. The honeymoon was definitely over. Apparently, as with all the women in my life, it was just a matter of time.

"Apology? From a couple of wet-behind-the-flaps millennials? I couldn't give a damn *less*. Just chaps my ass at the lack of common sense, not especially from Mister Uppity moviemaker back there, but from his partner, who, up until now, I had considered surprisingly wise for her age."

She sauntered past, tight-lipped and stiff of gait, not responding until she'd already vanished beneath the tarp.

"Let's move on, Deron. There are still several post-production issues to cover before we let you go."

Let me go? Sounds as if I'd been handed a pink-slip, Holly-weird style. Inhaling deeply, I allowed myself a few tranquil moments of meditation before following her lead. At the same time, I decided to take the high road upon resuming conversation. After all, I was the much older and presumably wiser—least my own words come back to haunt me—of those present.

She and Paul sat facing the set, where Dixon hunched over, silently fiddling with the equipment.

The sergeant's set chair had already been positioned between the two, with Dee-dee on the right and Paul's chair on the left.

As I gently rolled the chair back, Dee-dee dynamited any tentative plans for a peace treaty with a single sentence, spoken in the same stern, stilted tone as our earlier clash.

"If you thought that retro set in bad taste, brace yourself, soldier. Ron?"

"Almost there. You got this?" Dixon replied, still bowed over and turning knobs, something different about his tone, though hard to define.

"Sure. For now," she countered, staring straight ahead, unblinking and as cold as the symbolic sliver of ice gradually making it up my spine.

"I'll take care of the other then. Shout out if you need me, before, that is, before it's totally necessary."

It hit me as he made a b-line for the tarp and ducked beneath it, that he never bothered to turn around. His usually robotic monotone had held a tint of emotion, a nervous twinge that spoke to a building apprehension. The excitement of the project being on the verge of completion? Maybe. I had my doubts.

"More surprises I take it?" I said amiable enough, to which Dee-dee simply nodded and pointed a tiny remote she'd been palming straight out and engaging its inner tracking system.

"Miss Chang, is it really necessary I sit through this again? I was thinking of calling a cab and heading on back ho..."

Paul sounded bone-tired, and unless I misjudged his overall deportment, ready to be relocated to basically anywhere but where he presently sat.

"Just sit tight, Paul. We discussed this already. I *need* you here," she interrupted sternly as the monitor lightened. Stern and shockingly condescending. I was beginning to wonder if I'd somehow been transported to some bizarre alternate universe. Regardless, as snowy static cleared to a rear view of a not-yet-recognizable interviewee, it was as if I'd chugged a triple-espresso with a Red Bull chaser, all signs of weariness and fatigue from my own interview having flown the coup and replaced by a triple-helping of intrigue.

~ * ~

Video Interview with Paul Holliman

(Duration: 10:16. Forwarded to the 4:23 mark)
"I repeated, um, ordered the suspect, ugh, Brook...Brookens to drop his weapon. I'd never been forced to fire on a suspect or ever unholster and aim my firearm at one, for that matter. Not sure if I showed it in my actions or in the grain of my voice, but I've...I'd never been so scared, before or since. My plan, well, what I *wanted* was to provide a stall, a diversion until backup arrived and hope that increased firepower would convince him there was no winning, no way out except suicide by cop. Guess, well, I *know* I'd overestimated my lack of intimidation skills while underestimating the workings of the psychotic mind. Eight weeks' worth of scenarios at the academy wasn't quite the same as staring down the barrel of the real thing. Kinda knew I was in neck-deep upon staring into those shot-glass eyes. Brookens wasn't just riding the backroads to Nutsville, he'd long since arrived and been elected Mayor.

"Never felt the shot that put me on my back. I was standing in a shooter's stance, both boots set tight as I'd already dug 'em clean through the snow and ice clear through to the pavement. Next thing I knew, I was sprawled flat with snowflakes and ice specks blurring my vision while packing both nostrils and the inside of my opened mouth.

"I'd played some football in high school, and it was like I'd taken a humdinger of a clothesline tackle across the chest that had laid me out but good. There was a weird numbing sensation at my rib cage and I had to fight not to black out between blinking the wintry buildup out of my eyes. I remember wondering why I wasn't able to get up or at least turn over onto my side, like a gravitational pull had me bound to that damn pavement. I heard voices—the volume going up and down like a radio station not quite in range—but wasn't able to comprehend more than a scattered word every so often.

"I think I did black out a few times, but time was fractured. It was during one of these drifting-between spells that Deron was leaning over me, his face directly over mine one second and gone the next. I must've come too late to whatever he was telling me, as the only actual dialogue I remember was something to the effect of '...*gotta finish this now*' and '...*worry, deputy. It's the least I do for you.*' From there, I must've drifted again, as I woke to find myself on my stomach just outside the open door's threshold. By this time, the pain was still dull but growing increasingly aggressive, but I was able to lift my head by performing a mini-sit-up.

"What I saw, though it was kind of like peering through a fishing net for the majority of the maybe thirty seconds the vision held 'til my head was forced back down by yet another fainting spell, was Deron...standing over Brookens, who was on his back with the arm I could visualize spread wide with the hand pinned underneath Deron's boot. I can...could only speculate the other hand was similarly trapped on the opposite side. Brookens was...whispering something I couldn't make out, blood leaking from his nose and lips, and...smiling like a loon all the while. That much I...cannot, won't *ever* forget. Mess that his face was, he would just break into this lunatic grin whenever there was a pause in his sermon. I don't recall Deron speaking back until the very end, when he...raised my Glock and fired. My sight darkened about the same time

Brookens' head whipped back onto that carpet. Might've been my imagination, but I swear the man was beaming like a Cheshire cat 'til the very end.

"I awoke in the back of ambulance with the sirens blaring and two techies seated on either side.

"It would be three days and just as many surgeries before I was able to field questions, first from my department rep, then the state and finally the federal boys, and I was finding it damn strange that all the above were tossing around the word 'hero' and continuously patting me on the back. The diagnosis was handed out on day three by the head surgeon with my girlfriend, mother and sister in attendance. Not exactly an easy verdict to believe, much less accept. I was gonna walk again, by god. Hell, I'd show 'em. I'd someday run in the next department sponsored ten K. Yep, the infamous 'denial' stage swallowed my soul hook, line and sinker. Lasted all of a week to ten days. In between, I either wasn't able or willing to discuss the shooting with anyone, though to be honest details were fuzzy at best until months later, when I'd started counseling with a state-sponsored shrink. By then, Deron's take on the incident was all but set in stone and, well, who was I to shun my newly found hero status? Life was shitty enough, right? The whole 'tossed me his gun and saved our asses' thing was all I had left to hang onto, sanity-wise, to the point where I think I started believing it myself.

"The press conferences and TV appearances started to dry up soon enough, but I have to admit to thoroughly enjoying star-status back in the ol' hometown. I was Pine Bluff's golden boy and that suited me just fine, well, as long as I didn't dwell on pesky details like truth and accuracy. You see, it wasn't just my body that was paralyzed. My conscience was equally lifeless.

"As far as legalities, I wasn't able to completely corroborate Deron's take but surprise! No one cared. Brookens had been a confirmed mad dog that needed putting down and I'd aided in that particular euthanization, so little details like truth didn't matter.

"As a former law enforcement officer, admittedly of short duration, I can't sit here in good faith and agree with Deron Barrow's method of extermination. That's officially. *Unofficially*, and considering the two men's past relations and the mass slaughter of innocents that incurred that night, he did society a favor. Fifteen-plus years after the fact (*lowers head briefly*) and with my health gone to hell recently, I felt it vital to shed the false hero label I've hauled around like a stinking second skin. The random pats on the back from those in the hometown were bad enough—year upon year of false praise, a large portion of it as insincere as a politician's promise—but then a few months back, on the anniversary of the shooting came the compound fracture of the camel's hump, psychologically speaking.

"The mayor himself showed up on my front door to ask me to be the guest of honor at what they were calling '*A celebration of survival and perseverance*' at the city hall. Ironic as hell—fitting as well, as I see it—that ya'll came calling just a few weeks later. While I politely turned down the city's offer, I saw this as a chance to clear the air about what really went down, at least from my limited perspective.

"I want to make this clear (*raises a hand, exposed palm directly at camera*) that this isn't about discrediting or dishonoring Barrow or his actions. The man was fighting for his life as well as others. He saw a big picture that was solidly cloaked from the rest of us. He did what he thought he had to do. I can't say I'd have done the same. I have no basis within the scenario those two shared.

"All I know for sure is this; Deron Barrow was probably the only man on earth with the stones to do what he did, while also being the only one with the right to do so."

~ * ~

"You're shitting me, right? Tell me this is just some lowball, ill-conceived gag gone horribly wrong," Deron inquired softly, staring blankly at the monitor, the image having transformed to white static a half-minute earlier. His entire body hung slack and slightly slumped, as if slowly awakening from a prolonged slumber or heavily medicated state. In the surrounding silence—all-engulfing save a low whirring hum from the disc player—he pondered yet again the validity of an alternate universe—specifically one where up was down, down was up and reality was suddenly, hopelessly skewed.

"Paul's recording concluded no more than a half-hour before yours began," Dee-dee replied flatly, her slim arms folded defiantly as she turned slowly towards him. "Packs one hell of a punch, wouldn't you say? Like rock-hard knuckles to an unbraced gut, yeah?"

The smile she displayed, so gradually executed to be compared to a gradually uncoiling reptile, briefly held Barrow's squint-eyed glare in a hypnotic vice.

"Just hang onto that regulation stache, sarge," she continued, eyes practically ablaze. "You ain't heard nothing yet."

"Mi-Miss Chang?"

At the sound of Paul Holliman's weary, trembling voice, the temporary spell shattered, Barrow turned towards the source. If naturally pallid, the man's features were now ghost-like to the point of translucent, his Adam's apple bouncing wildly as he raised a shaky hand as if requesting permission to continue.

"Not now, Paul," Dee-dee scolded, waving him off while rising from the chair and walking casually over to power-down the monitor. "Allow me at least a *few* fleeting moments of pleasure to witness the squirming discomfort, the comedic look of befuddlement on display from our treasured guest and star of the show."

His chair rolled back with a series of resounding creaks before Barrow hopped free of its confining space, standing stiffly upon release as his stage throne spun recklessly away.

"Enough. Sincerely, what was *that* horseshit?"

Swinging around to face him, Diandra's eyes bounced from one man to another, finally landing on Paul and nodding stiffly as if to cue him for a response.

As an additional prompt, Barrow stepped between the two with hands atop hips and, jowls reddening and teeth gritted, stared down at the wheelchair-bound man like a gunfighter sizing up his opponent for a noonday duel.

"Paul? This is a gag, right? Oh, I get it. You recorded *that* and then reshot with the version we both know as truth, yeah?"

After briefing lowering his head and running a hand through a severely tangled coif, Paul Holliman could be heard inhaling deeply before his chin eventually lifted—blinking madly as if staring into a bright light—his tone weirdly mechanical and void of genuine emotion.

"I j-just couldn't lie anymore, Deron. All these years. So many...sleepless nights. A man can survive so many things, so many losses both mentally and physically that he...or she can push or lock away and refused to revisit but living such a falsehood for...for gain or notoriety has its own symptoms that gnaw and grind at the mind 'til the only salvation; the only way to reverse the condition is through confession. I...apologize for the timing. I really, *really* do, but to properly cleanse myself, I needed the widest format possible. When Miss Chang and Mister Dixon came along and asked me to participate, it was almost like a, well, a sign that this was my *last* best chance. I...truly hope you understand. Like I said," he paused, gesturing with a disjointed wave towards the lifeless monitor, "I have not and *will* not ever alter my...opinion that what you did was right, morally and spiritually. Brookens deserved to die that night. You did what any right-thinking person would've given the situation and, well, your history with him. But...it was time, past time, to explain what I really *remember* seeing, and it wasn't what I've been told I saw for the last fifteen years."

Jaw muscles working furiously, Barrow alternated hard, squinty glances between Paul and Dee-dee, finally executing a full-body slump and cackling aloud while side-stepping away with an explosive series of loud handclaps.

"Oh-kay then," he bellowed, facing a far wall and dropping to one knee as if to pray, "No punchline forthcoming then."

"No, Deron," Paul answered weakly but again with little resembling sincerity.

Shifting gracefully while remaining crouched, Barrow focused solely on Paul as Dee-dee leaned casually against the desk's squared edge, fingering her iPhone with shocking disinterest.

"So now that we've established this segment as completely spoof-free, I have a, *no*, I have several questions, Paul, if you don't mind. Well, actually, even if you *do*."

"Miss Chang? Could I...be excused from the premises please? I'm really not feeling too well," Holliman blurted nervously, bloodshot eyes darting wildly as if searching for the quickest escape route.

Dee-dee stared him down like annoyed adult to troublesome child.

"Hold your ground, Paul. We had this discussion before Deron's arrival, remember? We knew this wouldn't be easy. Facing the truth after so many years of spouting the same lie so often..." the cold glare averted towards Deron, "...that even the source starts to think of it as truth."

"Yeah, well, there's a liar here all right," Barrow said calmly, standing with hands now propped lazily atop hips; his deportment as a whole switching gears rapidly from anger-fueled pacer to thoroughly fatigued weakling.

"Or maybe, just maybe Paul deserves the benefit of a doubt I seem immune to. Maybe what he remembers from that night has been gradually altered as time passed, whether by dreams or some sort of psychosis or," he paused to raise a forefinger airborne, "a form of brainwashing."

Pushing away from the desk, Dee-dee practically darted forward to center the space between the two men. Sneakers planted wide, arms spread wide and eyes ablaze, she appeared to be prepping for her own personal sermon-on-the-mount. As the dialogue began, she pointed perfectly manicured fingernails pointed at both subjects simultaneously as if to keep each at bay.

"He *insists*, Deron, that this revelation is not a recent development. He insists he's been withholding the truth for fifteen years due to fear of rocking the boat on what the public, not to mention law enforcement, desperately wanted to hear. The details of Len Brookens' death needed to be self-defense related for all concerned. Crazy bad man dies in to-the-death duel with brave, stalwart old advisory, the headlines must read. Brookens lying helpless and unarmed while taking that fatal bullet would never do."

"There are police and medical examiner reports, not just text but crime-scene photos that disprove even the slightest possibility that the kill-shot happened the way he's describing."

Barrow's delivery, so-matter-of-fact and confident, appeared to strike a target dead-center, whether or not that had been its purpose or not, as Paul Holliman wheeled slowly in reverse, his ultra-pasty features now gleaming in a fresh layer of sweat.

"He's...I re-really need to...go now if...I can just c-call a cab," he babbled, blinkingly rapidly while focusing solely on Dee-dee, whose bizarre, accusatory stance remained stiffly intact.

"Police reports can be altered to fit whatever agenda is desired," she said coldly. "This we know, as can crime scenes."

Barrow paced forward, mouth agape, elbows bent, hands out and palms up, his brow so severely creased and his facial features so badly distorted he appeared some abstract painting showcasing a man at the breaking point of absolute anguish.

"What the hell is this exactly? So now *I'm* a murderer?"

"Mercy killing is more like it," Paul answered timidly, wincing almost immediately upon enunciating the last word and no doubt feeling Dee-dee Chang's searing glare. "L-Listen Deron, I don't...think anyone is gonna cast doubts on your decision to put that mad bastard out of his misery. I certainly don't."

"You tossed me that Glock, Paul," Barrow spat through gnashed teeth, fists clenched tightly at his sides. "Rolled over and crawled to the edge of that open door on nothing more than an unhuman grit and determination. Arm-strength propelled, dragging mostly dead weight and in what had to be extreme pain, you saved our collective bacons. Why sell yourself short at this juncture in your life? What *possible* purpose does it serve to belittle your own heroism while simultaneously transforming me to villain and Brookens to helpless victim?"

Gripping the chair's rims, the fingers of each hand possessing a purplish tint, Paul's mouth opened and closed several times as if to reply, the lower lip noticeably trembling. The mask of befuddlement he wore was stereotypical of the 'deer in the headlights' look of one without a clue how to proceed in the face of insurmountable odds. Obviously deflated, his head descended just as Dee-dee effortlessly stepped in as his verbal proxy.

"Repressed memories are often the hardest to pull from the depths of a traumatized mind. He went with your version of the story for obvious reasons at the time."

"My *story* is backed by the overwhelming forensic evidence found at that crime scene," Barrow railed. "According to this updated adaptation, I plugged a prone Brookens and then by supernatural teleportation, relocated the blood spatter from the back of his skull from the carpeted floor onto the wall behind 'im. Not only that, I altered the trajectory of the kill-shot from a downward angle to almost perfectly straight. Guess I used a pinkie finger, yeah? And then there's the little matter of the slug that damn near nicked my ear on its way to kissing the west wall. Now, being that I had all of about five ticks after the shooting before being cuffed and forced to smooch carpet, explain how I found the time to plug Brookens, magically relocate his spatter, and then scoop up the shotgun, fire a shot into the wall, wipe off my prints and place it back near his body. Sorry, but neither Sergeant Claymore nor his alter-ego was ever issued the superpower to freeze *or* alter time."

Seemingly unfazed, Dee-dee's tone remained stoically indifferent.

"Once again, police records can and have been altered to suit whatever agen..."

"*HORSE...SHIT!*"

In the aftermath of the combination shriek/growl, Barrow took a step back and took in a trio of deep breaths, each ensuing exhale released a bit slower than the last.

"I was there, lady, up close and personal, remember? And so was *he...*" he nodded towards Paul Holliman, now staring into the slightly-cracked concrete flooring with a look of utter detachment, "...now, I can't honestly say if, given the chance, I wouldn't have put a round in Brookens whether or not he was armed or not, but, being that he most certainly was, I've never had a reason to go all hypothetical. It was either me...or him. He fired...I fired. He missed. I did not. Roll credits."

Commencing a slow, deliberate pace within a space covering no more than ten feet, Barrow had, miraculously, shelved the volcanic anger of moments before and if anything resembled a middle-aged yet well-toned for his age professor concluding a lecture of only mild importance. "Please correct me if I'm off-base here, but if this is about creating some...false narrative to juice up the proceedings, you've stooped to a level I sure as hell never thought possible from folks I've trusted since the get-go to tell this story the right, and *only* way it could be told. "

"Deron, this...Paul's revelation was as big a shock to us as yourself," Dee-dee injected somewhat callously despite the attempted amiability of her words. "Still, we cannot, in good faith, omit such a dramatic reveal. I understand it changes the narrative somewhat, but in reality does nothing to alter such a predetermined outcome. Bottom line is that the project's core audience are past viewers and avid fans of what you accomplished as Claymore. The true-crime elements are for those mostly unfamiliar with both the sergeant and the man behind the character."

Barrow's casual pace halted in mid-step, wrists crossed at his lower back remaining in place even as he regarded the young filmmaker with a comically-creased mug that screamed befuddlement.

"Changes the narrative *somewhat?* It's more accurate to assume that the reveal in question will plant a seed of doubt in every viewer, fanboy or casual viewer, the doubt being that perhaps good ol' Ace got away with nothing short of an execution-style killing."

In light of Diandra Chang's blank-stared non-response, Barrow spun on a heel towards Holliman, who had, unconsciously or not, wheeled another dozen feet closer to the warehouse's nearest exit.

"Talk to me, Paul," he pleaded, hands extended palms up, head slightly tilted. "The truth I know is what we lived through, what we survived, and what you said on the video isn't even close, man."

Holliman held Barrow's glare for a full minute, jaw set tight and only occasionally loosening a degree before re-clenching, before twisting the chair in Dee-dee's direction and rolling full-bore until the space between them was an arms-reach away. Stopping so suddenly it briefly appeared he might tip forward from the seat, his words dripped with pent-up emotional overload, a heady mix of pity, shame and barely restrained rage.

"I'm d-done here, Miss Chang. You read me? No…more. I…did my bit, okay? They'll be no more takes. DONE!"

With that, he spun around and wheeled back towards the exit, only to be cut off by the lunging figure of Barrow, who effectively blocked his path with legs splayed and arms held straight out.

"Just hang on a second there, deputy."

Gaze effectively averted from the human barricade, Holliman's tone returned to its earlier state of guarded stoicism.

"Outta my way, Deron. I…got nothing more to say on this subject…ever."

"Did my bit? Did…my bit? You know, Paul, one might assume in utilizing this particular term, you were hinting at some choreographed set of lines, as in *acting* a part, playing a role. Gotta say, for the life of me I cannot drudge up another logical use that fits."

"I need to call a cab, Deron. Give me some space, please."

"Now that I think back, there were parts of that interview that appeared…heavily edited. Heavily cut, as if you'd…misread a cue-card or misremembered a line."

"Damn it, let me by!" he roared but with little actual fire, as if all remaining embers had been sufficiently doused. "I…need to get home to my…m-my meds."

Stepping forward, Barrow placed a hand gently atop the seated man's left shoulder, which instantly trembled beneath his touch.

"Paul, you saved my hide fifteen years ago. I can never, *ever* properly repay you. Truth is, I've never been able to properly accept that fact. I…hoped…hope the money helped.

"Brother, I have no right to ask for anything more from you. I might not understand why you're doing this, but whatever the reason, I'm sure it's justified in your mind, otherwise you would've considered it."

"Barrow...D-Deron...you wouldn't...you c-can't begin to..." Holliman stuttered, eyes brimming with tears, "...this isn't...personal, o-okay? Not personal."

"If you say so," Barrow replied softly before back-peddling gingerly away and first pulling and then holding the exit door ajar.

"Take care, Paul."

Dee-dee bellowed between cupped hands, and, as if the gesture itself wasn't enough of a testament to sarcastic spite, her smarmy tone most certainly was.

"So very disappointed that you refuse to stick around, Paul, but we'll talk soon, okaaaay?"

The chair had rolled forward a scant few inches before halting several feet from the potential liberation of the exit and outer handicap ramp.

A sigh, labored and pained; a chin briefly lowered to a borderline-emasculated breastbone. The turn was so gradual at its inception to be executed in virtual slow motion, the eventual three-sixty taking what seemed like several minutes to complete.

"So then, you gonna tell him now, or shall I?" Paul inquired sourly, formerly pasty complexion glowing a rosy red at the cheekbones and forehead.

Alternating glowers between his producer—her flippant expression unchanged—and the man most responsible for his continued existence, Barrow intervened once it was obvious a reply to Holliman's curious query was not forthcoming.

"Looks like that ball just rolled onto your side of the court, deputy."

"Miss Chang, you should know that breaking promises is small potatoes for me these days," Paul said through lips pursed so tightly he resembled a stage ventriloquist of old, sans the wooden dummy atop his lap. "When I said I was done here, more than a small portion had nothing to do with that damn interview. I told you, *both* of you, not to invite him here. I could've...*might've* made it if we'd just taped and I'd left before he arrived. Tiny consolation that it is, there is gratification in knowing I'm not a total douchebag. Mostly sure, but not completely soulless."

Though speaking indirectly to Paul, Barrow regarded Dee-dee with a cocked brow.

"So it wasn't a shaky or repressed memory behind that dog-shit rendition but an outright lie? Well, so much for that *recent* revelation caught on camera, right Dee?"

Shrugging nonchalantly, Dee-dee strolled back to the set and collapsed into the Claymore-reserved chair with a heavy groan.

"Fine then. *Great* even. Lengthy bouts of deception just aren't my bag. The goal was to get this thing in the can with a set DVR release and hopefully a fifty-or-seventy-five spot in cinema showings, then just set back and let the press and social-media detectives come to us. Heady stuff I know, but hey, a gal can dream, right? At the very least, following weeks and weeks of banter, we'd finally settled on a title. One I'm sure is self-explanatory to such a decorated vet: *The Blue Falcon*, courtesy of your old friend Conrad Boland."

"Ah hell, enough already," Barrow waved her off impatiently while approaching the set with Paul following gradually along the same path.

"Currently I'm wondering how it is I'm just now being introduced to a young woman I *thought* I knew at least somewhat but who is suddenly a total stranger in both manner and personality. That, and just how on God's green earth that stranger convinced a man like Paul Holliman to go full Judas."

"Smug, overbearing assholes of your stature rarely deserve honest explanations, Barrow," a somewhat familiar but also strangely alien voice rang out from behind the stage tarp.

"But as long as the bubble of dishonor has burst..." Ronald Dixon continued, emerging from hiding toting a cardboard box in folded arms and a backpack strapped between narrow shoulders. "...why not go full circle while we're all in attendance?"

"About time Mister Happy came out of hiding," Barrow said sourly, stopping a dozen feet short of the reimaged set-piece, the initial twinge of nostalgia he'd felt upon that initial viewing now replaced by a sickening sense of dizzying vertigo.

"Get to you in a minute, Sergeant Sham," Dixon replied curtly, slamming the box onto the ancient oak desk and whirling towards Paul Holliman with an accusing finger leading the way.

"I expected so much more of you, Holliman. I mean, I can...*we* can sympathize your plight; the razor-wire chains of emotion pulling you in opposite directions and all that shit, but I never truly thought you'd cave so easily. I guess the impotency of that interview session should've served as a big ol' red flag, what with the multiple takes and shitload of snips and tucks in the aftermath."

"It's called a change of heart, buddy-boy," Paul snapped back, jaw-jutted and head thrown back. "Something you'd know nothing about, apparently."

"Snappy *and* sassy, I'll give you credit. Hope that rediscovered chutzpah helps pay off all those overdue bills, since this unsuspected bout with conscience all but cancels out our agreement."

"Maybe not, boy, but at least I've regained sole ownership of my soul. One more false statement and I'm pretty damn sure my tongue would've snapped off its roller."

Their brief dialogue having evidently concluded, the two men discarded each other's presence, Dixon turning his back and rummaging through the box and Holliman wheeling cautiously towards a slack-jawed Deron Barrow. Diandra Chang, brushing silently between the two men, joined her partner at the desk, leaning in and whispering inaudibly into his left ear.

"I just couldn't go through with it, man," Paul offered, parked just to Barrow's right, head tilted upward. "Not with you here, staring me down. No way. Haven't slept a solid wink in two days. Can't eat or even down a glass of water without wanting to upchuck.

"Feels good to know I haven't yet reached rock bottom in the scum pond of humanity. It was close, but it appears my nostrils are still levitating just above the water line."

A dozen tension-filled seconds ticked by—Paul swallowing hard and his gaze darkening as if expecting the harshest of retorts—until Barrow peered over and down at the other man, his jaw muscles initially clenched tight but instantly loosening once their gazes locked.

"They...paid you to lie?"

"Affirmative, a tidy sum."

"All to slander a name already spattered with enough mud to paint a mural?"

"Afraid so. Tracked me down several months back and laid out the plan, as well as the proposed fee."

"The...plan. Well, don't I feel like a horse's exposed hind-end," Barrow half-whispered while briefly turning his attention back to his producers, still whispering back and forth as Dixon appeared to be readying the disc player for still another taped review.

"I'll get to their motivations soon enough, what I know of 'em at least."

Barrow again dropped shakily to one knee, perhaps to ensure he and Holliman conversed eye-to-eye.

"But what would...what amount of monetary gain could possibly turn you? Or was it something else? I might've missed a month here and there on your...the allowance, that is unless you changed mailing addres..."

"I got the money, Deron," Paul snarled. "Like clockwork. Appreciated it. Always."

"So, from this," Barrow pointed a finger in the general vicinity of the set, "I surmise a raise in allowance was in order."

Hands folded in his lap with fingers intertwined, Holliman shrugged.

"Since being sentenced to life in this damn chariot, I didn't turn to any of the usual suspects for my vice of choice. No booze, well, maybe a little booze, but no pain pill, meth or crack addiction. Can't say the same for gambling. Sports, online poker, you name it, I'll wager on it and lose...regularly. Cost me my wife a few years back. My home soon after. No excuses. I tried GA, but obviously true effort was lacking. Hey, your chosen sum wasn't the question as far as you and I go. Honestly, I'd have preferred some face time, not some fucking pity payoff. "

Obviously shamed, Barrow briefly averted his line of sight back to the producers, their stiff poses and animated gestures suggesting a building disagreement of some magnitude, although the conversation was still far too muted to comprehend.

"I'm sorry, Paul. I just...never knew what to say. Believe me, it wasn't snobbery on my part. It was the guilt, plain and simple. Brookens' victims were...are my victims."

"Never wanted your sympathy, Barrow. Just your friendship; that rare comradery of those who damn near die together within the same space but manage to breathe another day."

Barrow reached over, somewhat tentatively, and laid a bare palm over the top of the other man's folded hands and applied a gentle tap.

"It's never too late, bud, that is if you'll grant me the opportunity."

Holliman nodded, lips parting to respond when Ron Dixon's shrieking dialogue slashed the amiable mood like a descending axe blade.

"Well, isn't that just the sweetest thing? Over here, you two. *Now*, if you please."

Dee-dee and Dixon bookended a trio of chairs, a wide space set between the center seat and the far-left offering, obviously reserved for Paul.

"For the answers you desire," Dee-dee brayed directly at Barrow with a gracefully-executed *'welcome to the show'* sweeping gesture of her right arm, though her eyes held little of the stereotypical gleaming spark, "Two interviews, no waiting. Run time? Ten, maybe twelve minutes max. Questions and answers to follow."

Sharing perfectly synchronized sighs of frustration, the two men nodded in unison as if also telepathically communicating an unwritten agreement or secret pact.

Standing, Barrow then walked behind Paul Holliman's chair and gripped its navigational handles. As utterly betrayed as he felt—his slowly twisted gut and ringing ears just two of a multitude of symptoms—there was a legitimate fear that a burst of uncontrolled violence was forthcoming, especially considering Dixon's openly chiding comments. He didn't trust his own temper, nor the penchant for stupidity the younger man seemed to embrace.

"No thanks, Miss Chang. I'll pass, since I trust Paul's answers on why he was bribed to lie in order to make me the true villain of your 'honest biography.' You two can officially kiss my ass. Add *that* little nugget to your epilogue, with my full permission."

Steering the chair towards the exit, Barrow yelled over one shoulder even as, in the background, Ronald Dixon turned towards the cardboard box he'd retrieved from behind the set and began digging frantically with both hands.

"Oh, and don't even think about releasing that work of fiction without my say-so. I have several former contacts who've spent a lifetime practicing civil law, and I won't hesitate to sue your collective bloomers off."

The wheelchair abruptly ceased all forward movement upon a booming retort and subsequent spark ricocheting off stone flooring, the impact mere inches from the exit door.

"I won't ask again," Ron Dixon was heard to say, his words barely audible over the shrill, whimpering pleas of his fellow producer.

Eleven

Re-Shoot(s)

"Everyone settled in and comfy?"

Dixon stood with his back to the monitor, the long barrel of the blue-steel three-fifty-seven rotating with clockwork efficiency between Holliman and Barrow in precise two-second intervals.

"Ron, th-this is not what I, what we discussed as a-an option," Diandra Chang whispered hoarsely from the opposite end of the desk, her sneakered feet dancing about like a small child desperately in need of a potty break. "There was no talk of a...of using that...*thing* to threaten or intimidate. It's just the kind of Neanderthal behavior I thought we were fighting against."

The Magnum's sites now firmly set on Barrow's upper torso, Dixon scolded his partner without benefit of meeting her tear-streaked visage.

"Dee, your way was never going to work. Didn't I say so numerous times? The crime scene debunks even the slightest possibility things went down any other way than what Barrow says. Short of him confessing into the camera lens, his putrid legacy of bravery and sappy patriotism remains mostly unscathed, other than to that small minority that senses what a complete charlatan he is and always has been. Now, without further delay..."

"You can't just...*hold* them here. They have the right to lea..."

"Quiet, Diandra, *please*. Barrow needs to pocket that ego, perk up his ears and hopefully understand just what his reckless actions truly birthed all those years ago. Take my word, it's so much more than *you* even know."

Barrow and Holliman, parked side by side with Chang sitting to their left, exchanged a silent glance, the former executing a firm nod as if to communicate a cloak of confidence that was, in truth, as false as the documentary's proposed narrative.

"Ten minutes of their precious time isn't too much to ask. They can press charges in the aftermath, if so desired. Waste of time, since it'll basically come down to their word against ours. Hey, be great for publicity though," Dixon grinned devilishly, then suddenly hesitated—surprisingly steady aim still intact—to address his partner with an angry scowl that instantly aged him a decade-plus.

"Please press play, Diandra. I love ya like a sister, but all this teary-eyed sympathy is staring to grate my last nerve."

Standing with great pains, shoulders slumped and head slightly bowed, she strolled over and initiated the video player with a visibly shaking hand before retaking her seat with a worn and weary expression that screamed inner conflict.

Back-stepping to the desk's far corner, Dixon took a knee while striking a side-pose that allowed both a clear view of the monitor and his self-assigned charges.

"If I recall correctly, I'm up to plate first."

Hands tucked deep inside his pants pockets, Barrow leaned back with legs splayed and hands tucked casually behind his head.

"I'm braced," he spat indifferently, Paul Holliman's equally sardonic grunt the perfect bookend as the monitor flashed to light.

~ * ~

Video interview with Ronald Dixon

"Well, where to begin? How Deron Barrow and his television personality alter-ego have affected every aspect of my life starting around age four up 'til present day.

"As a young child, I hadn't a clue of course. I was just a bit player in the grand scheme, making short cameo appearances in the Oliver Twist role. Not exactly an orphan, at least technically, but damn close. My mother, Louise, had snagged the starring role upon my father's permanent exit from the set. *(Insert grainy color photo—Polaroid instamatic quality—of Ronald Dixon, age three, being held tightly by his mother while his father stands directly behind them with his hands resting atop the mother's shoulders)* She had little choice, you see. Unemployed, basically unskilled and left to raise me alone, she took center stage by default. Growing up in rural Indiana, I suffered little in comparison to my mother. Obviously, I lacked the maturity, but I must've also mastered the art of blocking out the pain of growing up in abstract poverty as the neighborhood bastard.

"Louise had inherited a sum from Dad's employer but past debts and a build-up of tardy monthly bills quickly ate the gist away—she and Dad had recently purchased a timeshare in Florida and a brand-spanking new Ford T-Bird to celebrate—and within a year or so it had dissipated altogether. Loved my mother to death but in retrospect neither she nor Dad were very good with money. She worked two, sometimes three jobs to support us, forced to forego such conveniences as dating, even though at the time of my Dad's passing she was still a very young woman in her late twenties. Not beautiful but not at all unattractive, though admittedly it is difficult for a son to gauge such things. Bless her overprotective heart, she did her best to shield her only son from the myriad of financial struggles. While I didn't dress in the latest trendy styles, at least my jeans weren't riddled with patches either. We rarely experienced the luxury of eating out, but occasionally she would afford me enough of an allowance to go to the local drive-in with my friends or to the local burger stand for eats *(Insert photo of teenage Ronald Dixon poised between two male friends of equal age, all smiling happily).*

"I remember she worked constantly, nights included when necessary, to keep the lights on, water running and gas stove lit. The neighborhood was low rent and rough, but I didn't know better since I'd been raised on its precarious grounds. Regardless of putting in a fourteen or sixteen hour day, Louise made me her lone focus, drilling me like a fire-spouting DI if my grades slipped even a single degree, and this was all the way through high school and into my early community college/pre film-school days. But you see, by the time I'd turned eighteen, this boy already had a set goal. Clear as crystal she was, and nothing was going to stop me from not only reaching that fictional brass ring but claiming it as my own. Ronald Dixon was going to make movies. Pen 'em, produce 'em and maybe even direct 'em. Biggest triple-threat since Spielberg, yes sir (*laughs, shrugs*). Well, that was the plan anyway.

"But I digress; it wasn't until a few days after I'd turned thirteen that my mother told me the truth about my father. I guess she figured I was finally old enough to handle the truth, first handing me a small envelope stuffed with old photos, most of which displayed Dad toting me around in various stages of toddler-hood, either sucking a pacifier or donning a diaper, and then regaling me with what Paul Harvey—my mom's favorite radio program back in the day—always referred to as 'the rest of the story.'

"As the photos went, I was most intrigued by those showcasing my father wearing the uniform of a soldier, either solid green fatigues and matching baseball cap or dress blues complete with a tie and shiny black shoes (*Insert photo of man standing stiffly—presumably at attention—in dress blue uniform, a US flag pictured in the background*). I was keyed in like any teenage boy would be in seeing their sire toting a firearm and looking all tough and Alpha-like, especially a kid without a single clear-cut memory of the person in question. Even though I was more of the bookworm, non-physical-contact type kid, just the thought of my old man being some old school warrior waging battle on some exotic foreign landscape birthed some serious chills, especially once Louise told me he'd served on an Air Force base in Korea. Damned if I wasn't ready to run out and purchase the first G.I. Joe doll (*laughs, clears throat*), oh, sorry, action figure, that I could find on sale.

"(*Sighs*) Well, all the chills and thrills dissipated once she revealed that he'd also perished on that faraway peninsula. By the time the story concluded, I was in tears, blubbering and sobbing and genuinely pissed off for possibly the first time in my young life without the incident being labeled a tantrum. This was adult-like anger: balled-up fists, gritted teeth, scalp-tingling and spouting every form of profanity I'd learned, all the while fighting off my mom's desperate attempts to console. I didn't know it at the time, of course, but my life's mission was set into motion that very day.

"The passing of time did nothing to steer me onto calmer waters. Neither did the many relationships I'd established that might've served as some life-changing diversion. Girlfriends came and went with no palpable effect, as did the many college drinking buddies. Nope, nary a ripple. Didn't know it at the time, but I was firmly on course to mission completion from the very moment that the former Louise Gale Waters of Peoria, Illinois entrusted to her only child that his father, Airman Harold James Bachman, had been murdered in cold blood at the hands of some doped-up lunatic named Brookens, shot to death while investigating a domestic dispute just miles outside the fenced perimeter of Kunsan Air Base in an area nicknamed '*American Town.*'

"As time passed, natural curiosity grew to full-blown obsession and by the time college graduation loomed, I'd requested and was mailed a base police report detailing the circumstances of my father's murder, this only after numerous delays by DOD officials. To my surprise, they were only lightly redacted and mostly intact. The report even included the Korean SP portion, included I could only surmise since the incident occurred off-base. I later had those translated into English and discovered some very interesting tidbits conspicuously left off the American G.I. version.

"It was within the muddled pages of this poorly written chronicle that I first became aware of the name Deron Barrow, a senior-airman who'd been the ranking airman on scene that night.

"Barrow had even supplied a lengthy supplemental narrative to his supervisor's initial report, describing not only in graphic detail Len Brookens' psychotic behavior in attacking and assaulting his spouse to the degree of broken bones and a severe concussion but also the fatal shooting of my father and attempted murder of Barrow himself.

"Weird, but Barrow was a much better writer than his superior, the typed text coming off in part like a work of dramatic fiction. Hey, I was no literary critic, certainly not at that age, but even so I could detect a strong sense of fraud within the man's overstated prose. Something stank in Denmark, or better yet South Korea. I had no doubt Brookens was a madman by definition, but Barrow's version was like reading the bad draft of some amateur crime-noir short-story. It reeked of fabrication, of purposeful diversion. I just didn't buy it as written as being completely truthful, plus which, there was the subject of Brookens himself before that night, a highly respected non-commissioned officer. What can alter a man so dramatically, you ask?

"Well, as it turned out, his transformation from professional, highly trained leader-of-men into a drooling loose-cannon killer-without-conscience wasn't due to some undiagnosed brain-tumor or single traumatic event, but an ever-growing Jones for illegally obtained medication.

"Infamously called 'speed or beanies' in the States, they were referred to as 'happy medicine' by the troops, and were highly addictive and, if consumed regularly, mind-altering. To refer back to the report completed by the Korean security police, it was here I found hints of suspicion in just how Brookens had obtained the amphetamines in question, and it turned out not to be the usual suspect, that being his Korean-born partner, who could've walked into any local pharmacy and purchased unlimited amounts, as prescriptions from reputable physicians were not law at that time. No, there was viable suspicion that Sergeant Brookens snared his stash at a reduced price from none other than the SP-in-charge that evening: Senior-Airman Deron Barrow. A supplemental report signed by the base assistant commander, a Colonel Vickers, confirmed that following an extensive investigation that included interviews with numerous witnesses, both stationed personnel and A-Town locals, confirmed that suspicion. The package even included a copy of the typed orders ordering Barrow back to the states for trial and possible sentencing on multiple charges of possession and distribution of restricted, illegal substances. I remember feeling a surge of satisfaction upon reading of his discharge; that moment of elation fading away just as rapidly upon the realization that a General Discharge from the military had been the lone punishment doled out.

"Somehow, some way, I was able to swallow my anger and hold it at bay for years on end, though it was never, ever completely digested, just stored deep down in my gut like some faintly throbbing tumor. I dutifully followed my dream of learning the craft of writing and filmmaking, driven by an inner force I could never quite pin down. Following graduation, I wrote and directed two short films before a chance meeting with Diandra and the beginning of our partnership. Though fine-tuning our skills on those other films, our passion project involved the triumphs and many tragedies surrounding one Deron Barrow. What rekindled my interest in this very personal story was again a singular incident of utter coincidence.

"I'd traveled to a Little Rock TV for research on a potential short film concerning the race riots of the sixties when I'd spotted a still photo hanging on a stretch of hallway wall dedicated to the station's present and former celebrities. My escort had to shake me quite forcefully to break my trance and the unblinking eye contact I'd made with the subject of that black and white pic; that being the sneering mug of Sergeant Ace Claymore, a haphazardly-scribbled message just underneath his jutting chin reading '*Best square yourselves away, troops, or I'll put a boot to all your worthless tails! Deron Barrow.*' From there, finding our elusive subject wasn't too difficult. Playing internet detective and utilizing the web's many tracking tools, I was able to pin down his locale to a rural Mississippi town only a few hours from Little Rock. The rest of the story, save former Deputy-Sheriff Paul Holliman's shocking confession, is outlined in our film. We've...had to rethink our motives for making this film.

"Listen, I...I've spent (*leans back, rubs eyes, sighs heavily*) the formative years of my life riding a rollercoaster of emotions when it comes to the subject of Deron Barrow and just how much he had to do with my father's murder. We watched countless hours of his portrayal of Ace Claymore and interviewed co-workers, former wives and bosses before meeting face-to-face with an offer. On the day of intros, I was a bundle of jumbled nerves and had no earthly idea how I'd react. Over the years, I'd experienced intense bouts of suspicion, disgust, distrust, anger and a burning hatred of a man I'd never met. I watched my mother work herself into an early grave to support a bastard son, the deceased father of which was never fated to fulfill an unknown potential that just might have seen them both live long, happy lives together.

"Now, months into the process and with the finish line clearly in sight, I don't feel an ounce of guilt in prejudging the man. I've found him to be the same arrogant, self-serving prick I'd always envisioned. Deputy Holliman's shocking revelation is, to me, the happiest ending I could have ever envisioned, and surely the most deserving. Deron Barrow's actions have initiated misery and suffering to so many and I'll be damned if he deserves any form of praise. If he cannot be convicted in a court of law for his many crimes against humanity, the least we can do is see him condemned in the court of public opinion.

"In my humble, admittedly prejudiced opinion (*grins devilishly*), it couldn't happen to a nicer guy."

Video interview with Diandra Chang

I found her medical records when packing away her things for storage. She'd just passed a week earlier from complications from a major stroke; the second such stroke in a six-month period. My stepbrother, ex-stepfather and I all insisted an autopsy be performed and the results definitely justified our insistence. While the base doctors had treated her merely for the broken wrist and fingers, fractured ribs and jaw and what they diagnosed as a mild concussion, the autopsy revealed something infinity more sinister. Chronic traumatic encephalopathy, the big, badass younger sibling of post-concussion syndrome, more recently brought into the national spotlight due to several noted professional football players suffering from the same condition, a few of which were pushed to commit suicide.

No one knew of the potential ramifications of too many blows to the head until the dawn of the 21st century, surely not two full decades earlier. There was no such known ailment in the nineteen eighties, so passing the buck of blame on some base doctor with limited resources would've been short-sighted, even for a naïve seventeen-year-old just looking for someone to accuse other the man more than likely responsible.

She'd spoken very little of my biological father, no matter how the level of my incessant curiosity, but would occasionally produce some rare photo of him, almost always decked out in uniform and almost never smiling. In fact, I'd never witnessed my father's smile until packing her things and discovering a worn picture album rotting away in the attic. In some pathetic, feeble attempt to keep her only daughter properly distanced from his very existence, she'd apparently held back all but the impersonal military pictures. I guess it was her way of tossing me the occasional crumb but not the entire meal. Not surprising, in retrospect. Mother had never told me of the events that most likely led to her mind gradually deteriorating. No, it was my stepfather, a kind but spineless man a full decade mother's senior that had dropped that particular bombshell the night mother had suffered that first massive stroke, pulling me to the side in the hospital waiting room.

He said Mother had insisted they never tell, mostly in the fear that I would immediately seek out my real father for some sort of half-assed reconciliation. Why had I not struck out on such an odyssey before then, you ask? I was, after all, a college freshman at the time. Pretty simple. Cruel as shit but logical as far as plots to hoodwink and undermine a child go. I'd been told at an early age, perhaps as young as three or four, that my father was deceased, killed in a tragic plane crash while serving his country overseas. As devastating as this deception had been, I never dared broach the subject once Mother was able to return home following an almost six-week rehab. I was able to stay with her a full week afterwards before returning to the dorm, all the while trying to comprehend her reasoning. To keep her little girl safely distanced from potential danger and sure disappointment. I got it, at least to a degree. But damn it, the man was my father!

True to my stepdad's sad, tragic tale, internet research had proven even the grisliest details to be fact. Regardless, I secretly plotted and planned a reunion with the person most infamously known as an unhinged killer. At that time, I couldn't give two shits what state facility booby-hatch he called home. I would procure the necessary passkey, by god. This I promised to myself. Fate is a real sadistic bitch, you know (*leans towards the camera, winks*)? Less than a week after returning to campus, I'd run dry on useable research on the 'net and sought out professional help, that being a private detective. With spring classes over a month away, there was ample time for a road-trip, no matter the distance. Money might be an issue if things progressed, but I'd saved a decent stash from a trio of part-time jobs and was more than willing to blow the wad if necessary.

Literally the day after speaking via landline to a local investigator about possibly taking on my missing parent case—even got a student discount, who knew? (*laughs*)—my stepbrother called. Father was dead; shot in some fleabag motel in Arkansas. It didn't end there, oh mercy *no*. He hadn't gone willfully or peacefully, claiming several lives on his way out and, for the coup de grace, even crippling a deputy sheriff for life. Here I was, barely twenty years old, and tasked to pass on this latest bit of grand news to my ailing mother, who'd long since stopped watching television except for her daily soaps, as she'd written off the world as a whole as a lost cause. I took a few days to decompress my own emotions and even considered not telling her at all, figuring it could only further damage her deteriorating health.

It wasn't until I found out through Jake, my stepbrother, that my stepdad was planning on breaking the news to her that I interceded. As I said, Gary—that's stepdad—was a nice enough man but not the sharpest tack in the bag. He later told me he and Leah—that's Mom—had vowed never to keep secrets. Gary didn't argue when I'd insisted I break the news. After all, Len Brookens had been my father and I the result of he and mother's early love, however eventually misguided.

As it turned out, my concerns for her mental and physical states and what the news might evoke from each was equally imprudent. Leah Mai Chang Brookens Watkins, as clear-eyed and coherent as I'd seen her in years, impressed with her cool, calm temperament and, following a moment of quiet introspection, had moved from her favorite couch—oxygen bottle dragging smoothly near badly swollen ankles—and applied a gentle hug and tap to the upper back of her only daughter, as if naturally sensing that I'd needed consoling far more than herself. (*Shrugs*) It's logical to assume that dredging up sympathy from a severely abused ex-spouse is no small task, but a person only has one father, so I guess it's really no surprise that I ended up curled into my mom's bosom like an infant with diaper rash, crying my fool eyes out.

It wasn't long afterward that mom descended further and further down into a blank-eyed funk before that final, fatal stroke.

So, here I was, between my freshman and sophomore years and still undecided on a major, now elder-less and literally steering blind down life's increasingly murky highway. I found myself studying Leah's medical records with a level of curiosity and intensity that my college texts could only dream of. To that end, I decided to drop out for a semester for additional research into both the possible causes of her condition and even more intently, my father's life before and after he'd been labeled just another dope-addled mass-murderer.

Long story shortened, I eventually settled on a Master's and what I hoped would be a long, lucrative career in documentary filmmaking. Point of order: I did not...repeat, *did not* enter this field solely in order to exact some sort of cinematic revenge against Deron Barrow. The idea for this documentary wasn't birthed until a little over a year ago, following my partner and I's last effort. Of course, with our mutual interest in the subject, I guess it was only natural we would eventually broach the possibility. Once Ron and I had co-written a first draft manuscript of the film we wanted to make, we both understood the risks, that being further cementing Barrow's legend as a redemptive hero-type. We agreed that if, once all interviews and research was complete, the story of Deron Barrow and his fictional alter-ego shone such a light, we would take our lumps and live with the results.

A decade and a half led me here, now, chronicling the life of a man who essentially aided and abided in the tragic deaths of both my parents.

Please don't misunderstand. I don't want to come off as overly callous. It's not like I don't believe in second chances for those deserving, but if the level of one's crimes serves as a barometer for the redemption they can hope to later achieve, Deron Barrow had one hell of a steep mountain to scale.

As of the date of this filming, nothing has come to light that elevates him past ground level, at least in this girl's opinion. This man fed my father's addiction for a profit, was hailed by many as a hero in his capture and walked away practically unscathed. While Len Brookens was shipped from mental health facility to prison and back again over a period of years, Barrow gained notoriety as a celebrity host, that is until a former superior came forward to tell the world the truth—(*pauses, flashes a left-handed salute*)—and thank you Chief Boland for your honorable service, not to mention our film's title.

Still, Barrow moved seamlessly on to his next gig and even remarried to his present spouse, seemingly impervious to the type of misery he'd caused to so many others. I truly believe that night in Pine Bluff was meant to be his comeuppance, my father's obvious insanity notwithstanding, but lo and behold, Mister Barrow managed to dodge the bullet yet again.

However inadvertently, however far out of reach of law enforcement, he played a much bigger role in the destructive of so many generations of lives—with branches spreading from coast-to-coast—than he ever *positively* impacted as some brutish, square-jawed lout spouting comically outdated, patriotic dribble into a camera lens.

And now, with Ex-Deputy Holliman's shocking testimony, that sadistic bitch I spoke of earlier seems to have deemed it fitting that a slice, however minute *(holds up left hand, the forefinger and thumb balanced less than an inch apart)*, of justice might finally be served in the honor of all the lives so severely altered by Deron Barrow's reckless actions.

~ * ~

"I really don't know what you want me to say here. I've stated my regrets, countless times. I've said how those regrets have haunted me; dogged my every move and affected every relationship and job decision I've ever made since the mid-eighties. It...I find it...*astonishing* that this entire sham production was...is about a revenge you feel justified in seeking since, in you two's highly prejudiced opinions, I simply haven't *suffered* enough? Why not just end *all* our collective miseries by proving you have the balls to use that thing, Dixon?"

Once static and white noise had repossessed the monitor screen, Barrow alternated steely-eyed glances at the two hosts, eventually landing with an accompanying scowl at Ronald Dixon, whose steady aim remained unaltered.

"Tell you what, cupcake, you either find the inner fortitude to aim and fire in the next thirty seconds, or I'm apt to confiscate it with extreme prejudice."

Dixon, lips drawn tight and tinted purple from constant pressure, remained silent while alternating glances from his seated foil towards his standing partner, the latter of which had cloaked her mouth with visibly trembling hands.

"I get it, all right? I...get...it," Barrow continued, pounding each kneecap with a balled fist to emphasize those final three words before turning to Diandra, his tone quickly shifting from barely-restrained rage to a quiet desperation that saw the clenched fists unclench and instantly transform into full, palms exposed and fingers-splayed pleading mode.

"Dee, your father was a monster *long* before I handed him the very first pill. He was a chronic abuser of not only your mother, but a checklist of others unfortunate enough to step in his path in and around A-Town. Cocky shit considered himself the unofficial mayor, untouchable and completely above the law. I'd arrived seven months into his tour and it was made very clear that neither the light colonel, captain or lieutenant assigned were really in charge. Simply put, Len Brookens was King Shit and those beneath him served as his favorite turds.

"He was also a known adulterer whose favorite weekend pastime was Friday and Saturday night jaunts into the town clubs, getting loaded on Soju, jungle juice and yes, illegal barbiturates and then paying off and whacking around the whore of his choosing. We all knew this. *Command* knew this. But then you see, Brookens was one hell of an NCO. A born leader. You wanna know the truth? The god's honest truth I've *never* told anyone, to include my last two wives?"

Standing, hands tucked at his back, Barrow shot Holliman a quick glance before turning to face the exit, as if unable to continue if making eye contact with anyone present. Stumbling a step forward from the set, Diandra Chang's entire frame shimmied, her slim arms hugging herself as if fighting a sudden chill.

"I fed that crazy bastard as many of those brain-melters as he would eat, all at a special discount price even lower than my usual. You wanna know why? I wanted, no hell, *prayed* that the bastard would either overdose in his sleep or pick a fight with the wrong hooker and find a knife-blade pulled across his gullet. I wanted that son of a bitch gone, for whatever reason! I...just wanted him *gone*. After that night on the peninsula, I figured he'd never breathe free air again. All that confessed, please allow me to inquire..." he spun on a heel, a flawless, textbook about-face his fictional alter-ego could be proud of, "...directly to my two scheming producers who despise me no end; you blame me entirely for not only his behavior and actions, but for being forced, by fucking gunpoint no less, to end his reign of terror? Please expound if you don't mind or, for shit's sake, even if you *do*."

It was Ronald Dixon who supplied an immediate reply, strolling purposely forward and past a perpetually wide-eyed Paul Holliman, leading with the handgun's stubby barrel.

"Enough preaching already, Barrow. Jesus, it's like you've been reading off the same worn cue-card."

The younger man halted an arm's length away, waving the firearm like a chalkboard pointer from Barrow towards Diandra and back again.

"So, you gonna tell her or am I?"

Barrow blinked once, twice, a third time, lips pursed tight, his steely glare boring into Dixon's own in what appeared to be the beginnings of a Herculean stare-off.

"Don't go all dense on me. You know exactly to what I refer. Selfish prick that you've proven to be, I figured you deserve first refusal, though I gotta tell you, keeping this particular whopper of a secret for all these weeks has been the hardest thing I've *ever* done."

"Boy, I've more than reached my limit on all the speculative fiction bullshit. Let me guess: another surprise guest stashed behind that tarp that you two bribed to continue the smear campaign," Barrow said, nodding towards the set and flap of tent beyond.

To this, Dixon side-stepped to the left in order to address his partner while also keeping the Magnum's aim steady in the area of Barrow's upper chest.

"Fine, just remember I offered," he scolded the latter before turning his eyes back to the former.

"Last month while you were in Chicago interviewing the former Maggie Jensen, you know, when I told you I would stay in Little Rock to work on the editing?"

Diandra nodded solemnly.

"Well, not quite. Instead, I flew down to Fort Walton Beach to meet with and hopefully cajole an interview from Seo Yoon Robertson, your mother's best friend from their Kunsan days."

Head tilting dramatically to the right, Diandra's expression was one of pained befuddlement, as if awakening from a deep slumber due to intense abdominal cramps.

"What? For *what* purpose?"

"She'd contacted me first. Remember that initial list of probable interviewees? We mailed feelers to 'em all. A few weeks later, about the time construction kicked off on these sets and we'd just flown back from the Conrad Boland interview, I'd checked our in-town P.O. Box and found my curiosity instantly piqued by a package addressed directly to myself but without a return addy.

"It was about the size of a man's size-ten shoebox, wrapped in plain brown paper and tied off with a single, slim white thread. I opened it right there in the post office parking lot. Two and a half hours later, with building cramps in my neck and a serious case of eyestrain, I pulled from that lot a total wreck with nary a single clue how to proceed. I cannot recall *ever* being more emotionally torn, or at least since the day my mother broke down and confessed to truth about my father's death."

Dixon paused long enough to ensure Barrow hadn't shifted position—the man stood statue-still, as if paralyzed by his own mystification—while simultaneously regrouping for what was likely to be the main thrust of his tale.

"What, so you're telling me is that Seo Yoon mailed us a pair of Mother's old shoes?" Diandra asked sourly, throwing both hands airborne while failing miserably to a woeful attempt to act annoyingly disinterested.

"To the *chase*, Dixon," Barrow spat in much more convincing take, "Before moss begins to form."

"Assorted letters tucked inside a journal. The journal was Leah's. As for the letters, a few were Seo Yoon's, but those weren't the ones that..." Dixon paused, reaching up with his free hand to execute a rapid but vigorous eye-message before turning towards Barrow, his slightly upturned lips visibly quivering. "...there were two that stood out from the pack rather dramatically, mainly due to the initials applied to their conclusion. The initials '*DB*.' The handwriting I've since compared with our contract paperwork.

"Now, are you sure you wouldn't prefer picking up from here, Barrow? Heaven forbid I accidentally misquote a major point."

Left brow severely arched, Barrow's lips had only started to part to reply when Diandra intervened, her shrill pronouncement delivered as she fast-walked forward to take up position directly between the two men and, as such, act as a human barricade against the pointed Magnum.

"He...y-you wrote my mother?" she blared, head swiveling wildly as to never address either man for more than a split-second before transferring focus. "Wh-when? Why would you...ever contact..."

Barrow, placing hands on hips, stared past her towards Dixon, who had repositioned the gun barrel over Diandra's left shoulder until it realigned directly at the head of his potential target.

"We...had a past. We were acquainted before the incident. I was...worried for her in the aftermath and, well, felt partly...responsible, I guess."

"Acquaintances? *Really*?" Dixon yowled, briefly tossing his head back in apparent disbelief, his newfound aim unwavering. "I'd say that's putting it mildly. *Tell* her, damn it!"

Studying the floor at his booted feet, a tight-lipped Barrow took the fifth even as Dixon side-stepped to Diandra's right and cut the distance between the two men to an arm's length.

"I read the letters, dumbass, and the journal, many times over. Why would either woman lie? Why would they fabricate such a story?"

Diandra, frantic in both movement and tone, leapt between them yet again, facing down her partner with upraised fists as if to goad a physical skirmish.

"What is it, Ron? For god's sake, what did my moth...what did *he* do?" she queried, concluding with a nod Barrow's way.

"Fine," Barrow spat through gritted teeth. "Leah and..." pausing, he stared down at his own slowly shifting shoes, like an overgrown child's confession of wrong-doing, "...we had a...friendship of sorts, or at least were forming the basis of one when the shit came down. She knew I worked for Brook...her husband, at least indirectly. One night I was on town patrol and she pulled me aside in an alleyway that split two of the least populated clubs. Didn't want us seen fraternizing, for obvious reasons. I remember she was sporting a helluva shiner that appeared recently applied."

As Diandra had, perhaps instinctively, back-stepped until she stood side-by-side with her business partner, both her expression and overall deportment had deteriorated to that of someone on the cusp of utter collapse. Dixon, on the other hand, maintained the same sour, distrustful scowl that had become his norm whenever Barrow spoke.

"Brookens was abusing her, both physically and mentally and she hoped I could, I don't know, intervene on her behalf to his superiors. But hey, you have to remember this was the eighties and the attitude towards domestic disputes was a far cry from anything resembling a me-too movement. What happened behind closed doors between couples generally stayed that way, and if anything, Korean culture was even more lenient, figuring a wife or girlfriend needed a good belt every now and then. I tried to console her best I could, but to report Brookens would've not only been a colossal waste of time, but more than likely resulted in a world of hurt for yours truly."

"Oh yeah, Barrow, you consoled her all right. Please explain to her daughter the technique you perfected for said comfort," Dixon sneered, reaching out with his free arm towards his visibly shaking partner and pulling her close.

Once Barrow's response consisted of a heavy sigh and mild shoulder shrug, Dixon raised the Magnum until the prospective target could look directly into its dark muzzle.

"Well now, who's sprouting moss now? Speak now or forever own those lies. How about, for once, try a little honesty? I hear it's good for the soul, even one as coal-black as your own."

Peering upward, Barrow swallowed hard.

"We, well, we did have an affair."

Diandra's throaty gasp was barely audible. Oppositely, Ron Dixon's cackle echoed through the mostly hollowed-out warehouse like small-arms fire. Barrow seemed to ignore each while resuming, as if rehearsing into a mirror into an empty room. Paul Holliman, meanwhile, had rolled back until his chair was within inches of impacting the exit door, his breathing as haggard as his visage.

"Short-lived but...it was what it was. She was hurting. I was there. Hey..." he continued flatly, raising both arms in mock surrender, "...it wasn't anything inclusive by a long shot. I was *there* for a dozen or more 'Ville girls during that tour, protracted as it was. For the record, it ended long before that night in their hooch."

Breaking Diandra's grip, Dixon lunged forward until his gun-hand was less than an extended arm's reach from Barrow, who nonetheless refused to flinch.

"Well, not according to Seo Yoon's letters, or for that matter, what she told me when we spoke face-to-face. She flat refused to be part of any film that glorified, and I quote..." he shot his partner a brief, forlorn glance, "...shit. Just...*shit*. I'm sorry, Dee. I...wasn't sure how to ever say this to you, but it certainly wasn't in front of this piece of trash."

"W-what?" she stammered, her reddened cheeks smeared with tears both fresh and semi-dried.

"Seo Yoon said she'd never be a part of glorifying a...rapist. She'd hinted at something similar in her letter and there's a vague passage in your mom's journal, though her writing leaves room for speculation. Maybe she was just too embarrassed to confess, even in her own private journal, or didn't want to relive it in some future reading. Miss Robertson wasn't nearly so guarded. Before rushing me out of her home, she made it very clear how disgusted she was that such a 'vile' man—her word exactly—be celebrated when, in a just world, he should've been rotting in prison."

Diandra, mouth hanging partially agape and eyes blinking rapidly, began to wheeze, a raspy growl from the back of her throat that continued unabated, seemingly without the need for a fresh intake of oxygen.

"Dee...Diandra, I did *not* rape your mother," Barrow said in a monotone so unemotional it sounded almost robotic, a stark contrast to his pleading hand gestures and stooped posture. "I would swear on a mountain of Bibles. Any...*our* actions were consensual."

As Diandra stumbled away to the left, head in hands and whimpering softly, Dixon resumed the unofficial interrogation, wild-eyed and with whitish spittle flying from his lips.

"Answer us this then: *why* would Seo Yoon lie? She had no motive to do so. None that I could detect other than a sincere disgust for all things Deron Barrow."

Though standing firmly in place, Barrow bowed up as to prep a physical assault.

"Eat shit, boy. Ya know, you're a walking, talking internet news-rag come to life, spouting fake news like it's bound gospel."

Keeping his aim firmly on Barrow, he side-stepped gradually towards Diandra, reaching out with his free hand and grasping her trembling left shoulder before applying a trio of light pats to same.

"Oh well, he said—she said, right, Barrow? You're obviously going to deny any wrongdoing for all of eternity, and we have no way to prove guilt three-plus decades later. So, on to chapter two then, what say?

"Shame is, much like the previous allegation, there's no proof and in truth, I might actually believe whatever denials come. First things first, however."

Applying just enough force to spin her ever-so-gradually towards him—Diandra appeared utterly drained, a lifeless husk—Dixon kneeled to even their height and, for the first time since brandishing the weapon, allowed his full attention be diverted from Barrow.

"Diandra, I wish I'd addressed it long before now but I truly thought the decent thing was at least give the man a chance, deserved or not.

"I've had both samples tested and re-tested."

"Sa-samples?" she mumbled, appearing semi-catatonic, a thin line of drool dripping from her lower lip.

"Barrow's from a drinking glass left at the apartment, and yours from multiple sources: a Starbuck's cup and, I pray you can forgive me, a blood sample from a used Kotex pad."

Like a prerecorded scene freeze-framed to pause, all movement briefly ceased to exclude Diandra's rapid blinking and a slight twitch at the left corner of Deron Barrow's mouth.

"DNA verified," Dixon concluded, the Magnum's gleaming barrel beginning a gradual dip until it pointed into the concrete at his feet.

"Oh bullshit," Barrow spat. "What kind of insane PR stunt is this, Dixon? Jesus, how low *can* you possibly go?"

Arms pumping forcefully, Holliman rolled forward at a frantic pace, braking less than a full yard from Ron Dixon's brown oxfords.

"I concur, wholeheartedly. Just what is this, Dixon? Some half-baked Maury Poorvitch episode? The hidden camera capturing everything you hoped it would?

"*Povich,* Paul, and no, it is not. No cameras, no script, no scam. I wish to whatever God would allow such cruelty that it was, but the testing was completed at two different labs and the result was the same from each."

As Diandra appeared to descend further and further into a self-imposed stupor and Barrow fell to one knee with head bowed, nodding slowly from side to side like the hand of a slightly defective grandfather clock, Holliman—pale, haggard features creased in a crinkled mask of disbelief and anger—alone was able to continue the dialogue.

"Then, why use this particular time and place to reveal this...discovery if not for some good old-fashioned shock value? There had to be a better way, boy, and surely without holding at least one of the parties involved at gunpoint. Please advise and or expound."

"I'm not the one on trial here, Holliman. You want to interrogate anyone, try your buddy over there. *That* woman..." Dixon's eyes briefly turned to Diandra, his voice noticeably cracking "...has been lied to her entire life. *That* walking excrement..." hesitating to address Barrow through a tight, frigid squint, tone instantly as icy as the stare accompanying it, "...is solely responsible. She deserves an explanation; he needs to provide same, and he will do so, even if I have to blow off his fucking kneecaps!"

Greatly strained as it was, several moments of relative silence ensued, shattered only slightly by Diandra's gasping sobs and a slowly building groan whose source is soon revealed as Barrow, who lifts his head so gradually, so painstakingly, as if hoisting a great weight.

"I...Dee...I didn't...had no idea. You have to beli..." Barrow began, lips parting and closing again several times as if struggling for the appropriate response, when a sudden influx of outside light, accompanied by a resounding screech, directed all attention spans present—save a dazed, weirdly unfazed Diandra Chang—instantly towards the exit door, pushed fully agape as a shadowy figure limped slowly into frame.

"Sorry it took me so long, partner, but since ya didn't provide me an actual street address, I drove by roughly two dozen similar warehouses until I spotted your ride."

Gasping for breath, a rail-thin Lance Garrett stepped inside just far enough to allow the metal door to shut behind him, the derby-style cane propped atop his left shoulder gleaming off the overhead lights, this temporary brightness quickly ignored in lieu of the small handgun tucked within the palm of his right hand.

"You're one lucky SOB, pal. I usually keep my cell on mute when napping. Believe I picked up about the time Ronnie-boy over there was spoutin' something about it all comin' down to your word over his or some-such drama."

Barrow patted his left front pants pocket before reaching in to retrieve his own cell, displaying it clearly towards Dixon before re-pocketing.

"Bless Jenny for teaching me speed dial on this damn thing."

Giving the trio remaining a quick once over, the miniature firearm's snub-nosed barrel roughly half the length of the thumb propped on its hammer, Garrett's gaze finally rested on Paul Holliman.

"You the deputy that saved Deron's bacon all those years back?"

Holliman nodded silently and looked to Barrow, who returned the gesture before providing official intros.

"Lance Garrett, meet Paul Holliman."

"Paul," Garrett said with nod of his own before taking a few short steps forward while directly addressing Dixon. "Ronnie, you might wanna holster that peashooter. Not only have I got the drop on ya from an experience standpoint, but I dialed nine-one-one as a precaution before ever exiting my ride. Just a matter of minutes before Little Rock's finest come to ca..."

"This what you *do*, Garrett? Provide support and, if necessary, alibis for bottom-barrel scumbags?" the younger man interrupted, his complexion plumb-red, his gun-hand rocking and reeling as if struck by a vicious tremor. His own aim unwavering and utterly without even the slightest movement, Garrett's smarmy, tight-lipped smile and gunslinger's squint were, considering the circumstances, the epitome of cool.

"Nope. Don't put my ass on the line for anyone but those I know to be good people. You know, salt-of-the-earth types. Far from perfect—name somebody who is—but those whose back I will proudly have. Now, how 'bout lowering that cannon before you accidentally plug either your own foot or someone else's?"

As if on cue, Dixon's gun hand instantly stilled.

"Not a chance, old man, at least until someone wearing a badge instructs us both to do so simultaneously. As for 'having the drop on me,' don't count it. Both Dee and I are expert marksman thanks to a previous project on gun control."

"Figures," Garrett scoffed. "So, this some new-fangled court of law? Judge, Jury *and* Executioner Dixon, I presume."

"No one I know more deserving of a little back-alley justice."

"Evidence overwhelming, is it?"

"I'd say so."

"What gives you the *say*?"

"That man has destroyed countless lives. Well past time that lifetime free-pass card he's been toting around for decades was permanently revoked."

"Not for you to decide, or her, or anybody else who didn't witness firsthand whatever the hell it is you're accusing him of."

"Our film will suffice for now, and I'll make damn sure it gets the nationwide publicity it deserves. *Bank* on it. Outside distractions like marriage, children, or even career hold no interest for me now. I have but one goal in life, and that's burying that son-of-a-bitch."

Careful not to turn his back on Dixon, Barrow slowly backed away until he drew even with Garrett.

"Slander is easier to prove, and rest assured I'll sue the shit outta you, buddy-boy. The lone admission I will, willingly, confess to is the...my affair with Leah. As for...the...that *other* claim, I'm gonna need my own paternity tests run, if you don't mind."

"Or even if you *do*," Garrett concluded for him, the two men sharing a brief glance and understanding nod.

Paul Holliman wheeled forward and faced them both, jaw set tight and gaze directed downward, his head gradually rising as to confess the wickedest of sins. In that brief interlude of relative silence, the shrill wailing of a distant siren could be heard.

"You can count on me, Deron. I'm...so, *so* sorry for even considering his...the...their bribe. I promise to make it up any way I ca…"

With cheetah-speed and agility, Diandra covered the short distance between herself and Dixon in a single leap, a shrill, whistle-like whine escaping the back of her throat.

"Dee, wha—?" her longtime partner managed as the Magnum was yanked away in a brutal swipe and an equally fierce hip-check sent him sprawling onto the concrete.

Paul Holliman, the right wheel of the chair temporarily sticking in a wide crack in same, had just enough time to twist his head towards the source of the melee when the initial blast—the booming retort like a bazooka ignited within a coal tunnel—sheared away the majority of his lower jaw. As Holliman's twitching form tumbled from the chair, Lance Garrett instinctively took a knee while firing the Smith & Wesson small-frame thirty-eight at a somewhat awkward sideways angle. Deron Barrow—the upper portion of his tee and left shoulder spattered in blackish-crimson gore—having executed a clumsy combat roll, concluded the movement by kicking out with his left foot and, finding the empty chair, sent it spinning forward in a half-wheelie.

Crouching in a classic shooter's pose almost immediately upon pilfering the forty-four, a squinting Diandra Chang was just lining up a second shot when her left kneecap exploded.

Her weight naturally shifting to the undamaged leg, she tilted hard to the right, eventually sitting with both legs splayed out in front and arms extended to reset her aim. Paul Hollman's wheelchair nicked her scalp and overturned, its intended target seemingly oblivious to its passing.

Bug-eyed, teeth gnashing and nostrils flaring wildly, her straight black hair hung over the right side of her face like a dark shroud, Diandra was hardly recognizable as the same person, a Jekyll/Hyde transformation of tragic proportions.

As the two shooters each took aim, the distance between them approximately ten yards, a pair of equally desperate, distinct voices pleaded instructions to each.

"D-Dee...STOP!" Ron Dixon was shouting, belly-crawling over with an arm outstretched.

"The gun-hand, Tank! Go for her gun-hand!" Deron Barrow bellowed from the opposite side, having struck the coiled pose of a football lineman tensed for the quarterback's signal.

"Ra-ra-raaaa-piiiiissst!!" Diandra screeched between gritted teeth, the Magnum's barrel gaining a steady bead on its semi-crouched target, the trigger yanked just as Dixon's hand clasped her right ankle and pulled her off-center.

Barrow leapt to his left like a sprinter at the sound of the starting gun.

Tank Garrett's carefully aimed follow-up shot followed a precise trajectory at Diandra's right shoulder—the attached arm and hand being her primary gun-hand.

The three-fifty-seven round sailed the length of Barrow's parallel form to graze his right heel and peel away a quarter-sized section of sneaker in the process, ending its trek by loosening a sizable chunk of stone from the warehouse wall.

The thirty-eight slug, sadly unable to comply with its human master's intended agenda due to a sudden, unexpected alteration of its intended target, soldiered on without hesitation nor conscience.

Instead of impacting the soft tissue of Diandra's shoulder or, if an inch or thereabouts off-route, perhaps her upper bicep, it split the flesh just above her left eye and dug a weaving grove—her head being gradually forced to the right—through orbital, nasal and temporal bones before exiting the zygomatic arch in a projectile glut of blood, bone and brain matter. Like a marionette with severed strings, she was officially expired upon landing in Dixon's open arms, her limp form hugged tightly to his heaving torso as a torrent of crimson life-source gushed forth from two separate wounds.

Mouth agape but somehow unable to reboot the power to speak, Deron Barrow crawled towards the fallen pair—his injured heel producing a winding, blackish-red slug trail in its wake-discovering he was weirdly deaf to Ronald Dixon's anguish-fueled screams, the younger man having propped both himself and his deceased partner into a sitting position.

It wasn't until he got to within reaching distance of the young woman who just might be his daughter that a hand plopped down upon his left shoulder, the accompanying grip forceful but strangely gentle as well. He turned his head briefly to see Tank Garrett's wincing mug parked just above his own, his old friend's lips mouthing words as inaudible as Dixon's heartfelt cries of agony. Never very efficient at lip-reading, he nevertheless thought he made out something about '*staying out of the line*' or '*the line isn't safe, partner*' or some such foreboding dialogue. Regardless, Barrow either felt no sense of impending danger or, more perhaps more apt, was no longer capable of defining fear.

All movement around him, his own sluggish actions included, slowed to a virtual crawl, as if controlled by some magical remote device that he prayed would soon see fit to press rewind on the whole tragic, abominable mess.

Propping himself up next to Diandra's slumped form, he clearly saw Dixon pull the Magnum from her grasp but, at least for that frozen moment in time, found the act of consoling the dead a higher priority than the younger man's possibly fatal agenda.

As Barrow struggled to rise to one knee, Diandra's full weight shifted to his waiting shoulder, her undamaged right eye partially open and gazing accusingly into his tear-filled own. Peering sluggishly over her blood-drenched left shoulder, he took note of Dixon's comically maniacal expression, the googly-eyed, teeth-gnashing, spittle-coated chin and mangled, cow-licked coif so extremely out of character, and couldn't help but giggle aloud. Immediately in the aftermath, there came the sober realization that whatever insanity reigned at present wasn't solely tied to the young film producer.

Muffled retort aside, Barrow winced in seeing the Magnum's

natural recoil force Dixon's right hand back as if yanked via some invisible wire, the revolver's barrel-end still leaking a single, pencil-thin tendril of smoke as the younger man braced for another shot.

That attempt was, at least for the moment, not to be, as Dixon's left bicep birthed a dime-sized hole from which a considerable leak soon sprung. The younger man's head flung back, eyes clamped, lips parted and teeth bared, the tormented howl that ensued of unknown decibel level to the man sitting a mere arm's reach away.

Trance effectively shattered, Barrow gently pulled out from under Diandra's body weight, purposefully placing her stomach first as to cloak the horrendous wounds to her once flawless facial features.

He allowed the briefest of glances to search out his old friend while tensing to spring to, at the moment, destination unknown. To his right stood—albeit shakily—Ron Dixon, debilitated left arm hanging limp at his side, the right swinging gradually around as to line up that previously plotted sequel-shot. To this left, in the direction of the exit door in which they'd both stood just moments ago, was nothing but empty floor space save Paul Holliman's fast-cooling corpse. Swinging his head in a wider arc, he caught the blurred glimpse of a limping, slightly humpbacked figure streaking towards the set and specifically, the bunker desk mockup of one Sergeant Ace Claymore, ironically a mockup of sorts himself. Somewhere in the far distance, Barrow heard his friend's pleaded cries, though like that previous exchange only a precious few words were even semi-comprehensible.

Thighs aching for release, Barrow turned his full attention back to Dixon, whose one-eighty turn had reached approximately the one-fifty point, while concentrating exclusively on Tank Garrett's raspy baritone—muted as it was, as if his friend were shouting from the recesses of a deep, dark mine—yelling the same identical refrain continuously, like an old vinyl record with a stuck needle. "Get DOWN! Get...DOWN!" he screamed over and over until the mysterious wall of dulled sound collapsed like the shattering of glass and Barrow's muted hearing returned in full DOLBY. In addition to Tank's scolding instruction and Ronald Dixon's wet gasps—the younger man alternated these with a sporadic cough, equally moist—there came a virtual concerto of squawking, warbling sirens from just beyond the warehouse walls.

"...Deron, get your ass down! You're dead center, partner! Duck or dive but get the *hell* out of the way!" came the unedited version of Tank's croaking orders, their meaning registering almost immediately upon Barrow's regaining his previously shaky bearings.

Barrow stood directly between the two shooters, arms spread eagle-style, as if to ward off impending hot lead from either direction with an open palm.

"Best do as he says, Barrow," he heard Dixon say in a flat, emotionless monotone that spoke volumes of the young man's mental state, as did his movements; utterly tremor-free and borderline graceful, a dramatic change from just moments before while cradling the bloody corpse of his friend and partner. "Before I alter the current plan to kill him and then cripple you. Easily reversed that," he paused, sighing wearily with the Magnum's front sight aimed just above and to the right of Barrow's open left palm. "But putting you down quickly, like some rabid animal, wouldn't be doing her justice. That's Diandra, asshole, you know...your recently deceased spawn. I have to believe she agrees that you deserve no *less* than a few years hauling around an oxygen tank, perhaps the prisoner of a mechanized chair much like that of poor Holliman's. After all, the suffering of others has always been your trademark specialty, right? Only fitting the tables are turned before you're allowed to waste away in a steaming bowl of your own self-righteousness. But, first things first..."

The round didn't quite clear Barrow's outstretched fingers, essentially redacting the top half of the middle digit as if by some transparent saw blade, its ascending trek ending—and blowing a half-dollar sized hole through—the already-tattered flag hanging from the set's back wall.

In the aftermath, Tank Garret could be seen peeking timidly around the oak desk, the snub-nose leading the way like a groping proboscis.

"Whoops," Dixon grinned devilishly upon taking note of the partially severed appendage, still held airborne in an apparent act of defiance. "My bad."

"Do y-your worst to me, s-son," Barrow said through a pained grimace, fresh beads of sweat pooling on his forehead and cheeks, the jagged digit leaking copiously, "But *no* more collateral damage. It's me you want..." he concluded with a shrug, pose unchanged, "...and I'm not going anywhere."

"Damn it, Barrow, move your stupid ass!"

Tank's final plea was mostly drowned out as the entranceway door flung open with a resounding shriek, followed by chorus of bellowing voices and the multiple sources of same, the first combat crawling in and the other fully upright but both striking the same shooter's pose. Both appeared painfully young, the stooped officer's short-sleeve shirt displaying two yellow strips over dark blue, signifying he held the higher rank.

"Sir, drop the weapon, NOW!" commanded the stander—his quaking tone less-than-shocking considering the chubby, peach-fuzz cheeks on display—concentrating his weapon on the closer target, that being a statuesque Ronald Dixon.

"Lower that firearm and on your knees, hands locked behind your head!" ordered the second in a firmer voice that, unlike his partner, indicated at least a semblance of experience, squinting through his Beretta nine-millimeter's sights in the direction of the set, where Tank squatted at the edge of the desk.

"No, no, not gonna happen...again," Dixon muttered, bloodshot gaze darting spasmodically between Diandra's still, splayed form and Barrow, who steadfastly refused to break eye contact despite law enforcement's sudden intrusion.

"I won't let you skate away scot-free from another tragedy, another senseless death while others, *innocents*, are unwilling handed the pain that y-you alone should be feeling."

"Son, toss it away," Barrow replied softly, the type of soft, borderline-patronizing dialogue one might usually associate when speaking to the mentally handicapped. "Lord knows, those boys won't hesitate mowing you down where you stand."

As the officers continued to repeatedly bark out the same orders virtually unaltered—Tank Garrett having quickly consented by tossing his firearm to one side, standing erect and placing his left hand at the back of his head, the right steering the cane he'd clearly shown to be only that—Ron Dixon had yet to acknowledge their presence.

"You...son of a b-bitch, you've d-done so...much...damage," he croaked just loud enough for Barrow to hear, the Magnum's barrel aimed directly between his eyes and literally within reaching distance. "How d-did...do you look into a mirror? How do you sleep?"

"Son...*Ron*," Barrow replied with a sad smile and slight nod of the head, lowering both arms so gradually it appeared each were being descended via invisible cables, "I made peace with those demons long ago. Think it's about time you did the same."

"Dixon, for shit's sake, do as they say!" Tank bellowed while slowly taking a knee, as directed by the more veteran of the two officers, the cane placed on the floor in front of him.

Fresh tracks of tears flowing freely down both stubble-infested cheeks, Dixon's lower lip quivered, soon to be followed by a barely visible tremor of his gun-hand.

"You got my dad killed. You murdered the man Dee thought was her father and raped her mom, never bothering to tell her the truth about her origin as full decades passed.

"Dee...died...at precisely the most...miserable moment in her entire life...because of you. I can't...let you walk away. I just can't. I...won't."

The lower-ranking patrolman had taken advantage of his intended target's lack of interest by taking two full steps forward and, allowed additional moments to concentrate, gained better control of his breathing while simultaneously shoring up his aim.

Barrow swallowed hard, arms now lowered to his sides, and, raising his head and jutting his chin, stared straight and unblinkingly into the younger man's tear-filled eyes.

"If you're telling the truth about that...paternity test, I..." he hesitated, voice cracking with emotion, broad shoulders trembling just slightly at first but intensifying in veracity as moments passed, gaze briefly shifting yet again to Diandra's prone, lifeless form and then back to Dixon, "...maybe I've...got it coming. But sincerely, I did...not know. Swear to god..." he sobbed, "...I had no...idea."

Lunging forth until the barrel-tip sat mere inches from Barrow's sweat-slickened forehead, Dixon's trigger finger visibly coiled.

"LIAR! F-fucking *L-LIAR*!!!"

The young officer fired just as Dixon repeated that first refrain, coincidentally at the precise moment the latter yanked the trigger on his own firearm, the former's strategically aiming for the gun-shoulder but instead nicking the elbow. This impact, minor as it was, served a major purpose in throwing off the trajectory of Dixon's close-range effort, which cleared the top-half of Barrow's right ear by mere inches. Yelping in apparent shock, his lanky frame twisting to directly face the officers, Dixon managed to swap gun-hands from right to left and, consciously or not, raised it chest-level as if lining up one or both for return fire.

Neither Tank Garrett—reaching out with futile helplessness with a groping hand—or a kneeling Deron Barrow—bloodied palm frantically attempting to slap away the newly acquired deafness from his right ear—found sufficient time for any type of verbal warning to the young man, both understanding it was only a matter of seconds before he would be riddled with bullets.

Though it appeared that Dixon was indeed preparing to retaliate, the revolver had actually begun to slip from his loosening grasp just as the officers proceeded to act on their training.

The shots rang out in unison, likely sounding like a single blast from outside the warehouse walls. For a frozen moment in time, all appeared relatively unchanged from before this latest ear-splitting concerto, all save a single individual's positioning.

Barrow's desperate lunge, a pirouette performed solely, and quite ironically, with his surgically reconstructed knee leading the charge, halted with his back to the officers and face-to-face—literally, as in perhaps three inches apart—with Ron Dixon.

"Oh god, n-no," Tank whispered, struggling to stand with aid from the reacquired cane and stumbling towards the pair, who momentarily appeared as impromptu dance partners waiting for a cue.

As the larger man's knees gave out and he toppled slowly forward, Dixon backed up a half-step, legs braced and arms held straight out, the palms of both hands held up as if performing street pantomime.

"Wh-what did...you do?" he whimpered as Barrow's body weight collapsed onto his open palms.

The two officers shuffled forward, guns still drawn and aimed at their intended target, the higher ranking sending the dropped Magnum spinning away with a forceful kick. Dixon had, meanwhile, allowed Barrow's limp form to slump to the concrete surface, though he continued to maintain a hold on both the larger man's shoulders.

"Back away, sir," the youngest directed towards Dixon, though noticeably absent of the earlier confidence, perhaps envisioning a rather dicey shooting-board hearing in his future. Dixon did so, shambling back on his heels and bloodied hands that left fresh finger tracks in their wake. Instructed to lie on his stomach with hands linked at the lower back, Dixon did so only after a lengthy scowl, head tilted and right eye cocked quizzically at the fallen man, as if he was a complete, utter stranger.

The ranked officer regarded Barrow only briefly before utilizing his shoulder-mic to request emergency medical services while the other cuffed Dixon and assisted him into a sitting position. Removing a pair of blue-tinted surgical-type gloves from his belt, the former then began applying direct pressure to the separate wounds on Barrow's back, the lower of the two a quarter-sized hole at his left latissimus dorsi, the higher—and easily more concerning—a similarly-sized indention on the spine side of the levator scapulae region.

Having confiscated both discarded firearms, the younger officer executed a quick but thorough frisk of Tank's person before squatting over Diandra's still form and, making official what was painfully obvious considering her wounds and the amount of crimson spillage, performed the perfunctory check for an active pulse. Afterwards, he stumbled over—face ghost-pale and gait noticeably wobbly—and did the same for Paul Holliman.

Awarded temporary clearance, cane balanced atop a knee, Tank peered down at his friend and, placing a hand gently atop one shoulder, managed to croak a query as much to himself as Barrow.

"Je-Jesus, partner. What were you thinking?"

"T-the k-kid's...oh-okay?" Barrow gasped, laying chest down with his head turned to the right and cheek planted firmly against the slightly cracked stone, a small blood bubble forming at the corner of his mouth.

"Nary a scratch, pal, all thanks to that jackass move. Listen man, the girl, I was aiming for her shoul..."

"Say n-no more, T-Tank. I...we know th-this and we'll make...damn s-sure the law knows."

"Listen, the cop, the one that looks like he just learned to recognize the blade end of a razor 'bout three days ago, he was lookin' damn piqued in the aftermath. Just so ya know."

Barrow sighed as if relieved, a pained smile forming before abruptly transforming into a teeth-gnashing grimace.

"N-no ha-hard feelings. I...knew what I was d-doing. Only h-had a blink to...decide. Two roads to...t-travel. I made my...c-choice."

Groaning, Barrow's entire frame appeared to tense—Tank's hand instinctively moving away—before relaxing just as quickly.

"Just hang on, partner. The patch 'em up and move 'em out squad is on its way."

"I...s-saw them c-cuff the k-kid. Shell-s-shocked. I might've s-spared him a bullet but...not t-the m-misery that c-comes with...losing all you k-know."

Hearing his friend's confession, though hardly a shock, Tank found the itch too bothersome not to scratch.

"Why, Deron? He'd as soon spit on your grave, and damn if you didn't just give him a prime opportunity to do just that."

"H-he was d-due, T-Tank," came the barely audible reply, bookended by a series of hacking coughs that coated his lips a dark maroon, "...and m-maybe so...w-was I."

EMS and fire arrived less than ten minutes later, along with three additional PD units and, last and easily the standout because of its ominous markings, a white van from the medical examiner's office.

By the time all had entered the warehouse and begun performing their individual rolls, Deron Barrow had long since lost consciousness and Ronald Dixon was practically catatonic and had to be literally carried to the waiting cruiser.

Paul Holliman's body was the first to be removed, followed by Diandra, both loaded and driven off as Barrow was being treated by a trio of technicians, the oldest of which—a chubby, balding man wearing a walrus mustache so colossal it appeared a real-life homage to Yosemite Sam—almost immediately recognized his patient, referring to him as 'that TV sergeant guy from late-night Saturdays.'

Tank asked for permission to accompany his old friend in the same ambulance but was immediately rebuffed and instead ordered to the local precinct for interrogation. As the only remaining witness coherent enough to question, he knew they weren't exactly going to be thrilled with his lack of pertinent knowledge, no doubt labeling him either purposely obtuse or worse, guilty as hell.

While being led away to a waiting cruiser, he was able to inquire to one of the techies concerning Barrow's status, the reply a curt, dismissive shrug of the shoulders that didn't exactly exude confidence.

Never a religious man by nature, though he had gained renewed interest in the many months since the diagnosis, Lance Garrett said a silent prayer for his old friend while being steered towards the precinct.

A similar invocation—accompanied by an audible sob he was unable to suppress—was completed for the young lady he'd been forced to fire upon, obviously troubled and as much a victim of her own frenzied emotions as the bullet that had accidentally ended her life.

All told, it took a scant eighteen minutes through moderate traffic to travel from the warzone of that rented warehouse to the nearest precinct.

By the time a trio of officers accompanied him to the first of three interview rooms deep within the surprisingly massive 12th Street Substation, the veteran of countless firefights and armed skirmishes over four-plus decades of military and private security services did so on the shakiest of legs.

Epilogue

At Ease

26 November 2019

Little Rock

Audio recording – Speaker recognized as Lance Garrett

Just hang on, partner. Turkey Day wouldn't be the same without your ugly mug parked at our table. Whispered this at the big guy's bedside just yesterday. He passed on a few short hours later. Complications from the paralysis. Autonomic dysreflexia the doc called it. Blood pressure dropped off the charts. Breathing stopped. According to both his surgeon and rehab team, it was a damn miracle he'd lasted this long. I'm sure they figured such dialogue would be a comfort. Guess I, we, should be thankful for every day, every minute we'd had since the shooting, considerin' we were told his chances of survival that muggy August day were calculated at less than twenty percent.

Jenny took it particularly hard. Strange considerin' how severely strained their relationship, but then tragedies tend to bring folks who once cared so deeply back together. Heard her tell Wendy she was flyin' back to the homeland after the funeral as she no longer had any reason to stay in-country. Not surprisin' really. She's still young, quite attractive and still has a lot of life yet to navigate.

Gave Misty a ring this mornin' to break the news, a call I'd been dreadin' so badly I even tried dumpin' the responsibility on Wendy before realizing it should come from no one but yours truly. Misty and I had been jawing regularly since the incident, and she even made that long trek from Lincoln to the IC unit several times just to hold Deron's hand.

While she is the ultra-ballsy type, a tough cookie with youthful strength on her side, it was how her mom would react that I fretted over. Grace Winslow had accumulated quite a laundry-list of health issues the past few years, to the point that Misty had purposely avoided telling her about the shooting or Deron's deteriorating state, though as the news went national, I figured it might be a degree worse to find out that way. In fairness to her long suffering, it's not my say.

I wasn't about to ask if she planned on spillin' the whole can of beans to her mother anytime soon. If nothin' else, Grace deserved the truth so the monthly allotments she'd been dolin' out for damn near fifteen years could cease. Talk about dread. I can only imagine. Before hangin' up, she asked I call her back with the date of the service and that she'd be booking tickets for both herself and, hopefully, Grace as well. Bless 'em both. Good folks.

Eric told me that our home landline hadn't stopped lightin' up since Deron's passing, vultures from both the publishing and film industry practically droolin' over the respective rights. Damn their greedy eyes, they couldn't wait 'til the body is sufficiently cold before pickin' at its bones. Jackass media are even worse, if that's possible, suddenly so solemn and ready to grieve over a man they seemed to revel in crucifying a few months back. The hell with the lot of 'em. Drained and weak as I feel most days, I'll be damned if I won't do my best to bloody the nose of the first so-called reporter with the testicular fortitude to ask me for an interview. Flick rights would've legally fell back into the laps of *Foul Play Films*, 'cept they went belly-up weeks before the incident, yet another factoid kept under wraps by the late Miss Chang and Mister Dixon. Seems they'd both maxed out several credit cards in the process of the project maintaining a pulse and planned on pirating the rights upon completion.

Probably come down to who owns the deepest pockets, as most things eventually do. Legally, with Dixon serving a five-to-eight year stretch in the Tucker Unit for one count of attempted murder and three for aggravated assault with a deadly weapon, and of course Diandra deceased, the rights to their unfinished docu-flick sits firmly in purgatory until a court can decide its fate, and that ain't liable to see first light 'til Dixon gets paroled. Gonna be a hot potato when the day comes, even with many of the principals gone, including the main man himself.

In the many weeks spent between surgeries, Deron often spoke of the pair with a strange mix of respect and, damned if I know exactly why, *awe*. Respect for their conviction, however misplaced, and awe for being able to plaster a smiling face onto so much repressed hatred. I could tell how it was eatin' 'im up inside, especially the memory of Diandra's Oscar-worthy façade at their many face-to-face meetings. Being that he'd never warmed up to Dixon from the word go, apparently the kid couldn't pull off the act like his partner, he was able to shrug that off without a second thought. It was Diandra's performance that served to gut-punch 'im something fierce. Said he'd felt a warmness, even an attraction, just being near her. He simply couldn't wrap his head around how it could've all been an act. I told 'im she'd had a lifetime to prepare for said performance. Not sure that served to sweeten the sourness, so to speak, but it was the best I could come up with.

As for Deron's unpublished biography, Jenny has exclusive rights to *The Mask Beneath the Mask*, and told Wendy there's no plans to shop it around. I gotta respect her decision, her bein' his legal heir and all, but I also know how proud Deron was of that manuscript and that he put a shit-ton of work into it. Be a damn shame if it just sits in some dusty drawer in the PI collecting mouse droppings.

Remarkably, he even managed to add the concluding segment—what was to be, ironically, the beginning of the end—to his personal journal via verbal recollections to yours truly, who subsequently passed 'em on to Wendy for official put-it-on-paper-purposes.

Happy to say there are a few bright spots littered among the many tragedies. The morning after Deron's passing, I spoke to Maggie Carpenter, who said she'd sold the idea to the new suits-in-charge at KATV to run a special primetime showing of one of Deron's most popular Claymore episodes as a tribute. I know myself and my clan will happily and proudly park ourselves in front of the boob tube that night, popped corn and cold brew at the ready. Hope that night comes sooner than later, considerin' my own sorry state these days. Let's just say that stage four Parkinson's ain't for the squeamish and leave it at that.

As for that previously mentioned memoir, there's another reason I'd like to see it in print someday, if for no other reason than to put to rest all the innuendo concernin' the interaction between Deron and Diandra's mom back in the day. Just weeks after the warehouse shooting, some Big Apple-based gossip rag called the '*Dog wags Tongue.com*' interviewed Seo Yoon Robertson, not a blessed clue how they even knew of her, and soon after published their exclusive interview. Goes without sayin' Deron came out soundin' like some droolin' serial rapist minus a soul. Fake-news media ate it up like the stinkin' hyenas most of 'em are.

Well, maybe a month goes by and I'm sittin' at Deron's bedside—Jenny had just left to go freshen up her coffee at the nurses' station—and he pulls me close, whisperin' in my ear where they kept their extra house-key hid and that he needs me to go by and pick somethin' up before Jenny or anybody else finds it on her own.

The next day I do just that and, stashed away near that old Selectric III was what he'd referred to as his '*alternate-ending*' version of the original manuscript, wherein a full eight pages of an as-of-yet unfinished chapter had been tapped out, unedited, raw and, like some secret director's cut, laid out separately from the rest of the pile. Can't say for sure why Deron wanted to keep those particular pages buried far away from pryin' eyes, but I'm sure he had his reasons. Could be he figured all the disbelievers would just see it as some pathetic attempt to save face but bein' as it contradicted all those bogus rape allegations, I aim to see it comes to light sooner than later. The open confession that the infamous beret left in Brookens' hooch was indeed Deron's was the lone jolt I'd noted, and all that does is cement the fact that he and Leah were most likely seeing each other on at least a semi-regular basis. Also served to contradict his original script's claim that the two's relationship was strictly platonic. I çan only surmise that specific denial was concocted to distance himself from justifying Brookens' bent on revenge. Can't say I blame 'im, considerin' the media and public-opinion crucifixion that would've surely followed.

As for the docudrama producers *slash* hangin' judges, I hear Ronald Dixon's family had initially plotted a civil suit, at least 'til they discovered what little remained of the Barrow estate. Diandra Chang's clan was all but non-existent save a distant uncle somewhere in Pusan, South Korea and rumor had it several new outlets in and around Hollyweird offered to fly 'em in and even pay his legal dues so he might sue the pants off Jenny or any and all other relatives tied to the Barrow name. Turns out the old dude was in the late stages of prostate cancer and couldn't quite recall a niece who had resided stateside. What a shame.

As for Dixon's DNA claims, which the media reported without properly substantiatin', the truth might've remained buried with Diandra's remains if not for the accused. If nothin' else, that allegation struck in Deron's craw like no other, surpassin' even the bogus rape charge. It was maybe a week after his third and last spinal surgery that he asked me, well, more like *begged* me, to find out if the kid's so-called factual test results were just that. I guess it came down to a man wanting to know the truth before the end. Using some of my old law-dog contacts and basically callin' in every chip I owned, I was able to gain access to a shred of bloodied cloth from Diandra Chang's shirt peeled off at the ME's office the night of the shooting and subsequently booked into evidence. That, along with a swab of Deron's saliva, was taken to one of the more respected crime-labs in the state and the results determined soon after.

For whatever limited time yours truly has left, the expression on Deron's pale, sickly face the night I passed on the results is the kind that stays with ya, for better or worse. At the time of the reveal itself, my stomach had been churnin' like a concrete mixer and my throat felt like it was packed with hot, jagged coals. I just didn't know how he would take it. I didn't...know what he wanted to hear. It was damned obvious I made the right choice. Lyin' never comes easy, especially when starin' into the face of the best friend you ever had. In the end, I just decided he might rest easier in the knowledge that his child wasn't killed in front of his eyes while tryin' to do the same to him.

As for this old war-dog, I'll be in attendance in two days hence when they lay Deron Joseph Barrow to rest. I've made damn sure he'll receive the military service he deserves, if not fully for that green, misguided airman who walked a not-quite-arrow-straight line, but the matured man who did his best to make amends for his younger version's many mistakes. True, I never knew the former, but I sure as hell did the latter, and have respected no other person as much.

Years ago, long before this cursed malady melted me into a wobbly husk of my former self, I purchased a life insurance policy, the amount of which even Wendy defined as overkill. Never been a believer in premonitions and such, but who can say? Something pushed me, cheap bastard that I was, to go overboard on what I thought my family would need in face of tragedy.

Regardless, my dear wife has vowed that in the weeks following the reaper tappin' my shoulder, that she would use a large portion to secure the film's rights and find a suitable producing outfit.

This recording will serve as the epilogue. By that time, I hope to be floatin' on a cloud, downin' a cold brew and chewin' the fat with the man known by so many as Sergeant Ace Claymore but who I personally refer to simply as friend.

A friend who flew from this world no longer a blue falcon but a majestic bald eagle.

About the Author

Born and raised in Alabama, Terry Lloyd Vinson is an Air Force veteran and the author of over twenty novels. He currently resides in Nashville with his wife, Liza, and a savage, ankle-chewing Maltipoo named Dexter.

Blacktop

Blacktop is a terror-filled road-trip atop the dark, isolated back-roads of West Texas. Equal parts action/thriller and sci-fi/horror whodunit, it guides readers through a shock-filled maze, beginning with the hijacking of a commercial bus and concluding with a furious battle royale pitting the ultimate in extraterrestrial evil versus the few survivors of that initial abduction.

PROLOGUE

Paying Respects

There are countless locales in the U.S. Southeast and Midwest where one might successfully deep-fry an egg atop broiling pavement during the dog days of summer. However, only in Texas, *West* Texas, to be precise, may one prepare the equivalent of an entire breakfast buffet off the same stretch of boiling blacktop. It is, in fact, the only place I know where a sudden downpour on a steaming-hot July afternoon actually *increases* the misery of those melting within its oppressive, muggy grip. Personally speaking, I'd find it impossible to choose between the two evils—from sucking in air directly from a lit furnace or so damned humid it's like inhaling over a bubbling caldron of swamp water.

In my fifty-eight years on God's green earth, I've known bone-chilling cold, skull-scalding hot and everything in-between, but this was an altogether new level of discomfort, severely altered state be damned. Over the past three decades, I've learned that we...*I* tolerate the cold a hell of a lot better. No doubt the thick wool Windowpane suit coating my outer hide did little to cool the effect, my inner tee and dress shirt pasted on like skin-tight scuba gear. However regrettable my choice of wardrobe, it was after all, my only suit of clothes, having recently replaced a classic pinstripe outfit that had hung in various closets for several decades, the inevitable switch made mandatory by a gradually inflating midsection. Though it's true we...*I* might appear a decade-plus younger than my actual age—one of the few perks of such a hellish existence—an overabundance of pure cane sugar in its many assorted guises trumps whatever fountain of youth one might've found.

As I recall, that old reliable, dark-blue striper hadn't seen much use in all that time, as appropriate occasions rarely surfaced. If memory serves, this was to be just the third funeral I'd attended at all and the first since my older brother's passing some thirty-three years previous. At the moment, I'd happily hand over the whole wretched, suffocating ensemble for a sleeveless tee and a frosty pitcher of Rocky Mountain spring water.

The nearly one hour drive to the burial site had been, pardon the expression, an insufferable death march whose duration felt three times longer. Despite a sparse caravan of no more than six or seven vehicles—the dusty, two-lane trail blazed by a vintage, rust-spotted, pock-marked hearse that had seen its better days, the best we could do on a shoestring budget—the absence of a clear radio station, my ride's woeful lack of AC, and a flat, barren, lifeless landscape all added up to a less-than-pleasurable transection from civilization to isolated boneyard.

As for the chosen site, its ultra-secluded location and ancient, long-neglected headstones might, under close scrutiny, raise suspicion. Not that there had been a slew of options, as months of research had born out. You can only string bait along for so many miles before the drawing scent fades.

At least the brief squall and accompanying deluge served to mat down the dust, which I'd been hacking and sneezing up since waking in that fleabag motel at just before dawn. Less than forty-eight hours spent between the vast borders of the Lone Star state, and I was quickly reminded of why I'd hardly regretted pulling up roots all those years ago. Sure, like I'd had a choice.

Purposely distancing myself from the rest of the caravan, I parked on the far side of the cemetery, the lone representative near a triangle-shaped assortment of ruddy-gray, squared grave-markers that looked to have been erected sometime between the civil war and WWII.

As thunder commenced to boom overhead, I decided to take the high road and seek out a semblance of cover to avoid instant disintegration by a random lightning strike. Yeah, *right*. Too little, too late for such wishful thinking. There was a job to do, and I had a major role in seeing it done.

Ducking between a rather flimsy-looking portable awning just as the storm seemed to let up a degree, rainwater having soaked through my socks to fill my penny loafers, I marveled that the rickety structure had withstood the burnt. Attendance is, not at all surprisingly, fairly sparse. The shock would've been if the opposite had been true, considering the circumstances. There was a palpable relief in the knowledge that, so far anyhow, there wasn't a single face present that wasn't at least vaguely familiar from past travels.

I was just about to pull a smoke from my inner suit pocket—its condition hopefully unaffected from the sudden saturation due to it being of the vapor, e-cigarette variety—when a quick peek over the top edge of rain-spattered bifocals instantly ceased all movement, not to mention the power to breathe. Damn. Instant paralysis at the mere sight; every nerve-ending on fire, lit up and revved to the red line by a single vision that wouldn't have meant beans to anyone save the congregation on hand.

As it is, I felt a cold chill override the stifling heat, sliding the length of and attaching itself to the whole of my spine like some reptilian icicle. For all intents and purposes, I might as well have been standing knee-deep in a snowdrift with blowing sleet and hail slapping all exposed flesh instead of lukewarm rain. Removing the spectacles with a noticeably shaking hand, I found myself helpless to steady, I used a semi-dry hanky pulled from a rear pants pocket to wipe the wetness from each lens, all the while entranced by the source as if half-expecting it to vanish between blinks. A half-dozen such orbital flutters later, and it did not. It was as genuine as the cloudburst that had proceeded its arrival, as if magically teleported on site by same. I found no humor in the outlandish possibility, as I'd witnessed stranger. Oh, *hell yes*, I surely had, as the man accompanying the sealed coffin could similarly attest.

The subject of this sudden, overpowering, full-body paralysis had either A: Not noticed or recognized me as of yet, B: Had achieved both but didn't give a good damn, or most disturbing of all C: Had achieved both and was presently strategizing my impending destruction.

I felt my limbs begin to rejuvenate with the help of simple logic. First off, in the many moons since our last meeting, roughly thirty-two years, the chances of being recognized were remote at best, despite the dramatically reduced aging process. Still, there had been some less-than-subtle alternations. For one, I'd lost the majority of the stringy, shoulder-length mop I'd sported in those days. That, and the twenty to twenty-five pounds of extra padding and a dramatic shift in overall body shape, and I hardly resembled that wiry, shaggy-doo scallywag of my reckless youth. Moreover, even if proper identification were somehow achieved, why would it even matter anymore? It wasn't as if I could be viewed as a viable threat. *Despised* perhaps as most traitors are but surely not feared.

With that, I managed to free the rust from both knees, pocketing the specs—really just part of what was an admittedly pathetic disguise—blowing out a sigh of pure relief while side-stepping over to a back row of lined, mostly vacated patio-type chairs and taking up position in the center seat.

Glancing casually around, I counted a grand total of thirteen attendees of assorted shapes, sizes and ages. Lucky thirteen, or at least I...*we* hoped.

The torrential rains had subsided to a light sprinkle, the blustery monsoon-like winds reduced to nothing more than a mild but unbearably humid breeze that was anything but refreshing. Maintaining as bland an expression as possible, I took note of the wide swatch allowed the entity by my fellow attendees, the entire front row conspicuously vacant save that lone stranger. We all understood the potential hazards of being found out too soon. I could only speak for myself, but the tension in the air weighed like a blanket of lead.

Four men, all several decades younger than the majority of those present and decked out in matching, plain brown suits and suitably grim, downtrodden expressions, carefully extracted a slick, dark-stained mahogany coffin from the back of the aged hearse and sauntered gradually over with heads slightly bowed. I, of course, was privy to their true identities, though was damn near reduced to guffawing aloud at the very sight. Two sets of identical twins they were, each pair resembling a present-day American actor of prominent fame. Of course, we'd received no forewarning of such bone-headed disguises, and it was far too late to backtrack. We could only hope such a blatantly reckless fuck-up went unnoticed for as long as it took for the Hollywood look-a-likes to do what they'd been trained to do.

The pastor, white-haired and similarly dour, followed a few steps behind. The mortician, rail-thin and bug-eyed, his shiny, bald dome the color of a ripe radish beneath a newly birthed sun, brought up the rear in a shambling gait I couldn't help but identify with every *living dead* flick I'd ever seen.

A plan, years in the making, dozens upon dozens of secret rendezvous at the most desolate of locales, and there still remained a shadow of a doubt wide enough to cloak all of West Texas, even odds on events concluding in either giddy success or total, bend-over-and-grip your ankles disaster.

As the preordained date had neared, I'd tried like hell to replace all the fear and apprehension with positive vibes; the eternal optimist barricading all negativity. Finally, no longer able to stomach the self-delusion, I instead settled on finding a suitable middle ground in the relief of impending closure, be it bad or good. Just the mere prospect of that final curtain falling on a horror show that had long-since ran its course served to recharge some seriously drained batteries.

That in mind, I'd driven countless miles despite a budding case of hemorrhoids, disregarding a sense of foreboding so stout I'd hadn't managed a decent night's sleep in over a week. I could only pray this new, wholly bizarre, improbable and, *hopefully*, unexpected twist would allow a closing chapter to be added to that long-dormant manuscript; a musty, yellowed manuscript patiently awaiting a finale worthy of its proceeding chapters. Only then could the fictional book in question be closed on a non-fictional tale even the most open-minded reader would surely dismiss as, in keeping with the Midwest setting, a load of steaming cow manure.

The Hollywood pallbearers soon straddled the appointed gravesite and slowly lowered the box with grace and gentleness. In the aftermath, they stood with arms pinned tightly at their sides, staring straight ahead, impassive to a fault. Trained well, no doubt, to display the least amount of emotion possible, least they accidentally come off as either insincere in sympathy or jaded with indifference. Neutral is the new apathy, it seems, while donning the mask of deceit. The Four Horseman of the burial set had it down to a fine, stone-faced art. Ludicrous ID choices aside, their group act, suitably stoic and downtrodden, was a convincing-enough one.

The pastor, his pale, drooping jowls having grown rosy-red from the heat, bowed his head to lead us in prayer. I couldn't help but peek around at the mid-prayer point. The entity's head remained propped upright, its steely, emotionless eyes no doubt pulled wide and unblinking. Surely it didn't suspect, or at least have a clue of the *vastness* of the charade, otherwise there would've been at least a trace of a hint. Either that or it was so damn smug, so confident in its power, that it just didn't give a shit.

Devotion complete amid a muffled chorus of amens, there was a short pause as the pastor sidestepped away with a well-worn bible clutched to his chest. As my eyes remained glued to the back of the entity's head, tunnel-vision by its truest definition, I was briefly unaware of any and all movement outside the narrow passageway between it and myself.

Due to this, I first heard before actually viewing the sudden commotion. It began as a series of primal grunts and growls, accompanied by hurried steps, a series of gasps and a stern yet openly panic-leaden shriek of dialogue whose source was easily identified as that of the pastor. So cool, calm and steely-eyed during our practice sessions, the bald shit was coming apart at the seams, folding under the pressure like an aluminum can in the jaws of an industrial vice.

"For g-god's sake, disperse! *DISPERSE*! It knows! It k-knows!"

The entity stood, spreading its bare, spindly arms as if to receive a warm embrace while simultaneously releasing a low, hissing sound—a bizarre hybrid of leaking tire and rustling rattler—that I found nauseatingly familiar. As a sudden wave of dizziness took hold, I found that the internal time machine beckoned. It had sights to show me, a long-repressed reboot of a rainy summer night long ago...far away, and its hypnotic pull grew increasingly stout.

Having apparently left their assigned posts, the Tinsel-Town pallbearers rushed forward with legs and arms pumping. Donning similar masks of sneering, wild-eyed rage, their youthful faces so weirdly contorted they seemed to have instantly aged a decade or more, the target of the Four Horseman's sudden charge was certainly no mystery. By default, it could only have been either myself or the more obvious choice, as the sparse crowd between had scattered in panic—apparently heeding that chicken-shit preachers screeching advice—as if from an approaching tsunami, tripping and flipping over the majority of the patio chairs in their wake.

Surreal is a word I've strongly avoided using over the past three decades, but I found no other description quite as apt at the moment. *Déjà vu* was also on the banned verbiage checklist, though in fairness the odds of experiencing a similar escapade as remotely bizarre as that certain night in the Year of Our Lord nineteen eighty-three had always been a long shot at best.

That proclaimed, Webster's abridged possessed no more appropriate description and/or vibe to be claimed. Especially when, just as the Four Horseman dived forth as one towards the entity's prone, statuesque form, linked arm in arm like a segmented battering ram, I heard both the funeral director and pastor cry out in mortified unison.

Squinting past the impending brawl less than a dozen feet to my north, I saw the coffin lid splinter in two as if fractured from within by some inner detonation. The mortician and pastor had, respectively, sprinted in opposite directions, the latter having tossed the good book aside as to perhaps achieve better aerodynamics for his wind-milling arms. So much for planning. Spineless bastards. Good riddance. They'd have surely hindered or, worst case, completely sabotaged the mission with their jelly-kneed presence.

Thirty-one years is what people of my generation and cultural background might refer to as a "lengthy spell." A virtual lifetime of faintly recalled or completely voided memories.

As of that moment, the clear, detail-laden flashback that ensued reduced said timespan to one of the more vintage clichés in the book. It made it *truly* seem like only yesterday.

Also by the Author
at
Rogue Phoenix Press

In Sheep's Clothing

1880's, Utah territory: an entire unit of U.S. Calvary soldiers has vanished from between the walls of Fort Drake, a remote site surrounded on all sides by warring Indian tribes and whose lone mission had been to protect the local gold-miners of nearby South Pass City. A trio of snow-crested mountain ranges away at Fort Lagrange, Wyoming, golden-boy Lieutenant Drew Barron and three hand-picked subordinates are tasked with solving the mysterious disappearances, their laborious quest littered with assorted dangers; roaming marauders, bloodthirsty wolves and a blizzard of epic proportions. At trek's end, Fort Drake is found to be deserted until a trio of unlikely allies crawl forth from hiding just as the frigid grounds fall under attack yet again, the survivors forced to barricade themselves within the cramped confines of the post armory. Faced with dwindling supplies, bone-chilling temperatures and a relentless enemy poised just outside their rickety safe-haven, Lieutenant Barron and those within his care will soon discover they have yet to confront the worst that the newly dubbed 'Fort Dread' has to offer.

www.ingramcontent.com/pod-product-compliance
Lightning Source LLC
Chambersburg PA
CBHW061942170626
46813CB00006B/2498